Glenda Adams is the author of
of short stories *The Hottest N*
novel, *Games of the Strong*; a
Franklin Award winner *Danci*
third novel, won the 1990 Age
for Fiction.

Glenda Adams was born in Sydney and has spent
several years in New York City teaching fiction writing
at Columbia University. She is currently lecturing at the
University of Technology, Sydney.

To my dear friend Lorri,

Bon Voyage!

and all happy wishes

to a great mate.

Lots of love

Elizabeth

June '91.

IMPRINT

Longleg

GLENDA ADAMS

ANGUS
& ROBERTSON

An imprint of HarperCollins*Publishers*

AUTHOR'S ACKNOWLEDGEMENTS

The author gratefully acknowledges the support of the Literature Board of the Australia Council and of the MacDowell Colony.

*Collins/Angus & Robertson Publishers'
creative writing programme is
assisted by the Australia Council,
the Australian goverment's arts advisory.
and support organisation.*

*All characters in this book are
entirely fictitious, and no reference
is intended to any living person.*

*AN ANGUS & ROBERTSON BOOK
An imprint of HarperCollinsPublishers*

*First published in hardback in Australia in 1990
by CollinsAngus & Robertson Publishers Pty Limited
This Imprint edition published in Australia in 1991 by
CollinsAngus&Robertson Publishers Pty Limited (ACN 009 913 517)
A Division of HarperCollinsPublishers (Australia) Pty Limited
Unit 4, Eden Park, 31 Waterloo Road, North Ryde
NSW 2113, Australia*

*William Collins Publishers Ltd
31 View Road, Glenfield, Auckland 10, New Zealand*

*Angus & Robertson (UK)
77-85 Fulham Palace Road, London W6 8JB, United Kingdom*

Copyright © Glenda Adams 1990

*This book is copyright.
Apart from any fair dealing for the purposes of private study,
research, criticism or review, as permitted under the Copyright
Act, no part may be reproduced by any process without written
permission. Inquiries should be addressed to the publishers.*

*National Library of Australia
Cataloguing-in-Publication data:*

*Adams, Glenda, 1940 –
   Longleg.*

   ISBN 0 207 16916 0

   I. Title.

A823.3

*Cover photograph courtesy of the author
Printed in Australia by Globe Press*

 5 4 3 2 1
95 94 93 92 91

Part I

It took William Badger some time to understand that he was going to be left behind, deliberately abandoned, what seemed like a thousand miles from home. His mother had simply asked if he would like a nice seaside holiday, and he had said yes.

His father was in the corner of the kitchen at the time, his back to William, mixing stale bread and raisins and milk, making something they called heavy (because it was indeed very heavy), which they pretended was real cake. William was eating his Vita Brits, Vita British he secretly called them, British submarines surfacing through the milk, so that when he swallowed them he felt he was acquiring strength, the steel and the courage of the navy at war with the enemy, even though the war had been won several years before.

William was still searching for an appropriate name for his inseparable companion and best mate. Dash, perhaps. William Dash. Billy Dash. They would share the same first name. Williams Badger and Dash.

Rose Badger pulled out a chair and sat opposite William, her elbows on the table, her chin in her hands. 'Wouldn't that be simply super? A lovely, delicious, adorable exquisite seaside holiday?'

William looked carefully at his yellow-haired mother, the youngest, loveliest mother in the world, then over at his father, at the counter next to the sink, a tea towel tucked into his trousers as an apron, the oldest father in the world, with grey, creased elbows and a back that bent so that the shoulder blades protruded, fin-like, and caused the shirt to fall loosely like the skirt of a dress, down his back, the oldest father with a back now curved over a cracked mixing bowl and hands whose skin looked like old work gloves, squeezing the bread and dried fruit and milk together.

William pretended to consider his mother's proposition. It could be a joke. She could be teasing him. 'I wouldn't mind going to the beach,' he answered, not overtly keen, but not surly.

'There's no need to go,' said his father. 'I can set up the hose and the spinning rose, if the boy needs to get into some water to get cool.'

Rose Badger looked at her watch and tapped her foot in its white open-toed shoe. Peep toes the women called them. Watching the tapping foot, William thought his mother might well begin to twirl. He rather hoped she would.

'Don't be silly,' Rose Badger said to the bent back at the sink. 'The boy needs a holiday. He needs the salt in his hair, the broken shells under his feet.'

Even at this early hour she was fully dressed in stockings and a good dress, with lipstick. Every morning she wore a different dress—she owned seven dresses—ready to answer any summons. She could just put on her hat, pick up her purse and a suitcase and go back to England. Every morning when he set out for school William felt that she might not be there when he got home. Now in her navy blue dress with the polka dots and white shoes she was ready to walk out the door and take him to the beach.

'Why wait another minute, another second?' she said.

'He'll get sunburnt,' said Wally Badger, still kneading the mixture. 'And so will you. Neither of you are equipped for this sun.' He held up his brown creased arm and turned it this way and that, to show them the kind of skin they ought to have if they were contemplating the beach. To William the arm looked like a lizard, and if he squinted at it, to make it blurry, the hand turning back and forth at the end of the arm was a head, searching the air for flies.

'He'll be careful,' said Rose. 'He's the most careful boy in the world.'

William knew that was true. He was a careful boy.

'Zinc cream is the ticket,' said Rose.

'And you need to keep a hat on,' said William, although he had no intention of wearing a hat, like a baby, when he was at the beach or of wearing zinc cream on his nose. He could see them both lying on the sand, his mother sitting with one leg bent, her hands clasped around her knee, her head thrown back, smiling, with her eyes closed, and him lying on his back beside her, his arms and legs straight out like a gingerbread man.

'A good seaside holiday is what he needs, and me, too,' said Rose.

Rose Badger still sounded as if she had stepped from the pages of an English storybook. She referred to the nice boys at school as William's chums, and to the wicked ones who tormented him as rotters. These days, to tease him—and she liked a good tease—she chased him through the house reciting the stories and poems he no longer liked, the ones he in fact now hated, which she had read to him when he was very young, when he loved her voice so much that he never was able to object and say that he was getting too old for poems about snails and fairies behind curtains and sick dormice. He was ten years old, and these days he ran away holding his ears, and she pursued him, reciting, warbling, those poems, following him right into his room, where he hid under the bed. She knelt by the bed and threw aside the bedspread and lying on the floor, her head at his level, sang, 'James, James, Morrison, Morrison, Wetherby George Dupree, took great care of his mother, though he was only three.' She loved to tease. Full of fun was how his father described her.

William could squirm out from under the bed and

wriggle past her, while she got to her feet more slowly and set out in pursuit again, saying those words, 'James James Morrison Morrison said to his mother said he, "You must never go down to the end of the town without consulting me." ' Then changing the words to 'William, William, Badger, Badger, said to his mother said he.'

Despite his dislike of the poems, William often murmured as he set off for school, having said goodbye to his mother in her dress, stockings, shoes and lipstick, 'She must never go down to the end of the town without consulting me,' chanting in time to his footsteps. It was always possible she would go to the end of the town and beyond, to the edge of the continent and be gone when he returned. And so every afternoon he hurried home from school, never went with the other boys to the golf links, because he had to prevent her slipping away without consulting him. Consult. William quite liked the word.

Now in the kitchen William said to his mother, 'Mumma needs a good holiday at the beach, too.'

Wally Badger, without turning around, said, 'Everyone could do with a good holiday at the beach. I don't know anyone who couldn't do with a good holiday. But is it wise? That's the issue here.'

'Dadda could come, too,' said William. He was far too old to be saying Dadda and Mumma, but it seemed to please them.

'Your Dadda has to work,' said Rose.

'But he doesn't *go* to work,' said William. And that was true. Wally Badger sat on the front veranda, or made stew in the kitchen, or mended his motorbike in the driveway.

'Your Dadda has work to *do*,' said Rose, irritated at William's pedantry.

'It had better not be for long,' said Wally Badger.

'We won't be away long,' said William. 'I have to be back to start school.' He wanted to cheer his father up, reassure him, but he did not mind how long the holiday would be. It was the day after Christmas, Boxing Day, and school would not start again for weeks. 'Father,' he added. That was what he would call his Dadda from now on.

'Father?' said Rose immediately. '*Father*?' And she burst into laughter.

William could see his mother was ready for something, something daring. Her eyes and cheeks were bright, her feet tap-tapping. She had been in this state for more than a week now, ever since their terrible drive in the borrowed car to Ama's place before Christmas.

'You wait in the dining room,' Rose said to William. 'I need to discuss something with your Dadda.'

William slid off the kitchen chair, the flaking paint of the wooden seat scratching his bare legs.

'And make your noise,' said Rose after him, 'so that we have our privacy. Sing. Or hum.'

William stamped his way out of the kitchen and along the hall into the dining room, where he went down on all fours and made growling noises. He prowled the perimeter of the room on his hands and knees, bumping into furniture, letting out wild howls, while Rose and Wally Badger argued in the kitchen.

He bumped noisily into the armchair, into the table leg, and into the sideboard, the door of which flew open. William halted, sinking back on his heels before the table linens heaped in disorder on the shelves of the sideboard. The shelves of linen were in a terrible mess. This Christmas, just the day before, Rose had not used any of them. She had stood in front of the sideboard, opened the doors and bent to look in, then slammed them shut with the same vigour with which she had slammed shut the door of the borrowed Morris Minor when they visited Ama. She said why bother about a fancy table, what was the point, and she set the table in the kitchen with their usual placemats and their everyday serviettes in their everyday serviette rings. Wally Badger had lifted each place setting and carried it to the dining table, saying 'Christmas is Christmas,' and so they had ended up eating Christmas dinner in the dining room after all.

William took each cloth out gently, refolded it, and placed it neatly on the floor beside him, until he had a stack of cloths and a stack of napkins and a stack of doilies. His growling softened, then ceased altogether. He quite liked to fold things, put things in order. He was a careful boy. His shoes, when they were not on his feet but beneath his bed waiting for his feet, always stood side by side, neat little friends, twins, inseparable companions, best mates, who could chat to each other as they waited all night for their master to arise and press them into service. On his desk his ruler was straight, parallel to the front of the desk, and his two pencils lay beside the ruler. He could tell when Rose had been in his room to steal something, because a shoe was kicked slightly aside, a pencil was resting at an angle.

Rose came into his room to plunder his emergency supplies when he was sleeping or at school. For several years he had been saving all the sweets he was given at Christmas and on his birthday. Every creamy toffee, every chocolate, every Violet Crumble Bar from one year to the next were hidden in brown paper bags in his room, ready for an emergency. If ever something were to happen, a catastrophe, a flood, an earthquake, he would survive, if he were careful, rationing the supplies to keep him and his inseparable companion alive. Recently he had carried out a quality test of the supplies and had unwrapped a Violet Crumble Bar, the oldest piece in his collection, possibly three years old, just to examine it, and when he cut it in half with his penknife, he found that the honeycomb within had turned moist and soft. So he had taken to dating the wrappings and periodically examining the oldest, eating it if it had deteriorated. But Rose found his supplies no matter where he hid them. The sweets were now under his mattress, but it was only a matter of time before she plundered them. When he got back from the beach holiday he would leave a decoy supply, the oldest sweets or his least favourite, in an easy place, with his socks for instance, where Rose could find them, while the real hoard would be hidden more cunningly elsewhere.

'William?' Rose called from the kitchen, reacting to the silence from the dining room.

Folding and ordering the table linen, William knew he was too old to growl and pretend to be an animal, just so that his parents could talk without his hearing. Nevertheless he banged one fist on the floor, to make a steady noise, as he peered into the dark, empty shelves of the sideboard. All the linen was in neat piles on the floor. He leant forward on his knees so that he could reach in, and he tapped the toes of his shoes on the floor, to keep up the noise.

He ran his hands through the dark within the sideboard, in case he had missed a doily or a napkin, and his hands stumbled upon a box that rustled with paper.

It was a shoe box filled with papers and photographs. William's feet stopped tapping. The photos were old, brown, like the one of his father in army uniform that hung in the hallway. The photos contained men and women he did not know: a boy with long blond hair wearing knickers and a lace collar; a tall man with a moustache, his arms folded across his chest, and beside him a woman, . dark, in a loose dress, barefoot, with long dark hair that looked as if it had never been brushed and one foot turned slightly, the knee bent, as if she might run off. William studied her. There was something about the eyebrows. This wild woman might be Ama, his grandmother, his father's mother, who lived outside Sydney, whom he had seen only three or four times in his life. But it might not be Ama at all. The woman in the photograph was too young, too agile. Perhaps the tall, stern man beside her was Apa, whom he had never seen, who had died long before William was born.

Also in the box were documents bearing various names, some familiar, some strange, the handwriting often difficult to follow: Badger, MacKenzie, Walter. But especially· interesting was the name Longleg. He could decipher the first name, William, since it was his own, and then Longleg. William Longleg.

'William?' from the kitchen. William resumed thumping, slow, thoughtful.

His inseparable companion could be William Longleg, not Dash. It was a name that would carry its owner far, striding off across unexplored territories as he stuck faithfully to his leader, his partner, William Badger, who was sitting for the moment in a dark dining room in a fibro house in a grid of straight streets to the west of the city of Sydney.

For years William had requested a companion as a present. He had begged for one. He had in mind a store dummy, a mannequin exactly his size, a boy, the kind he had seen displaying the clothes in the children's department at David Jones'. His dummy, if only he were given one, would share his room, wear his clothes, sit beside him, be his friend.

'Dummy?' Rose laughed when he mentioned this longing. 'You don't need a dummy, you are one.' And she chased after him, trying to tickle him. Once she had promised him a dummy, but produced only a rubber dummy, the pacifier that was given to babies to suck to stop them crying. At Christmas and on his birthday there had never been a real boy dummy when he awakened.

The day before, waiting for him when he went into the dining room to look at his stocking hanging from the mantelpiece, were two books, a pair of new grey school socks, a washer (face flannel his mother called it) onto which Rose had stitched eyes and a smiling mouth to make it seem more like a gift instead of something useful, and a Rex bar, his least favourite sweet, which he planned to leave in his decoy hoard for Rose to steal, when they got back from the beach holiday. Rose had bent down and kissed the top of his head, his short curls, when she came in and found him reading one of his new books. 'We don't have the money, pet, for many gifts,' she whispered.

But now he had a name for this boy, this companion, whenever he arrived. William Longleg. Billy Longleg.

William shut the doors of the sideboard and leant against them, his legs stretched out in front of him.

The two books, which were his father's Christmas gift, pleased him well enough. One, he knew, was from the second-hand shop, because it was leather, ripped and cracked, that looked as if it was a hundred years old. It was called *Underground, or Life Below the Surface*, with more than a thousand pages.

'It's a dirty book,' said Rose, thrusting the tome aside and holding up her fingers smudged with brown from the crumbling worn leather. 'And heavy enough to press flowers in. You can pick a rose and press the life out of it in a book like that.'

That night in bed William had read parts of it, smudging his hands and the sheet, about life under the ground, disasters and nefarious goings on. There was the inundation of mines. Boys pulling carts of coal on their hands and knees in Belgium were drowned when the mine flooded. The water rushed in so strongly that all the air and gas in the mine were compressed and forced out through fissures in the earth with the power of gunpowder, sometimes overturning houses on the surface. Miners trapped without supplies for thirteen days in a pocket of air underground ate their leather belts, their candles, and the rotten wood of the timber supports, crumbling it in the water first. But when the miners were reached through a bore hole, it was light they craved, rather than food, for the darkness had made the place more horrible than anything they had ever imagined.

Inundation. Another beautiful word to murmur. William had read about the gambling hells of Germany, where a man who had traversed the rose-strewn road to ruin ended up with a snake in his stomach, about a beautiful English girl who was led through temptation to despair and suicide, about the illicit ivory trade in Africa, about subversives who bombed public buildings, and about the underworld of Paris, where vast numbers of unchaste women, even married women, indulged in love and passion with gallants and lovers, ignoring the rules of respectable society.

The second book was *Out Back and Other Poems*, slender, with pages of thick pink cardboard and a picture of a wandering swagman on the cover. William would sit on the beach near his mother at dusk, learning the poems, when he had finished with swimming and running along the sand and around the rocks collecting shells and flotsam. And *Underground* he would read alone at night under the covers, while his mother slept.

'William?'

William gave a start and, guilty, resumed banging and growling, forgetting his resolve no longer to oblige his mother and father in that way. They had stopped talking and must have been listening to his daydreaming, through the kitchen wall.

'William Badger. Quick, quick, quick. Make haste.' Rose was at the doorway looking down at him as he banged and growled. Her eyes were bright and wide open, not blinking. She looked as if she might laugh at him.

William leapt to his feet, embarrassed.

'Now?' he squeaked, and followed Rose back into the kitchen, where she stood at the table and tapped her fingers.

'Hurry up and get dressed and pack your things and we'll set out.'

His father was still standing, shifting bowls and dishes in the sink.

'Tell the boy it won't be for long,' said Wally Badger.

But William did not mind how long it would be.

'Wear your school uniform,' said Rose. 'But pack your shorts and sandals. Wear the good socks, the new Christmas ones with the elastic, and take the old ones for messing around in. And don't forget your bathers.'

Rose Badger spun around, the skirt of her polka-dotted navy blue dress flaring out. Rose Badger could not stand women who went about in what they called housedresses, ragged old sacks that made them look like the side of a bus. Wreck of the Hesperus she called those other housewives, who, when the doorbell rang, had to make a dash for the bedroom to change their clothes. 'Totally lacking in any kind of charm,' Rose said.

'Totally lacking in charm,' was how she referred to anyone she despised. For some years William thought she was saying 'totally lacking in chum,' which seemed appropriate for a despicable person with no friends, and such a pronouncement coming from his mother made him want a companion, a chum, more than ever, so that he would not be totally lacking in chum and therefore despicable. But he had no friends. If only she would get him a store dummy to be his chum, his chum William Longleg.

Standing in the kitchen doorway Rose Badger began to sing her song. '*Sah ein Knab ein Röslein rot, Röslein auf der Heiden*'. Quickly, quickly, William lazybones, hurry, hurry, run, William, run.' And she pursued him with pinching fingers. 'The rose will stick you with her thorns so that you'll always remember her,' she said and changed the pinching movement to poking, jabbing her fingers at his arms, so that he had to duck out of the way.

'Easy,' muttered Wally Badger to his baking pan. He was pressing the heavy into the pan with the heel of his palm.

Rose was so excited that William was sure she would start to twirl. She was able to twirl and twirl until William knew she must fall down, the way he fell down if he spun around and rolled across the carpet or the grass, as if the flat surface were sloping. But when his mother twirled, she kept her right foot in one spot, using it as a pivot, and used the left foot as if she were on a scooter, pushing herself around and around, her arms held out at shoulder level, and she threw back her head and laughed. William could see under her dress when she twirled, her slip and the tops of her stockings, whose seams were always straight. He was both excited that she could be so carefree and competent at twirling and also uneasy that she was capable of such abandon. Only after many, many revolutions did she flop onto the lounge, almost flying into it, so that there was a moment when her whole body was completely in the air, after her feet had left the floor, as she flung herself at the brown couch, and before her body touched the cushions.

'I'm really the passionate European type,' she called to him as he sat with his legs crossed on the carpet, gazing up at her. 'I'm not really English at all.' She fanned herself with both hands, still laughing, shaking her head so that her yellow hair danced off her neck. 'I have to keep it secret.'

'Why?' William always asked.

But Rose continued as if there had been no question. 'No one can know. And so I'm always a stranger. But they called me Rose, English Rose, to trick everyone. Rose. Rosie. Rosette. Rosina. A hedge rose. Wild, wild Rose. That's what my name should be.' And she hummed her song to herself, forgetting William sitting on the floor on the other side of the room, humming until she came to the words she loved. 'And I'll stick you with my thorns, so that you'll always remember me.'

William at first believed that the language, the nonsense words she sang, was the language for singing, distinct from the language used for speaking, until once—it was when he was very young, during the war, before his mother brought him to Australia—a man shouted at Rose Badger for singing that song. The man was a stranger, passing the house, and Rose was sweeping the front path, singing the song, with William sitting on the front steps. William could remember it clearly.

'Bloody traitor,' the man shouted.

'Same to you,' Rose retorted, uncharacteristically shouting, uncharacteristically vulgar. Nevertheless, she picked William up and took him inside. Much later, when William tried to ask about that shouting man, his mother said that some people were ignorant, particularly the English.

But Rose kept on singing indoors, especially during air-raids, until another man, this time in the air-raid shelter, said, 'I'd be careful if I were you. Someone'll turn you in as a spy.'

'I sing,' Rose replied, 'in order to survive. Music knows no politics, no wars. My father sang. He always sang. He knew every song in the world, every language in the world. And I sing, too. Among my people, everyone sings.'

Even as a small boy in London, William could see that singing made his mother feel better. It seemed to protect her. In the far western suburbs of Sydney, Rose Badger often broke into song, sometimes humming, sometimes singing the words loudly, an incantation or a spell, as she stood in the kitchen or walked along the street or sat in the bus if the upstairs of the double decker was empty, as if suddenly assailed by enemies, warding off evil. She sang as if she were holding up a crucifix to a vampire.

That particular night, when the man in the air-raid shelter had scolded her, William had been curled up under his eiderdown on his bed, watching the searchlights criss-crossing the black sky when the air-raid sirens went off. He was always watching for German aeroplanes. His mother ran into his room.

'Couldn't we just get under the bed, in the dark, like a cave,' William said. 'You and me.' He could still watch the searchlights from under the bed.

But Rose picked him up, eiderdown and all, and ran with him across the road to the shelter in the basement of the big house on the corner that was filled with boarders. Since Rose was alone—her husband was off in the Far East it was said and William did not even know he had a father—the woman who ran the boarding house included her and William in the shelter. While they sat in the dark

in the cellar, along with all the boarders, the woman—
William remembered her vaguely, she never smiled—gave
him a rubber ring to put in his mouth so that he would
not bite off his tongue when the bombs dropped. Sometimes
the woman brought her handkerchief collection with her
and allowed William to play with it. If he was awake
and had tired of being clutched and whispered to by his
mother, he sat on the floor at his mother's feet, lifting
out the dozens of beautiful handkerchiefs, unfolding and
arranging them in families.

That particular night he was sitting on his mother's
knee in his pyjamas, wrapped in his eiderdown. Then the
woman held out the box of handkerchiefs and he slid to
the floor to lay them out. Rose declared that everyone
should have a personal theme song, which they would all
sing each time they were gathered together in the shelter,
to ward off the bombs.

'She's full of fun, isn't she?' the woman responded. She
seemed glad to have someone like Rose in her shelter so
that her boarders would be entertained.

'Your song,' Rose said to the gruff man in the corner
who would bring up the business of being a spy, 'is "Lazy
Bones Sitting in the Sun",' which made everyone laugh,
since that man, Rose told William, was known never to
stop working, cutting the grass, mending the fence, painting
the guttering, and on Sundays the landlady of the boarding
house had to confine him to inconspicuous tasks inside the
house or the garage, so as not to offend the churchgoers.

William had all the handkerchiefs with small dots laid
out side by side on the mat on the floor of the cellar and
was separating the white handkerchiefs with embroidery
from the plain whites, giving them names.

'What's my song, then?' asked the landlady, the woman
with the handkerchiefs who never smiled, as if to jolly

things along, to encourage Rose and her boarders to have a bit of fun.

Rose hesitated a moment and said, ' "Run, Rabbit, Run",' and everyone laughed again, because it was known that this woman had relatives in Australia. When they were all gathered in the shelter she often read out their letters, causing everyone to hoot and laugh when those Australians talked about eating rabbits.

'And William has two songs, "I Miss My Swiss" and "Little Mister Baggy Breeches".'

His mother had a cake tin at home on whose lid was painted a Dutch boy in baggy trousers and clogs standing in front of a windmill beside a Dutch girl in a white bonnet who was kissing his cheek. Often Rose took this tin and held it next to her face and sang 'Little Mister Baggy Breeches, I love you,' swaying to the music. William's mother had the most beautiful voice in the world. Then she sang 'I miss my Swiss, my Swiss miss misses me.' But William, when he tried to sing it, managed only to stammer 'I miss my miss, my miss miss misses me.'

'What's *your* song, then?' asked the landlady.

And Rose sang softly *'Heidenröslein'* all the way through. *'Sah' ein Knab' ein Röslein rot, Röslein auf der Heiden, war so jung und morgenschön, lief er schnell es nah' zu seh'n.'* A boy saw a red hedge rose, so young and beautiful, that he ran up to see it closely, so young and beautiful that he wanted to pick it, take it from its hedge. The rose told him that if he broke her off, she would prick him with her thorns so that he would never forget her. The boy picked her, and the rose pricked him.

Everyone applauded, except the gruff Lazy-bones man.

'That sounds suspicious to me,' he said. The talking and laughing subsided. 'I'd be careful if I were you. Someone'll turn you in as a spy.'

'She has to be extra careful,' someone volunteered.

'With no husband, no family, no background, it would draw attention,' said the landlady.

Rose, angry, switched to a different kind of song, to please those around her, a song of nonsense syllables called 'Chickery Chic Cha-la Cha-la.' To William the words sounded no different from the words of *'Heidenröslein'*. But that was the night, Rose told William, that she decided they would go to Australia after the war and find Wally Badger, William's father. She needed room to sing. But after they went to Australia on the boat and managed to find Wally Badger he, too, told her to quit singing those songs because it gave people the wrong impression, even out in Sydney, and even though the war was over.

Once, when she hummed in the train as they were going to town, William reminded her to be extra careful.

'Pardon me for breathing,' she said. 'For living.' For a while Rose stopped singing and took to breathing instead of singing. She demonstrated to William the idea of space. If you weren't allowed to sing, then at least you needed space to breathe. She often stood breathing deeply, her diaphragm lifting and falling. She patted her chest, beneath the collar bones. 'You lift here,' she said, breathing again, 'you let this part of you reach to heaven, just breathing, like a lark singing to God.' And she began to twirl, around and around. That was the first time Rose twirled. 'You need room,' she gasped.

Sitting on the brown couch, taking deep breaths after she had twirled, fanning her neck with her hand, Rose said, 'I should have been born with hair black as a raven's. In Napoli or Madrid. I'm a gypsy at heart. A wanderer.' She knew a song about wandering, and whenever she talked about moving, travelling, she liked to hum that tune. She could easily wander off, while William had his back turned, while he was reading a book, taking a bath. And so he tried to be near, watching, especially when she twirled. 'And your father would love me more, I think, if I were darker,' Rose often said.

'But you're beautiful,' William protested.

Rose shook her head. 'There's no telling with men. Some want the opposite to themselves, that's why he chose me, but he is at heart drawn to the dark, the exotic, as I was to him, believe me. You'll see when it's your time.'

In the kitchen the day after Christmas, Rose was wearing the navy blue dress with the full circle skirt cut on the bias that she particularly liked to twirl in, and announced their seaside holiday. 'We'll borrow Mr Stanley's Morris. He won't be needing it, since it's Boxing Day and a holiday.' It was Mr Stanley's Morris that Rose had borrowed for their drive to Ama's.

'Isn't Father coming?' William asked, looking back at his father. 'We could go on the motorbike. We wouldn't have to borrow the car.' Wally Badger's Harley Davidson was able to take the three of them chugging along, William riding on the pillion seat behind his father, Rose in the wooden sidecar that was big enough for her to lie down in.

'Pet, Dadda has to work tomorrow,' said Rose. 'He has work to do. He needs rest today.'

'And my leg,' said Wally Badger, mumbling, pushing the pan of heavy into the oven. But his leg had not stopped him from riding the bike in the past.

Wally Badger got his leg in the First World War, when he was only seventeen. Suspended from a nail in the garage were his army boots, and hanging in the hall just outside the kitchen door was that brown photograph of him as a soldier, in his digger's hat, sitting in a cane chair in a military hospital in Egypt with ten other soldiers, some in pith helmets, some in shorts, recovering from influenza. Wally Badger looked as if he were the liveliest and cheekiest of the group, one elbow propped on the back of the chair, one leg crossed over the other—he had not yet got his leg—so different from this old man with the shoulder blades like shark fins who seemed to swim slowly about the house. Once William had taken the photo out of the frame and found a message written on the back in indelible pencil. 'Dear Ama and Apa, this is one more hospital group. I must have at least thirty different kinds. Ladies come each day and take our photos and then send them to us for us to send home. I leave again today for Greece or Gallipoli. Love Wally.' And that was when he had got his leg.

'Were you a hero?' William asked, when Wally found him studying the young men in the photograph. 'You must have been extra brave, extra courageous.'

Wally did not exactly deny it, but he also added, 'I was one of the lucky ones.'

'Then you must have been extra careful,' said William.

'Extra something,' said Wally. 'The rest of them are pressing down the ground in Turkey and Greece.' When the next war came around, Wally Badger found himself in England, taking a look at certain coalmining procedures so that he could report back to the colliery where he worked north of Sydney. That was when he had come across young Rose, who was working in the office, keeping track of the shipments and doing the bookkeeping, and glad to be paid attention to by an older man. 'They're more like babies, older men,' Rose used to say, 'although they don't know this.' And she would add, whispering, 'They like to have a young woman so that it at least *looks* as if they are lusty and vigorous.'

'We're do-ers, we Badgers,' Wally Badger said from his chair on the veranda in Sydney, where he sat all the time, no longer working, because of his leg, the oldest father William had ever seen. Once a year, on Anzac Day, he rode his Harley Davidson to the station and took the electric train to town in order to buy a red crepe-paper Flanders poppy from one of the women holding trays of poppies on the ramp at Wynyard. Sometimes he went to Martin Place to watch the ceremonies at the cenotaph, although he never marched with the other returned servicemen, and sometimes, depending on his leg, he just bought the poppy, stuck it in his buttonhole, and took the train straight home, to sit once again on the veranda.

'With or without a gammy leg, we Badgers are do-ers,' he said, tapping his leg with his pipe.

After Wally Badger had worn the red paper poppy for a week or so, he gave it to William, who placed it carefully in a tobacco tin, along with the silver paper he saved from his chocolates and old pencil stubs.

'Just hurry and pack your suitcase,' said Rose Badger to William, 'and we'll be off to the seaside.'

But William knew the sea was miles away. 'How will Mr Stanley get his Morris back?' he asked, adding, 'Mother?'

'*Mother*?' Rose laughed and leant over to kiss his forehead. 'Let me be the one to worry about that, pet.'

Wally Badger pulled the pan of heavy from the oven to test it. 'You won't be gone for long, son. You'll see.'

William took out all his clothes: two pairs of shorts, two shirts, two pairs of underpants, two singlets—vests his mother called them—and his striped pyjamas.

'And your new face flannel,' Rose called. Sometimes he felt he knew a whole other language, and he sometimes imagined speaking this language to astonish the boys at school, to demonstrate his power to wield words and name objects in order to subdue those boys, his enemies, although he also knew that such a verbal display would not win him friends, would only induce more torment.

'I'm going to fetch Mr Stanley's Morris,' Rose called again. Fetch was another one of those words. Consult. Inundation. Fetch. The excited pitch of her voice produced in William both elation and fear.

The front door slammed and Rose Badger's footsteps tapped across the wooden veranda, skipped down the front steps and then down the cement path to the front gate. The gate squeaked open and banged shut behind her, and her footsteps trotted across the footpath. Then there was silence as she crossed the strip of grass, then the trotting sound again as she crossed the road to the Stanleys' opposite.

Rose Badger had borrowed Stanleys' Morris a few weeks earlier, having been summoned by Ama.

'You don't have to go,' Wally had said, uneasy.

'Why not?' asked Rose.

'She's just an old woman. A troublemaker.'

'She wants to see me. It's not much for an old woman to ask,' said Rose. 'Not that she has ever liked me, nor I her.'

'It costs a lot in the train,' said Wally Badger.

'I'll borrow Stanleys' Morris,' said Rose.

'Take William with you,' said Wally Badger. 'I can manage here. He'll be good company.'

William leapt to his feet and stood beside his mother, ever on duty, ready to go.

Rose shrugged. 'The boy has got school.'

'He can miss a day of school. It's the end of the year,' said Wally Badger.

William could see that his father really wanted him to accompany his mother. 'I'd like to go,' he volunteered.

'It's me she wants to see,' said Rose.

'He'll like an exciting car ride,' said Wally Badger, ignoring her. 'And it's part of his education to see things, to get to know his environment, his own grandmother.'

'Why not,' Rose repeated, but it was no longer a question. She smiled, a small smile, not her old smile. She reached up to touch William's cheek rather absently and for a moment she looked right into his eyes. 'You're a good boy, William. The gentleman.'

William smiled down at her. He would not mind at all going in the car to Ama's in the bush, even though he was frightened of her, lurking in her house all alone.

The next morning William found his school clothes laid out over the ironing board in the kitchen—the grey flannel shorts, grey shirt, grey blazer, green cap, grey socks, his best clothes—and his mother standing by the sink, wearing her white hexagonal hat with the netting that covered her forehead and eyes and nose, even as she made the tea and eggs and toast for breakfast.

'Here,' said Wally Badger, and pressed a pound note into Rose's hand. 'I'd come, too, but my leg, as you know. And I have to work. The boy will be good company. He's closer to you in age than I am.'

William had never thought of it like that. It was true. He was ten, his mother thirty, his father fifty-five.

Rose was wearing her sundress, red and white pinstripes that came with a white bolero that could be worn when bare shoulders were not appropriate or when it got chilly. 'It's not you she wants to see,' she said to Wally Badger, who sat at the kitchen table as if it were an ordinary morning, as if his wife and son were not going on a long drive to see his own mother, whom they rarely saw, not even once a year. He picked up the paper, smoked his pipe, and propped his leg on the fourth chair at the table. 'An escaped convict around Jindabyne,' he announced.

'There aren't any convicts any more,' said William, puncturing the yoke of his fried egg.

'Hurry, William, we have to get a start,' said Rose. 'We have a lot to get through today.'

'Escaped from the jail down there,' said Wally.

'With a bit of luck we'll meet him,' said Rose. 'A bit of excitement at last.'

'It's way down south, so it's not likely,' said Wally sharply. 'But in any case don't pick up anyone hitchhiking as you drive out.'

'If one is to have varied and interesting experiences,' said Rose, 'then picking up hitchhikers, it seems to me, qualifies.'

William ate steadily. He would have to be alert to threats from without as well as to erratic behaviour from his mother. Wally Badger turned the page and went on to sports. The photo of the escaped convict was now facing William and he memorised it, trying to visualise the clean-shaven face covered with stubble, since that was how he imagined escaped convicts to be.

'Time to go,' said Rose. She drew on her white gloves, clamped her handbag under her arm, and sailed down the hallway. William leapt to his feet and followed.

'It might turn chilly,' Wally called after them as they got in the Morris. 'You'd better wear a cardigan. That dress is a bit bare.'

Rose, half in the car, got out again and ostentatiously put on the white bolero before getting into the driver's seat. William scrambled in beside her, and they took off, leaving Wally Badger leaning against the front gate. After Rose turned the first corner and was out of sight of Wally Badger, she stopped the car and took the bolero off, throwing it behind her onto the back seat.

On the seat between Rose and William were a jar of

ginger and a tin of shortbread for Ama, two extravagant purchases befitting the apparent gravity of the occasion and, as Rose said, it was the Christmas season, too. The jar was of teal blue ceramic and the tin was painted with a Stuart tartan pattern, both of which William wished they could keep and place alongside the Dutch-boy tin on top of their new refrigerator.

'Ama has a sweet tooth,' said Rose. 'We give her such things to tame her, as one offers sugar to a horse.'

The drive to Ama's house took all morning. Rose pointed the car north and drove earnestly for two hours without stopping, announcing the names of the rural suburbs as they passed through them. William sat uneasily beside his lovely mother, watching her, upright in the driver's seat, the little hexagon anchored to her neat hair, her arms stretched out before her, her hands in their white gloves clasping the wheel at ten to two, the left hand every now and then reaching down to change gear. He noted the way her little feet pressed the clutch and accelerator.

Rose darted a glance at William, sitting so seriously beside her.

'I love a man in uniform,' Rose said. 'And here you are, so smart and grown-up in your school uniform.'

'Dadda wore a uniform,' said William, struggling to connect his mother and father.

'Not really, not when I met him, unless you call an old cardigan a uniform.' She laughed.

'But the photo.'

'That was a different war. He was already forty-something and wearing a cardigan when I met him.'

William was silent. He wished that the impudent young man in the brown photo in the hospital in Egypt in one war had been the one who met his lively young mother in London in the next war.

'My father wore a uniform,' said Rose. 'And my grand-father. And now you. A family of uniforms.'

William sat quietly. If he said nothing she would continue like this, reminiscing, and he would get to know things he would never find out by asking. Above all, he should not ask a question, because all she did in reply was tickle him or tell him to stop pestering her.

'They had two uniforms each,' said Rose. 'Summer and winter.'

'In London?' William could not help himself.

Rose pulled in for petrol at a service station and poked William's arm. 'See?' She pointed at the long low building in front of them. 'In this country if it's not longest, or tallest, it's the first.' She was pointing at a sign: 'The First Jigsaw Gallery in the Southern Hemisphere.'

Rose paid the attendant for the petrol and pulled over to one side to park. She flung open the door and all in one movement leapt out, slammed the door behind her, strode off, without consulting William, and was already halfway across the cement yard in front of the jigsaw gallery before William had even opened his door.

William eased himself out of the car, closed his door, and followed his mother. She had disappeared into a building with four solid walls, which would contain her. He could not possibly lose her here. It was not as if she had taken off along a street with alleys and doorways into any of which she could swerve and vanish if he took his eyes off her for a moment.

But when he stepped inside the tin shed that contained the gallery, William found that his mother had indeed disappeared. The shed was divided into two parts, the front section a gift shop with carvings and boomerangs and serviette rings. William walked quickly through the displays of souvenirs. Perhaps Rose had bent down to fix her shoe.

Then he saw a doorway that led from the shop into the back section. The walls of this dark room were covered with jigsaw puzzles depicting scenes from all over the world. According to a card fixed to the wall, the puzzles had been assembled and lacquered by the wife of the service station owner. Rose Badger was there, standing before 'The Tower of London'. William moved to her side. She moved on to 'A Swiss Resort', and when he followed, to 'Alpine Scene'.

'That is my country,' she said, waving her hand at the European scenes. Every time he came close to her, she stepped away.

William followed her, contemplating the puzzles, tessellated and glowing under the lacquer, trying to grasp the idea of the world, the idea of other places, his mother's idea of the world. The farthest he had been from home, apart from that first voyage from England, was Ama's house which was in the bush, but only a couple of hours from his house. Perhaps he, William, should find a way to take his mother on the boat to England and Europe. That was what she needed.

Rose passed quickly by 'Washington Crossing the Delaware', 'A Day on the River', and 'Beach Scene, Hawaii', with William in pursuit, then tapped in her little shoes out the door and through the shop back to the car.

'I'll take you to Europe,' said William, 'as soon as I have earned some money.'

Rose laughed. 'William William Badger Badger,' she said.

She started the car, pointed it north again, and sped out of the service station, changing from first to second to third gear in a few yards.

'We'll start saving,' said William. He thought about ways for his mother to save money—he could eat less, and he could be more careful with his clothes, so that they would not get torn or muddy and have to be replaced. He could urge her not to buy any new dresses for a while, since the ones she already owned were beautiful.

They were on a straight stretch of road, with few houses. Rose was staring straight ahead. And suddenly William remembered the escaped convict. The convict might have managed to make his way north, skirting Sydney, and this was where he would be lurking. William suddenly had a good and daring idea. When the felon leapt out and pretended to hitch a ride, and when William saw his mother's right foot leave the accelerator and move across to the brake, then William himself would courageously stretch out his own right foot, across his mother's left leg, which would be manipulating the clutch, and bring it down on top of her right foot, pressing it back on the accelerator, forcing her to continue driving, preventing her from stopping. But to carry out this plan, he would have to sit very close to her with his leg ready, otherwise he would lose precious seconds and they would be doomed. He pretended to be looking interestedly out his window as he slid toward his mother, an inch at a time, until he was pressed against her.

'You're too old to be clinging to me like this,' Rose complained, shrugging her shoulder and wriggling her whole body, trying to shake him off her. 'You're smothering me. We're in the most spacious country in the world and you're on top of me. We might as well be in a bus at peak hour, or joined at the hip.' William did not budge. 'Can't you give me some room?'

Finally, even though it might mean that she would tease him and later mock him about his dependence, he said, 'I like to be close to you.'

'Like a tiny boy,' she said. But for the moment she

had no choice but to let him stay pressed beside her as they bumped along.

After a while, she said, 'For me, the earth has not stopped rocking since 1946.'

William thought of her spinning round and round in her full circle skirt in the lounge room.

'One day,' Rose continued, 'perhaps I'll take you to the docks, where we stepped ashore. Don't you remember?'

William badly wanted to remember the ship and the voyage and the stepping ashore, but there was nothing. He could summon only his bed in his room in London and the air-raid shelter in the dark cellar of the boarding house and the songs and then nothing, until Sydney.

'We'd been at sea for so long, six weeks, that when I set foot on the firm earth in Sydney I nearly fell over,' said Rose. 'It was like getting off a merry-go-round or a moving bus. Everything was back to front. It felt as if the ship were steady and the ground was swaying, tipping, underneath my feet. Someone had to catch me.' She began to swing the steering wheel back and forth, with both hands, like a cancan girl holding up her skirts and swinging them back and forth while she did the high kicks. 'For me the planet is always rocking. See?' The car lurched to the right and the left, onto the shoulder of the road and into the lane of the oncoming traffic. William fell against the door, then against his mother.

'Scared?' she asked.

William sat straight. If he nodded she would swing the car even more, teasing him. Back and forth they went, zigzagging along the road, deserted for the moment. Rose began to hum a song, not the rose song, but his song from the air-raid shelter, 'I miss my Swiss my Swiss miss misses me.' Then she sang 'I miss my miss my miss miss misses me,' poking fun of William's early attempts to sing the words. Then William reached out his right hand and placed it on the steering wheel. It was the most daring, sweeping movement he had ever made, reaching out, clamping his right hand around the steering wheel and holding it straight, defying his mother's attempts to turn it with both her hands.

'We'll have an accident if you don't let go,' she said.

But he held on. With his left hand he braced himself against the passenger door. She tugged at the wheel, trying to wrench it away from him, then took one hand off the wheel and grabbed his wrist. Still he would not let go. As she shook his wrist and kept one hand on the wheel and as he gripped the wheel even more tightly, the car began to wobble. Suddenly she took both hands off the wheel altogether, leaving William to steer with his one hand. He was still pushing on the wheel, against her attempts to turn it, and the car veered off to the right, toward an oncoming car.

'You naughty boy,' said Rose. She placed both hands on the wheel again and straightened the car. After a few moments, William took his hand away. Rose jiggled the wheel a few times, mildly, so that the car shuddered a little. William understood that she was having the last word. He stared ahead, as if he were concentrating on the road, but from the corner of his eye he watched Rose's hands.

'You never could say it, those words,' Rose said.

Finally Rose turned off the paved road onto a side road that began as asphalt, then turned into gravel and then dirt. They passed a dairy, bumped down a hill, with the bush growing wilder and thicker on each side, until they came to the fence and gate made of chicken wire, enclosing the three acres of bush in the middle of which sat Ama's house.

'Why do we call her Ama?' William asked.

Rose did not answer, or else she did not know. When

he asked Wally Badger once, he said it was just a name that she had been given as a child. 'In those days everyone was given a special name as a child, and that was hers. Mary was called Sally, Elizabeth was called Mim, and so on.'

William liked Ama's house, but Ama herself terrified him. Her skin was brown and leathery, and she never addressed him directly. She called him 'the boy', the way his father sometimes called him the boy, saying 'give the boy a cup of tea,' or 'give the boy four lumps of sugar,' or else she called him a villain, when he did something wrong, something that displeased her, as in 'tell the villain not to lean against the fly screen,' and 'the villain should pick up his socks.' The worst thing that had happened— and he could not bear to think of it, always skirted around it in his memory if he could—concerned the socks. He had left them on the veranda floor once, when he had gone to dip his feet in the pond. Ama had told him to pick up his socks, not to leave them lying on the floor, but he had run off, and when he had come back half an hour later and gone to put on his socks, he found that they had been nailed to the floor.

'She's wild,' was all Rose had said. 'Like an untamed animal.'

Ama's house was made of fibro, a square box of a structure with a veranda on all four sides and a tin roof that sat like a shallow cone over it all, extending beyond the veranda. The veranda was stuffed with scraps of fabric that Ama cut up and heaped in piles on boxes and tables, ready to use to make rugs and quilts and dresses. The whole house smelled of cloth, and smoke, because the stove in the kitchen and the water heater in the bathroom used wood fuel, and the fire in the fireplace in the kitchen was always burning. What William liked was the bush surrounding Ama's house and the little paths she had hacked through the growth, which led to unexpected treats and surprises: the pond in which a giant red fish circled, and farther on, beyond the pond and around several bends in the flagstone path, a stone igloo that he could crawl in, and around another bend a clearing with four stone benches arranged in a square around a dirt floor that he could draw on with a stick, with the trees meeting overhead, turning the clearing into a cave of foliage and stone. Ama had once kept a pet wallaby, until the people up the road at the dairy reported her and she had to give it up. After that, for months, she saved the contents of her chamber pot and when it got dark she carried the pot in her arms up the dirt road then stood on tiptoe to slosh the contents over the gate onto the driveway of the dairy farmer's house. 'That'll teach them a lesson,' she said. But even after the wallaby had gone, wild animals continued to come to her for food. Three lizards came every day—a blue-tongue, a frill-neck, and a goanna. They crawled out of the bush and lay in the sun on the square of cement outside the backdoor, waiting for milk and bread.

'The woman is brilliant, coarse but brilliant,' Rose whispered to William. 'This country is full of brilliant women hidden in the bush with no way out.'

'She could get out if she wanted to,' said William. 'She could walk down the path and up the road to the train.'

'Her rugs win prizes,' said Rose. 'At the Show. The knitting she does is as fine as the Irish knitters', finer. Your Ama is a gifted woman. But she's a hard woman, too. This country makes hardworking women hard as nails.'

Ama seemed not to like William very much, nor did she seem to like his pretty mother.

'She probably doesn't want us to come,' said William. 'We should go home.'

Ama had no telephone, and he was afraid they would startle her, catch her in the middle of some secret ritual and make her angry. And he did not want to see the blue chamber pot.

'She is the one who asked me to come,' said Rose. 'She sent word.'

Rose pushed open the gate, a square of chicken wire attached to a square wooden frame that scraped along the ground as it opened. They passed through the gate, and stepped up the flagstones through the bushes which leant out and scratched at William's sleeves leaving burrs sticking to the grey flannel. They walked up the path for minutes, perhaps a quarter of a mile, perhaps half a mile, a mile, two miles, a long, long way, until they faced the square fibro house with the tin roof and veranda enclosed in rusting fly wire. The piles of bright fabric stacked against the wire caused it to bulge outwards in places. The front steps were formed by two loose blocks of cement, secured neither to the ground nor to each other, so that they wobbled when a visitor stood on them to reach the door and the veranda. Ama avoided these steps altogether, simply making the big step from the ground to the veranda floor in one movement, hauling herself up with a grunt. Before they reached the steps, William could see Ama behind the screen, standing there, a shadowy figure. But the figure faded as they approached, and when Rose balanced herself on the top cement block and banged the door against the jamb several times, like knocking, to let Ama know they were there, the space behind the screen where William had seen her, was empty.

'She must be at the back and can't hear us,' said Rose and led William around the side of the house to the back, where indeed they found Ama sitting in the sun on the wooden step outside the back door, as if she had been

there for some time, so that William doubted that he had
seen her lurking in the gloom of the veranda a moment
before and believed it was Ama's double, a shade, that
he had seen. Around her, piled against the wall of the
back veranda, were pieces of iron, tyres, rusted scythes,
an old lawn mower, saucepans and broken plates. She sat
with her legs apart, her long skirt hitched up to her knees.
She was wearing men's argyle socks, pulled up the calf
as far as they would go, and men's black lace-up shoes,
old and brown with dust. Lying near her toes basking on
the cement at the bottom of the step were two of her
lizards. She did not seem surprised to see Rose and
William—she did not even look up when they rounded
the corner of the house. She sat looking at the lizards,
her eyes half-closed. The blue-tongue was darting its tongue
in and out, and the frill-neck flared up its frill at the sound
of the newcomers. But they did not scuttle off into the
bush. They stayed before Ama, who held out to them chunks
of stale bread, which they nipped rapidly from her fingers.

Rose and William stood still and watched until the lizards
had finished eating and lapped at the milk in the cracked
blue saucer at Ama's feet. Then Ama stood up, slowly, her
hands rubbing the small of her back, as she straightened
her body. 'The kidney,' was what she said to them. At first
William heard, 'The kid,' and thought she was referring
to him, as the kid, in the same way that she called him
the boy, but then remembered that Ama had only one
kidney, another remarkable and frightening thing about her.

'You're here,' she said, without smiling, looking Rose
up and down, then peering over Rose's shoulder at William,
hanging back behind his mother. 'There's another one like
him,' Ama said, moving her jaw slightly toward William
and smiling a narrow smile, keeping her lips together.

Rose turned to William, her face blank. 'You can go

and play,' she said, before turning away from him,
dismissing him, and stepping into the dark house,
disappearing behind the rusted wire screen, to the dark
kitchen where the kettle was always at boiling point on
the fire.

'Spitting image,' William heard Ama's voice pronounce
as he ran off.

William dashed off thankfully, along the path that led
to the right, disappearing into the gum trees and bushes,
winding to the fish pond, which was now covered by a
sheet of chicken wire. He no longer had any desire to
dip his feet in. He would never again take off his shoes
and socks at Ama's. If he sat still and stared through the
surface of the water, he could glimpse the lone red fish
gliding among the plants growing in the murky pond. She
had seen one like him, another one like him. He thought
about that and finally was sure that his grandmother meant
that she had found a store mannequin for him to play with,
a boy dummy, and that if he went back to the house he
would find it there, dressed in school clothes, ready to
be taken home and be his companion. Bill, Billy something.
He had not yet found a suitable surname. 'Come on Billy,
let's climb this tree.' 'Billy, come here a minute, what
do you want to play?' 'Billy, I can't get up, I've hurt my
leg, a bad break I think. You'll have to carry me to safety
on your back.' He and Billy would be inseparable. 'They
got me, Billy,' he said. 'I had discovered Hitler hiding
in his bunker, I was lying on my stomach, the bullets in
my belt digging into my stomach—actually I was wearing
two bullet belts, crossing over my chest. I was in the
entrance to the bunker. Hitler had not seen me. He was
sitting in a rocking chair, wearing boots, but one leg was
resting on a stool—he has a bad leg, no one knows that
about Hitler, he tried to hide it—and the foot on the ground

was rocking the chair back and forth, which made it difficult for me to take good aim. But finally I got the sights set just below a medal he was wearing on his jacket on the left side and was about to squeeze the trigger, when they jumped me. They had been having afternoon tea and came back. When they jumped me they hurt my leg, broke it in several places, I think. But I managed to fight them off, throwing them on their backs, wounding them, giving me enough time to get into the forest. But I can't go on with this leg, Billy. I've got a bad leg. You've got to help me.' And Billy, his best mate, answered, 'Billy Badger, I'm right here.'

William poked a stick through the wire into the water, trying to stir the red fish out of its hiding place. Ama called the fish Goldie. Perhaps his mother would somehow manage to conceal Billy and save him until Christmas, and he would be standing beside the mantelpiece on Christmas morning.

William walked along the stone paths, hitting the bushes with a stick, with Billy beside him. He heard a thin voice, a woman's voice, Rose's voice, saying goodbye. The wind carried the voice to him. He ran back along the path to the house. It was possible that Rose and Ama wanted him to receive his present, the dummy that Ama had found, which was just like him.

He saw Rose standing before the front steps, her hat on, holding her handbag, clearly on the point of departure. He thought he could see Ama in the gloom of the veranda, as he had seen her when they arrived. As he emerged from the bushes, Rose started to walk down the path leading to the front gate. 'Don't you want to look for Bluey and Frilly?' Ama's voice croaked from within, and she rattled the door at him. 'Come on, come and say hello to Bluey and Frilly. You can pat them.'

William saw that Rose had not hesitated or turned. He was going to be left, she was leaving without him. And he tore after her, down the path, clutching her hand when he caught up with her, slowing down, matching his steps to hers, expecting her to try to shake herself free of his grasp. But her hand hung limply in his, and she seemed not to notice that he was there beside her. He decided that he should remain quiet for the whole journey home, not remind her that he existed, in case she remembered she had intended to leave him. He dropped her hand gently, minimising his presence, and fell into step behind her, walking on the grass on the shoulder of the path when he could and tiptoeing when he was compelled to walk on the flagstones, so that she would not be aware of his footsteps. All the way to the car Rose looked at the ground before her, hardly blinking, hardly breathing, but humming softly her song.

Rose started the car and headed south, home. William sat near the door and stared ahead, silent, but chanting slowly to himself. 'William William Badger Badger said to his mother said he, "You must never go down to the end of the town without consulting me." '

By ignoring his mother, he seemed perversely to attract her attention, when for the first time in his life he did not want it at all.

'Aren't you sorry you are an only child?' his mother asked suddenly, then laughed. 'I just wondered. Aren't you lonely? They say only children are always lonely.'

Halfway through the journey she spoke again. 'If you have ever been tormented, even once, then you remain tormented for the rest of your life.'

William knew that.

Rose hummed softly. 'Little Mister Baggy Breeches, I love you.' She eyed William, then getting no reaction she began turning the wheel in large movements, to the right and left, so that they waltzed back and forth across the deserted road. William stared steadily ahead. 'Not afraid any more, I see,' said Rose. 'Good.' And she began to hum again, her own song, and as the journey home progressed, her song got louder, and when she lifted her eyes and saw William sitting against the door, she seemed to smile as she sang, '*Knabe sprach ich breche dich, Röslein auf der Heiden,*' and she beckoned William to her. '*Röslein sprach ich steche dich, wennst du ewig denkst an mich.*' When she sang '*Ich steche dich,*' Rose poked William in the ribs with her finger, really jabbed him, so that it hurt even through his grey blazer.

'You were going to leave me,' William said, carefully phrasing a statement rather than a question.

Suddenly Rose stopped the car and leapt out, slamming the door. They were in the middle of a suburb that was like a town. William had seen the signpost that announced Parramatta. Rose stood still for a moment in the middle of the wide footpath alongside the main street, then suddenly lifted her arms and started spinning.

'See,' she cried, 'this is what it was like, when I got off the boat. The earth was moving.'

Her skirt was flaring out. Her arms, with the white gloves on the hands, were outstretched. Her little hat sat tight on her head like a lid. She pivoted the right foot on the spot, and pushed with her left. Her eyes, like a dancer's, were fixed on one spot, and she spun her head quickly as she turned to fix her eyes on the spot again. She spun like this for perhaps fifty turns. It was late afternoon. Men who had been drilling the roads, loading and unloading the trucks, were getting off work. Some were sitting on the kerb smoking, some were gathered around the doors of a pub, beer mugs in their hands. Although William remained in the car, hunched over, frowning in embarrassment, he found he was counting the turns. Rose had not twirled outdoors before, in such a space, on such a firm surface. The carpet at home was soft, the lounge chairs and walls too close. Here she was like a spinning top that could veer in any direction and still keep spinning, perhaps even going up or down steps. Sixty, sixty-one. Two men, having completed a delivery of beer barrels to the service entrance of the hotel, stood beside their truck and watched this young spinning woman, with the red and white striped dress flared out almost parallel to the ground. One of the men whistled. The other began to clap.

'Atta girl,' he called and started counting, from one, although William was up to sixty-eight. The clapping man's friend stopped whistling and joined in clapping rhythmically and chanting the numbers, twenty-one, twenty-two, twenty-three. A head poked out the window of the hotel. Passers-by stopped to watch. Passengers in a passing bus peered out. Rose, smiling, straight and bright, kept spinning. One hundred and four, William counted. A dozen or more men had gathered, laughing, clapping, and then they fell silent, suddenly uneasy at this extraordinary display. The yellow-haired woman was possibly drunk, and in public. It was not normal to spin like that. But around she went. William knew she could go on forever.

'All right,' cried one of the men, 'We'll shout you a beer.'

But Rose kept spinning. William emerged from the car and blushing furiously walked up to his mother. Her skirt caught on his chest and bunched up, and the onlookers cheered at the glimpse of her stocking tops. For a moment Rose faltered, missing her step. But when she saw it was William standing close to her, she simply laughed lightly and moved away from him as she retrieved the rhythm of her spinning. William followed her, and she spun farther away from him. He considered grabbing at her dress. He did not like all these strangers watching, several of them openly ogling, and sniggering to one another. Rose spun away from her son, toward the two delivery men. As her skirt hit the legs of one of the men, the one who had offered the beer, he stepped forward and simply placed his hands on her waist, stopping her dead in mid-spin. She stood erect in front of him, her back to him, her arms still out. He stood behind her and slightly to one side, his big workman's hands on the white belt of the striped dress. They stood like two dancers in the final pose of a *pas de deux*. Rose's legs were neatly together, her skirt continued to swirl slightly, completing the revolution she had begun. The man's friend applauded. The other bystanders smiled and clapped. Rose, surprised to be standing in that position in contact with a strange man, with an audience, brought her hands to her sides.

'Now you've earned a beer,' said the man.

Rose took his hands from her waist and stepped forward as if she had not heard him. She walked toward William, slowly, because with all that turning, despite her expertise, he knew she could easily lose her balance.

'That's what it was like, when we landed from that ship,' she pronounced. 'I was dizzy and the ground was tipping, and that's what it has been like ever since. I've been rocking on solid ground—or rather, I've been standing still and the ground has been rocking me. That's what it has been like. Can you imagine life, for someone like me—the earth slanted and the ocean firm?'

'Can we have something to eat?' William asked gravely, almost whispering. He wished his mother would not announce her thoughts to the world at large.

Rose spun round to face the man behind her. 'I would love to have a beer.'

'Squeeze me?' the man said.

'That beer,' said Rose.

William went to her side. 'Mother,' he said urgently, then, 'Mumma!'

'And my boy here will have a lemonade,' said Rose.

'Sounds like a good diarrhoea,' said the man.

Rose fanned at her neck. 'I'm hot from all that.'

'I bet you like dancing,' said the man. 'I can see you'd be an all-right dancer.'

William tugged at his mother's arm, trying to haul her back to the Morris Minor. Rose stumbled and tried to shake William off. 'If you pull at me one more time I'll hit you,' she said.

'Hey, what's the big diarrhoea?' the man said to William. He took Rose's other arm and pulled her away from William. 'We're all going to have a drink.'

William, angry, let Rose go and she fell against the stranger, who also staggered back a step or two before steadying himself. Then arm in arm his mother and the stranger walked along the street, and William followed, his heels like firecrackers hitting the asphalt road.

The door to the ladies' lounge in the pub was blocked by drinkers, men standing around talking to the few women in the lounge.

'Squeeze me, squeeze me,' said the man as he manoeuvred Rose ahead of him. 'Let the lady through, squeeze me.'

Once they were seated the man said, 'I tell you what, what'll you have? A shandy for the lady and a lemonade for the boy, right?'

Rose told him the story of her arrival and her subsequent life in the western suburbs.

'I tell you what,' said the man. 'So that you can recapture that feel of the sea, to get as close to the feeling as possible, why don't you just go to town and get the ferry out to

Manly, get the feel of the water, walk around for a minute or two, along The Corso, take a look at the sharks, and the beach.'

Rose was smiling and pretty as William liked to see her. At least she was happy, although he hated this pub and hated this man and his strange, crude talk.

'I don't want to go there,' cried William. 'Mother, Mumma, I want to go home.'

He had to get his mother away. 'Let's go back to Dadda now,' he said, standing up. 'My father's waiting for us,' he explained to the awful man. He could not even begin to imagine what he would say to his father when they got back.

'And you could leave the boy on Fort Denison in the middle of the harbour,' said the man. 'Pinchgut. That's where they put the convicts. He looks like a bit of a terror to me.' He looked at William standing rigid and sedate in his uniform. 'A spell in the old dungeons would do him good.'

Rose and the man got up and walked out of the pub. 'Allow me to escort you to the car,' the man said.

As they passed an old church, Rose swerved from the street to take a look at the tombstones. 'A graveyard,' she laughed, a sound approaching a cackle. 'Just the place for me.'

'It's about the oldest cemetery in the southern hemisphere,' said the man.

'It would be,' said Rose bitterly.

William trailed behind them. The man stood on the footpath. Just one moment at a time, William thought. It did not matter. Whatever his mother wanted to do, she could do. He would monitor her, just follow, and step forward when needed to save her life.

Rose drifted among the old gravestones, many of them

overgrown with weeds. She bent down and held back the grasses, reading the inscriptions.

'Here's one for Rose,' she cried, and recited ' "Here lies little Rose. A bud to bloom in heaven." That's me, Rose, a bud to bloom in heaven. They heard I was coming and they made me my tombstone already.' She laughed until tears came to her eyes. Then she stood up and spread out her arms and turned around, a hundred and eighty degrees. But then she stopped and said only, 'Fancy that.'

When they returned to the man waiting on the footpath, she said, 'They have my tombstone in there. "A bud to bloom in heaven", that's me.'

'You look to me as if you've bloomed already,' said the man, 'already blooming here on earth.'

'And where is the one just like me?' William asked when he and Rose were back in the car.

Rose looked at him, puzzled, and continued to drive in silence until they drew up in front of their house.

'Poor little Rose,' she said.

'I thought she had a boy for me,' William insisted, and since Rose looked puzzled again, he added, 'Ama. You know, a store dummy, a boy for me to play with, another one like me.'

But there had been no boy for him that Christmas. He vowed that when he was grown and had children, boys or girls, he would buy them life-size friends. He would go around to all the shops and buy the broken ones and mend them to provide his children with companions. Once he had seen broken arms and legs and torsos in big boxes in corners in David Jones' in town. Yesterday, Christmas Day, all he found when he got up and went into the lounge room were the books, the socks, the washcloth and the Rex bar.

In his room this Boxing Day William could now smell the heavy baking in the oven. He liked eating it, even though it was poor man's food, something they made to use up the stale bread, so as not to waste a scrap of food. 'Once you've been through a depression,' Wally Badger said, 'you can't waste anything ever again.'

'And when you're poor,' said Rose, 'like the Badgers, and it looks as if you'll be poor for the rest of your life, you don't waste anything either.'

After the visit to Ama's and the wild twirling in Parramatta, Rose had been listless, sitting at the kitchen table or standing by the sink staring out the kitchen window at nothing in the backyard, while Wally Badger moved silently around her, hovering, trying to please, avoiding any provocation, any argument, not speaking, until suddenly, after a few days, he said he had a good idea.

'Why don't you borrow Stanleys' Morris and go to town?'

'Why would I want to go to town?' Rose said, finally responding.

'It'll do you good, to go to town, buy a dress, how about that? For Christmas?' His voice was husky, lilting, striving for sincerity.

'What would I need a dress for?' Rose said.

'Or go to Rose Bay,' said Wally Badger. 'Just the place for my little Rose.'

'Do they have a cemetery there?' Rose asked.

'Come on, say you'll do it,' said Wally Badger. 'They have flying boats at Rose Bay. You can watch them and make sure they don't fall in the drink.'

'I don't need to go anywhere,' said Rose.

'Take William with you,' said Wally Badger. 'I can manage here. He'll be good company.'

William leapt to his feet and stood beside his mother.

'Listen son,' said Wally Badger. 'As you go through town, look up and see if you can see the AWA tower. I had a friend who used to work there. Communications. It's the wave of the future, communications, and the AWA tower is the tallest building in the southern hemisphere. Maybe you'll be a communicator. The world would be a better place if we all just communicated.'

Rose Badger snorted, the strongest response she had had to anything for several days. Unwittingly, Wally Badger had goaded her into a kind of liveliness. 'I wouldn't call that stack of steel a *building*,' she said. 'It's a structure. The tallest *structure*, perhaps. And there's not much competition. You have to see Europe to see real buildings.'

Usually it was the flowers that angered her, especially the waratah, the state flower.

'The shape,' she said, screwing up her face, 'round and hard, and the colour, like blood.'

'And keep an eye out for the Harbour Bridge, son,' Wally went on quietly. 'I was watching when they opened it, when that fellow on his horse rode out in front of the premier and cut the ribbon.' He was standing leaning against the stove, oven cloths in his hands, ready to retrieve whatever it was he was preparing for dinner that day. 'The longest, single-span bridge in the world.'

Rose snorted again. It was always like this. When Wally Badger said this was the oldest land mass, Rose Badger said she could believe it, it certainly looked decrepit and shabby enough. When Wally Badger said the longest stretch of straight railway line in the world was between Perth and Adelaide, Rose Badger said she would have thought that that was the kind of thing a normal country would try to keep quiet about, instead of drawing attention to it. Just as a woman cleverly masks her worst features, so should a country.

'It's part of his education to see things, get to know his country's history.'

'History?' said Rose, arching her eyebrows.

Wally Badger brightened, increased his enthusiasm. Rose was coming back to life. 'First settlement in Australia, and all that.' Now he was deliberately provoking her.

'Ah, of course,' said Rose, sinking back into her chair. 'First, oldest, longest, tallest.' If Wally Badger had told her all this—longest, oldest, tallest, etcetera—before she left Southampton on the *Strathnaver* she would have walked right back down the gangplank and stayed in the northern hemisphere. She had not come all the way from England to hear colonials boasting. And Wally Badger responded mildly that he was not the one who had made her come to Australia.

'It's a national sickness. Chronic,' said Rose Badger, sniffing, and drumming her fingers on the kitchen table.

'And the boy's got to have some national pride.' Wally Badger was practically singing. Rose was alive again. 'What if there's another war?' He let the oven door bang, and for a moment William thought that his old father might begin to dance, do a jig, even twirl, so animated had he become. 'He might have to fight for his country one day. He needs national pride. If we're invaded he'd have to join the resistance and sabotage the enemy. You've got to have strong convictions to do that.'

Rose looked at him sharply. 'What are you so elated about?'

Wally Badger quieted down immediately. His good spirits might in the end cause her listlessness and detachment to return. He pulled out a chair for Rose and resumed his deferential hovering. He gently pressed her to borrow the car for the day and get away, as if he were a doctor and this was his prescription for the restoration of her health and good spirits. 'Why not pop over and ask Mr Stanley opposite if you can borrow the Morris for a day?'

'Why not,' Rose repeated.

William would happily go to Sydney and see the sights with her. Maybe she would be her old self.

'And he can make sure I don't get on a boat and sail away, won't you William? Or jump on the flying boat and fly off—if it doesn't fall in the drink, as you would put it. William can be my keeper,' Rose said, looking away toward the saucepans on the stove, not moving from her chair. Nevertheless, this woman sitting on the shabby wooden chair was still far from the pretty young mother who could lift her chest and breathe, as a lark preparing to sing to God, who could twirl and leave the ground.

Rose did not muster the energy to leave the house and go to town until today when, her face flushed and wild, she announced the seaside holiday. But by then Wally Badger did not want her to go at all.

William placed his two books, the Christmas gifts, in his suitcase, along with his clothes. They fitted easily into the big brown schoolcase that his father said he would be needing when he went back to school at the end of January. 'If you're going to be studious, son, you'll be needing something to carry the books in. If there's no war, maybe you'll be prime minister, something to do with running the country and making sure that poor people are taken care of.'

William lifted his mattress and considered packing his sweets collection. But since this was not an emergency, he would take only one item, a Cadbury's Caramello bar that he had received at Christmas a year before. He left the new Rex bar under his pillow for Rose to find when they returned from their holiday.

William dressed in his school clothes, and crammed the

cap on his short, short hair. Rose believed in the fortnightly haircut. She cut it herself. He always had the shortest hair of any boy at school, shaved almost, up the sides, and a few incipient curls in a bunch on the top of his skull. Sometimes he prevailed and managed to allow his hair to grow uninterrupted for a month. But after their trip to Ama's, Rose had seized him and cut his hair, so that he would look decent at Christmas. He liked to keep his head covered, so naked did he feel, and for that reason had grown fond of the green school cap. The old socks, whose elastic had slackened so that they piled in a heap around his ankles, he packed as instructed. Then he buttoned his collar and tied the green and white school tie. He hated school, but quite liked the uniform.

In the kitchen on this sunny morning, the day after Christmas, with the temperature at eighty-five degrees, Wally Badger was sitting at the table, still wearing the tea towel tucked into his belt.

'It won't be for long, son,' he said. 'Going to the seaside is just something she wants to do. Bit of an interest for her. She likes to see the ocean.'

'I like the beach all right,' said William. And he, too, thought the change would be good for his mother. He could see to it that she got rest and was not worried. He thought he knew how to handle her now, not to react too much to anything.

His father turned away. Rose Badger's footsteps were on the path again, then the steps and the veranda, and then the screen door burst open. She was humming one of her tunes in a determined way.

'Ready?' she cried, as she poked her head around the kitchen door. 'We're taking the bus and the train after all.' She disappeared into the hallway, then reappeared in the doorway with her white straw hat, which she placed on her head, slightly to one side, and pinned in place with several hatpins, bending her knees and looking into the glass of the framed photograph hanging on the wall, the young men in uniforms in Egypt, about to go off to Gallipoli or Greece. 'There'll be wind on the ferry, and hats off indoors.' William whipped off his cap. She looked at him, then touched the lapels of his jacket. 'I love a man in uniform, and with a good haircut.' She passed her hand over his hair, which was so short he could feel her hands on his skull, and he shivered.

Wally Badger was looking at her, glum, angry.

'Mr Stanley wouldn't let me have the Morris Minor,' said Rose gaily. 'He has just washed and polished it and he doesn't want it to get dirty. So he says. But really, he's a bit of a dog in the manger. I returned it safely last time.'

'So why don't you just call it a day and stay home?' said Wally Badger.

Rose shrugged. 'The bus and the train won't take all that long. And William will take care of me, won't you William.'

'Wait a mo, the heavy's almost ready,' said Wally Badger. He opened the oven and poked at the pan. 'You can take some with you. But maybe you should sit down and have a cuppa first.'

'We have miles to go.' Rose pretended she was riding a horse, making little galloping movements with her feet, urging her horse on with one hand hitting gently on the rump, and she sang a few bars. ' "Who goes there so late, through night and wind?" We can't wait for the heavy.' And she spun around again, once, snapping her fingers above her head.

'Listen, son,' said Wally Badger. 'When you get out at Wynyard, don't forget to look up and see if you can see the AWA tower.'

'Tallest, longest, oldest,' Rose Badger mimicked.

William was standing before his father in his uniform, his suitcase at his feet on the green linoleum, as if he were ready for inspection.

'And at the foot of the Harbour Bridge on the northern side,' Wally Badger went on, 'is the Olympic Pool. Longest swimming pool in the southern hemisphere.' And before Rose could say anything or groan, he added, 'It's for the boy's own good, his general knowledge. Maybe he'll be a quiz kid one day.'

'What a little man!' Rose exclaimed, touching William on the lapels of his jacket as he stood at attention.

'Wait just a sec,' said Wally Badger. He pulled the steaming baked bread out of the oven and placed it on top of the stove. 'It really should cool first,' he said, cutting it into squares and wrapping several pieces, soggy and hot, in greaseproof paper. 'Eat it, son,' said Wally Badger. 'There's nutrition in bread and raisins.'

'In Pompeii,' said William, 'they found bread in the oven when they excavated. Stale bread.'

'Who told you that?' Rose asked. She stuffed the little package of heavy into her purse, wrinkling her nose as if it were a dead fish.

'My *Underground* book,' said William. 'My Christmas book.'

'This stuff,' said Rose, 'which we may, just may, have eaten *in extremis* during the war, is fit only to be used as a poultice when you want to draw out a splinter or burst a boil. Or to feed to pigs.'

Wally Badger placed the remainder of the heavy in the Dutch-boy cake tin, and Rose began to sing 'Little Mister Baggy Breeches, I love you,' but William turned away.

'Mother,' he said, frowning, reproaching her.

William followed Rose, who was practically skipping, in her white peep toes with the wedge heels, with her handbag clamped under her arm, this summer day, along the footpath. She would have burst into a run if it weren't for William with his green cap down over his forehead and his suitcase. She slowed her sprightly pace so that he could manage to walk beside her, as her escort, on the side near the road.

'A gentleman always walks nearest the kerb,' she said, 'so that the slops hit him and not his lady.'

'Where's your suitcase?' William asked.

Rose made a little polka step and did not reply. She never answered questions.

At the bus stop at the corner they had to wait for twenty minutes. William stood with his eyes closed, in order to guess if the bus would be a double decker or single, with stairs outside or in, painted in camouflage or red or the new green that was becoming more frequent these days. He also forced himself to guess whether there would be a soldier on the bus with a limb missing. When they went out, they often saw young men on crutches with part of a leg missing, one trouser leg pinned up, home from the war, hauling themselves off and onto the platform of the bus.

The bus was a double decker, green, which meant stairs inside. William had guessed double decker red with outside stairs. A bad omen, to be wrong on two out of three possibilities. And on the back platform there was no soldier, only two girls in cotton dresses waiting to alight. Rose dashed onto the bus even before the bus was stationary, past the giggling girls. William stood back, allowing them off, then climbed onto the platform and turned around to look at the girls on the kerb. They were about his age. One in particular had caught his attention, the girl whose

dress was white with pink flowers and puffed sleeves. From
one of the sleeves came a slim brown arm and from the
other nothing. One puffed sleeve of the dress did not have
an arm emerging from it. This girl had only one arm.
And she was only ten or eleven years old. When she saw
William staring, she poked out her tongue, then pointed
at him and cried, 'Stare, stare like a bear.' William lowered
his eyes, mortified not only because the girl had caught
him in his rude staring but also because the passengers
downstairs now turned and were staring at him, too.

Rose had already skipped to the top deck and found
a seat at the front. William climbed the stairs slowly, his
suitcase banging, and sat beside her.

'You don't mind if I have the window, do you?' said
Rose.

'Where are we going?' William asked.

Rose laughed and after a suitable silence, so that it would
not look as if she were answering his question, she said,
'It's a surprise.'

William watched his mother as he would an actor in
a play. She was doing a lot of laughing this morning, arching
her neck, opening her mouth, showing her teeth, making
entrances, speaking lines, making exits.

'I wish,' said William, 'that I had only one arm.'

'What rubbish,' said Rose, suddenly angry. 'Don't ever
let me hear you say anything like that again.'

William was taken aback at her anger. 'But I would
have got it in the war, fighting the enemy,' he explained.

'Be grateful that you have two arms and two legs and
a head, although sometimes I wonder about the head.'

She looked out the window. William took out his
notepad and pencil and wrote down his wrong guess about
the colour and structure of the bus. He was keeping a
tally, to find out how many times he was right and how

many wrong. He decided that he could not allow the girl with one arm to count as a maimed soldier and felt proud of his honesty. Then he sat silently, looking at his knees, waiting for the play to unfold, for the scene in which Rose would reveal their destination.

'We're nearly at the station,' Rose said, and taking a quick look at her face, William could see that she was in good spirits again.

'When we get to town,' Rose continued, 'I'll show you the Quay, near where we stepped ashore.'

'Where was I?' William asked.

'Boys always have trouble remembering,' said Rose. 'I was the quoits champion of the whole ship. I got the rope ring on the stick every time. Girls have wonderful memories. They remember everything. It's a burden women must bear. Memory.'

By this time they were at the station and Rose stood up and was trotting down the stairs of the bus.

They took the electric train to Wynyard. William read all the billboards as they passed. Periodic signs announced, mysteriously, 'Only 10 miles to Griffiths Bros. tea', 'Only 8 miles to Griffiths Bros. tea'. At Strathfield, where the train waited for a few minutes, he had time to study a billboard that seemed to advocate that children eat bananas. The faces of a girl and a boy, larger than life, looking like twins and smiling at a bunch of bananas, attracted him, particularly the girl, who had straight black hair worn in what was called a Chinese cut, a fringe across her forehead almost touching her eyebrows, meeting at right angles the hair at the side, which fell straight down to her chin. Her face, framed squarely by this hair, was radiant as it gazed at the bananas. And on the billboard next to her, facing her, was a smiling boy with red hair and freckles recommending ETA peanut butter.

Rose nudged him. 'See that handle?' She was pointing to the corner of the carriage at a chain and handle hanging from the ceiling. 'That's the emergency brake. It makes the train stop. The naughtiest thing you could ever do is pull that just for fun. You'd go straight to jail.'

The last thing he would do on this earth, William thought, would be to pull such a chain.

At the top of the Wynyard ramp at George Street, where Wally Badger bought his Flanders poppy on Anzac Day, William craned his neck trying to see the AWA tower, without success. The street was too narrow and the immediate buildings too high. Then they took a tram to the Quay, where the harbour stretched before them, and William noted the bridge, without comment, since he did not want to provoke his mother's predictable scorn.

But of course she could read his thoughts. 'The coathanger,' said Rose, following William's gaze. 'That is what they call it, and that is what it is. They should have made a tunnel. The longest tunnel in the southern hemisphere. At least we wouldn't have to look at it.'

William resumed reading billboards at the Quay. 'Manly: Seven Miles from Sydney and a Thousand Miles from Care'.

Rose led William to the wharf where they boarded a green and white ferry.

'Where's Care?' William asked, pronouncing it Carray, making the analogy with cafe. He felt he should perhaps hold back, refuse to embark, instead of trotting along the gangplank behind his mother without knowing where he was going.

'Mmmm, you're adorable,' said Rose, pinching his cheeks. 'My little man. So manly.'

But she did not answer his question.

William sat on the ferry seat on the upper deck next to his mother, watching her white gloves tapping on her handbag as if she were playing the piano and her toes wriggling, and yes, she was humming 'Heidenröslein'. 'War so jung und morgenschön, lief er schnell es nah' zu seh'n.'

The ferry passed Fort Denison—Rose pointed it out— and William turned away, feeling queasy, remembering the dungeons and the convicts.

'You're going to have a holiday in Manly,' Rose announced. Then she opened her purse and brought out the package of heavy and handed it to him.

This was the part in the play where he was being told his destination. William noted the word 'you', not 'we', and felt a tremendous uneasiness. And Manly.

'I won't go to Manly,' cried William. That was where the stranger his mother had met in Parramatta had suggested they go.

'There's a lady who runs a boarding house,' said his mother. 'An English lady. That's where you'll be staying.'

That was when William knew he was going to be left, just as he would have been left at Ama's if he had not been alert enough to prevent it. He had always expected it. But this time, in the ferry gliding across the harbour to Manly, William saw that he had cooperated in the plan, walked right into the trap.

'This English lady really loves children. And there's the beach every day.'

'It won't be for long,' Wally Badger had said. 'Where's your suitcase?' William had asked his mother. 'How would *you* like a nice seaside holiday?' Rose had asked him. The signs had all been there, and he, a veteran Vita British, had not taken sufficient note. He was going to be left behind miles and miles from home, seven miles from Sydney and a thousand miles from Care.

'Here we are,' Rose announced gaily. 'Isn't it just lovely?'

They stepped down the gangplank onto the wharf when the ferry pulled in to Manly. William walked after his mother, lugging his suitcase, treading deliberately on the cracks in the footpath, keeping up with her clicking white heels. He walked with his head down, as if pulled along on a lead, and did not look toward the aquarium, which was nearby, not even when Rose shuddered and said, 'Ooooh, sharks, horrible things.' He walked with his head down a few paces behind Rose, not turning to look at the dodgem cars or the ferris wheel in the amusement park, and as they traversed The Corso, although he knew the ocean must be ahead because he could hear the waves crashing and the shouts of the bathers, he refused to look at the sea. Rose turned left along the beachfront and after a while, left again, along a street that ran back from the beach. William could see the bare legs and sandy feet of the beachgoers on the cement as he passed, and in the rubbish receptacles he could see discarded lolly papers and sheets of newspaper greasy from fish and chips. And then something black, with a white skull and crossbones made him look up briefly. Before him was a street vendor's stand, and among the multicoloured balloons and windmills and kewpie dolls on sticks attached to the stand was a solitary black balloon, with a skull and crossbones stencilled on in white, dancing around on the end of its stick. William lowered his head again, and only when Rose announced brightly 'Here we are, isn't it just lovely?' did he raise his head.

They were standing outside an ordinary suburban house—shiny, plum-coloured brick with an orange tiled roof and an open veranda, before which grew hydrangea bushes. Inside the slatted wooden fence at the street ran a privet hedge. The house itself looked too solid for its size—like a fort. The front steps curved, as if they were leading to a mansion rather than a squat square of dark bricks, the colour William hated most when it came to bricks. The wall of the veranda, also constructed of the same plum brick, rose to above waist level and was wide enough to sit on or even to lie on. The columns rising from the veranda wall to the roof were square and also of brick. So solid was the veranda that it looked as if it had been a solid wall, indeed a fort, out of which squares had been cut so that it could merit being called a veranda, yet still resist cannonballs fired by the enemy.

On this veranda sat several men reading newspapers and magazines. From the street William could see with a quick glance the tops of their heads and the soles of their shoes propped up on the veranda wall. One set of feet was bare, just soles and toes.

Rose Badger held the gate open for William with one hand, and with the other clutched her throat and wrinkled up her face. 'I can't stand privet,' she gasped. 'Such an offensive smell.'

William stood still, not stepping forward through the gate.

'Actually,' Rose said, 'you should hold the gate open for me, that's what gentlemen do,' but since William was rooted to the footpath and unlikely to move unless forced to, she continued to stand holding the gate open for him, tapping one foot, still moving one hand about her throat, nose and mouth, warding off the smell of the privet. Then she dropped the hand to her side, composed her features, and smiled brightly. William knew that the smile belonged to the play, the continuing performance he was watching this day.

'Look smart,' said Rose Badger. 'Once we're settled in, we'll go to the beach and get an ice-cream and have a swim.'

William looked at her full of hope. She had said 'we'. 'We're settled in' and 'we'll go to the beach'. So, it had all been just her sense of fun, to mislead him, tease him. A kind of joke.

The men on the veranda looked up over their newspapers at the sound of the gate opening and at the sound of a woman's voice. They watched, taking in the image of a pretty young woman with yellow hair and sparkling white hat and gloves and shoes. Rose pulled William through the gate, closed it, then turned and walked snappily up the path to the steps.

William, invisible in his grey uniform, walked solidly behind her. As long as she was in his sight, even just the heels of her shoes, there was a chance he could remain with her, leave with her when she left. But she had said 'we'. Surely she was going to stay after all. It had all been just her sense of fun, to mislead him. She liked a joke, a good tease.

As Rose reached the top step, a tall, thin, unsmiling woman emerged from the house wearing a straight, dark skirt and a blouse with a round collar buttoned to the neck. Her brown hair was rolled back over her ears into a bun at the base of her neck. 'Badger, isn't it?' Rose leant up and gave this woman a quick peck on the cheek. 'Mrs Badger?' said the woman. 'Lovely to see you.'

'Miss Bucket,' William heard Rose say. 'Ah.' His mother had stopped on the top step and so he had stopped, her shadow, one step below. And still the woman, Miss Bucket, did not smile.

The three men on the veranda were watching, William knew that. The feet of the man sitting nearest the steps came down off the veranda wall. William could see the bare toes without having to look up. Then a face appeared before his face. This man had bent down, leaning his chest

on his knees, his face almost lower than his knees, so that
he had to look up to look at William, and he forced William
to look at him. The man bending down close to William
was young, with curly brown hair. He winked at William
and smiled, showing a missing tooth at the side of his mouth.
'How are you going, Smoodger?' he said. William lowered
his gaze further, to his own polished black shoes and new
grey socks, but he had managed to notice that the man
was not wearing a shirt and that his trousers were rolled
up almost to his knees. Beyond this man were the feet
of the two other men, one in black shoes with the laces
loose and without socks, the other in sandals and socks,
the holiday garb of working men.

Miss Bucket steered Rose and William past the men
on the veranda, positioning herself beside the front door.
Her body blocked the men so that Rose and William could
not see them fully as they passed into the house, as if the
men were something to be hidden from polite society, like
dirty laundry. Miss Bucket followed them into the hallway
then ushered them into her living room.

'This room, of course, is private,' she said to Rose,
inclining her head toward the veranda. 'You know how
it is with boarders. Not this handsome young man here,
of course.' She tilted her head at William. 'Those others.
One finds that so many of them don't know how to behave,
let alone speak.' She indicated the sofa where Rose should
sit and a chair for William. 'You've had lunch,' she stated
rather than asked.

'We had a picnic on the ferry,' said Rose.

William wondered at the lies of adults. They had eaten
heavy on the ferry, just a chunk of bread and raisins, nothing
that could be called lunch. He was hungry but immediately
he resolved to bear his hunger and not to eat at all until
he was taken home.

'Then I'll make tea,' and Miss Bucket left the room.

'Sh, pet,' said Rose, as if William might object and want lunch. 'It's past their lunchtime anyway. This is a boarding house, with hours. You'll have to eat lots for dinner. And you can always put Dadda's heavy under your pillow and eat it if you get hungry tonight.'

So he *was* going to be left. It was not a joke. It had been foolish to imagine that she might be staying with him after all. All these years, all those dresses and those stockings every day, this was what she had been preparing for. This was the day he was to be left.

'I won't stay,' said William. It never occurred to him to ask why he was being left. It had always seemed to be one of the possibilities, that children would be left somewhere. He had always trailed along after his mother, as children are supposed to do, but in the end such loyalty amounted to nothing. She was going somewhere, he knew. But why could he not remain with Dadda at home?

'We came all this way, to wonderful Manly,' said Rose, with exaggerated indignation, still on stage. 'You said you wanted a seaside holiday, you said you liked the beach.' She looked at him, her lip trembling slightly. 'And you should take off your cap indoors.'

Miss Bucket appeared with the tea tray, on which sat a teapot, two cups and saucers, and a glass of milk for William. On a plate beside the teapot lay three arrowroot biscuits. 'What a fine young man you've brought me,' she said.

William sat without moving, practically without breathing. He was looking at his knees, in particular at the scar on his left kneecap that had come from a dog bite when he was much smaller. To get to school he had to pass a house with a dog whose only reason for existing on this planet was to rush out when William passed. 'Just

show it you're not afraid,' Rose always told him. 'Show
it who's in charge,' his father said. 'It'll tire of the game
soon.' But the dog never tired, and every now and then
it caught William and bit him. He had a small scar on
his cheek and this bigger scar on his kneecap.

'Your cap, William,' whispered his mother.

William whipped off his green school cap and placed
it on his knee, over the scar.

'Put it on your suitcase, silly,' said Rose.

'He'll love it here,' said Miss Bucket. 'And it's not as
if we're strangers.'

William looked up at her quickly, examining the face,
then looked down again. He had never seen her before.
He looked at his mother, alarmed, but she was busy holding
her teacup.

'I love children,' said Miss Bucket, 'as you know.' She
leant forward and placed a finger under William's chin
and tried to raise his head and have him look at her. William
used all his force to keep his head lowered, to resist her
finger. It seemed that adults always wanted to poke at
children. 'In fact, I have a recipe for preserving children,'
said Miss Bucket. 'I got it from a cook book a relative
sent me.'

William swallowed in panic. All he knew about
preserving were the peaches and plums in jars on the pantry
shelf at home. And Egyptian mummies.

Miss Bucket took her finger away and sat back in her
chair. 'Shy,' she said over his head at Rose. Then to William
she said, 'Take one grass-grown field, half a dozen children
or more, several dogs, preferably puppies, one brook, and
some pebbles. Into the field pour children and dogs.'

She knew about the dog. She was going to put him
in a field with dogs.

'Allow to mix well,' Miss Bucket continued. 'Pour brook

over pebbles until slightly frothy. When children are nicely brown, cool in a warm bath. When dry, serve with milk and fresh gingerbread.' She held out the biscuit plate to William, and William took one and ate it, forgetting that he was not going to eat. Miss Bucket was the witch, escaped from the fairy tale, offering him goodies, out to get him, with a plan to cook and preserve him as soon as his mother left.

'That's delightful, isn't it William?' Rose said. 'What a delicious recipe.'

'Have another bickie,' said Miss Bucket. 'There's a good little chappie.'

William looked at his mother, who had taken only tea, no biscuit. He was trying to transmit to her the information that Miss Bucket was a child murderer. Rose nodded at him, smiling. 'You may take another biscuit.'

'And if you like, as a special treat since it's Boxing Day,' said Miss Bucket, 'you can dip your arrowroot biscuit into your milk.'

William sat like a rock with his milk in one hand and the second biscuit in the other. He was not going to eat it this time. His suitcase was at his feet, on top of it his green cap.

'Go on, dip it in,' Miss Bucket said.

William shook his head. 'I'm not allowed to dip them in when we're out. Only at home.' William was startled to hear the loudness of his own voice.

'Don't stretch the truth, William.' Rose laughed, exposed in her double standards, one set of manners for home, another for public. She raised her eyes to the ceiling. 'Children,' she said and laughed some more. 'Once I let him dip his biscuit in, when he was sick.'

Miss Bucket said, 'What a priceless pet. And he'll have such a nice healthy time here. You won't know him when you see him. He'll be brown as a loaf of bread and plump. Good enough to gobble up.'

Miss Bucket stood up. 'You must be longing to see your room, hummmm?' She led them out of the sitting room along the hallway past several doors. 'We are just a small cosy group here, just a few good working people. They think of this as home, as family. It's just like being back in London for me.' One door stood open, showing a tiny room with two single beds along the walls, parallel to each other, with a night table between them, a wardrobe at the foot of one bed, a chair at the foot of the other. The floor space in the room was like the aisle in a train carriage. Miss Bucket paused and quickly drew the door shut. 'Two of the young men are in there,' she said. 'They're like brothers.'

At the end of the hall was the bathroom, the door was half open. Miss Bucket stood in front of the door, blocking their view, again something unsavoury to be hidden from sight, and as she steered them to the left, she closed the bathroom door, giving a little cough as if to cover up her action. 'Men,' she said. 'I simply can't get them to keep doors closed.'

They passed through the kitchen to the back porch, where a young woman stood ironing at an ironing board. The porch was small, ten feet by six, and was enclosed, the brick wall of the kitchen and a back bedroom forming two walls, and fibro the bottom half of the other two walls and louvered glass the top half. At the far end was a daybed and a set of shelves, like a bookshelf. Above the shelves were several nails driven into the brick on which hung garden tools—a sickle, a trowel, and secateurs. The near end, where they were standing, was the public passage, carrying the general traffic from the kitchen to the backyard, the lavatory and the laundry. Through the louvres, and beyond the sheets that hung on the clotheslines in the backyard, William saw a little shed against the back fence and for a moment he believed that Miss Bucket would lead them across the porch, through the backdoor and down the steps, across the grass, under the sheets to that shed. He dared to hope that it might be his room. But Miss Bucket shepherded them around the ironing board, nodding at the young woman ironing, and opened the door to the bedroom that adjoined the porch.

'Excuse us,' said Miss Bucket, 'we're showing this young gentleman to his room.'

'Is that so?' said the young woman, looking from Rose to William, giving a bit of a smile.

Rose looked away, not wanting to engage in any kind of talk with Miss Bucket's boarders. The young woman winked at William, and pursed her lips at him. She was wearing a housecoat of pink cotton and scuffs on her feet, while she ironed a full white petticoat with frills. She looked like a little girl, with her hair in a fringe straight across her forehead and hanging down the sides of her face to her chin, as if her face were encased in a helmet, like the girl with the bananas on the billboard at Strathfield.

As the young woman stood to one side to allow Miss Bucket and her guests past into the bedroom, Miss Bucket said, with emphasis, 'Thank you muchly, Gert.'

Inside the room, Miss Bucket whispered, 'I wish they wouldn't iron on holidays. It's so hard to live a civilised life, on top of all the other problems.'

A single bed stood along one wall beneath a window that gave onto the backyard and the washing on the line. 'Of course, it's a holiday for everyone except those of us who run boarding houses,' said Miss Bucket indicating the washing. 'For us, it's unceasing. Three hundred and sixty-four days.'

'It's adorable,' said Rose, nodding at the room, which was about the size of the room they had seen off the hallway, shared by the two men. 'And all for you, William, all by yourself.'

William stood just inside the door, his suitcase in one hand, his cap in the other.

'Put your suitcase down, William,' said Rose.

William saw himself as a puppet, a dummy, with his owner manipulating his movements, the way he would have to move Billy Longleg about, when he arrived. He placed his suitcase beside him on the floor.

'Here's a little chest of drawers where you can put your things.' Rose opened the top drawer, then looked up at Miss Bucket. 'Someone's things are still here.'

'He'll have just the bottom drawer,' said Miss Bucket. 'The others are for storage, bedding and clothes, old clothes, and so on. You know how it is, finding room for everything in a house full of people.'

'One drawer is ample,' said Rose, 'isn't it, William?' She looked at him still standing by the door. 'And unbutton your blazer, now that we're here.'

William unbuttoned his blazer.

'You can take it off altogether,' said Rose, and held out her hand to take it from him.

'I'm not hot,' said William. He would not change out of his school clothes or unpack his bag. He would remain ready to walk out the door and return home, the moment his mother came back for him. There was no way to stop her leaving without him, leaving him behind, but he could at least be ready to leave when she returned.

'I have to fly, darling,' said Rose. She knelt down in front of him and flicked at his lapels, brushing something off.

'What about the beach, and the ice-cream?'

'I'll just leave you to say goodbye,' said Miss Bucket and withdrew.

'Be a good boy, won't you? Make mumma proud of her little man, won't you?'

William could not look at her. She was too lovely. As lovely as a film star. He would cry.

'Get lots of good sunshine.' She kissed him on the cheek.

'When will someone come to get me?' William mumbled.

'Soon,' said Rose, answering his question directly. 'Very soon. Not long. If you liked it here you could even go to school.'

William thought he might faint. School was weeks away. She was going to leave him here for weeks.

'Do what Miss Bucket says,' said Rose. 'I'll be back in no time. You'll see. Mumma has some things to see to.'

'I can see to things with you,' William pleaded. When Rose shook her head, with a smile, and said 'They're grown-up things,' he said, 'Then I can keep Dadda company at home.'

But again she shook her head. 'This'll be a nice change for you. Nice climate, sea breezes, different from the dust and heat in the western suburbs.' She stood up.

William was terribly afraid. He had no idea where she was going.

'I'll be back very, very, very soon,' she said. 'I have a suggestion. Why don't you learn all the poems in your Christmas book of poems, and when I come back, you can recite them to me. I'll expect you to know the poems by heart.'

'But you wouldn't like them,' said William. 'They're about the outback.'

'I'll like them if it's my little man saying them.'

She gripped his shoulder for a moment, then she was gone. William remained standing inside the door, next to his suitcase. He could hear Miss Bucket calling out her goodbyes from down the hall. He heard the front door close, heard his mother's shoes tripping down the steps, the gate opening, the shoes trotting along the street, along The Corso, past the amusement park and the aquarium, up the gangplank onto the ferry. He heard the pistons of the ferry starting up. After the ferry he had difficulty hearing anything. He did not know where she was going. She could be anywhere. And still he remained by the door, his cap in hand, ready to leave. He stared out the window, then looked around the room. Under the bed he saw a pair of pink slippers, and hanging behind the door a woman's pink milanese nightgown.

Miss Bucket came in and looked around, surprised to see William there. 'I thought you'd be begging to go to the beach already.'

William shook his head.

'Listen,' said Miss Bucket. 'I have to rearrange things a bit. I'd forgotten that someone was coming back and would be needing this room. The person whose room this is is coming back, you see.' Miss Bucket opened the top drawer and pulled out a tortoiseshell hairbrush and comb and a hand mirror, and a photograph of a young laughing woman. 'A relation,' she said.

William nodded. She would have to send him home now, if the room was taken. He would go home to his father. Miss Bucket arranged the items on top of the chest of drawers. William thought he could remember the way home. After the ferry, there was the tram, the train, and the bus. He picked up his suitcase. 'I'll just be going then,' he said.

'I didn't mean that,' said Miss Bucket, making a dry

laughing sound. 'You're charming. And your mother is right, you are like a little man, a little old man, so stern and severe.' She beckoned to him to follow her. 'We're going to put you on the porch here. There's plenty of room.' William did not move. She took the suitcase from him.

Since William would not entrust his suitcase to anyone, he held on and trailed after Miss Bucket onto the porch. The ironing board had been folded up and was leaning against the wall near the daybed. The young woman with straight hair, Gert, had disappeared.

'This'll be more fun here,' said Miss Bucket. 'A bit like camping out. You boys like adventure, they tell me. You can pretend it's wartime, with people all jolly together. You still remember the war, don't you?'

William stood by the daybed, looking down at the faded stripes on the cotton bedspread.

'Change your clothes. That uniform is ridiculous for this weather. What can your mother be thinking of? Go and explore until dinner time. You'll hear the bell. The beach isn't all that far. Just down the road, to the left when you go out the gate.' Miss Bucket sounded impatient.

'I'll just wait here, thanks,' said William.

The young man with the missing tooth poked his head around the door that led from the kitchen. 'Miss B., how about some afternoon tea, now that you've finished with your fancy guests.' He winked at William.

'Ah, tea,' said Miss Bucket.

William allowed himself to put his case down, and he perched on the very edge of the bed. His hands clutched the cotton bedspread. His mother had not left him any money, beyond his sixpence pocket money, although he had seen her pressing pound notes into Miss Bucket's hands. He thought he could find his way home, but he had no money to pay for the ferry and the tram and the train and bus. If he walked continuously for several days and nights, he would make it. He could find the bridge, the longest single-span in the world, and keep his eye on the AWA tower, use it as his marker. But what if his mother came back while he was on the road? She could be here the next day or the day after, if the things she had to see to were quickly concluded. She would not be able to find him. He could not even go to the beach. If he were not there when she came to get him, she might go away again.

So William stayed sitting on the bed. He could hear Miss Bucket in the kitchen washing the teacups and saucers. He heard her banging pots on the stove and chopping things on the chopping board, muttering, preparing dinner. The boarding house guests passed back and forth through the porch to get to the lavatory in the backyard. William did not look up, although they passed across one end of the room that was to be his bedroom, seeing only their feet and trouser legs, or in the case of the young woman, the hem of her housecoat.

'Hello Smoodger,' the man with the missing tooth said once, as he passed. William recognised the voice, then saw the bare feet. 'Hey, Smoodger, come here, come on, I'll show you something.' But William remained resolutely still. Then on his way back from the lavatory, the man said, 'Jeeze, look out, I've never seen such a big one!'

William looked up. The man was pointing up at the ceiling, then he pointed over William's shoulder at the wall, where the gardening implements hung, as if at some kind of menacing creature. William stared, following the line of the finger, trying to make out the danger. The man, while pointing, edged toward William, saying, 'Can't you see it? Look, up there!' While William's gaze was still fixed on the ceiling, the man reached out and pinched William's bare leg, just above the scar on his knee.

'Ow!' cried William, clapping his hands over the spot. He blushed and wanted to cry.

'Got him!' cried the man, holding up his forefinger and thumb, pressed together as if they had captured and squashed an insect. 'Biggest bloody mosquito I've ever seen in my life.' He held his finger and thumb close to his face and examined them. 'Lucky I got him, he had already drunk a schooner of your blood, young Smoodger, drinking as if it was five to six at the corner pub.' He made a show of holding up the finger and thumb. 'He's still wriggling, the bugger,' then he bent down and placed his finger and thumb in front of William's nose. 'Want to see him?'

William leaned back, away from the man's hand, shifting back on the bed so that his back was against the fibro wall and his legs and feet stuck straight out in front of him. He felt ridiculously childish. The man, shaking his head, leant over, placed his finger and thumb near his foot, then opened them as if dropping whatever it was he had caught, making a show of treading on it, grinding it into the porch floor with the ball of his bare foot.

'That wasn't a mosquito,' said William. 'You're a liar. You pinched me.'

Miss Bucket in the kitchen clicked her tongue.

The man, squatting now on the floor next to William's bed, raised his voice so that Miss Bucket would be sure to hear and jerked his head toward the kitchen to indicate to William that he should pay attention. 'A great, bloody, and I do mean bloody Miss B. in the pure sense of the word,' and he nodded at William. 'A bloody, great torpedo, right?'

'I don't believe you,' said William, resisting the man's attempts to get him to collude with him against Miss Bucket.

'Stop that, Roy,' said Miss Bucket. 'That's quite enough, thank you muchly.'

The man, Roy, got up, gave the floor a final grind with his foot, and shaking his head, left the porch. 'I bloody well saved a kid's life, Miss B.,' he said at the door of the kitchen. 'That mozzie was as good as a vampire. Would have sucked the boy dry, then what would his mother say? She'd take back all the money she's given you, wouldn't she? She'd need it to go out to the shops and buy a new boy, to go to the Boy Department at David Jones' and get a completely new boy for herself.'

William examined the floor where the mosquito had supposedly been squashed, but saw nothing. 'Bloody great liar,' he said, then loudly, so that Miss Bucket could hear, 'Great bloody liar.' He waited a few seconds, then when he heard nothing coming from the kitchen, yelled, 'bloody,' then, 'bugger.'

William sat on the bed, his head bowed, for the rest of the afternoon, until dinner time.

Rather than just one store dummy, he thought he would like to own several. A boy his own age, of course, a kind of twin, with whom he could share every thought. Then perhaps a larger one, an older boy, like a big brother, who would wear long trousers—William could hunt through Wally Badger's old clothes for discarded trousers, although it would be tough to find any, since Wally Badger wore the same trousers for years and years—the same good brown ones for best, the ragged brown ones around the house. William thought he could possibly also accommodate a smaller dummy, a younger brother, and perhaps even a younger sister. The littlies. He and his twin, Billy Longleg, could look after the little ones, buy them things, take them to the cinema. But the girl would need a dress, unless she were a tomboy and preferred to wear shorts, like her brothers. William and Billy could take the littlies to the beach, on the bus and the train and the tram and the ferry and along The Corso to the yellow sand. But that line of thought brought him back to Manly, where he now sat, more alone than he had ever been in his life.

The hem of a young woman's dress and her sandals were standing in front of him.

'Dinner,' was all she said.

She bent over and placed her forehead against his, trying to push his head back a little and look into his eyes.

'Come on, one eye,' she said.

But William leant away. Although he had been forced to raise his head and show his face, that did not mean he had to look at her, and he slid his eyes sideways, so that he could see through the louvres, without turning his head. This was a different young woman, not Gert with the hair helmet.

'Don't you know one eye?' said the young woman. 'You put your foreheads together and stare at each other and the other person's eyes merge, they become one. One eye.'

She picked up William's hand, rigid on the bedspread. 'Dinner,' she said again.

William pulled his hand away, and placed both hands beneath his thighs, so that he was sitting on them and no one could grab them. He kept his head bowed, his neck tense, ready to resist if she should place her finger under his chin.

The young woman, he could see out of the corner of his eye, was pretty. Her hair was brown, cut short, with a fringe in a sickle shape covering half her forehead.

'My mother will be here any minute to get me,' he mumbled. He could not bear the thought of sitting at a table with all those strangers, adults, all of them turning on him, mocking him, giving him a good tease.

'We'll see her if she comes,' said the young woman. 'She'll have to walk right past the dining room—we'll leave the door open and you can keep your eye out for her. I'll keep my eye out, too. Come on.'

She took his arm and he allowed her to pull him off the bed, resisting only slightly. She led him through the kitchen, where Miss Bucket was untying her apron.

The young woman paused, as if to allow William and Miss Bucket to recognise each other and exchange some formality.

'When is my mother coming?' William asked.

Miss Bucket hung the apron, a stiff oilcloth rectangle, on the back of the door. 'Soon,' she said.

The young woman led William on, along the hallway and into one of the side rooms, the dining room. Carefully and conspicuously she opened the door wide, pushing it back so that it was touching the wall.

The man called Roy and the two others who had been on the front veranda were already sitting at the table along with Gert. Roy had tied his table napkin around his neck and was sitting like a little boy with his knife and fork clutched in his fists, pointing upwards to the ceiling. At the entry of William and the young woman he quickly pulled the napkin onto his lap and replaced the knife and fork on the table. When he saw that it was not Miss Bucket, he picked them up again, this time as if they were drumsticks and began to tap out a rhythm on the table, dah d'dit, d'dit, dah dit, dah dit, dit, d'dah dit, as if he were playing a drum.

'We're leaving the door open so that the boy can see his mother when she comes to get him. He wouldn't want to miss her,' announced the young woman who had become William's protector.

Roy dropped his knife and fork and made a show of laughing, opening his mouth and showing the gap in his teeth. 'His mother? What have you been telling the little smoodger?' He winked at William. 'We're friends, the boy and me.'

William stood in one spot, just inside the door. The young woman had to pull him to one of the chairs, where a plate smaller than the others had been placed, and a table napkin rested not in a ring but folded beside the plate.

'She's probably run off,' said Roy. Every time he spoke, and several times during every outburst, he winked at William. 'They often do that. She's English, right?' When William, standing pale and straight nodded, Roy said, 'Well, there you are. They can't take it, the English, out here.'

'She's probably not English,' said William, blushing as he tried to change the meaning of what this man with the missing tooth was saying, tried to defend his mother. 'She's a wanderer. Possibly a gypsy.' And then he stopped, hearing what he was saying, realising that if she were a gypsy, his prospects of being picked up were even more remote.

'Don't tease him,' said Gert.

'Who's teasing?' said Roy. Then to William he said, 'I bet your mum hates the way we do things here, right?' And then he whispered to Gert, who sat next to him, 'Like our Miss B.' He raised his voice, 'Hey, Miss B., did you drop the leg of lamb on the floor and have to cook a new one?' And he tapped out another rhythm on the table with his knife and fork, softly, d'dah dah dit, dah dah dah, d'dit, d'd'dit, dah dah dah, dah dit.

'Patience is a virtue,' called Miss Bucket from the kitchen.

'Come on,' Roy said, 'tell us what your mum hates here.'

William said nothing. He was afraid to hear this kind

of talk. He had been expecting something like this for years and now it was happening, exactly as he had imagined it. The young woman who had led him in now pressed down on his shoulders, forcing him to slide onto his chair. His legs caught on the table cloth and began to pull it, causing the glass of water in front of his plate to teeter and his knife to fall to the floor.

The young woman, his guide, caught the glass and steadied it, looked quickly at the door and then straightened the cloth, bending down to retrieve the knife, blowing on it, then replacing it next to William's plate.

'Tell us,' Roy insisted, then said, 'Dah, dit, d'dah d'dit.'

William couldn't bear the attention, and so he answered, in order to free himself. 'Billycans. Milk delivered in billycans.'

'Milk in billycans? Is that all?'

'Insects get in and float in it,' said William. 'Flies.'

'See what I told you,' said Roy. 'They can't take it, the English. Too squeamish.'

'I'm English, too,' said William, taking a different line of defence. 'I was born there.'

'Ah, but you're a man. You can take whatever gets dished out, even what you'll be called on to eat here,' said Roy.

The table fell silent, looking to Roy to keep the noise going. Roy was looking unconcernedly around the room. William was thankful that no one was attending to him for the moment.

'Just be careful of swamps and the snakes,' said Roy suddenly.

'Don't tease him, Roy,' said William's young woman with the sickle-shaped half fringe, whom William had had a chance to consider and decide that she was the prettier of the two young women.

'That's Heather,' said Roy. 'She'll watch over you, since her room is at the end of the porch, near your bed.'

So this was the relation Miss Bucket had referred to, the one with the pink nightie on the hook on the door and the pink slippers under the bed.

Miss Bucket was still clattering with plates and pots in the kitchen.

'She said the room was for a relation,' said William.

The men at the table and the two young women laughed.

'She's the cat's mother,' corrected Gert.

And that caused everyone to guffaw and hoot again.

Roy leant over and whispered loudly at William, 'That room has always been Heather's. Miss B. just pretended it was empty, so that your mother could go off with a clear conscience.'

So Miss Bucket was a liar. What a treacherous world. It was too late now to warn his mother. It was too late.

'If Heather really is her relation,' Roy went on, 'Miss B. has been keeping a big secret. A very big secret all round.'

They were all still giggling like a class of schoolchildren when Miss Bucket came in with a plate of little white rissoles. She stood at her place at the head of the table and began dishing them out, two onto each plate as it was passed up to her. When Roy's plate was passed back to him, Roy turned his rissoles over and over with his fork and peered at them from different angles. Miss Bucket was annoyed.

'Mock fish,' she declared.

'Watch out for the swampy places, oozing with water, around the rocks,' said Roy to William. They all seemed to address William when they spoke. If he had not been there, they would have had nothing to say. 'That's where the mock fish lurk.'

William frowned, worried.

'Don't take any notice of him,' said Heather.

'They're poisonous, mock fish. And don't forget the savage, bloodthirsty flowers. We have them, you know, flesheaters. That's probably what scared your mum. The death trap flowers. I'd say that was it. That's why she's gone off. They grow all around these parts, waiting for some flesh to walk by. This is their peak season, December to March. They've got green and white faces and pink hairy ears, and mouths with hinges, and they can catch creatures and eat them. It's easier for them to catch children than adults, so watch out.'

Miss Bucket finished serving the rissoles and returned the dish to the kitchen.

'Don't take any notice of Roy,' said Heather. 'Listen, I tell you what, tomorrow I'll make jumping frogs for pudding, how about that?'

William had not changed his expression. He was pushing the white rissole around on his plate, afraid of the mock fish and the jumping frogs and the swamps in which they swam.

'It's only grated potato and flour and egg,' whispered Heather. 'It won't bite. It's not really fish. It's Miss B.'s way to not buy meat with the money we all pay her.'

'I've got a very hungry plant just out the back,' said Roy, 'at this very moment. I have to feed it every day. I'll show it to you later.'

'It's only a ginger beer plant,' said Heather.

'If,' said Roy, holding up his hand to stop her, 'if I don't give it a teaspoon of ginger and a teaspoon of sugar every day, it crawls up to the house across the back porch, devouring everything in its way until it gets to the kitchen and helps itself. You'll see. The sugar bowl is often found turned over on the floor in the mornings, and there's bits of sugar and stuff in a trail across the floor and across the porch, right past your bed. But now that you're here, it won't need to go as far as the kitchen.'

'Roy!' said Heather.

Miss Bucket returned to sit down and Roy fell silent.

'Can I make jumping frogs for pudding tomorrow night?' Heather asked. 'For the boy. To make him feel at home.'

Miss Bucket hesitated.

'I'll pay for the frogs and everything, of course,' said Heather.

Miss Bucket nodded. 'You can and you may,' she said.

'She'll go by the swamp and wrestle with the flesh-eating plants to get the frogs,' said Roy, 'risking her own life, so that William here can have an amusing pudding.'

William did not want to eat jumping frogs. 'Please don't bother,' he said. He would have to make sure he stayed awake all night—he intended to anyhow, in case his mother came—but now with the devouring plant he would have to be very careful, and who knew just how far those frogs could jump if they were motivated.

'They often find bits of bodies inside the plants,' said Roy. 'When they open them up, they find the bits the flower couldn't digest.'

'What bits are they?' Gert asked, and everyone began giggling again.

William considered Gert's hair and her face and decided that Heather was definitely the prettier by far.

'And if you try to press a flower like that, one of the types that eats flesh, if you try to tame it or kill it and press it in a heavy book, you'll find it simply gobbles up the paper. It hollows out a cave inside the book by eating the pages, then grabs your fingers when you go to open the book. It eats your fingers.'

'That's enough. Roy, you're distracting the boy,' said Miss Bucket. 'William, eat your dinner.'

William put down his knife and fork. 'I eat only peanut butter,' he said. 'That's all I eat. ETA peanut butter.'

'You ate those biscuits smartly enough this afternoon,' said Miss Bucket.

'Peanut butter and biscuits,' said William. 'That's all. And bananas.'

After dinner William stood at the front gate, waiting. The book of poems was in the pocket of his blazer and *Underground, or Life Below the Surface* was under one arm. After a while he leaned sideways, against the privet hedge, which gave a little, and he found he could squeeze between the hedge and the wooden fence next to the gate. He could sit down on the earth at the base of the hedge—the privet smell did not bother him as it bothered his mother, sneezing and clutching her throat whenever they passed one—and watch for Rose Badger through the spaces in the fence. It was still light enough for him to see the words of the poems in his book, and he began to say the words over and over in time to the footsteps of passers-by. 'With seldom a track that a man can trust, or a mountain peak to guide,' he murmured. Every pair of high heels tapping on the footpath could be Rose. 'All day long in the dust and heat—when summer is on the track—With stinted stomach and blistered feet, they carry their swags Out Back.' He wondered if that was where Rose was, outback, with blistered feet and a stinted stomach. But it was not likely. She was not the type to go outback. She did not even like the suburbs, and hated the bush.

William opened the large leather *Underground* volume and rested it on his knees. He moved his finger slowly down the page of contents and considered the chapter headings: The Diamond Fields of South Africa, dust storms and heavy rains, individual instances of good luck; The Underground Railroad in London; The Gambling Halls of Germany, rose-strewn roads to ruin; Subterranean Dwellings; Accidents in Shafts, eight hours of mortal agony, an accident caused by rats; Burglars and Burglaries, underground for dishonest purposes; the Under-world of Paris, the immorality and licentiousness of Paris, actresses and champagne, bloodthirsty viragoes and desperate cut-throats; Dungeons, shut up in the dark cells, a night of horror, Peter the Great Torturing his son; Graves and Their Construction.

When it was quite dark Miss Bucket came looking for him, calling his name. William considered staying hidden in the hedge all night, but it was uncomfortable, and Miss Bucket's calling voice persisted so loudly and unpleasantly that he crawled out onto the path.

'Bedtime,' she said, when William appeared in the bright light of the hallway, speaking to him as if he were five or six years old.

He walked up the steps and down the hall, through the kitchen onto the back porch, and lay on his bed on top of the covers in his clothes, so that when Rose came, he could just get up and walk out with her. He could hear Roy and the other men talking in the backyard outside the louvres.

'If you don't get in your pyjamas by yourself, I'll have to put them on you,' said Miss Bucket.

Although William knew he could get the better of Miss Bucket in a fight and prevent her taking his clothes off him, the thought of her touching him and ripping at his blazer and shirt, possibly tearing them, so that he would not look at all neat when his mother came, made him decide to get into his pyjamas, even before Miss Bucket said, 'And if you don't go right to sleep or are too rowdy, then I'll have to use something. When we were children and disobeyed our parents they used chloroform to quiet us down and put us to sleep. I'm sure I must have some chloroform somewhere.'

William grabbed his pyjamas and raced across the backyard past the men and under the clothesline to the lavatory, where he put on his striped pyjamas.

'Hello?' he heard Roy say. 'Who was that, Phar Lap?'

William sat on the toilet seat holding his neatly folded school uniform, afraid to go back past the men, vulnerable in his nightclothes. Finally, when someone banged on the door and said, 'The lav isn't your bedroom, son. We've all got to use the dunny,' he flung open the door and raced back to the porch.

He folded his school clothes again, carefully, so that they would not crease and placed this bundle on his bed, between his pillow and the porch wall. Then he lay on his back on the bed, his hands behind his head, staring at the ceiling, mumbling his poem, while Roy and the other men stood out the back smoking and laughing and Heather and Gert trotted back and forth across the porch, retorting to the 'Hellos' and 'What have we heres' from the men with a 'Get out' or 'Come off it.' From her room at the other end of the porch Heather called out through the louvres now and then, 'Stop it, Roy.'

'For time means tucker and tramp you must, where the scrubs and plains are wide, with seldom a track that a man can trust, or a mountain peak to guide,' said William softly.

Miss Bucket appeared only once, poking her head around the kitchen door to check on him. He was able to close his eyes and feign sleep and thus avoid her chloroform. In one of the books he had had when he was much younger, even before the 'James, James, Morrison, Morrison' poem, was a picture of a boy in his pyjamas at a fork in the road. One way was broad, smooth, beautiful, enticing, the other narrow, overgrown, thorny, difficult. In the story the boy had chosen the easy path and met with nothing but disaster and corruption and sin. It was only a bad dream, however—that was why the boy was wearing pyjamas— and at the end of the story he woke up in his own bed.

The lavatory and the backyard were lively places, with the boarders trecking back and forth across the porch. This pleased William, since the noise helped him stay awake. He dimly heard Heather calling to the men from her room to 'Take off, won't you. People are trying to sleep.'

'Take off?' said Roy. 'Give me some money and a car and I'll take off like a bride's nightie, you'll see.'

'Pipe down, Roy,' Heather retorted.

'Like a pink, slippery nightie.'

And then it was morning and William sat on his bed while the men polished their shoes ready for work. Roy spat on his shoes and rubbed the spittle in. 'Very good for leather,' he said and then, 'What else didn't she like, your mum, come on, I bet there's a whole list.'

William was cocking his head and squinting, looking for signs of sugar on the floor. 'Cockroaches,' he said absently. 'They're too big.'

'And they fall in the milk in the billycan, right? Next to the flies, right?' Roy laughed. 'What else?'

'The flowers,' said William.

'Right,' said Roy. 'Because they gobble you up.'

'Because the colours are wrong,' said William.

'Leave him alone,' said Heather, coming out of her room in her cotton dress and nylon stockings, carrying her shoes. She set them down and began to polish them, ready for the office. 'The boy's mum will be back soon.'

'Don't count on it,' said Roy. 'The *Himalaya*'s leaving today, tomorrow, some time, for London. Maybe she's on it.'

William had not considered the possibility of his mother's making a journey by ship. He took a deep breath, feeling a new great fear. Then to re-establish the calm he knew he had to maintain—if he panicked and collapsed it would only make things worse—he said to Roy, 'You must have fed the plant. There's no sugar that I can see on the floor.'

William's voice was even a little taunting. He was pleased to be able to challenge the truth of Roy's story, to challenge Roy himself.

Dressed in his grey uniform William spent the day near the front gate, tucked in his nest between the hedge and the fence. By pressing back against the privet he was able to make the space rounder, cosier, more like a cave, the branches and leaves giving a little behind his back and coming forward around him at the sides.

'And dirty and careless and old he wore, as his lamp of hope grew dim; He tramped for years til the swag he bore seemed part of himself to him.' As William chanted he formed the twigs of the hedge into shelves and niches, where he intended to place his books and his pocket money, his notebook and pencil. If only he had brought his supply of sweets from home, he could have stored that, too. If only he had known it would be an emergency.

Nevertheless he continued to expect Rose at any moment, and he intended to recite all the stanzas of the poem to her, as she had requested.

He sat with his notebook and pencil ready to write something down, he was not sure what. He tried writing down the number plates of the cars that passed, then descriptions of every passer-by, as if he were a detective, documenting the activities in the street and in the pocket-handkerchief park opposite Miss Bucket's front gate. In between observations he copied important paragraphs from *Underground*, descriptions of the lives of those who delved and dared, of curious deeds, hidden localities and lives.

Exploring subterranean tombs, travellers got lost and perished for want of food and light. Exploring a tomb at Thebes one adventurer was moved to recite 'The Last Rose of Summer'. As they groped their way through black, dirty, dusty passages his companion, a man called Jack, got stuck in a passage so narrow that he filled it as a cork filled the neck of a bottle, and was like a number ten gun wad forced into a number eight barrel. Jack opened his mouth to spout a verse of poetry and got a bat between his teeth before he finished the first line.

A truck pulled up opposite, a council truck, and several men jumped out with a long two-handled saw and began to saw at the trunk of the palm tree that grew just inside the railing fence of the park. In one hour they felled the tree, laid it along the grassy strip, cut off its branches, which they threw onto their truck, and drove off. Left behind, like a beached whale, was the long grey trunk of the palm, looking very interesting indeed. William wrote this event down. After a while, he crept out of his lair, through the gate and across the street, to examine the thing. He took out his penknife and poked at it. The wood seemed fairly soft. He scooped out a chunk of wood, and then some more. And suddenly he had a plan. He would carve out a canoe. He ran back to get his pencil from its shelf in the hedge, then back again to the tree trunk, on which he marked out the area to be hollowed out. Then he began work, systematically carving up little squares and scooping them out. He worked feverishly, and every now and then he retreated to the hedge to rest and jot down his progress in his notebook. 'Six inches in fifteen minutes,' he wrote. 'The wood is pretty soft.'

After lunch, he resumed his position at the hedge, now and then darting across the road, to hack at the tree trunk. At one stage, instead of returning to the hedge to write, he sat on the top bar of the railing fence, swinging his legs, contemplating his canoe. Suddenly he rolled backwards, as if he were on monkey bars, and hung by his knees, his finger tips an inch or so above the ground, and hanging upside down he looked across at Miss Bucket's inverted gate and the hedge. As he hung there the carving of the canoe, all his efforts, seemed stupid, and he dropped from the rail, letting his hands go flat against the ground as he brought his legs over his head to thump on the ground. When he stood up he bumped his head on the lower rail, quite a hard knock, and he ran back across the road, inside the gate, and crept into his nest in the hedge, where he allowed himself to cry. These were his first tears in months, years. He cried there, for several minutes, his wrists pressed against his eyes, biting his lips, trying to muffle the animal noises that came from his throat. Then he opened *Underground* and copied out a few sentences about the ghastly display of skulls and bones in the catacombs of Paris, a few more lines about a man broiled alive in the caverns of Naples, a few more about the women of gay and coquettish disposition who prefer lovers to husbands, who completely unbend, cast reserve to the breezes, take easy positions, blow small clouds of smoke at the frescoed ceiling, or keep time to the clinking of champagne glasses with their symmetrical feet, and then a paragraph about the flooding of a mine on the Loire, where five out of a hundred and ten men survived the inundation for thirteen days. 'The energy and tenacity of life are great, and few men ever know how much they can undergo until they are driven to make the experiment.'

At dinner the second night Heather said to William, 'Come on, say your poem.' Again, all comments were directed at William, and he wondered how they had managed before he arrived. 'We've all heard you. And I can hear you from my bed. Come on, say it. And then we'll have jumping frogs.'

'He hasn't even unpacked,' said Miss Bucket. 'And he refuses to go to the beach.' She placed a peanut butter sandwich on a plate in front of him.

'There's threepence-worth of dinner,' said Roy.

'It's what the boy said he wants,' she said defensively.

'That'll save on the mock meat,' muttered Roy, then to William in a jolly voice he said, 'On the weekend I'll take you to the beach. We'll have a good swim in the Pacific Ocean and say hello to the sharks, what do you say to that?'

'I can't,' said William. 'My mother is coming for me.'

'Listen, son,' said Roy, 'I think you'd better come to the beach with me. I'll tell you why.' He looked around the table. 'It's a fact. I'll tell you a true story. I come from Western Australia, you see, and there's a town there called Vasse, and do you know why it's called Vasse?'

William looked at him gravely, without even shaking his head.

'There's a river called Vasse, too. Where it lets out into the Indian Ocean there's the longest jetty in Australia, so it's an important place. It's called Vasse because it's named after a sailor called Vasse. A Frenchman. Those French came exploring in the olden days and by mistake they left Mr Vasse behind. They left him and sailed off, back north, to France and the continent.' He looked around. 'Poor Mr Vasse was left standing on the beach, all alone, the only white man down here, while his ship sailed off home. He just stood there on the beach, never leaving it, looking out to sea, hoping to see his mates turn the ship around and come back for him. He stood there until he died. That's why it's called Vasse.'

'Roy,' said Heather.

'It's a fact,' said Roy. 'My oath. Now,' he said to William, 'since we think your mum has run off back to England on the boat for a quick look-see, then it follows that she'll be coming back on the boat, if she comes back.'

'When she comes back, Roy,' said Heather.

'She said she was coming to get me soon,' said William.

'She said if she isn't back, he can start school here,' said Miss Bucket.

William kept swallowing, his throat dry. How did these people know all this about his family and his life, things he did not know himself.

'So,' said Roy, 'I reckon coming to the beach with me will kill two kookaburras with one stone. First, you've got to vary your lookout. If you stay by the front gate all the time, you're going to die there, like Vasse. We'd have to change the name of Manly to something else, Unmanly, or Billy, after you, Billy, who died there. And think of the expense, changing all the maps and everything from Manly to Billy. And frankly, I don't think it's a good name for a place. I wouldn't be happy living in Billy. Sounds like a billycan, and in summer you'd think you were getting broiled alive all the time in a billycan, every time you said the name of where you lived. I live in Billy.'

'Roy.'

'You have to vary your movements, so death can't find you. And second, if you stand on the beach and look out to sea, you'll be the first to see your mother's ship coming in.'

Heather got up and went to the kitchen, patting William's shoulder as she passed his chair.

'You can check the ocean every day for ships, then you can go and wait at the gate,' Roy continued, 'because it will take her a little bit of time to get off the boat at the Quay and then catch the ferry here to get you. You'll easily have time to get from the beach to the front gate before she gets here.'

Heather entered bearing the dessert on a tray, little glass bowls of green jelly in which sat chocolate Freddo frogs, half in and half out of the jelly.

'Oink, oink,' said Roy.

'That's pigs, not frogs,' said Heather.

'So what do frogs say?' asked Roy.

Heather shrugged and looked at William.

'What do frogs say?' Roy asked him.

William hesitated. 'Croak,' he said dully.

'That's it, the boy's a genius,' cried Roy. 'Croak, croak. Show us how it goes.'

William was silent. Then suddenly he made his growl, 'Rrrp, rrrp,' several times, very loudly, the animal growl he made when Rose wanted to talk privately with Wally Badger and ordered him to make noises.

Roy applauded.

'That's enough,' said Miss Bucket.

'See,' said Heather, smiling at William. 'They're like frogs about to jump out of a green pond. Get it? Jumping frogs?'

William could eat the jumping frogs after all, at least the green jelly part. He spared the frog itself, licking it clean of jelly and slipping it in his pocket. He would start a new emergency collection. When Heather saw that his dish was empty, she gave him a second one. 'I made extra,' she said, and William saved that frog, too, eating only the jelly. 'I knew you'd like them,' said Heather. 'But now you have to tell us your poem.'

William could see no escape. He had accepted her jumping frogs. And also he quite liked her.

'During the war,' Miss Bucket suddenly said, 'we used to sing songs. We weren't afraid to entertain each other. His mother gave us each a song to sing.'

William closed his eyes. So this Miss Bucket was the handkerchief woman in the air-raid shelter. That's what she had meant when she said that first day that they were not exactly strangers. 'My song was "Run Rabbit Run",' said Miss Bucket, and she smiled around the table at her boarders. There was silence for a moment, then Miss Bucket stood up and removed plates. Roy laughed into his hands. 'Rabbit,' he chortled. 'That accounts for all the rabbit we get to eat here. I think you are better off with peanut butter after all, Billy Boy.'

'Come on,' said Heather to William, drawing out the words, 'the poem.'

And with his eyes still closed William mumbled the poem.

'He tramped away from the shanty there, when the days were long and hot. With never a soul to know or care if he died on the track or not.'

'Just like poor Vasse,' said Roy. 'Not a soul knew or cared if he died on the beach or not.'

Every morning William dressed in his school uniform and good socks and waited in his cubby hole at the front fence. Miss Bucket did not seem to care, as long as he was out of the house. Even in the rain he could sit there, protected by the overhang of the hedge. Every day he learned two more lines of the poem. 'And dirty and careless and old he wore, as his lamp of hope grew dim; He tramped for years til the swag he bore seemed part of himself to him.'

And every day he wrote down more important facts

from *Underground*. Some diamonds explode. Many priestesses of Venus sin without satisfaction, and laugh without gaiety. The lowest pariahs accost strangers at night and smoke cigars in the street. Peter the Great stood calmly by while his son died in agony. Vienna, Naples, St Petersburg, Berlin, London, New York have reputations as the wickedest of cities. Stockholm has more illegitimate children than any other European capital. Brigandage is rapidly becoming a thing of the past in most parts of Europe, thanks to the introduction of the railways. Earthquakes in California benefit mine owners by opening up new rich chambers of ore.

He carved out more of his canoe, methodically, half-heartedly, his initial zest having subsided. Now and then he sat on the top rail of the fence along the park, throwing himself backwards to hang by his knees, but no longer bumping his head when he got up.

One morning, William was sitting under the hedge as usual when Roy's head appeared over the fence above him.

'It's beach day,' he said. 'Come on, maybe we'll see her boat coming back and you can wave to her.'

'She didn't go to England,' said William. He agreed to go to the beach with Roy, just in case, but refused to change into shorts and his bathing suit.

'Then we'll just take them with us,' said Roy, rolling William's suit in a towel and placing it around William's neck, as he did with his own suit and towel.

Heather came with them, wearing a blue skirt and sandals, not a full circle, not cut on the bias, William noted, but gathered. As they walked along the street toward the beach, she put her hand on William's shoulder and hummed a tune.

'I like poetry, too,' she said. 'My mother, who is dead now, always said if you couldn't play the piano or an instrument, then at least you should be able to recite a poem. My speciality is "The Man from Snowy River" and "*La Belle Dame Sans Merci*", which means the beautiful lady without mercy.'

'Sounds like all women I know, beautiful or otherwise,' said Roy. 'They never show us poor men any mercy, right William?'

'And I can do most of "*Morte d'Arthur*",' said Heather, 'which means the death of Arthur.'

'Death,' said Roy, 'don't mention Death. You're talking about nothing but death and dead, while we're trying to trick Death. Poor old Arthur, Artie, didn't manage to pull it off, whoever he may be.'

'King Arthur,' said Heather.

'What we want is to get Death's attention away from William here, waiting on the beach,' said Roy. 'We don't want to have to write Morte William, do we? What about "The Man From Iron Bark". I seem to remember that. The man from Iron Bark visited the barber, didn't he? Better to be thinking of hair cuts and shaves than Death. Hey!' Roy stopped short, pointing at the street vendor on the corner selling the balloons and windmills and kewpie dolls on sticks that William had glimpsed when Rose brought him along The Corso to the boarding house. The black one with the skull and crossbones was still there. 'You see what you've done! There's Death,' cried Roy, 'just lying in wait. We'd better buy it immediately and get control over old Death.' He paid sixpence for the balloon and gave it to William. 'Hold onto him tight. Here's what you have to do. You have to hold onto him until we get to the beach, then you cut him loose—you take him off his stick and let him fly off. That's how you get rid of Death.'

William took the balloon gingerly and held it stiffly before him on its stick.

'I'll tell you exactly when to let him go,' said Roy.

When they reached the sand, Roy and Heather stooped to take off their shoes. William said he would not bother, he was just going to stand on the sand and watch the horizon. He did not intend to swim or anything.

'Think of it like this,' said Roy. 'After we let Death here go and send him on his way, you're safe. You could easily stand in the water and keep cool and at the same time watch the horizon, and if you saw her boat, then you'd still have time to get dried and dressed before the boat docked and she came on over here to get you.'

William shook his head and walked for a few steps keeping his legs stiff, not bending the knee.

'You can change like this,' Roy called after him. Roy wrapped his towel around his waist and slipped his trousers off and his trunks on.

'It's easy,' Roy said. 'No one'll see anything you don't want them to see.'

William turned away and resumed walking, both legs straight, like a robot, a puppet, gripping the black balloon. Perhaps he had broken both his legs once, and now although he could walk he could never bend his knees again. But both legs seemed improbable, and keeping both legs stiff was hard to maintain on sand. Perhaps it was just one leg that had been broken and was now permanently stiff. So he walked to the water's edge, keeping one leg straight, limping along. He had broken the leg when he had fallen out of something, out of a hammock, perhaps, or off the back of a bus. He had been quite little, sitting on his mother's lap on the back seat just next to the back platform and the bus had jolted and turned a corner rather suddenly, and his mother's grip on him had been too slack, not tight enough, and he had rolled off her knee, across the platform and onto the road, where a car ran over his leg. And now

he could never bend his knee again. Or a bomb had dropped
when they were in the underground shelter in London,
a direct hit. A beam had fallen across his leg as he lay
with his head in his mother's lap and pinned him down.
His mother had been killed instantly. Everyone else was
unconscious. They were trapped for days. He stayed alive
by chewing on the wooden beam that lay across his body.
And now he could not bend his knee ever again.

William heard hoots and yells behind him and turned
just as Roy tackled him and threw him to the sand. William
kicked and punched at Roy's back, forgetting about his
impaired leg, letting the balloon go. Sand was getting in
the pockets of his trousers and his blazer and into his socks
and shoes. Roy ran after the black balloon rolling along
the sand at the water's edge and caught it.

'Now,' he said, taking the balloon off its stick and
handing the balloon back to William, 'now let him go,
send him off.'

William flung the balloon away from him, standing on
tiptoe as he let it go. It flew off unhampered by its stick,
then, beyond the swimmers in the surf, it fell into the water.

'That'll teach Death a lesson,' said Roy, shaking his
fist at the sea. 'Into the drink with Death.' He flicked
sand at William, who, having watched the balloon
disappear, resumed spitting the sand out of his mouth and
shrugging in an effort to shake the sand off his clothes.

'Come on,' said Roy. 'Now you can give swimming
a try.'

William agreed to give it a try, not that he wanted
to swim of course, but he reasoned that the water would
wash the sand off.

He wrapped his towel around his waist, the way Roy
had done, and wriggled out of his grey flannel trousers
and into his bathing trunks. Once his legs and chest were

bare, he found himself running down the sand, past Heather standing at the water's edge hugging herself, straight into the sea, shouting when the cold water hit his chest and took his breath away, then laughing.

'Attaboy,' cried Roy, abreast of him. Then he dived under the water and grabbed William's legs and William kicked back, laughing and sputtering, and when Roy came up for air, William cleverly ducked him from behind. Then together they turned on Heather, in water up to her ankles, hunched over and shivering. They splashed her while she shrieked and begged them to stop.

'The beautiful lady without mercy,' cried Roy, and William kept splashing her, while Roy seized her and carried her in, until the water was up to his waist. Then he dropped her.

William forgot to keep his eye on the horizon.

Later, when they all lay on the sand, Roy propped himself on one elbow and said, 'I'll tell you something. Without us down here in Australia, the world wouldn't be able to spin properly, you know that, don't you.'

William looked interested.

'Oh, Roy,' said Heather. 'Not again.'

'It's a fact,' said Roy. 'We're doing the world a very big favour. If we all got on boats right now and went back north to the old country, back to where we came from, the world would spin out of control and we'd all be dead. That's why we have to stay here. It's a kind of public service, a service to the whole of the human race. That's probably why William and his mother came here in the first place. It was very noble of them, if you think about it. They sent word up to Europe that they needed a few more people down here, because the world was tilting, a population explosion in the north, and William's mum very gallantly volunteered to bring herself and her boy here. When it began to tilt again, Miss B. offered to come down, her finest hour.'

'My mother came because my father was here,' said William. 'They met during the war. Then he came here. And after I was born, my mother came, too.'

'That's what she told you,' said Roy. 'She didn't want anyone to think she was boasting, about helping mankind. But the real reason they send people down here is that as Europe gets more crowded—and they're having babies by the millions up there—then the world gets out of balance, and they have to pack some off down here. It's how this whole country got started in the first place.'

'Don't listen to him,' said Heather. 'You'll fail history and geography if you take him seriously.'

'It's a fact,' said Roy. 'The world is a giant seesaw, poised on its axis, and to keep it steady, we down here have to press hard into the ground, doing coalmining and everything, so that the Europeans up there are free to do their art and their music and think clever thoughts above the ground. They couldn't do it without us down here keeping things steady, tamping the ground down. The world wouldn't spin properly. My oath.'

Roy sat up and smoothed out the sand in front of him. 'Here, I'll pass on to you a secret, something that might come in very handy in the future.' With his finger he wrote the letter S in the sand and next to it he punched his finger into the sand three times, forming three dots. Then he wrote the letter O, with three dashes after it, then S again, with three dots. 'SOS, see?' said Roy and he pointed at the dots and dashes as he said, 'D'd'dit, dah dah dah, d'd'dit. Three shorts, three longs, three shorts.'

William repeated the dots and dashes in the sand.

'Morse code,' said Roy. 'If you did it very big, an aeroplane could see it from the sky. If you banged it on a rubbish bin with a stick, it could be heard miles off. A useful thing for a man to know.' And suddenly he turned on William and beat out the rhythm of shorts and longs on his shoulder. William scuttled away from him, then as Roy pursued him, William got up and ran, Roy chasing him, until Roy grabbed him, threw him to the ground and sat on him, beating out on his chest d'd'dit, dah dah dah, d'd'dit while William struggled and giggled and kicked trying to be free. When Roy had finished, the two of them stood up and walked back to Heather and their towels, Roy's hand resting comfortably on William's shoulder. 'I'll show you the other letters,' he said, 'and the punctuation. It might just come in handy for a man like you who is likely to have adventures.'

On the way back to the boarding house, the three of them linked arms and trod heavily on the ground, to weigh down their end of the planet.

'My mother said the ground was swaying when we stepped off the boat,' said William.

'You got here just in the nick of time then, in time to steady the planet,' said Roy. 'And that's why your mum will eventually come back. When the world begins to slant a bit, she'll know and she'll have to come back to save us all. A brave and courageous lady.'

'She wouldn't go back to England,' said William, 'without consulting me. And especially not if she knew it would tilt the world. She probably just went straight home to my father, Walter Badger. They probably had to discuss something in private.'

When they got to the front gate William ducked into the hedge and emerged holding his notebook.

'To write down the rest of the morse code,' he said.

Inside the boarding house was a letter from Wally Badger.

'You certainly must be having a good time,' he wrote. 'I think you may be running short of cash and I am enclosing one pound to help you along. There is really little to write about. I miss you of course and will be extra glad when you return. It is not so good with both yourself and your mother gone. All for now, will write again soon. Love from Dadda.' So, Rose had not gone home to discuss something at all. She had really gone off and Wally Badger did not know.

William had been at the boarding house for several weeks. He had memorised all the letters of the morse code, and often he sat in the hedge tapping out messages. His hair was covering his ears, and Roy had begun to call him Wilhelmina, but William would not let them cut it. It was his measure of time, like carving out a few more inches of the tree trunk, whose cavity now was big enough for him to sit in. For the first time his head felt covered and protected. He began to transcribe into morse code his favourite passages from *Underground*.

'When school starts, you'll have to get that hair cut,' said Miss Bucket.

'I'm not going to school here,' said William. 'My school is at home.'

'We'll have to call you little Rose, soon,' said Roy. 'Rosebud. That's what you'll look like, a little girl.'

After that William let Roy take him to the barber shop to get his hair cut. It was Saturday and drizzling, not a beach day.

'Short back and sides,' Roy told the barber.

'Not too short,' William tried to say, but the big white cape swirled over him and the paper was tucked noisily around the neck. It seemed that the barber could not hear him, no matter how much he made his mouth move— he knew it moved because he saw it in the mirror, saw the lips moving like a goldfish, mouthing the words 'not too short.'

The barber clipped up his neck and over his ears, zealous as barbers always seemed to be, knowing what heads needed in the way of a cut better than their customers.

Released, William scurried into a sweet shop and spent some of his pound on chocolates and crumble bars. All the way home, beside Roy, he tried to draw his head into his collar. He felt bald and helpless again and did not want to be seen, and he could feel the rain on his scalp. At the gate he ducked away from Roy and squeezed into the hedge. As he suspected, the hedge was thick enough to keep his cave completely dry. He took out the sweets and placed them in the little forks formed by the branches of the hedge, next to the Freddo frogs, then sat still, watching, moving his eyes from chocolate bar to chocolate bar, reassuring himself that each one was dry, not in the line of a stray drip. After a while he took down his notebook and read his morse code notes from *Underground*, about the adventuress who was more interesting at forty than in the flush of her glowing youth, accosting strangers at night on the boulevards, asking loungers in the cafes to buy her coffee and wine, smoking cigars in the street, often arrested for brawls, intoxication and pilfering.

'We stepped into a dismal vestibule,' he read. 'A few steps brought us into the hall—it should have been called a cellar—and in it were some fifty of the most villainous-looking men and coarsest women I had ever had the misfortune to encounter. It was evident at a glance that they were thieves, robbers and assassins; the slightest acquaintance with phrenology and physiognomy made that clear—that some of them were of the sneak, some of the burglar, and others of the desperado order. The place was dimly lighted with a few sputtering candles; the ceiling low, the air mephitic. The women, if they might be termed such, were more brutal and bloodthirsty in their dispositions, judging from their expression, than the men themselves. One Amazon, who had a mustache and slight whiskers, had committed two murders.'

He turned back to the book to transcribe yet another passage, and as he wrote in the dots and dashes he proclaimed the words out loud.

' "There is a young person I have not noticed before," I said to my companion, pointing to the left. "Who is he? He can't be a thief. He must have gotten into this company by mistake." The man I had designated could not have been more than twenty. He had a fresh, handsome face, and when he smiled, as he often did, his smile lighted up his countenance as sunshine lights up a landscape. It was hard to associate him with crime or vice of any kind . . . The detective laughed and said, "You mean the Badger. He is one of the greatest scamps in all Paris, and one of the most desperate scoundrels. There is nothing in the world he would not do for money. If I were not here, and anybody were to offer him five francs, he would walk up to you, salute you politely, and blow your brains out, regarding it as a capital joke. The Badger is well-educated, and is reputed to be the son of a prominent lawyer by an actress. He ran away from home, and turned thief on instinct. He is absolutely without fear and without conscience. That crime is natural to him is proved by his enjoyment of it." '

The Badger. William read this description of this lovely young man several times, savouring the words: scamp, reputed, prominent, scoundrel.

He sat back against the hedge, astonished, breathless, alert, energetic. The Badger, underground, in Paris. Surely it was he. He was The Badger. In Paris, Europe, Northern Hemisphere, Earth.

William placed the book carefully in its place in the hedge, leapt out of his cave and dashed across the road. He thought he might sit in his canoe in the rain and plan some action, some crime. They had shaved his head in jail, from which he had cunningly extricated himself. Now he somehow had to hide the telltale short hair of the escaped convict. The unkempt stubble on the face of older criminals was not his problem. He was too youthful a criminal to have stubble. He took out his handkerchief and tied a knot in each of the corners, forming a convenient skull cap, which he pulled on over his short hair. He was busy looking from side to side, checking that no one was around to see this escaped criminal, so that he did not notice that his canoe had gone until he was actually climbing over the railing of the fence. It had been there when he set out with Roy for the barber's, he was certain. But in the short time they had been away, something had come along and dragged it off. He could see the marks in the grass, as if the canoe had resisted and had had to be subdued.

William sat on the top railing of the fence, feeling the raindrops soaking through the handkerchief and settling on his scalp. The Badger. Fresh, handsome, and a desperate scoundrel. He had put in thirty or sixty or a thousand hours carving out the canoe. When Rose came, and she must come soon, how pleased she would be to see him like this, in his school uniform, and his short, short hair. As the rain fell and began to penetrate the wool of his uniform the cloth began to smell. Rose would certainly not be pleased that he was sitting in the rain, ruining the good cloth.

William threw himself backwards from the rail, intending to swing by his legs a little, to let the rain soak in, to get as soaked as he possibly could. He stretched his fingertips so that they touched the mud that had formed on the ground along the fence. He would get as dirty as he possibly could, too, since he was The Badger of the Paris underworld, not William Badger, son of Rose and Wally. But because the rail was wet, his legs slipped and the force of his throw pulled them right off the railing, and as he replayed it in his mind, sitting there in the mud, nursing his left wrist, which took the full force of the fall, he saw himself like a boy in a cartoon, falling straight down on his hand, with his head, then his body and legs following, compressing, like a concertina.

When he looked down at his wrist he saw it had grown, swollen, so that it was wider than his hand and his forearm. And it hurt. He got to his feet and holding his wrist walked across the road and up the front path and steps, past the two men on the veranda, with their feet on the brick, their heads in their papers, into the front parlour, the private parlour, where Miss Bucket sat having tea.

But before she could scold him for interrupting and for ruining his clothes and muddying her carpet, he simply held out his left wrist, resting on his right hand, as if he were offering her a plate of biscuits.

'What have you done now,' Miss Bucket said rather than asked, and with a sigh went to find Roy, who was sitting on the back porch, near William's bed, reading the paper, leaning back on the two legs of the chair, which with the weight of his body was leaving indentations in the linoleum.

'Stop that at once,' said Miss Bucket, taking Roy by surprise. 'That is no way to treat a chair. And look what you've done to the floor.'

Roy snapped the chair forward onto its front legs and stood up. Miss Bucket beckoned William into view. He had followed her through the house and stood behind her, holding his wrist. He stepped forward, an exhibit. Miss Bucket pointed at the boy's wrist.

'He'll have to be sent home now. Lucky he is packed already.'

William had never unpacked. Every morning during all these weeks he had made sure his things were all in his suitcase and that he could leave at a minute's notice. 'I have no choice,' said Miss Bucket. Roy was examining the wrist. 'Go to the corner and telephone his father,' said Miss Bucket. 'It's raining. I can't go out myself.'

'We don't have a telephone at home, Miss Bucket,' said William. 'I'll go back by myself, I have almost a pound note for fares.'

Miss Bucket was tapping her fingers, irritated, d'd'dit, d'd'dit, d'd'dit, over and over, SSS, a long hiss. 'Surely someone in the vicinity has a phone,' she said.

William thought for a moment. 'The Stanleys opposite.' The Stanleys had everything. A car, hot water, and a telephone.

Miss Bucket went to look up the phone book. Roy led William over to the bed and sat him on it.

When he tried to remove William's muddy shoes and socks and jacket, William pulled away, still cradling his wrist. 'I'm leaving,' he said.

'The bedspread will get dirty,' said Roy. 'You're all muddy.'

William glowered at Roy.

Then suddenly Roy started laughing. 'Did you really call her Miss Bucket?' he asked. 'Is that what you've been calling her all this time?'

William nodded.

'Bucket?' Roy hooted. 'Hey, Heather, come here,' and he hooted with laughter again. Heather's head appeared around the door. 'The boy's been calling our Miss B. Bucket.'

Heather giggled.

'As in kick the bucket,' said Roy. 'Very appropriate, the boy's got a sense of humour.' He turned to William, sitting pale and trembling on the bed. His wrist was throbbing.

'It's Barkit,' said Roy. 'Miss Baaaarkit.'

And Miss Barkit appeared at the kitchen door with Stanleys' phone number and sent Roy to the corner phone to get the message to Wally Badger. When he returned he saw that William's wrist had swollen to such an extent that it was pressing against his jacket cuff, and he took Miss Barkit's secateurs from the wall and half cut half ripped the sleeve open to the elbow.

Wally Badger's Harley Davidson pulled up and his shoes passed by William, who was crouched in the hedge gathering his chocolates and his books and notebook and pencil as best he could with one hand. His wrist was painful, but as he squatted to place the objects in a brown paper bag, he was able to rest the injured wrist on his thigh. He crammed a crumble bar into his mouth. This qualified as an emergency. He did not even hear the motorbike pull up, and he had not recognised the shoes as his father's. It was not until Miss Barkit shook the hedge, sending raindrops down onto him and his possessions, and peered around and down at him and said, 'Your father's here,' that he knew he had been called for. Then his father's face peered down, old and grizzled. William was ashamed that this man, more than fifty years old, was his father, and he was ashamed that the awful Miss Barkit should see him.

As his father tucked him into the side car, covering him with a blanket and a tarpaulin, William asked for his mother, and Wally Badger coughed and said she must have gone off.

'But don't worry, son. If we can't find your own mother, we'll get you another one. Whatever happens you won't be without one, I guarantee you that.'

After the hospital Wally Badger brought William home. His broken wrist was in plaster and resting in a sling. Dandelions were growing in the cracks in the front path. The wire in the screen door had come loose and peeled back in one corner. Cartons filled with newspapers were stacked in the hallway. Wally Badger seemed awkward, a little formal, as he stood aside to allow William to precede him into the kitchen. The sink was stacked high with dirty dishes.

'A cup of tea, then,' said Wally, who then had to lift several dirty cups and plates out of the sink in order to fill the kettle. 'Dadda will just make a nice cuppa.'

'Where did she go?' William asked Wally, who only shook his head.

William went to his room and felt under the pillow. The Rex bar was still there. And under the mattress his emergency supplies rested untouched, proof that Rose had not come home at all after leaving William at Miss Barkit's. He lay on his bed holding his injured, plastered wrist in his good hand. He would read *Underground, or Life Below the Surface*, all thousand and more pages, searching for more information on the nefarious life of The Badger and his terrible crimes. A broken wrist was one of the occupational hazards of the violent life of the criminal.

After a while, they found Rose and she was brought back home. William knew it was his mother because she was wearing the white shoes with the peep toes, although they were grubby and had not been cleaned in a while, and he recognised the navy-blue dress, although the full circle skirt cut on the bias now drooped unevenly in the front and the back. Her hair, however, was black. The two men who brought her back led her up the cracked cement path, one on either side, propping her up, and they practically lifted her up the three wooden steps that led to the wooden veranda and stood her there, letting go of her to see if she could stand on her own, watching her sway a little. William knew it was his mother even though her hair was black and her eyes were downcast, like a criminal just captured. She had been gone for several months.

William's father, the oldest father in the world, eased himself up from his chair on the veranda and with the other two men watched her sway for a moment before going forward and taking her arm.

'You're home now, Mumma,' he said. 'The boy's here. And me. We'll take care of you.'

Rose raised her eyes to look at her husband, Wally Badger, and made a smile that to William seemed to sneer. William, who was standing by the screen door, now dashed to her side and put his cheek lightly against the sleeve of her dress.

She lowered her head to him and rubbed one hand over his yellow hair which, under Wally Badger's care, had grown full and curly, its yellow almost as bright as Rose's hair had been.

'Why don't you twirl?' he suggested, as if he were a doctor encouraging a patient to take an aspirin. 'You're wearing your dress, cut on the bias. And it'll do you good. To twirl.'

She twisted his hair in her fingers.

'What did they do to your hair, mother?' he asked, glaring at the men who had brought her.

'Hair,' said his father, 'is only hair. As long as you have some, it can always grow back. Hair is the least of it.'

'You can even shave your hair right off,' said William,

using something approaching a bedside manner, attempting some kind of jollity, 'and you think you'll be bald like that for the rest of your life, but it grows back.' He wanted to reassure his mother that he bore no grudge because of those haircuts of the past.

'Mumma's tired. Leave her alone,' said Wally.

'We'll go then,' said one of the men.

Wally Badger nodded, and the two men lit cigarettes then went down the front steps doing a kind of after-you dance to see who would precede the other down the narrow path to the gate.

William held the screen door open so that Wally Badger could lead Rose Badger inside the house. 'Mumma can just come into the bedroom right here and lie down and take off her shoes. I'll cover Mumma with something,' said Wally. But Rose veered to the left as soon as they were in the hallway and forced them to follow her into the lounge room. William stopped in the doorway. Perhaps she was going to spin after all, and snap her fingers and laugh. But she sank into the couch and sat there with her chin in her hands.

'So this is it, then, is it?' she said.

'This is it,' said Wally Badger.

She looked at William. 'How's the little man?' she asked. 'What can you do?'

'I learned the poem,' William said.

His father waved him out of the room. Since they did not order him to make a noise—and he would not have obeyed if they had, The Badger was beyond that now—he simply waited quietly in the hallway, sitting on the floor a few feet from the lounge room door. He was not going to let his mother out of his sight again. But all he heard, before his father shut the door, was his mother saying, 'spitting image'.

When the door opened again and his father emerged, William got up and crept in to sit in the armchair opposite his mother.

'For my birthday,' he said, 'I would still like to have a boy, a store dummy, you know, the same as me. Spitting image.'

Rose stood up slowly. 'You can tell me the poem now, William,' she said. However she did not stop to listen but walked down the hall toward the kitchen.

'The old year went and the new returned, in the withering weeks of drought,' William said, trailing after her.

Rose walked into the kitchen and around the table. William recited the whole poem, all eight stanzas, slowly, just to keep himself with her. Rose circled the table and returned to the hall. She wandered through the house and out onto the front veranda, William following reciting, where she sat down on the front steps.

He sat down next to his mother, pressed against her side. 'All day long in the flies and heat the men of the outside track, With stinted stomachs and blistered feet must carry their swags Out Back,' he murmured.

When he finished the poem and Rose said nothing, he said, 'That's it, the whole poem.'

She sighed. 'That's very good indeed.' But she was gazing off across the street, as if the Stanleys' brick house opposite were not there at all.

'We'll have some good times now,' she said. 'I'll take you all around, you'll see, you and me.'

'Where were you?' he asked.

'Your father said he is going to buy me a car. I'll drive you places. You'll see.'

Wally Badger wanted to buy a Holden, Australian made, but Rose Badger wanted something British or European, something of quality and taste, in keeping with her personality.

'A car reflects on you the way your shoes and handbag do,' she said, automatically. Nevertheless, her shoes now were dirty and she had not even carried a handbag. 'One of those Morris Minors would be good.'

These days Wally Badger was doing whatever Rose wanted. She had been back only a few weeks, and Wally was watching her carefully, bringing her tea in bed in the mornings, telling her how pretty she looked every day. He set up the ironing board for her to iron her dresses after washing day, but she was no longer so particular about wearing a different frock every day of the week, and she did not seem to care if it was wrinkled or not.

'If this is it, Wally, then this is it,' she said. She went to her rag bag, where she kept the mending and the worn-out clothes, and pulled out one of her old dresses. 'This will do for around the house.'

'Wear your striped dress, the sundress,' said William from behind his cereal bowl. There was still hope that she would resume her twirling and laughing.

'Pipe down, William,' Rose said.

William had never heard his mother use a slang expression, his surprise overcoming his hurt at being snapped at.

So Wally Badger bought a second-hand Morris Minor, light blue.

'Why don't you drive somewhere, Mumma,' Wally said from his porch chair, his leg propped on the veranda rail. Rose stood in the front doorway, behind the torn screen door, her arms folded.

'I'll fix the wire in that door while you're gone,' said Wally.

William sat sideways on the top step, leaning against

the veranda post. When he looked up at his mother, she seemed blurry, fuzzy in outline behind the screen, blending into the dark of the hallway behind her.

'If this is it, this is it,' said Rose. 'Why bother to go anywhere else?'

'Come on, Rose, we Badgers are do-ers, travellers, take the boy and explore a bit.' He tapped his leg, then tapped at his pipe, which had a hole in the stem where his tooth, his eye tooth, the one with the point, had clamped shut on it over the years. 'Unfortunately I can't, but the boy will be good company.'

'We Badgers,' said Rose bitterly.

'You could buy a new dress,' suggested William. 'You could become an adventuress, more interesting at forty than in the flush of glowing youth.'

'That's no way to talk to your Mumma,' said Wally.

'Perhaps I'll drive up the street and have a schooner at the pub,' said Rose. 'Coming, William?'

William looked at his father, who placed his pipe in his mouth—William heard the click of the eye tooth slipping into its hole in the stem—and nodded. William nodded back, moving his head only slightly, so that Rose would not perceive their collusion.

William enjoyed the responsibility, accompanying his mother, not letting her out of his sight, guaranteeing always to bring her safely home. If only he had realized, when she had taken him to Manly, that he could have been the one in charge. As he saw it now, he really should have ordered his mother home that day after Christmas. He should have refused to disembark from the ferry. He should have stayed there and let it carry them both back to the Quay and home. But then the swirling memory of her, excited in her sundress and white shoes, interfered and he knew that nothing would have changed what had happened then. Now, she was different. And so was he.

Rose ran a comb through her hair and ran lipstick roughly around her mouth, a rapid circle, without looking in the mirror or in the glass of the photograph hanging in the hall. Then she walked, swinging the car keys around one finger, to the car, parked in the street. William followed. He was wearing his old school trousers, and his old school shoes and a grey cardigan. He would have changed for this outing, to please his mother, but she no longer seemed to care, and if he had gone to his bedroom to change and let her out of his sight she could easily have driven off without him.

At the pub Rose parked, swung her legs out of the car and walked to the ladies lounge without looking back to see if William was with her. He scrambled out and followed. They passed the tiled bar, from which the men spilled out onto the street. As Rose passed, several of the men swayed toward her, waving their mugs.

'Here's to you,' cried one of the men.

'Here's to you, too,' responded Rose, raising her hand as if she were holding a mug of beer.

William was astonished. She had never spoken to strangers in the street—except for that one time in Parramatta—and especially not drinkers at a pub. She used to cross to the other side of the street when they passed a pub, calling it a glorified toilet.

In the lounge were several young women, a couple of them with their husbands, all drinking beer and laughing. Swarming around the drinkers and crawling on the floor were several children in their pyjamas and nighties, little children with thin blond hair, runny noses, sucking on bottles of milk. Even the bigger ones of five or so were sucking on bottles.

William had heard Rose say that it was no wonder the

country was full of drunks when they took their children drinking with them, started them off young. William feared that Rose, with her new ferocity, might join this crowd, just pull up a chair and begin drinking and talking. The drinkers stopped to watch as she entered. She stood at the door, at ease, and surveyed the room, then took an empty chair from one of the tables and, with a 'May I?', drew it over to the window and sat down. William went and stood beside her.

'You're smothering me,' said Rose. 'Bring a chair for yourself.'

William had to turn back to face the people, drinking and still watching them, in order to search out a chair. One young woman, with only one front tooth and long hair the colour and texture of dead grass, called 'Here, love,' and pointed to an empty chair next to her. William waded through the little children to fetch it.

'Thank you muchly,' he found himself saying. The phrase just sprang to his lips, and he blushed.

'Thank you muchly!' the young woman echoed, and she and her companions burst into laughter.

William placed his chair at the window, facing his mother, as if they were in a train carriage going on a journey. His mother gave an exaggerated sigh and looked out the window, drawing her chair a couple of inches farther away from him.

'Where did you go?' William asked Rose. 'That time.'

Rose waited several seconds, staring out the window, then turned her face to look at him for a moment, then back to the window.

'Anyway, William, it's clear you've worn the wrong clothes,' she said.

'I didn't have time to get into my good trousers,' he said.

She smiled, not at William but at her reflection in the window. 'I mean, you should have worn your pyjamas, like all the other kiddies here.'

'Where?' he persisted, smarting at her calling him a kiddy.

Rose sighed and looked exasperated. 'Would you please stop badgering me?' she snapped, loudly, so that everyone in the ladies lounge turned to look at them.

William looked away from Rose, pushed his chair back several inches, and decided to try very hard indeed never to look at his mother or ask her for anything ever again.

'Just stop badgering me,' Rose repeated.

Part II

William never imagined that he would willingly lower himself into a hole in the ground, yet he was lying on his stomach, his cheek against the floor of the underground tunnel, aware of each grain of limestone imprinting on his skin, his arms stretched out along the rock floor in front of him, the fingers of his right hand still gripping his carbide lamp. The grit pressed into the skin of his knee at the tear in his trousers, the trousers he had torn several months before when he had fallen down in the street. As he breathed, deeply, pretending that his back was his chest, forcing it up with each inhalation to see if it would touch the roof of the tunnel just a few inches above, he realised that the earth could indeed move, could adjust itself, a minor earthquake, like the pages of a heavy book closing, and he would be squashed. He would become a relic, a remnant. They would place a marker on the grassy, sunny hillside dozens of feet above declaring that he lay under the ground, pressed, flattened, a flower robbed of its juices at the peak of its flowering, having bloomed and been rudely halted, pressed flat. Here rests William Badger.

William arched his neck and chin so that he was looking at the soles of the boots splayed in front of him, a few inches before his face. They were Meg's boots, wonderful boots indeed, encasing Meg's neat little symmetrical feet. William had had ample opportunity to admire the uppers of the boots when they were above ground, brown leather ankle boots, perfectly laced, with the bows of the laces tucked down inside the tongue out of harm's way, tiny boots with, he now saw, treacherous cleats on the underside. He had felt the cleats through his sneakers when Meg had stepped on him, back in the light of day, in that other world on the surface that he might never see again. But he had never had a chance to examine the boots in this way, at leisure, at close range.

He rested his cheek on the limestone again, his neck still arched and his head craned back, contemplating more thoroughly the cleats of Meg's boots, a whole world, a system, that she carried around beneath her on her soles. The cleats were arranged in a way that reminded him of the obstacles of a pinball machine, and as he lay waiting for the squirming forward to resume, he imagined shooting a ball up from Meg's toe on a route that wove around each cleat in turn, leaving no cleat neglected, uncircled. He was acutely aware that he lacked boots himself, although he thought that if he dared to go on with this madness, this caving, this spelunking, this hiking and mountain climbing underground, beneath the surface of the planet, he would need footwear with cleats. Possibly he could find a pair of used boots at the army disposal store and tack cleats on. Then he remembered Wally Badger's old army boots, hanging from a nail in the garage. They would do. If he ever got to the surface again, he would go back to see Wally and Rose Badger, the folks, whom he had seen only once since he had run off to the city. He did not want to see them, but he needed the boots and it was Christmas time, and Wally Badger had written to say that Rose had not left the house for six months and that he himself had spent three weeks in hospital. Until then Wally had been maintaining the house, mowing the lawn, mending things, shopping for food, cooking, washing the clothes. But Rose still refused to leave the house even to go out back to the laundry or to hang the clothes on the line. William could go home and say simply Merry Christmas, or rather Happy Christmas, since merry implied some kind of licentious and immoral drunkenness, seize the boots, and return to the city in time to go caving again with Meg and Jack and the other Trogs over the New Year weekend.

The cleats on Meg's boots had become a moonscape, bald knolls with traces of soil and vegetation on the plains between. Then as William studied this terrain, plotting a path through it, the protrusions suddenly appeared to be indentations, and rather than hills he found himself avoiding ditches, much more dangerous than hills. William blinked, and the ditches became mounds again. He shifted the focus of his eyes again and found he could make the cleats invert at will. He swivelled his eyes, searching for another object on which to test this new-found magic. The rock floor of the tunnel was gritty, but the particles were too uniform and blended too easily with the solid rock, possessing a gritty reluctance to bend before his magic. He slid his gaze back to the cleats and with his new extravagant regard forced them to palpitate under his gaze, inverting from knoll to ditch and back again. He took a deep, powerful breath, which swelled his back and his shoulders. That giant gesture brought the roof of the tunnel close to him and he became again a mere man, a young man in his prime, immobilised beneath the surface of the earth. He slid his eyes to the roof of the tunnel, carefully resolving not to panic. They could all die; the other Trogs would be missed; their families would know they had disappeared; no one knew that William Badger was with them; no one at all would miss him. There would be no carved stone on the hilltop above to mark his underground death.

When Meg had urged him to join the Trogs and come with her on this caving weekend, he had imagined it would entail more or less walking into a cavern, perhaps scrambling a little up a steep rock face to the cave entrance, then walking in, upright, australopithecus seeking shelter, or Tarzan entering the cave frequented by ivory thieves. When he discovered that entering the cave meant wriggling into a hole in the ground and squirming along a tunnel, William said he would stay behind above ground and look after the camp. How had he agreed to join this madness?

William rubbed his cheek against the rock floor, as if against a favourite eiderdown, and took a shallow breath. The limestone grit dug further into his knee as he breathed. He feared that his back would brush the tunnel roof, thereby demonstrating again how hopeless his situation was and how foolish he had been to agree to follow the others as they traipsed up over the grassy, golden hill several hours earlier. How misleadingly exhilarating it had been to search for the hole in the hill that signified the entrance to the caves, how childishly proud he had been when he was the one to locate the hole, beneath a tuft of grass and shout, 'Hey, I've found it.' Meg and the others, spread out over the hillside like a party searching for a dead body, had immediately abandoned their search, given up the kicking at the grass, the stamping and the swaying of the arms from side to side as they pushed aside bushes and grasses, and they had come rushing to him. Jack, the leader, had yelled encouragement, slapping him on the back, saying, 'That's more like it, Billy Boy,' which he took as great praise. Meg, in her smudged white boilersuit and hard hat with the carbide lamp fixed to the brim, had leapt upon him, her legs about his waist, one arm around his shoulder, the other arm vertical, the index finger pointing, reaching to the heavens.

As she leapt on him her helmet had snicked his ear, which began to smart, throb, and no doubt turned as red as a crybaby's face. But William could attend to that later. When Meg and the Trogs had descended into the hole in the ground, he could walk back to the camp at the foot of the grassy slope and kneel by the creek to dip his flaming ear in the cool water. But for the moment, with Meg upon him in a delightful way—he felt her boots locked together against his buttocks—yelping with happiness and praising him for being so acute as to detect the cave entrance, which was well known as a tricky entrance (other cavers had been known to spend the entire weekend searching for the entrance and to have returned to Sydney without finding the caves at all), he ignored his ignited ear and placed both his arms around Meg's waist, lifting his face from the studs on the placket of her boilersuit, which were scraping his nose and chin, to look up at her, allowing the upward reach of his neck and face to stretch his mouth into a smile, a genuine, pleased smile. He had this boilersuited bundle of a girl in his arms, at last.

The other six—there were nine in the group—came hooting and bounding across the slope to where Jack and William, with Meg straddling him, were standing next to the cave entrance. Eager to be the first, Jack sat on the grass at the edge of the hole and lowered his legs in, appearing, at the moment before he eased his whole body in, to be a legless man. 'I'll make a preliminary check,' he said, 'just to make sure that this is in fact the entrance and not a wombat hole.' He seemed to slide in almost horizontally rather than vertically, as if he were getting into bed, slipping between blankets of pale green tufted grass, until only his head and one arm remained visible. William had blinked and changed the focus of his eyes, making things blur, and he had seen a man drowning in the ocean, raising one arm to signal for help. Jack's head and arm slipped from view through the grass, and for a moment his fingertips gripping the grass at the perimeter of the hole could be seen before they, too, slid under the ground.

William held on to Meg, rather more tightly than he intended, startled at the disappearance of Jack into what was, after all, solid earth, and he was only dimly aware of her struggling—she had unlocked her boots and let her legs drop toward the ground, but William continued to hold her tightly and since he was much taller than she, she was dangling, flailing her legs, bumping her boots against his shins as she tried to get him to let her go and place her on the ground.

'Put me down,' she gasped. She had both hands on his shoulders, pushing herself away from his chest, so that her only point of contact apart from her hands braced against him was her pelvis held against his stomach. William was still watching the grass where Jack had disappeared, and he felt that he, or better someone else, should jump in and save him, haul him to the surface. Now aware of Meg's struggle and its increasing vigour, William wondered what was preventing her from reaching the ground, if that was what she wanted, until the pressure of her hands on his chest and her buttocks against his clasped hands made him realize that it was his grip that held her to him. And releasing her suddenly he allowed her to slide down his body, and again in the space of a few minutes he was startled, this time at the unexpected and unearned pleasure as she slid past his own pelvis. Suddenly the smarting in his ear flared up again, and he cupped one hand over it. Instead of hitting the ground Meg's boots landed on William's feet, which wore only canvas sneakers. He was preoccupied for the moment with the pain in his insteps and in his ear and with the pleasant residue of Meg's body against his, pleasure inserted between two pains.

Meg stepped back off his feet, impatiently pulling down the legs and crotch of her boilersuit, which had ridden up as she slid down William's body.

It was William's discovery of the cave entrance that had resulted in this physical disarray.

'Well done,' said Meg.

Jack had not reappeared. Once Jack had vanished under the earth, the grass seemed to close over the entrance, like water, so that once again it was difficult to see that there was a hole in the ground. William squinted at the approximate spot, then stepped forward to kneel beside it. He intended to call out, 'Hey, Jack, mate, you all right?' but when he thrust the grass tufts aside with one hand and bent his head down to call out he found that he was not by the entrance at all. He was looking at the solid ground. Quickly he stood up. He looked around, moving his eyes systematically from left to right, as if he were mowing a lawn. Then as his eyes traversed the small area of the slope where the entrance simply had to be, he saw a movement in the spiky grey-green and the spiky brown head of hair, belonging to Jack, poked through and gradually emerged. William stood spellbound, watching the brown tufts of Jack's hair rise uncannily, then the ears and face appear. Jack turned his head from left to right, licking his lips, as if they had got coated with some essential underground substance, then stretching his lips back to rid them of the traces of whatever it was and shaking his head a little he let out a hoot. 'We're in business.' His chin was now level with the ground and the grass framed his neck like a collar. He brought both arms up above his head, demonstrating that the hole was in fact wider than the protruding grasses made it appear, and then brought his palms down to rest on the surface, so that he could hoist himself out. His shoulders, torso and one leg then another emerged.

'It's the entrance all right,' he called out and stood up, dusting himself down and stamping a few times as if he had indeed just hauled himself out of the water and was shaking off droplets rather than limestone grit and bat droppings.

William stepped toward him, to thump his back or provide any service that might be needed. Perhaps it was then that he was aware that he wanted to go under with them all.

'Why don't you just put up a marker?' William asked, sensibly. 'Then you wouldn't have to search each time.'

Meg turned away, folded her arms, sighed, then turned back. 'Because,' she said, 'we can't defile the countryside.'

'Something tasteful,' said William, 'something in keeping.' He cast around for an idea. 'You could tie something to this bush.' He touched the leaves of a bush a few feet from the entrance. 'Something beautiful, of course, something natural.'

'And we don't want to make it easy for just anyone to find the caves,' said Meg. 'That would be irresponsible. Someone inexperienced could get into big trouble. There's a narrow tunnel in there that you have to negotiate before you get to the caverns and the river. Amateurs could get stuck.'

This was the tunnel William was now lying in, face down, breathing as if his back were his chest. He had not really meant to go under with the others, despite the momentary urge he felt witnessing Jack's exhilaration when he emerged from his reconnaissance mission. William had insisted he would be the cook and get the fire and dinner ready. He had walked away from Meg and Jack and the others down the slope to the pile of sleeping bags and haversacks while the Trogs were fiddling with their carbide lamps near the entrance, preparing to descend.

Meg followed William, calling back to Jack, 'Don't go in without me. Just a sec.'

William heard her boots thumping on the grassy slope behind him, leaping along. He imagined her leaving the ground with each bound, sailing through the air, a troglodyte set free and bursting into flight. And then he felt her beside him, her right hand slipping into his left arm, and after a series of little steps to halt her rush down the slope she fell into step beside him. The force of her landing beside him and the sudden termination of her bounding and flying pulled him along a little, forcing him to trot for a few steps. Then they fell into a more sedate gait, arm in arm, like a couple taking a turn in a civilised European forest—the Schwarzwald or the Forêt des Soignes. William brought his right hand across to cover the back of Meg's right hand, resting now on his sleeve, and he looked down fondly at her grey fibreglass helmet with the carbide lamp on the brim giving off its nauseating aroma. And he felt such a great surge of warmth for this little female creature so firmly attached to him that he bent down and kissed the grey dome, just letting his lips brush the cool hardness. Meg, unaware of this devotion taking place on the crown of her helmet, gave a skip which, as her body lifted and fell, caused the helmet to rise and bump against William's lips, even as he straightened up. His upper lip was pushed against his teeth, which pierced the inside of his lip and he heard in his head the flesh crunch and tear and felt the trickle of blood within his mouth, and he felt a new sweet pain, the third to be incurred in just a few minutes. William swallowed and took his right hand from Meg's in order to press the sleeve of his sweatshirt against his mouth. Then Meg's face turned up to look at him. William cleared his throat, took his sleeve away from his mouth and pretended to be pushing his hair back from his forehead.

'Say,' said Meg, 'why don't you come under with us?'

'Underground? Beneath the surface?'

'It's a shame to come all this way and not see what it's like.' Meg stood back, her hand still on his arm, and surveyed his shirt and jeans and sneakers. 'It doesn't really matter that you don't have the right gear. It's a fairly benign cave. There are spare lamps. The helmet doesn't really matter. You just have to carry the lamp and push it ahead of you when you're crawling, and keep your head down.'

They reached the bottom of the hill and stood among the detritus of the camp, next to the creek. William gestured at the campsite, as if to say he had work to do right there.

'We'll just put the food somewhere safe and we can all cook it together when we come out. That's what we usually do, when there's no one like you to be caretaker and housekeeper and see to things.'

William must have agreed to go underground. He must have nodded at Meg, given some kind of sign. Meg called back up the slope, cupping her hand against her mouth. 'Wait up, he's coming, too.'

Meg was busily wrapping the meat in plastic bags. 'All you have to remember is to keep your shirt on. Never take off your shirt.'

'I have a good idea,' said William. 'We'll put the meat in the creek to keep it cool.' It seemed like a very clever idea, a suitable successor to his discovery of the cave entrance.

'We don't usually do that,' said Meg.

'It'll keep it cool,' said William.

He tied the plastic bags with string and placed them in the water at the edge of the creek, then he tied the string to the trunk of the tree that grew right at the water's edge. The steaks, tethered in plastic bags and moving about in the current, were like animals not yet slaughtered, obediently shifting about quietly in their pen awaiting the moment when they would be lifted out of the water, unwrapped, and tossed on the fire.

'Why would anyone want to take off his shirt anyway?' William asked.

'Some idiots come to a narrow neck in a tunnel and find their shoulders are too wide, and they think if they take off their clothes they'll squeeze through. But that can be fatal. If you can't get through with clothes on, you have to accept that you can't get through and go back.' Meg shrugged. 'It's a kind of underground hysteria or frenzy that can overtake you, a compulsion, like sailors when they hear the Sirens.'

They stood around the hole lighting their carbide lamps, the evil-smelling grey chunks of carbide lighting up, then sizzling. In the open air they cast no light, but the increase in the odour and the sizzling indicated that they were alight. Jack placed his helmet on his head and slid in first, followed by two of the others, then Meg. William, the amateur, the beginner, the weak link in the chain, without boots, without a boilersuit, without a helmet, holding his lamp in his hand, was to be placed in the middle, following Meg and followed by the remaining four.

The hole in the ground was vertical for only two feet or so, and William watched Meg insert herself, feet first, up to the hips, then she angled her body horizontally as she disappeared. 'Wait a few seconds, then you go,' said the Trog behind William.

William waited a few seconds, then a few more. He was not sure he could do it.

'Go on,' said the man behind him. 'You have to keep up the rhythm of the group.'

William sat on the edge of the hole then stood up, protruding from the ground from the thighs up. Looking down past his knees, he could see that the tunnel slanted off almost at a right angle to his sneakers. Meg had disappeared, but he could see the flickering light of her lamp on his sneakers, and terror of losing her prompted him to slide his legs along the tunnel, lowering his torso until he was sitting, and then sliding his legs and body farther along the tunnel until his head was lying at the bottom of the two-foot hole and his body was extended completely underground. He looked up through the grasses surrounding the perimeter of the hole to the pale, pale sky, bid the world goodbye, then wriggled farther into the tunnel, hauling himself along by the heels of his sneakers, discovering that the rubber soles did not have what could be called heels and provided little purchase. His lamp clattered along beside him as he used his elbows to help thrust his body forward. His knees hit a rock that hung low from the roof of the tunnel, and he gasped.

'Turn over,' Meg called from beyond his feet, her voice echoing. 'It's easier to move backwards if you're on your stomach.'

The feet of the Trog behind poked at his head. William turned over rapidly and squirmed backwards, trying to catch up with Meg, trying to avoid being struck in the head by the boots behind him.

Ahead he heard thudding and clanking, and then he felt his feet and legs drop suddenly and for a moment he was suspended, in the shape of a right angle, his upper body lying along the floor of the tunnel, his legs dangling.

'Ease yourself down,' said Meg. 'You'll be able to stand.'

William stretched down. He steadied himself, eased his upper body out of the tunnel, and found he was standing upright in a little cavern, a hollow sphere in the rock, next to little Meg, who turned her face up to him, but all he saw was the bright light, a single eye, coming from the lamp on her helmet. He held his own lamp up and watched the four men behind him emerge feet first, one by one, from the tunnel.

'Just remember where exactly in this cavern that tunnel is,' said Jack. 'For when we come back.'

'Can't we mark it?' William whispered to Meg.

She shook her head.

'Ah, right,' he said. 'Defiling the underground.'

William looked up at the lip of the tunnel memorising it. The cavern was pocked with similar bumps and shadows that could also be tunnels and could mislead unwary cavers as sailors of old had been misled by indentations in rocks and cliffs that falsely promised inlets and harbours.

With the nine of them in the miniature cavern, there was scarcely room to turn around. It was simply a fortuitous little space hollowed out by underground waters that served as a kind of anteroom to the main caves.

Then Jack was scrambling up another part of the rock wall and he hoisted himself into a black shadow that formed another tunnel, the exit from the anteroom. The second and third Trogs followed, then Meg. She was so short that she had trouble getting up to the first hand hold. William offered her his hands, linked, to give her a leg up. Meg placed her cleated boot in the stirrup formed by his hands and pushed up, and she too disappeared into the next tunnel. William followed. This section of the tunnel was higher, and having entered head first, they were able to crawl along on their hands and knees and proceed more rapidly. William felt that the tunnel was descending, and suddenly Meg called out, 'Drop,' and swivelled her body around so that she dropped feet first down to a lower level, then turned again and continued crawling. William mimicked her, pleased with the ease of it. 'Drop,' he called, and swivelled his body. Perhaps it was not so different from climbing a mountain above ground.

They crawled for what must have been several hundred feet. At times fissures and tunnels branched off to the right and left, and shining his lamp down some of these William could see that most of them narrowed and flattened and ended. When his back started to bump and scrape the roof of the tunnel, William understood that their tunnel was narrowing, and finally he was forced to lie flat on his stomach and to squirm instead of crawl. Again, the toes of his sneakers gave him little purchase and he had to rely on his elbows, and the sleeves of his thick sweatshirt came to feel like milanese, offering his elbows little cushioning against the rock floor. He grunted and hauled himself along, pushing his lamp in front. And then the underground file halted completely. William's lamp bumped into Meg's boots. Then he felt a jolt from behind as the helmet of the Trog behind him hit the soles of his sneakers.

He heard Jack's voice, far off and fuzzy, calling out, then the sound was repeated by the others, until Meg's voice coming back over her shoulder called 'Halt.' And William, catching on, called 'Halt,' back over his shoulder.

'Thanks a lot,' he heard the Trog behind him mutter then call out in his turn, 'Halt.' And the sound was repeated and receded back along the tunnel.

This was where he lay contemplating the cleats of Meg's boots, inverting the bumps to hollows and back again, and designing the stone for the top of the hill far above that would mark their grave. It would be a simple slab that would organise the surrounding chaotic tumble of grass and bushes and gum trees, giving a system to the surrounding countryside. The countryside would incline toward the apex of that hill, the tracks and dirt roads, the paved roads and the highways, would lead to that hill and the slab on top. The towns on the coast and the distant city would no longer be centres but on the periphery, inclining toward, paying obeisance to this hill.

But the earth did not move and crush them. And finally the caravan of underground squirmers inched forward again. William heard the echoes of grunts and curses from up front, and after a while, as he hauled himself along on his elbows once more, William saw what the trouble was. The tunnel narrowed so extremely that it seemed to be a mere slot that pressed in on his skull. Squirming directly into it was not going to work. His head was too round, his shoulders too wide, and the walls of the tunnel grasped at his shirt. Meg had got through without any trouble at all. But Jack and the two men second and third in line must have had to spend some time negotiating the narrow strait. Since the tunnel seemed to twist to the left ahead, William could no longer see Meg's feet, but he could hear the scraping of her boots receding as she now sped forward. He butted at the tunnel. Too much hair. He should be bald. Too much skull. He turned his head sideways, and nudged it into the slot. But then his shoulders were impossibly large, and flexed as they were with the effort of pushing and hauling, they seemed gigantic, freakish. He was expanding. He was becoming a giant. The shirt, the foolishly thick shirt his body was encumbered with, was holding him back. He withdrew his head and retreated a few feet.

'Hey!' came a cry as his feet knocked against the lamp of the man behind.

Ahead he heard singing. 'Laura, you're the face in the mystic night.' A woman's voice, soft and lovely, which he wanted to reach. The voice was calling him.

'Got to get out of this shirt,' William muttered. He knew he could get through in his skin alone. His hands were tugging at his shirt, pulling it up to his armpits.

'Get a move on,' came the voice from behind.

'My shirt!' William shouted. He was trying to tear off this imprisoning, restricting garment, a maddened man.

'Leave it on!' cried the voice behind. William felt a hand close around his ankle. 'Leave it on.' The hand pulled him back a little. 'Angle your body. Angle it!'

The grip on his ankle soothed William, and he lay quietly on the floor of the tunnel for a moment, allowing his body to deflate, to shrink. Then breathing slowly and shallowly, he edged his body sideways so that his right shoulder and hip were beginning to curve upward against the wall of the tunnel, and he turned his head to the right, placing his left cheek on the floor, and slid forward and thus came safely through the narrow strait. The tunnel enlarged, and he could crawl again, clattering and scrambling, bumping his lamp against the floor in his haste, making for the beautiful voice, leaving behind him the grunting and heavy breathing of the next Trog negotiating the treacherous rocks. The tunnel opened out to form a broad soft ledge, soft because the rock was covered with a fine and comforting dust. William found himself kneeling on a precipice. Below him, what seemed to be hundreds of feet but probably only twenty feet or so, were three lamps shining up the rock face and behind the lamps no doubt were three upturned faces belonging to Jack and the second and third Trogs. Meg was against the cliff, halfway between the ledge and the floor, nudging her way down. William lay down, his face jutting over the edge, holding out his lamp, and watched her descent. She was like a suction cup attached to the rock, sliding down. And then she jumped for the last few feet and was standing with Jack, who put his arm around her shoulder. They turned away, facing the black expanse of the cavern, and first Jack then Meg cupped their hands around their mouths and started yelling,

'Coo-ee!' The echoes bounced back. The cavern was vast. And then among the echoes of the coo-ees, there was a pinging sound, and William felt ghostly flutterings about his head. Bats. He let out a cry.

Now there were four lights aimed up at him.

'They're bumping into me,' cried William, covering his face with his hands. 'The bats are bumping into me.'

'Bats never bump into things,' Meg called up.

'Into me they bump,' said William.

'Impossible,' cried Meg. 'They never bump into things, not even into you, unless they're sick.'

William wanted to be down there with them, not hunched on this ledge like some old, infirm bird, under attack by sick bats, and he feared that the others, issuing forth from the tunnel behind would push him over head first. The clattering of boots and helmets was approaching from behind. Rapidly he turned around and swung his legs over the edge of the precipice.

'Wait!' cried Meg.

William looked down.

'You have to sing,' she said.

Sing? William thought about the word. He had never sung. Surely she had said swing, or spring.

'Sing!' called Jack. 'It's what we do when we get inside.'

Meg cupped her hands around her mouth. 'You have to sing a song. All the way through.'

'For God's sake sing,' hissed a voice beside him, 'so that we can all get on down.'

William sat back on the ledge and looked out into the black. He was going to have to sing a song.

'Come on,' said the man beside him, impatient. 'It's for luck, a Trog tradition, to ward off disaster under the ground.'

William cleared his throat and found himself uttering

the nonsense syllables he had heard his mother sing when
he was a boy. *'Sah ein Knab' ein Röslein steh'n, Röslein auf
der Heiden, war so jung und morgenschön, lief er schnell, es nah'
zu seh'n, sah's mit vielen Freuden.'* He knew all the words,
but had no idea what they meant. He liked the sound of
his voice echoing around the cavern. *'Und der wilde Knabe
brach's Röslein auf der Heiden, Röslein wehrte sich und stach, half
ihr doch kein Weh und Ach, musst' es eben leiden.'*

Meg was applauding from below, her round bright
carbide lamp smiling up at him.

William began the second stanza.

'That's enough,' said the Trog beside him. 'Climb down
now.' And William lowered himself over the edge as the
Trog remaining on the ledge began with 'Laura, you're
the face in the mystic night.'

Halfway down, William thought he would fall. He could
not find a foothold. Big boots were clattering down above
him. They would tread on his fingers if he did not hurry.
He could not see the rock face beneath him. His foot was
waving around, a thread of spider's web floating around
looking for something to attach itself to. 'Where is my
foot?' he called to Meg, a cry for help.

'It's at the end of your leg,' Jack called up.

Meg and the others below were laughing. William
started to laugh, and his fingers started laughing, too, and
letting go. He was going to fall off the rock face, killed
because of a piece of wittiness. Here lies William Badger.
He could hear the Trogs above him laughing. There could
be multiple deaths as they all dropped down the precipice
laughing.

But then Jack, the joker, climbed up a little way and
took hold of William's leg, pulling it onto a toehold.

'And that,' he said, 'is called pulling your leg.'

William dropped the last few feet to land beside Meg.

She put her arm around his waist. He was shaking. Phrases of 'Laura' were continuing to ring out overhead.

'That's our official Trog song,' Meg said. ' "Laura, you're the face in the mystic night." You'll have to learn it, too. It's quite difficult.'

And now when William looked down at her he found he was close enough to see beneath her lamp to her bright round face shining up at him.

William thought that he might be in love with Meg. He had met her the previous May, in the basement of David Jones', where he was a salesman in Pens and Pencils. He remembered the day because that morning on his way to work he had been accosted in Martin Place by a witch in a high pointed black hat, a black cape, and a front tooth blacked out. She blocked his way as he hastened to work, carrying his sandwich in a brown paper bag in one hand. He was a minute or two later than usual. He had overslept and then lain in bed for a few extra minutes, watching his roommate polish his shoes. Any delay now would mean that he would be late. This witch poked a little cardboard box under his chin, demanding money for a charity. Was it toward sending Olympic athletes somewhere?

'I don't have any change,' he said, stepping sideways.

'A pound will do,' the witch said, jingling the box and stepping sideways to block his way.

She was a student. It was Commem Day, prank day. Hundreds of students descended on the city once a year, dressed in costumes, and in addition to the pranks—throwing firecrackers and flour and balloons filled with water at each other and at the working public—they collected money for a charity. A bunch of educated louts was how one newspaper described them.

Sitting in the gutter as citizens made their way to their

offices, were two other witches, crouched over test tubes suspended over tripods and a camping stove. In the test tubes were eggs. They were frying eggs in the street.

William's witch was jumping up and down before him, rattling her box of coins.

'I can't give you a pound,' he muttered, trying again to step around her.

She danced from side to side, capering back and forth, preventing him from proceeding. Passers-by hid their smirks by covering their mouths with their hands or turning their heads away, laughing at him, William thought, glad that it was he and not they who had been singled out for this public display.

'Please,' he said. 'I have to work.'

'Work, work, work, off to work you go, that's all you all know,' she said.

William certainly knew how to work. In the midst of his public embarrassment he felt a certain bitterness. He had worked for years. For four years he had been a builder's labourer, had driven a truck and made deliveries, and now, as he strove for something cleaner, more orderly, more elevated, he sold pens and pencils in a department store. For four years he had been standing behind a counter selling pens and pencils and desk sets and ink, saving his money diligently for the time when he knew what it was he was going to do with himself.

'You need to dance a little, sing a little,' his witch was chanting. She suddenly seized his left hand in her right, clamped her left hand on his shoulder and started waltzing, singing 'Sweet Australian wattle in the bushland green'.

The other two witches were sitting watching and cackling, spooning egg into their mouths.

William tried to break free, to wrench his hand away, to pluck her hand from his shoulder with the hand that still gripped his lunch, but his witch held on. The two in the gutter were singing and clapping. William pulled his witch from side to side, building up a pendulous momentum, trying to fling her free.

'Just give us your pound,' she said, gasping as she clung to him. Then, as he threw her back and forth more roughly, she began to shriek, and then suddenly went limp, still without letting go. She just let her legs collapse and she drooped toward the pavement. Her left hand on his shoulder was sliding down his arm, still gripping tightly, and her right hand pulled his hand down with her. Unable to stop his violent swaying, William stumbled, tripping over the limp body at his feet, and he fell down on one knee beside her. He felt the knee of his trousers tear and his skin scrape along the cement. His lunch fell to the ground nearby.

'You don't have to assault me,' she said, but incredibly she was still hanging on to him. He could not get her to let go, as much as he tried to prise her loose with his free hand. He felt foolish indeed, a man rendered powerless by this young woman in witch's clothing. And then he saw his chance. Her hand, gripping his, was on the pavement near his foot, and without thinking what he was doing he trod on her hand and his, pressing with all his might. And it hurt her more than him, since her hand was gripping tightly and the knuckles were uppermost and bore the brunt of his shoe. The witch shrieked. The other two witches leapt up and came toward him. He lifted his shoe. The witch let go his hand and his arm, and he sprang up, jumped backwards, free, and turned and broke into a run, sprinting around the witch lying on the pavement, bounding off the kerb, toward the cenotaph in the middle of the road. He heard them burst into laughter as he ran.

When he got to work, at five minutes past nine, gasping from having run up Martin Place and along Castlereagh

Street, bounding through the employees' entrance and down the steps to the locker room, he stopped for a moment to examine his torn trouser leg and his knee, on which a medallion of blood had formed, similar to the skinned knees he had as a child when he fell off a bicycle or slipped on the gravel dribbling an imaginary soccer ball. It did not seem fair, really, that he had to stand among fountain pens and propelling pencils and leather desk sets, working for so little money, when those others, his own age, were out there larking around.

Of course Miss Block was standing by the counter in Pens and Pencils, looking busy, although she performed only one of the routine early morning tasks, the most spectacular, that of whisking off the white dustcloth that covered the display on top of the glass cases behind the counter overnight. She carried out this trick standing on tiptoe—she was a short woman, even in her high-heeled black shoes with the gillie ties—and spreading her arms, like a conductor about to ask an orchestra to strike the first note. With her fingertips she seized the corners of the cloth that fell down over the sliding doors of the glass case, then flicked her wrists so that the far corners of the cloth, which lay at the back of the case and which she could not even see, flew up and sailed toward the top of her brown curly head, a wave breaking on the sand, pulling the cloth up and over. Usually Miss Block was able to catch this cascade of cloth in her arms, the way a fireman might catch a baby thrown from the window of a burning building, cradling it for just a moment before handing it to William to fold. Only once or twice in four years had William seen the cloth misbehave and fly over her head so that for a moment she stood covered in white, a substantial ghost. At Christmas and Easter, when Santa

Claus and Easter Rabbits holding fountain pens in sacks and baskets made the unveiling of the display on top of the case trickier, Miss Block could nevertheless flick the cloth off and cause it to rise even higher as it flew to her without disturbing a single pen or pencil in the display.

But Miss Block did not dust or wipe. William did that, standing on a box to reach the back half of the case, for despite the cloth that warded them off by night, dust particles were free to gather from nine to five thirty. After dusting William left the floor at nine fifteen for three minutes to go to the men's room in order to wet the cloth that he used to wipe down the glass counter, always grubby from the hands and elbows of the previous day's customers.

This morning when he arrived five minutes late, the white dustcloth had already been folded—could Miss Block have done it herself?—and shoved out of sight, and Miss Block was looking busy indeed as she patrolled her counters, responsible not only for pens and pencils but also for stationery, opposite pens and pencils. As she walked she moved her hands about, as if she were engaged in conversation and was emphasising a point. This morning her hands seemed unusually animated. Miss Block was distracted.

The first customers had been let in and were fanning out through the store. Miss Block ignored William, actually turned away from him—he was grateful, because this gave him time to get behind his counter and hide his torn trousers and bloody knee—and walked over to Stationery where the girl there was already dusting and wiping.

'Sorry,' William mumbled at Miss Block's back as he slipped behind his counter and stooped to reach for the cheesecloth folded into a pad with which he wiped down the counter so that it would appear that he was not wasting a minute. In fact, he would get his tasks done more quickly

than if he had been there on the dot of nine. It was
difficult to bend his hurt knee, where the blood was
congealing and the joint stiffening. The cloth pad was
not there, but in its place was a new black docket book.
Perplexed, William straightened up, his weight on his good
leg. Then he saw that there was someone else behind
his counter, at the other end, a young woman who was
leaning over with her elbows on the glass counter top,
her face cupped in her hands, looking down through the
glass at the shelf on which lay the pen and pencil sets.
At first William believed that she was a customer who
had strayed out of her territory. She was wearing a black
dress, but it was no ordinary, workaday black dress that
a salesgirl might wear. It was made of a soft cloth, crepe
perhaps, with a satin sash and flowers of dull red
embroidered around the hem and on the right shoulder
like a corsage. The cloth that formed the shoulders and
sleeves of the dress was flimsy and transparent. William
could see the skin through it. The dress was something
a girl might wear to a dance, a cocktail party. Her straight
brown hair was parted in the middle and drawn back
into a bun at the nape of her neck, giving her a solemn,
old-fashioned look.

The cheesecloth pad rested on the counter in front of
her. Then Miss Block, completing her first circuit of the
day, rounded the corner of the counter and stood before
this young woman, as if she, Miss Block were the customer.

'We don't lean on counters at any juncture,' she said.
'They must have stressed that in your training sessions?'

William was standing in an exemplary way, alert, with
his back straight and hands clasped behind him, his feet
planted twelve inches apart, but he leant slightly to one
side so that his weight was off his hurt leg. He was trying
to look as if he had been on duty for hours.

The young woman straightened up rather too slowly, William observed.

'If you have queries,' Miss Block said, 'then bring them to me or to Mr Badger.' She nodded at William. 'Where is your docket book? Is it prepared, ready for service?'

The young woman looked around her—on the counter, under the counter, on the floor.

'You can't possibly have mislaid it in your first five minutes,' said Miss Block.

William reached for the new book he had just encountered and held it up.

'Good, good,' said Miss Block. 'Mr Badger is one of our experienced salesmen.'

William relaxed his stance a little. In the face of the several infringements already committed by this young woman, who seemed to be a new salesgirl, Miss Block had chosen to overlook his lateness and to praise him instead.

'This,' she said to William, 'is a new assistant, Miss Miss. She is on probation this week, while we assess whether she has an aptitude for retail.'

'M-m-miss . . . Miss. I didn't catch your name,' said William, when Miss Block moved away. He heard himself stammer and was surprised. M-m-miss, d'd'dit. 'Miss Miss?'

'Meese. Meg Meese,' said the young woman wearily, as if bored with her name. 'One day I'm going to change my name.'

'Are the counters prepared?' called Miss Block, wringing her hands. The cheesecloth pad had not been wielded at all and it was clear that the counters were not prepared for anything.

William took the cloth pad and refolded it, turning yesterday's grime to the inside and exposing a fresh white section to deal with today's.

'I'll just damp this down,' he said and limped off with

one stiff leg to the wash room, where he would take an extra minute or two to wash his knee. There was nothing he could do to improve the torn trouser leg. The trousers were ruined and would have to be used around the house and on weekends.

When he returned he saw Miss Block talking to Meg Meese, a stern look on her face. Then she walked off, leaving Meg standing forlorn and alone behind the counter, leaning on nothing. William began his systematic wiping of the glass, eradicating the fingerprints and smudges.

'She doesn't like my dress,' said Meg.

William realised that Miss Block's distraction this morning stemmed from Miss Meese's dress. And Miss Meese looked as if she might cry.

'It's quite a lovely dress,' he said, considering it. 'Gathered. And it falls very nicely. But perhaps . . .'

'I know, I know,' said Meg.

'Just stay behind the counter,' said William. 'It'll be all right,' although that would not solve the problem of the transparent shoulders. 'Look, I've torn my trousers.' He pointed to his knee, attempting to cheer her up with his own disarray. 'And if Miss Block sees, I'll be in trouble, too.'

'She's going to get me a cardigan,' said Meg, not even looking at William's tear. 'She keeps an old one in her locker, she said.'

Then there was a customer, a woman in a shiny teal coat of shot faille, tapping her fingers on the counter, and William hastened to show her every fountain pen in stock. He pushed the damp cloth toward Meg and gave her an encouraging nod, making a little wiping movement with his hand to indicate that she might feel better if she surrendered herself to retail for the time being, for the next few years, and did something.

When the customer pulled the lever of the plunger of one of the pens and went to fill it in the open ink bottle kept for testing, William caught her wrist and said gently, 'Just dip it in. Filling the pen is not permitted at any juncture.'

He glanced over at Meg, who was slowly pushing the cloth over the counter, and felt sorry for her.

The customer left buying only a plain lead pencil rather than a costlier fountain pen, and William was glad to be free of her, even though it would mean less commission at the end of the month. He wanted to comfort Meg Meese and show her how to wipe down the counter top, because he was rather pleased with his system, doing one section at a time, and raising the cloth in a scooping movement at the end of each stroke so that any loose particles would be lifted up and not fall back on the glass. But Meg Meese did not seem interested. She watched him, but seemed to be staring beyond his hand and the cloth.

'This is what we do first thing every morning. Wipe down the counters.' When he got to Meg's elbows, which were resting on the counter again, he waited for her to straighten up and lift them. 'We're not allowed to lean.'

'Oh, heavens,' said Meg crossly. She moved along the counter, peering down at the goods on the glass shelves below. 'We get commission, right?'

William scrubbed at the counter diligently.

'In that case,' said Meg, who had reached the leather goods and the gold fountain pens and pencils, 'it makes sense to concentrate on these, doesn't it?'

'People mostly want the cheap things,' said William.

'You'd have to sell twenty of those cheap pens to get the same commission as you would selling just one of these, wouldn't you?' She took out a gold fountain pen and pretended to write. 'Do you ever steal anything?'

'Of course not.' William paused to lean against the counter. It had never occurred to him to steal.

'No leaning!' Miss Block had completed another patrol. She was now carrying her old black cardigan, which she proffered to Meg.

William was suddenly weary, even though it was only nine thirty. But he had no choice. He had to stand there, leaning on nothing, from nine to five thirty every weekday and from nine to twelve on Saturday. He had finished high school. Rose had wanted him to leave as soon as he was old enough, at fifteen. She had wanted him to work and contribute to the household. She thought she could get new curtains on time payment if William were contributing a couple of pounds a week. But Wally Badger always said, 'Let the boy finish school.' And William did, but right after the final exams he left home, left Wally and Rose Badger, who spent their time watching each other and rarely talking to him, and he took the electric train to town and found a room in a boarding house in Glebe where he had one bed, one drawer in a chest of drawers, and two pegs to hang his clothes on, all for four pounds a week. And just two feet from his bed, running along the other wall, was a second bed, belonging to Ralph, the man with whom he shared this little room and the chest of drawers. William had taken to Ralph immediately. He was older, about thirty, and had worked long enough as a clerk in an insurance office to have saved enough money to put a deposit on a car and pay it off. That was the extent of Ralph's ambition, to possess a car. It was only that morning, as he had lain in bed watching Ralph polishing his shoes, that William remembered Roy from so many years before at Manly and realised that Ralph reminded him of Roy and that the little room he and Ralph shared was just like Roy's room at Miss Barkit's. He had not thought of Miss Barkit or Roy or that boarding house at all, perhaps not since he had been carried away from it nursing his broken wrist in the sidecar of Wally Badger's Harley Davidson. And then lying in bed he had remembered his humiliation when Roy and Heather—yes, that was the name of the pretty young woman in that back bedroom—had laughed at him for thinking Miss Barkit's name was Miss Bucket.

'We never lean against or sprawl upon the counters,' Miss Block reminded William, as she supervised Meg's putting on the black cardigan. 'We stand straight, with our hands at our sides or clasped in front, ready to be of assistance. And there are always counters and shelves to be dusted, boxes to be unpacked, displays to be checked and rearranged.' She moved off.

'She's like a battleship, no a destroyer, the way she cruises around these counters, as if they are islands and she has to patrol the seas in between.' Meg smiled at William, apparently happy that she was not the only one to be rebuked. 'How do you stand it?' she asked.

Miss Block was beside them again. 'We're starting the Mystery Shopper this week.' She looked from Meg to William. 'We don't know who he is, but if he comes to this counter and finds the service courteous and efficient, he will nominate you for a one-pound bonus.'

Meg nodded at Miss Block's back. 'One whole pound, for being subservient.'

'A pound is a pound,' said William.

'You work here all the time? Every day?' She was leaning on the counter again. 'Why don't you get a better job than this?'

'I'm not qualified for anything else.'

'You should train for something.'

'Why are you here then?'

'Don't tell them, but I'm only filling in time until I can be a secretary. The pay is good. There are good, dignified jobs for secretaries.'

William had sometimes thought about training for something. He, too, felt he was filling in time, waiting to make some move, take some action, but eight years had gone by and he still had not located what it was that he was awaiting.

'You passed the Leaving, didn't you?'

William nodded and moved off to see to a customer and began showing him all the brands of ink in stock. 'We find this one is the best,' he said. 'Swan.'

'Then there's nothing to stop you,' said Meg. 'I didn't do the Leaving. You have a big advantage already, but you've got to have ideas and imagination, like me, if you want to get anywhere.'

A woman tapped at the counter farther along, where the expensive leather desk sets and fountain pen and propelling pencil sets were. Meg moved to her.

'I want that one,' the woman said, pointing to a gold fountain pen. 'It's gold, isn't it?'

'Of course,' said Meg, although William knew she had no idea if it was or not.

'Thank you, sir,' William said to his customer, 'very much.'

'It's gold,' Meg said firmly, adding 'Madam,' loudly and deliberately, so that William could hear. And without even trying Meg sold a twenty-pound pen, while William sold two shillings-worth of ink.

All morning, like a soldier guarding a prisoner, Meg stood at that counter, selling one or two items for every ten or twelve that William sold at the cheap end of the counter. She had to ask William for help with writing up her docket book once or twice and she had to let him do a COD order, since that was a more complicated procedure. As William completed the forms, Meg stood beside him tapping her fingers on the counter. William listened to the message she tapped out. D'dah dit, dah dah dah, d'd'dit,dit. Over and over.

Rose. Meg was tapping out Rose, Rose, Rose.

'That's morse code,' he said.

'What is?' The tapping stopped.

William tapped his pencil on the hard black cover of the COD book, and said the code out loud. 'D'dah dit, dah dah dah, d'd'dit, dit.' He repeated it.

Meg joined in, and together they stood tapping and chanting softly, 'D'dah dit, dah dah dah, d'd'dit, dit.' Meg started to move her foot in time with the tapping, doing a little dance, and then at the approach of Miss Block, they both stopped and stood up straight.

'Rose is my m-m-mother's name,' said William, putting his hand over his mouth to stop this sudden onset of stammering.

'How do you know morse code?'

William cleared his throat. 'Someone taught it to me, that's all.' And again William was remembering Roy, whom he never thought of, and those terrible Manly days.

At one o'clock a salesgirl from Stationery came over to Pens and Pencils to relieve William while he went out to eat his sandwich.

'We shall make up a new schedule, when Miss Meese has had more experience and can be trusted to be responsible for Pens and Pencils on her own,' said Miss Block, 'but for today and all this week, Miss Meese, your schedule will be the same as Mr Badger's.'

Meg and William left the floor together and went to

their lockers. William's leg was still stiff from his fall. Then he discovered that his lunch was not there. He had left it on the footpath in Martin Place, where the witch had assaulted him.

Meg came and stood beside him, holding her brown paper bag. 'Where are we supposed to go for lunch?'

'I go to Hyde Park, when it's sunny,' said William. He was distressed by this disruption, this lack of lunch, which would change his routine. He would have to find a sandwich shop and wait in line. 'I have lost my lunch,' he said forlornly.

'You can share mine,' said Meg.

William stood with his head bowed. The distress at the waste of his peanut butter sandwich—it would have been kicked into the gutter, trodden on—was profound.

'Come on,' said Meg, and she led him out of the store, holding his hand for a moment and ready to drag him along with her. 'What happened to your leg?'

'I told you,' said William. 'I fell down. And these are my good trousers. Wool.'

They sat in Hyde Park on a bench. Meg handed him a devon and pickles sandwich. 'I've got two,' she said. 'It's far too much for me by myself, but my mother says you need your strength.' She bent over William's knee and examined the tear, shaking her head. 'You could try that invisible mending place at Wynyard, but I think it's too big, this rip.'

She positioned herself on the bench on William's left, then turned a little toward him, and rested her right elbow on the back of the bench allowing her hand to hang free from the wrist. She inclined her head to the right and crossed her left leg over her right.

'I'll tell you what I'm going to do. I'm going to learn shorthand and typing. At night.'

William was wondering whether he could swallow devon and pickles. For years he had never eaten anything but peanut butter for lunch.

'Why don't you do it, too?' Meg spoke earnestly, then took a tiny bite from her sandwich. 'You've got to ask questions, question your life.'

'You think I should be a male secretary?' said William. 'Who would hire a man?' He closed his eyes and took a bite from the sandwich, chewed rapidly and swallowed.

'You could be private secretary to some old man, a retired judge writing a book, who hated women.' Meg shrugged. 'Or a mason. They hate women. You could be secretary to the masons.' She pointed across the park to the building next to the museum. 'Look, there's their head-quarters. I know because my father's a mason. You just go in, say you're a secretary, and they'll take one look at you in your wool trousers and snap you up.' Meg paused. 'You'd be sitting down all day, once you got a job. And then you could do classes in something else at night. Get more training in something. Accounting, for instance. *Do* something with your life.'

'We Badgers are do-ers,' said William.

Meg chewed thoughtfully. 'And Rose would be pleased, I bet.'

'Who?'

'You know, your mother, Rose.' Meg cocked her head further to the right. 'Where are your parents? Are they alive?'

'My father and m-m-m.' William couldn't say the word. It was the letter M he could not get past. 'M-m-my m-m-.' It was a cement block higher than his head. He couldn't climb over it.

Meg swallowed and looked at him, surprised. 'Your mother?'

William nodded. 'She, and he, m-m-m-, the folks, they live in the western suburbs,' he blurted in a rush.

'What are they like?'

What were his parents like? William had no idea. He frowned, eating his sandwich without tasting it. 'They're like any parents. They live in a house. I don't see them now.'

'Why ever not?'

William shook his head. He had not been to see Wally and Rose for five years, having returned only that once since he had moved into his room in Glebe eight years before.

'They would help you better yourself, wouldn't they? Mine are going to pay the twenty pounds for the secretarial course.'

William shook his head again. 'You don't know them.'

'What sort of a name is Badger?'

'Name? It's just a name.'

'Where's Ratty and Mole?'

'What?'

'*Wind in the Willows*, silly. All those underground creatures.'

William was having trouble keeping up with this new salesgirl. Inside the store, where he had some authority by dint of his years in Pens and Pencils, this Meg Meese had looked to him for help. But now, divested of authority, he was floundering, and she was in charge. He felt like a lumbering, slow clod, like wooden clogs clinging to the feet of a nymph.

Suddenly he tapped out on the wooden bench, dah dah dah, d'dah d'dit, dah dah dit, d'dah, in an effort to regain his authority and possibly her admiration. 'Know what that is?'

Meg shook her head.

'Dah dah, dit, dah dah dit, dah dah, d'dit, d'dah dit,

d'dah dit. Meg Meese. You can't just change your name. It's not allowed.'

'A person can do what she wants,' said Meg. She adjusted the drape of her right arm along the bench back. 'I saw a painting once, a picture of a painting actually, an oil painting, in a book in a library. I often go to the library. By an artist called Picasso. The painting is called Olga. She had hair like mine, and a dress like this one—I copied hers when I made this dress—and she was sitting on a lovely chair covered by a black cloth with marvellous green leaves and grapes and a kind of yellow trumpet flower embroidered on it, with her arms like this. It was a picture of me.'

'How could it be a picture of you? Picasso never saw you.' William felt he was losing ground again, becoming a clog again.

'Things like that can happen, you know. In another part of the world, at another time altogether, things can happen, or have happened, and they are connected to you. That painting of Olga is me. I know it.' She wrinkled her nose. 'My given name has held me back, that name, made me set my sights low. That's why I'm going to secretarial school. I want doors to open.'

William was still tapping out morse code on the bench. Meg was still talking, confiding her secrets to him.

'And one day I'll go on a working holiday, to the continent, maybe live in Paris and get to know things there, while I work as a secretary somewhere, maybe at an embassy. That would be a good job. Haven't you ever wanted another name?'

William was startled and his tapping stopped. It was silly to want to change your name. But had not he wanted to be someone else, once? Longleg? Billy Longleg? But no, it was his invisible secret companion, not he, who was to have been Billy Longleg. 'Of course not,' he said. 'Listen, do you want me to teach you morse code? We can tap out messages at work. It could come in handy. It's something to know. You like to know things.'

'Right under Miss Block's nose,' said Meg.

William spread out the brown paper bag that had held Meg's sandwiches and began writing out the dots and dashes. Meg abandoned her languid Picasso pose, bringing her arm down and moving closer to William as he wrote A dot dash, B dash dot dot dot.

'And then there's a statue of George Sand, in stone, sitting like Olga, in exactly the same way,' said Meg before William had even reached C. 'George Sand is a woman, you know.'

'There are special combinations for "message ends", "over", "I am about to transmit",' said William, 'and all the punctuation signs. But you can learn those later.'

'That pose must mean something,' said Meg. 'It must symbolise something in art. Everything has a meaning in art.'

William thrust the paper bag at Meg and she studied the marks. 'The thing about that painting of Olga, besides the dress and the beautiful upholstery, were some black marks, squiggles, on the yellow wall behind the chair. Ochre, I think I'd call the colour of the wall, rather than yellow. The squiggles were like this.' She took the brown paper bag and the pencil from William, turned the bag over, and scribbled some vertical lines. 'As if a child had been naughty and drawn on the wall. The squiggles were just below Olga's fingertips. She could almost have made them with her own fingers.'

William took back the bag and looked at the erratic scribbling, then turned the bag over, back to the orderly dots and dashes of the morse code. He looked at this young woman beside him and did not know what to say.

'Or better still, like primitive messages on the wall of a cave, cave drawings,' said Meg. 'I like caves very, very much, don't you?'

'I don't know,' said William slowly. He had not considered caves for a long time. 'Morse code is messages, too. Like cave drawings in the air.'

'I like going into caves. I do it on weekends sometimes. We have a club, The Trogs we call ourselves. Short for Troglodytes.'

'Cavemen,' said William. He remembered what troglodytes were.

'Very good,' said Meg. 'Not many people know that word.'

'Or someone who chooses to live alone in seclusion, a recluse, or someone who lives in a primitive or degenerate fashion,' William elaborated. 'I used to know a lot about those who delve and dare underground in hidden localities, who follow ways that are dark and tricks that are vain.' And then he remembered The Badger. 'I can tell you about a famous criminal called The Badger, who lived underground with the bloodthirsty viragoes and desperate cutthroats amidst the immorality and licentiousness of Paris.'

Meg was now clasping her little hands at her bosom, smiling up at him. 'You, too, have existed in Paris! Like Olga!'

On pay day, when Miss Block brought around their pay envelopes, William saw that he had a few extra shillings in commission, and an extra pound attached to a note that indicated he had served the 'Mystery Shopper'. He showed the note to Meg, proud of his performance and feeling vindicated, wanting her to understand that it paid to be nice. Since he earned only seven pounds a week, a pound was important. And he was short of money because of the new wool trousers he had had to buy.

Meg held up the pound note, a crisp new one, and read the letter of commendation out loud. ' "You have contributed to David Jones' high standard of customer service through your careful and courteous attention to the Mystery Shopper" '.

Then she opened her envelope and examined her wages.

'I've got an extra two pounds ten,' she said. 'It's commission. I'll shout you lunch. A meat pie, if you like.'

As they sat on the park bench eating the meat pies Meg had bought, she reached into her pocket and took out a fountain pen with a mottled blue barrel and cap. She unscrewed the cap and held the gold nib before William's eyes.

'How did you steal it?' William gasped. 'I locked them all up, I'm sure I did.'

Miss Block would notice the empty case and William would be fired.

'Give it to me,' he said. He would put it back after lunch.

Meg leaned away shaking her head. 'It's mine,' she said.

'Why did you do that? I'll lose my job. And so will you.'

'It's a stupid job.'

'It's a job. And some of us have to work. We have no choice.'

'You're teaching me morse code and I'm going to teach you a new way to live,' said Meg. 'I like to help people, and you need help.

'Give me the pen,' said William standing up and holding out his hand. 'Please.' He swayed a little on his feet and thought he might fall. He could not bear to think that Meg had stolen a pen from his counter. He put his hand to his forehead.

'Hey,' said Meg, pulling him back to sit down on the bench and putting her arm around his waist. 'You do need help.'

'Why did you steal it?'

'Steal what? I told you, it's my pen. My mother gave it to me. It was my father's. William,' she said, drawing out his name. 'Mr Badger, you don't think I stole it, do you?'

'I think you stole it,' he said.

'Boy oh boy,' said Meg. 'Is it on the basis of knowledge or on evidence that you know that I stole that pen?'

'It's obvious,' said William. He was now clinging to the bench with both hands and still feared he might fall.

'Ah, obvious, is it? How do you know that you have lungs with which you breathe? How do you know that there is a centre to the earth?'

William was confused. 'Everyone knows that.'

'Know?' Meg was giggling, yet looking closely at William. 'No lizards need a hairbrush, some creatures that drink coffee are not fierce, no fossil can be crossed in love, no emperors are dentists.' She paused.

'How do you know to say all that?' William asked.

'Listen, seriously. If you say all dogs are faithful, it tends to imply that there are dogs, that dogs exist. But if you say all those who are free from sin may cast stones, it doesn't mean that there actually are any individuals free from sin, does it?'

William placed one hand on his forehead.

'It's just logic,' Meg said. 'No one is despised who can manage a crocodile.'

'What are you talking about?' whispered William. 'Please stop.' He had been transported to a foreign country, where he could not understand the language.

'I've taken a lot of courses at the WEA,' said Meg.
'Workers' Education. You know. I did Introduction to
Logic. I was going to do something called Aesthetics—
that's about the nature of beauty—but I thought it wouldn't
be as useful. I've done Beginning German, the Geology
of Sydney, caves and all that, and Upholstery. And next
I'm going to do typing and shorthand at the Tech. It's
the only way out of the DJ's basement.'

They stood up to walk back to work.

'I would have gone to Hungary in 1956,' said Meg. 'To
be a nurse. I would have nursed Hungarians wounded by
the Russians.'

'Why didn't you?' asked William.

'The only trouble is, I'm not a nurse.' Meg sighed. 'I
could have joined the underground.'

'What could you do for Hungarians?'

'They needed help. I could have written their story or
made broadcasts on short wave or smuggled out secret
documents. The only trouble is, I was too young. I would've
needed my parents' permission to even get a passport.'

When they got back to Pens and Pencils, William walked
swiftly to the counter to check the fountain pen display,
resisting the impulse to run, to get there ahead of Meg,
who trotted in front of him, nimbly ducking around the
customers in the aisles. When William got to the counter
Meg was sliding the glass doors of the case shut and stood
tapping her fingers on the counter, humming, smiling.

'You *did* steal it!' William exclaimed.

Meg's eyes were roaming about beyond William's head.

'That means you lied to me about it.' Lying was as
bad as stealing.

'I'm tired of being a worker, a slave, Miss Block's slave,'
said Meg. Then as William frowned, she laughed at him.
'You are so cautious and stodgy.'

Meg was waiting for William when he emerged at five thirty-five from the employees' entrance on Castlereagh Street at the end of the day. She scampered down Market Street with him to the bus stop in George Street, sometimes trotting by his side, sometimes moving ahead with a little skip so that she could turn to look up at him, walking sideways, almost backwards, for a few paces. If she had been a puppy William might have tripped over her. She was following him, yet although he was the one determining the route she was so eager to romp along that her exuberance led her to prance ahead now and then, anticipating his path.

'Where do you go now?' she asked, a pace in front of him, looking up at him.

'Home,' he said. 'I catch the bus to Glebe.'

'It's only five forty,' she said, falling into step beside him.

William stepped behind her to the other side, so that he was nearest the kerb.

'There's Cahill's,' Meg said, 'over there,' indicating the coffee shop across the road. 'You go down the stairs, you'd hardly know it's there. It's a good place to go when you're alone. I go there often. There's a counter with a magazine rack and you can have a waffle with ice-cream and maple syrup and read at the same time, without having to hold the magazine. Or raisin toast, you can have raisin toast, or something more substantial.'

William frowned as he continued walking, not sure if she was inviting him to eat with her. He never ate in restaurants or cafes. At the bus stop William stopped and Meg halted beside him, standing rather too close to him. William stepped sideways, away from her. She stepped next to him and he moved away again.

'Where do you go?' he asked. He stepped back another pace.

'Let's look in Dymock's window while we're waiting,' Meg said and drew him away from the bus stop to the books piled in the windows.

'I've read all their Penguins,' said Meg. 'Hemingway, Waugh, Huxley, Stella Gibbons—the orange Penguins, not the green—and I've read all their Everyman's Classics, *Bleak House*, everything. Have you?'

'Not really,' William said. 'Why do you read so much?'

'The more versatile and knowledgeable you are,' said Meg, 'the more successful you'll be as a private secretary. A secretary must read as widely as possible, because there are no limits to what might be expected of her. I go to all the continental films, too. Do you?'

'Not really,' said William.

'I've seen "One Summer of Happiness", "*La Ronde*", "*Gervaise*", "*Nana*", and "*Diabolique*".' She gave a shudder. 'That was really terrifying. The wife thinks she has killed the husband, but it's all a trick, a ruse, and he comes back to life, out of the bathtub. And I've seen "Bicycle Thief" and "The Railwayman".'

'Why do you go to so many films?'

'Because that's contemporary culture. When I'm a secretary in Paris, my employer will need to be able to discuss anything with me. I have to be cultured. And look, just down there at the Lyric.' She pointed across the road, past Beard Watson's to the little cinema in the next block. 'They've got something called "Wild Strawberries" showing now, and I am going to see that soon.' She paused. 'Want to come with me?'

'I don't know,' said William.

'Just come and look at the pictures outside,' Meg said and led him along the block and across the road to the cinema, where she stopped before the photographs displayed outside the theatre.

'Look at that!' Meg was pointing at the clock without hands and then a coffin lying on the road. 'You can be sure that that's symbolic,' she said. Then she pointed at a photograph of a blonde girl sitting on the grass. 'Swedish,' she said, then sadly, 'the trouble with being cultured is I've got no one to talk to about it.'

William looked down at this sad, strange girl by his side. 'I used to like poetry,' he said. 'I used to learn poems off by heart.' He tapped on the glass that covered the photographs, d'dah dit, dah dah dah, d'd'dit, dit.

'Poetry's good to know. You can quote things at the right time. Say something to me.'

'It's been a long time,' said William.

'Just try, just a line,' said Meg.

'It's called "Out Back".' He wanted very much to remember something, to show Meg that he did indeed like poetry, that he had the potential to be cultured. 'The old year went,' and he tapped in time to the line, d'dah dah dah, 'and the new returned,' d'd'dah d'dah. He struggled to remember. He could see the little pink book sitting on its shelf in a fork in the branches of the privet hedge, and the weighty *Underground, or Life Below the Surface* wedged into the hedge closer to the ground. He could see the sweets tucked higher up in the hedge, like stars watching over him. 'in the withering weeks of drought,' d'd'dah d'd'dah d'dah. He looked at Meg.

'That's really nice,' she said. 'And you were tapping out a message at the same time. What did it say?'

William tapped again. Dah dah dah, d'dah d'dit, dah dah dit, d'dah. Meg drew from her purse the brown paper bag on which William had written the morse code when they had sat together at lunchtime in Hyde Park.

'Do it again,' she said, 'slowly.'

And William obliged.

'Olga!' cried Meg. 'You tapped out Olga!' She was delighted. 'I know, let's have a cup of coffee at Repin's. It's just down here, near Wynyard.'

William hesitated, looking back toward the bus stop where he was supposed to be standing.

'Wouldn't you like to be someone else?' she asked.

William was silent.

'Where would you like to be from? England? Ireland? What about Sweden? You could be Swedish. Or German.' Meg studied the photographs behind the glass. 'We could have met on the boat coming out to Sydney and become fast friends. Or we could be related.

'You need a new name,' said Meg. 'You'd feel much better. In German class—I studied German for nine weeks at the WEA—we had to choose a name, and I said I was Olga, and the teacher always addressed me as Olga when she asked me a question. And do you know, I wasn't afraid to answer. I'm normally shy. But in that class, when I was Olga, I was not afraid to say things out loud.' She plucked at his sleeve. 'Come on.'

William let her lead him into Repin's Coffee Inn and to the only empty booth.

'I've got plenty of time until my secretarial class, and you're not going anywhere, are you?' Meg was now examining the menu. 'Raisin toast and coffee, black for me. Europeans always have coffee black after midday,' she said. She pulled out of her purse a packet of cigarettes and showed the pack to William. 'Cocktail Sobranis,' she said, and opened the case to show him the neat row of pastel-coloured cigarettes. She extracted a pink one and gave William her box of matches so that he could light it for her. Then she sat back, turning slightly so that her right arm rested on the back of the booth and she cocked her head slightly to the right. 'This is how Olga sits in the painting,' she reminded William, looking at him seriously. Then lifting a piece of toast she said, '*Bon appétit*. English is the only language that doesn't wish people well before they begin to eat.' She leant forward. 'Why don't you tell me something about the women of the demimonde? You mentioned them that lunchtime in the park.'

'They're bloodthirsty,' said William. 'They accost strangers at night on the boulevards. They ask loungers in the cafes to buy them coffee and wine. They make poses and smoke in the streets.'

Meg closed her eyes and smiled. 'Go on.'

'And sometimes they are arrested for brawls, intoxication and pilfering. These women might start out adventurous, good and kind, but in that wicked city they quickly become vain, given to licentiousness.'

'I'd love to *be* there,' said Meg dreamily.

'The adventuress is usually favoured by nature and carries her fair face and symmetrical form to the best market. Good and kind at first she has become what man has made of her; and in the vocation she has chosen, vanity and self are her impelling powers.'

'That sounds like poetry,' said Meg. 'Are you quoting something?'

William shrugged and nodded. 'Kind of.'

Meg sighed and flexed her shoulders, adjusting her arm so that it lay even more languidly across the leather back of the bench. 'Go on.'

'Her beauty is a commodity she offers to the highest bidder. She receives large sums, but she squanders them recklessly.' William was enjoying himself. He suddenly felt he could recite all the pages of *Underground*. It was as if he were reading the words from the pages, sitting under the hedge. He remembered everything. 'Display is her only passion. She shines in the Bois, bets desperately

at Baden, turns heads at Vienna, shocks the proprieties
of London.'

'That wouldn't be hard, from what I know about
London,' said Meg.

'But you haven't been there,' said William.

'I'm sure I've been there,' said Meg. 'I *must* have been
there at another time altogether. What else?'

'She interrupts the opera at Madrid and is the subject
of scandal in the *New York Herald*. But her career is
necessarily brief, for her reign must end when years begin
to tell. Between twenty and thirty-five her golden harvest
must be gathered.'

'That's not very fair, is it?' Meg murmured. 'Not fair
to women.'

'Then there are those who sin without satisfaction and
laugh without gaiety. They have a freedom that women,
however fallen, always enjoy in France. For some cocottes
the greatest ambition is to kick the hats from the heads
of their dancing partners and to throw their drapery into
the wildest confusion.'

'Drapery!' Meg laughed and with her left hand plucked
at her skirt and raised her knee under the table, pretending
to cancan. 'Go on. You really are quite cultured already,
you know.'

'They do their wooing in the presence of hundreds. They
make up their differences with petting words and copious
caresses and enact their melodramas regardless of envious
eyes and smiling lookers-on.'

William stopped his recitation. A woman holding a string
bag filled with parcels was standing beside their booth.

'May I sit here?' she inquired.

Meg opened her eyes. William moved over to the wall
to make room for the woman, who said, 'It's so crowded
this evening.'

'Please be velcome to sitz mit us,' said Meg, who did not change her pose.

As the woman placed her string bag next to Meg and then settled herself next to William, Meg winked at William.

Meg addressed William, '*Ah, Ingmar, das nicht gut*. *Frau sitz hier* now,' then she let off a string of words, '*Doppelgänger, Tafel, gehen, zwischen*.'

William had no idea what was going on and started tapping on the table, d'd'dit, dah dah dah, d'd'dit. Meg winked at him.

'You're from somewhere else, aren't you?' said the woman.

'*Ja, ja*, I from Germany,' said Meg.

'Germany? Really?' the woman replied.

'*Ja, ja*, but I escape as baby. Vater die, Mutter and me escape to London, then kaput, she die.'

'London? Really?'

'And this, my cousin Ingmar. No speak English. I teach English him. He is son of German countess. She Nazi, he not Nazi of course, just baby in war. But he must change name and hide. Ingmar,' Meg addressed William, 'say how you do.'

William was silent, appalled.

'Do not afraid, Ingmar,' said Meg.

'Certainly no need to be afraid in this country,' said the woman.

'Say how you do to lady, Ingmar.'

The woman turned to William and enunciated slowly, 'How do you do.'

'Answer lady please Ingmar,' said Meg. 'Say how you do.'

The woman was holding her hand out to William.

'How you do,' he finally blurted and shook the woman's hand.

'I,' said Meg grandly, 'am Olga. How you do.'

'You lived in London?'

Meg nodded.

'What part of London?'

'Oh, here, there, always move. My mama was also countess. Before war, bad war.'

'Really? We have a Russian prince where I live. In the eastern suburbs. He mows the lawns in our street and he mows the golf course. He is a real Russian prince, you know.'

'So sad. All money gone,' said Meg. She looked at her watch. 'Oh, we go now. The class in English begin soonly.' She stood up.

The woman stood up to allow William past.

'Thank you muchly,' he said as he slid out of the booth.

'Here, Ingmar, this is shilling, this is two shillings, you pay now. Good practice.'

Outside Meg burst into laughter. 'Wasn't that fun?'

'Why did you do that? She couldn't possibly have believed you.'

'She'll tell her family about us tonight. It's not every day you meet the son and the daughter of German countesses.'

'Why do you do that?'

They walked together back to the Market Street bus stop. Meg was quiet now, walking neatly at William's side. 'I do it,' she said, 'because if you pretend to have been somewhere or to be someone, after a while it feels as if you actually have been where you say you have been and you actually are that person. It isn't even lying. You really believe your own story, and you can make that story as wonderful or as sad as you wish. You can make your own life.'

At the bus stop they were silent for a while, until Meg said, 'And you have to *do* something.'

William shook his head.

'You know so much, about the world, about Paris and London and everywhere,' she said.

They fell silent again. It was now six thirty and the crowds at the bus stop had gone.

'Come to my class with me, come on,' said Meg. 'If you learn shorthand and typing you can be private secretary to a, a count, a diplomat, or someone important and cultured and you'll lead an interesting life. You speak well and you have a good vocabulary—boulevard, drapery, proprieties. You'd make a good private secretary.

'And now,' said Meg on the bus, 'you shall come with me to the secretarial course tonight.'

'I don't want to.'

'You must come. It's your passport. To a better life, with doors opening for you.' She shook her head impatiently. 'Don't you see, you have to *do* something, begin somewhere?'

At Railway Square, Meg hauled William off the bus with her and led him along Harris Street to the Tech and into the classroom, a large shabby room with thirty desks in rows, each with Underwoods sitting on top, and behind most of the typewriters sat young women, combing their hair, yawning, chatting.

When William entered, they all stared at him and some giggled at the sight of a man, the only man among them. He pulled back from Meg.

'They don't know anything,' Meg whispered fiercely. 'They're stupid, bound by tradition. Come on.' And she went up to two empty desks at the back, side by side, placed her purse on the floor beside one and beckoned William to the desk beside it.

William wanted to die, but it seemed simpler to do as he was told. And he could not bear to think of the gales of laughter that would follow him if he turned and ran.

A woman with grey hair, cut short, and wearing a navy-blue suit and pink blouse with a bow at the neck entered and stood in front of the class. William could see that the skirt was cut badly and he could also see that she had tucked her blouse not only into the skirt but into her corset as well, so that an inch or two of the grubby pink cotton of the corset showed all around the waistline of the skirt.

'Good evening, girls,' she said, and the girls tittered. 'I am Miss Fletcher. Sit neatly now. A good secretary never slouches. This is how we sit.' She turned the chair at the front of the class sideways and sat on it, to demonstrate. 'See how our backs are straight, and our feet are planted side by side, squarely on the floor. Our knees are together and we never cross our legs. The Queen sits like this all the time, if you take the time to notice. Do as I do, girls. Sit like the Queen.'

The students cleared their throats and sat appropriately. Again, a few giggled and turned to look at William.

'Even when your desk has a modesty panel—and all respectable employers provide modesty panels for their girls—you still sit in this pose.'

Miss Fletcher stood up and walked among the desks, checking the girls' posture. 'And if we have to stand, beside our employer's desk while he gives us instructions, or at the file cabinet, this is how we stand.' Miss Fletcher walked to the front of the class and stood with her feet slightly apart, her back straight. 'This is how the Queen stands, both feet parallel, weight distributed evenly.'

Then she caught sight of William. 'Are you sure you are in the right class?' she asked.

Before William could say no and flee, Meg put up her hand and said, 'He is going to be personal assistant to an

English baronet in Rome, who is writing his memoirs, and Mr Badger is required to learn shorthand and typing before taking up his position at the end of the year.' The tittering stopped and an awed silence fell over the class at this impressive credential. 'The baronet is his uncle, you see.'

'You should be aware that this is not just a shorthand and typing class,' said Miss Fletcher. 'We encompass all aspects of secretarial practice, including character and attitude. Our girls, our students, are not destined for the typing pool.'

'That's exactly what the baronet requires,' said Meg. 'That's why he's here.'

Miss Fletcher coughed her acceptance of William's presence. 'You may stay as long as you keep up and do the work.' Then she barked, 'Posture!' Her pupils sat up straight. 'The perfect secretary is born and not made. Be that as it may, if you have the right attitude, you can be improved through training.' She turned to the blackboard and began writing, speaking the words as she wrote her list. 'The personal qualities essential in a good secretary are: common sense, loyalty, punctuality, discretion, tact, a cheerful and equable temper, ability to take responsibility, orderliness, a quick, alert and sensible mind, a sense of proportion, enthusiasm for work, a high standard of achievement, technical skill, and also an ability to mix with people without embarrassment. Are you writing this down?' She turned to her pupils. 'I would recommend that for the rest of your life you write this down inside the cover of each shorthand notebook every time before you begin on a new notebook.'

'That wasn't so bad, was it?' Meg asked as they left the building two hours later and walked back to the bus stop at Railway Square.

'Why did you say that about the baronet? Why did you lie?' William asked.

'To get respect,' said Meg. 'It was only a story, not really lying, and if it is the only way to get respect from people who are limited, I say it's not a sin to lie.'

'No men are secretaries,' William insisted.

'Some secretaries are men,' Meg corrected. 'Times are changing. You'll see. You can be a pioneer. If you talk about something enough, it gets in your bones, in your blood, it becomes real.'

'And you are Olga in the same way?'

'Yes, I am Olga, and I have been in Paris, and I was painted by Picasso, and I made those marks on the wall with my fingers.'

'Like a cave drawing?'

'I like caves, and you will, too. It all comes together in that painting. The cultured side is represented by her sitting, on that upholstered chair in the salon, and the primitive side by the markings on the wall. I'll show you one day how nice caves really are, how nice it is to camp in the bush and then go under the ground into the caves and explore in the dark.'

William was not sure. 'Maybe. Caves aren't really very safe, you know.'

'There's no maybe about it. They've been safe havens, refuges, for man for millenniums, I mean millennia.'

Meg stood beside William for a few moments. 'You know what else I would have done? I would have gone to South Africa, too, to help those people in Sharpeville. They were killed just for wanting to go to school, and the people in charge, like kings in castles, never want change. I would have been a teacher, and been a nuisance to the wicked government.' She stood silently, looking off across the square. 'The only trouble is, I'm not a teacher.

But you,' she turned to William, 'you can do anything. And you have to *do* something.'

Meg went to the kerb, ready to cross the road. 'I catch the train now,' she said. 'See you tomorrow in Pens and Pencils, in the basement, but not for long. We're on the way up.' And as she said 'up', she waved at William and pointed at the sky.

William loved the secretarial class. He liked the orderliness of it. He liked placing the paper straight in the typewriter. He liked the tap-tap-tapping of the class as they typed in unison, like a chorus of morse code operators, fff jjj over and over, with the forefingers poised above their home keys and the thumb thumping down on the space bar between each trio of letters. He was already outlining the essay they had to write for the next lesson, on one of two topics: What do you think are the attributes of a good private secretary? Or: What kind of private secretary would you like to be? And they had to prepare for discussion two topics: Office machines will gradually eliminate the private secretary, and, A private secretary cannot be trained.

Looking ahead in the typing exercise book he saw he would soon be typing 'all is fair; sell us jars; a kid used a ready idea.' And beyond that: 'Joel got to that lake at four. He hooked a trout. Ask Gil or Kurt to look for Hale at the old house. Jill has a silk shirt. The shirt fits her just right. Joe Yale will take Paula Quat to the party Friday.'

William suddenly felt that he might indeed be the assistant to a person of importance by the time the new year came around.

By the time William went caving with Meg in December he was versed in filing (spike, box, concertina, loose leaf and card) and in keeping a postage book and petty cash book; he could eliminate jargon in a report or a letter; he knew how to fold quarto and foolscap letters, send telegrams, make trunk calls; he could use the correct form of address for doctors, clergymen, the mayor, the prime minister and a fellow of the Royal College of Surgeons; and he could take Pitman's at ninety words per minute and type everything—letters, lists, figures and fractions—at forty words per minute.

When the Trogs hoisted themselves out of the cave into the open air William, expecting to be dazzled by sunlight, found himself stumbling about in the dark. They had been underground for seven hours.

'That was good,' said Meg to William, 'for your first time. You'll get used to it.'

William breathed deliberately, calming himself down. Crawling back to the surface had made him anxious, looking in vain for light at the end of the tunnel. The longed-for emergence into the dark of the night instead of the light of day had taken him by surprise.

'I'll need boots,' he said. 'There are boots in the garage at home. I'll get them over Christmas.'

He put his arm around Meg's shoulder. She stepped away from him.

'How come you know German?' she asked.

'German?'

'That song you sang.'

William was astonished. 'That's German?'

Meg nodded and frowned at him. 'You didn't know?'

'My mother sang it all the time. Once.' He had had no idea that those nonsense words were German.

The other Trogs, having emerged, were stamping and jumping up and down, hooting with joy at the return.

'Is she German, then?' asked Meg.

William sat on the grass and held his knees. Was Rose German, then? She could not possibly be. He would have known. He shook his head. 'English,' he said. 'I was born there, in England.'

Meg shrugged. 'You should ask her, though.'

'Tucker,' yelled Jack. 'I could eat ten rabbits.'

The Trogs started to career down the hill, arms outstretched, gambolling like lambs.

'Probably,' said Meg, holding back from the others, remaining by William's side, 'you are the son of a German countess, hiding behind the name Badger in Sydney, Australia. I'd say that was the explanation. Come on!' She tugged at William, who got to his feet and attempted to mimic the frolicking of the Trogs, who were receding into the dark and shouting, 'Laura, you're the face in the mystic night.' The murky white of their soiled boilersuits, their outstretched arms, and the light of the lamps now dim made them look like twirling ghosts.

'You have to sing it, too,' Meg called back to him. 'It's the test you have to pass to be a Trog.'

William followed Meg in a series of modest leaps, mumbling the song, then suddenly tripped on a clump of grass or a rabbit hole and went sprawling forward. His momentum when he fell rolled him over several times on the grassy slope, scattering the soft ash from his lamp. He got up, picked up his lamp, and walked back down to the camp, where the dim lamps were bobbing around.

'Where's the meat?' cried Jack, who was building a fire.

'William, the meat,' said Meg, as William staggered into the camp.

He took one of the lamps that was still burning, went down to the bank of the creek and knelt down beside the tree trunk to which the steaks were tethered. The strings were slack instead of taut, and William could see that they were snaking like fronds of a water plant on the surface of the dark water, which tumbled along noisily over the rocks and pebbles. He hauled the strings in, like a fisherman, knowing there would be no catch. There were no plastic bags on the ends of the strings, and no steaks, only the severed tops of the bags still attached, like some new-fangled fishing fly. He leant forward and plunged his hands into the black water and groped around, overturning the stones. He took off his sneakers and socks and rolled up his trouser legs and stepped into the water, systematically overturning rocks, searching, moving slowly downstream in case the steaks had been carried off and lodged farther down.

'Bring on the tucker,' he heard Jack shout.

Then Meg was at the bank. 'Hurry up,' she said, then, 'What's wrong?'

'They're gone,' said William.

Meg was holding the strings. 'Gone!'

Then all the Trogs were at the bank.

'They're gone,' said William lamely, wishing he could hide, disappear, run off over hill and dale and never be seen again.

'Looks as if something ate them,' said Meg. 'Yabbies, probably.'

'What was the meat doing in the creek in the first place?' Jack asked, his voice booming across the creek, through the bush, and all the way back to Sydney.

'To keep cool,' said William humbly.

'That's the stupidest idea I ever heard,' boomed Jack.

'There's always bread and cheese,' said Meg. 'And beer.'

For a while everyone searched the water for the missing steaks.

'The stupidest idea I ever heard,' Jack kept repeating.

Finally they returned to the campfire in silence, leaving William standing in the creek with the water swirling above his knees, feeling more foolish and miserable than he had ever felt, and he had had his share of feeling foolish and miserable in his lifetime.

William borrowed Ralph's car and drove out to see Wally and Rose Badger on Christmas morning, arriving at eleven, thinking that would give him a decent amount of time to chat politely, to find the boots, to offer to help with anything that needed doing around the house, and to eat with them, before heading back to Glebe as soon as was decently possible. He had telephoned them—they had had a telephone for some years—and told Wally, who answered, that he would be coming.

'Very well, son,' Wally Badger had said.

'Don't forget to ask,' Meg had said the day before in Pens and Pencils.

'Ask?' William replied.

'You know, German, a countess, and all that. You sang that song. You have to *ask* questions to get answers.'

William pulled up at the kerb outside the house and sat for a moment, trembling, nervous. The house was shabby. The dandelions and paspalum mixed in with the grass in the front yard and in the driveway at the side were knee-high. As he stepped over the weeds growing in the cracks, which were more like fissures in the cement path that led to the front steps, he thought that he would spend an hour or so pulling them out before Christmas dinner. Even that would make a difference in the appearance of the house and assuage his guilt at not having helped his parents at all in the five years since he had last visited. The stump of the hibiscus tree that used to grow in the corner of the front garden was sticking up three feet or so above the long grass. William could chop that down and mow the lawn, or rather the combination of growths, before leaving. He should have worn the trousers with the torn knee, his caving outfit, instead of the trousers he wore every day to Pens and Pencils.

Instead of going up the front steps and into the house by the front door, he stepped through the long grass to the driveway and made his way through the undergrowth to the garage at the back. He would see if the boots were hanging on the nail and check what tools were in the garage. He would go caving again, only to be with Meg, as long as the Trogs forgave him for losing their steaks.

On the driveway were several motorbikes in various stages of assembly, protruding from the grass like ships that had foundered in a fierce storm. One hulk lacked a front wheel and was sitting rusted on wooden chocks. Another was lying on its side. The wooden sidecar from the old Harley Davidson sat on bricks near the fence. Littered around were engine parts, with the grass growing up around them, as if novelty biscuit cutters in the shape of exhaust pipes and mufflers and cogged wheels had been stamped into the grass. Mowing would not be simple.

In the garage, the door of which gaped open and had not been shut in years, the boots were on their nail. They were cracked and hard, the soles were peeling from the uppers. If William had stopped to think before making this journey, he would have known that they would be useless. They had not been touched for decades. How had he imagined that he could have worn the boots that had been worn by his father in the First World War. They had been claimed by nature, covered with cobwebs, attached to the garage wall like a hornet's nest.

Beneath the boots, leaning against the wall, was an axe. At least chopping down the stump at the front would be simple. William brought the axe out into the sun, running his fingers along the head, rusty and blunt, but it would do the job. He leant the axe against the wall of the house, then, since the back steps into the kitchen were clogged with garbage and boxes, he returned to the front of the house to resume his entry through the front door.

William was dreading facing Rose and Wally Badger. He knew he would not be able to look at his mother, no doubt still young, still pretty, or at his father, still the oldest father in the world. But he walked steadily, stepping over the bike parts, his face registering nothing of his internal panic. Cool as a cucumber, he supposed, as usual.

On the front veranda stood Wally Badger, the man who got his leg in Europe at the age of seventeen in one war, who had looked into coal shipments in another war, and since then had inhabited this veranda.

'Dadda,' said William before he could stop himself. The word had surged forth, ahead of Father, but this father, more bent and white and thin and more ancient than ever, now looked more like a Pop.

'Thought I heard something out back,' said Wally Badger.

William stayed on the path at the foot of the steps.

'How are you going?' William asked.

'You look as if you need a haircut, son,' said Wally.

William thought he saw a shadow behind the screen door, but the rip in the mesh was longer than before, and the section that had come loose was vibrating a little, probably from Wally's having just opened and shut the door. Then the curtains on the front window giving onto the veranda seemed to flicker.

'Feeling better?' William asked. 'After hospital?'

'Getting my strength back,' said Wally.

'What was wrong?' William asked.

Wally took in a breath through his nose, a long sniff, then banged at his trouser pockets, searching for his pipe, which he discovered in his shirt pocket when he thumped his heart.

'Nothing serious,' he said.

'But what? Three weeks is a long stay.'

Wally located his tobacco pouch and poked a wad into the bowl of the pipe. 'They don't know what they're talking about.'

'What did they say?'

'A lot of rubbish.' Wally Badger tamped the tobacco down. 'Malnutrition. They don't know anything, as long as they say something.'

William squinted off across the road at the house opposite. Stanleys' house. But the man now watering his garden with a bright green hose, while his wife and children stood watching, was a newcomer, not Mr Stanley. The hose must have been a Christmas present.

'How could it be malnutrition?' William asked. 'In this day and age? Weren't you eating enough food?' So many questions.

'They talk bosh at the hospital. It's because of my leg, I'm sure. You get an injury when you're young, it plays up when you're old.'

William looked back at his father. A blurry figure was definitely standing on the other side of the screen door. 'Christmas dinner is ready.' It was Rose Badger. 'We've been waiting an hour already.'

William walked slowly up the steps.

It was only just past eleven. He could not possibly be late.

'We eat early these days, son,' said Wally Badger.

Rose disappeared from the doorway into the dark interior of the house. Wally held the door open for William.

'After you,' William said, and held the door for Wally, who shook his head.

'No, son, you're the visitor, the guest. After you.'

In the house, more gloomy than ever after the bright sunlight outside, William saw that nothing had changed since he had visited five years before. Nothing had changed since he was a boy. The same rug on the linoleum on the hall floor, the same carpet and lounge suite arranged in the same way in the lounge room, the same chairs around the same table in the dining room. But there was more clutter. Newspapers were stacked on two of the four chairs at the table, and cardboard cartons filled with books and papers stood along the wall.

Wally waited for William to enter the dining room. The window shade was pulled down so that it reached beneath the window sill and the tassel touched the floor. It looked as if it had lost its spring and had not been raised for some time.

The table was set with three places, knives and forks laid directly on the dull wood, with no table cloth or place mats. The orange plastic salt and pepper shakers in the shape of tulips stood in the middle of the table, along with a bottle of tomato sauce.

Wally lifted the pile of newspapers from one of the chairs and shuffled with it to a corner where he let it drop. Puffs of dust rose and seemed to render opaque the narrow beam of sunlight that managed to stream in at one side of the window shade. Wally came back to the table and pulled out a chair for William as if he were a waiter seating a customer in a restaurant.

Rose came in from the kitchen with a plate in either hand. She was wearing a sundress, faded red and white stripes, which William recognised as the sundress she had worn when he was ten or so, the same dress in which

she had twirled in the main street of Parramatta. It was
remarkable that the dress still fitted her. It was even too
big and hung loosely. Her shoulders and torso were thinner.
And her hair, still blond, but duller and dry, was longer,
just pulled back to the nape of her neck and held by a
rubber band, ending untidily at her shoulder blades. She
set the two plates carelessly at one end of the table. On
one plate were six slices of ham, on the other three potatoes,
boiled in their jackets and cut in quarters.

She went back to the kitchen and returned with a packet
of bread and a packet of margarine and flung them on
the table. Then she sat down.

'How are you going?' William asked, glancing at her
briefly then lowering his eyes.

'There are two slices of ham each and a potato and
you can fill up on bread if you're still hungry.'

She did not look at William. They had given up looking
at each other years ago, after Manly.

'Well, *bon appétit*,' said William. 'English is the only
language that doesn't wish people happy eating when they
begin a meal.' He was talking mainly for his father's sake,
trying to act as if this were a normal family partaking
of a normal Christmas dinner.

'The English like to say grace instead,' said Rose. 'We
could say grace and ask for deliverance from our pain.'
She helped herself to her two slices of ham and pushed
the plate at William and Wally. 'But why bother?'

Once you had known torment, William recalled her
saying once, the torment was with you forever. He took
his two slices and passed the plate to Wally. This was
Christmas dinner. Across the road they would be having
a chicken or a turkey, with gravy and stuffing and roasted
potatoes and green vegetables. There was nothing green
here. No wonder his father was suffering from malnutrition.

But why did he not object? He knew enough about food to know about greens and protein and fats. Yet both Wally and Rose Badger, with their lifeless, sallow skin, looked as if they were in a concentration camp.

William ate his ham, his four pieces of potato, and took two slices of bread. It was twenty past eleven. As he took a dab of margarine with his knife, Rose said, 'Be careful with the margarine. We don't waste food here. I don't know how you do it in town, but here we don't have money to throw about.'

William thought he might just eat and then leave, at about a quarter to twelve. They did not want him here.

'Where's the Morris?' he asked. The car was not in the driveway.

'We sold it,' said Wally. 'Rose put the money in the bank.'

'Back to motorbikes, then?' said William.

'Don't have much time to fiddle with bikes. Rose wants me to sell the bits and pieces for what I can get and put the money in the bank. We walk to the shops these days.'

'I can help tidy things up in the yard after lunch,' said William. 'If you like.'

Christmas pudding was three pieces of heavy on a plate, one slice each. They finished their Christmas dinner at twenty five to twelve.

Rose hurried the plates back to the kitchen. Wally shuffled behind her with the salt and pepper and tomato sauce. 'Why don't you have a lie down?' he said to Rose. 'I'll see to the kitchen.'

'I'll help you,' said William. When he went into the kitchen Rose left and went to the bedroom and closed the door.

The kitchen was a mess. The counter tops were covered with paper bags, tins of food that had not been put away in the cupboards, boxes of odds and ends—a shoebox containing buttons, elastic, zippers, and safety pins, an old tobacco tin containing washers for the faucets.

'If that's the way you've been eating, no wonder you've been sick,' said William. 'If you're the one who does the shopping, why don't you make sure you get fruit and vegetables and meat?'

'Rose is the one who makes the list. She's making my pension stretch. She is saving money hand over fist. A thrifty little thing.'

'You both look as if you'll keel over.'

'I'm just old,' said Wally, scraping the plates over the rubbish bin, although there was nothing at all on the plates to scrape.

'And hot water, I see,' said William, noting the heater poised on the wall above the sink. He tucked a tea towel around his waist and turned on the hot water, ready to fill the basin and do the dishes. The hot water heater popped into life.

'Use cold,' Rose called from the bedroom.

William looked at Wally, surprised.

'No point wasting money,' said Wally. 'Hot water is like pouring money down the drain.' He took the plates, dipped them quickly in a pan of cold water on the counter next to the sink, giving them a rub with his bare hand, then setting them to drain. He repeated this with the forks, holding the tines under the water and rubbing at them with his finger and thumb.

'Do you have a bath in cold water, too?' William did not really want to know. He was filling the kettle with water and was about to turn on the gas burner to boil it. 'Tea? Coffee?' he said to Wally.

'We only boil water for tea once a day,' said Wally. 'At breakfast.'

Then William noticed that the refrigerator door was open and that items other than perishable food were stacked on the shelves—canned goods, washing powder.

'We don't need a fridge, either,' said Wally. 'It just gobbles up electricity.'

'What about milk? That can go off in minutes in this climate.'

'We don't use milk any more.' Wally turned away from him.

Either Wally Badger was committing suicide, slowly, or else Rose was murdering him, slowly. William wanted to shake his father until his teeth rattled and his head flew off. He rushed from the kitchen out the front door, took up the axe and started hacking at the hibiscus stump in the front yard. At first he tried chopping it, close to the ground, bringing the blunt blade in at an angle, first on one side, then the other, to form a V and topple the stump. But then he simply bashed at the stump until it broke. He threw the severed stump onto the ground near the double gates of the driveway. The gates were permanently open, anchored in place by the grass. The man opposite, still wielding his hose, was watching William with interest. William nodded at him in the way that neighbours were supposed to acknowledge one another when they found themselves in their gardens at the same time.

'Happy Christmas,' the man called.

William gave a wave, then, to avoid having to engage in any kind of conversation, he went quickly to the garage and hauled out into the sunlight the lawnmower, an old manual mower with blades that had not turned in years. Then he went back into the garage to look for oil of some sort. Against the back wall was an old can of oil, with cobwebs over it, probably the very can that William had used on his bicycle chain as a child. He oiled the screws and blades, every bit of metal he could see, and finally the blades consented to turn, giving out an irregular, chugging sound.

The children opposite started shrieking. Their father had turned the new green hose on them. They laughed and ducked out of reach around the side of their house, then crept out once more in order to be hosed again.

William seized an old cardboard box that was still intact, even though it had been left outdoors, protected from the rain and sun by an overhang from the roof at the back. He took this box to the driveway and started throwing the motorbike parts into it. He was a do-er. Even Meg would have to agree.

Wally Badger opened the back door, rolling down his sleeves, having finished whatever else he had found to do in the kitchen. He stood in the doorway watching William's fierce activity, which carried with it a silent but unmistakable disgust with Wally and Rose Badger and their life. Or perhaps it was terror that fuelled William's frenzy.

'Once these are in this box, you can take it all to a junkyard and see if you can get a few bob,' said William.

'Dinner's ready,' the woman opposite called, and her husband wound up his hose and disappeared inside with the children. Their turkey was done.

William filled one box with bike parts and hauled it to the front gate. He picked up the bike hulk that lay on its side and leant it against the fence, and he moved the bike without the wheel next to the sidecar.

'Hey,' he said to Wally Badger, who was still standing watching blankly. 'Why did you sell the car?'

'It was just using up money. Registration, repairs, insurance, and so on. We never went anywhere.'

William started mowing. He began with the driveway, pushing and hauling the old lawnmower as if it were a steamroller. The thick grass clogged the blades so that he had to stop every few minutes and pull the grass out by hand to enable the blades to turn again. He was going to mow the entire yard, front and back. Then he was leaving. He himself would buy the box of motorbike junk and dump it as soon as he found a ditch or a field on the road back to town.

Stones and small bits of metal were still thrown up by the mower, hitting him on the shins, even though before beginning to mow a new section he stopped and raked through the grass, pulling out the objects that could hurt him and jam the blades. At one thirty or so the family opposite came out and sat on the patio, the mother and father drinking tea, the children horsing around on the front lawn, playing with their Christmas toys and shouting.

All afternoon William mowed and raked. When he was mowing the strip of grass outside the front fence, between the footpath and the kerb, one of the children, a little boy of five or six, came to his front gate and swung on it for a while, watching, and then finally called out, 'I got the money bag in the pudding.' And his sister cried out, 'I got the ring.'

By three o'clock William had finished the front. He dragged the mower around to the back. This was a much harder job. An old double washing tub sat in the middle of the yard. Bricks were scattered everywhere. Hardened bags of cement from some project abandoned years ago lay in a heap.

But William was possessed. He hauled each object to the side, tugging, grunting in the heat. He picked up the garbage and rubbish that surrounded the garbage can and threw it in a thick paper sack that had once contained cement. He would take the garbage with him, too, and ditch it somewhere in the dark on the way home. He thought of going into the house for something cool to drink and then remembered that there was no refrigerator. He turned on the tap near the back door and dashed water over his face and arms, and when Rose called out, 'We have to pay water rates, remember,' he was not surprised.

He mowed and mowed and then clipped the weeds growing in the path. He chopped back the tufts of dandelions and other weeds that had sprung up at the door of the garage and pulled the doors shut. He lugged the box of bike parts to his car and dumped it on the back seat. He threw the tree stump into the boot. Then he closed the double gates, which squeaked and groaned on their hinges. Each task led to a new one. He ran back to the garage, seized the can of oil and raced back to the gates to oil the hinges. By seven o'clock he had done what was possible. The house looked tidier.

William stood at the front gate, staring feverishly at the house, looking for the next thing that teetered or groaned and was in need of help. Behind the screen door was a movement. Or was it simply the tear in the wire flapping. He went to the garage and threw open the doors, contemplating the bits and pieces of equipment and junk. In the corner stood a small fly screen. William wrenched it free of the surrounding boxes and took it back to the front door. He measured with his arm the length of the tear in the door and then held his arm against the window screen, memorising where to cut. Then he looked around for something to cut the screen with. The shears he had found in the garage were rusted rigid and had been thrown in with the motorbike parts to be disposed of. The axe was still leaning against the wall of the house. He placed the window screen on the grass and with little chopping movements, as precise as he could make them with such a large dull tool, he cut a rectangle larger than the tear in the door. He fitted the rectangle of wire mesh against the rip in the door, carefully peeling away several strands of wire around the four sides so that he could weave the patch into the screen of the door, covering the tear.

It was almost dark. His trousers were stained with grass—ruined, and once more he would need to buy a new pair—his hands were ingrained with dirt and rust, he was sweating, and his sneakers were filthy and stained. He thought that he was probably as insane as his parents and he had better get out of there before he was a prisoner forever. His mowing the lawn and tidying things up, disturbing the status quo of Wally and Rose's existence, was akin to a peasant's revolt at the gates of the castle, and those who ruled in the castle, he knew, when threatened with change responded with punishments and repression.

The house was dark. What could Wally and Rose possibly be doing? He would go in and give his father the five pounds, no ten, or twenty, all the money he had on him, apart from the money he would need for petrol. He would tell Wally once again that he had to eat or he would die. And William would never come home again.

William flung open the screen door. He was actually very pleased with the neat patch he had made. The appearance of the house was much improved. He felt his way down the hall, gloomy after the bright dusk outdoors. In the kitchen a light flickered. He found his father and mother at the kitchen table eating Jatz crackers straight from the packet and chunks of Velveeta. They were in pyjamas. On the table one candle was burning.

'Have something to eat, son,' said Wally Badger.

William turned on the light. Rose threw her arm up to cover her eyes against the sudden glare.

'Turn it off,' she screamed. 'Turn that light off.'

William looked at his father.

'I fixed the front door,' he said. 'And the lawn should last for a few weeks.'

Rose got up and came around the table, reaching past William to flick off the light. William grabbed her hand, wrenched it away from the light switch, and with his free hand, turned the light back on.

'Tell him to turn it off,' said Rose, struggling to free herself from William's grasp.

William held both her hands in his right hand. He could hang on forever if necessary, as he had hung on when she was swinging the steering wheel back and forth on their trip to Ama's in Stanleys' Morris Minor when he was a child.

'It'll kill her, son, to have the light on,' said Wally.

William stood with his legs apart, knees slightly bent, Rose's thin little wrists easily encompassed by his grip.

'Then let it kill her,' said William. 'This place is like a bloody tomb already.'

'Walter Badger, tell the child to do as I tell him and turn off the light.'

Wally Badger said nothing further.

'Why?' William asked. 'Why no lights? What is going on here?'

But no one answered his questions. William let Rose go, but he remained in front of the light switch, guarding it. She stood panting angrily in front of him.

'He'll be gone soon,' said Wally Badger to Rose. 'A light doesn't matter this once. It's Christmas, after all. And when he goes we'll turn it off.'

Rose turned on Wally. 'You agreed, no electricity. It's money going down the drain. You might as well stand at your front gate and throw your money into the street.'

She spun around and left the kitchen. The front door slammed. William heard her footsteps on the veranda and then on the front path. Then there was silence. She must be crossing the grass. The front gate would make some kind of sound if she opened it.

'You don't really need electric light, you know,' said Wally Badger. 'If you go to bed at eight or eight thirty and get up at five or six, you don't need lights at all.'

'She's mad,' said William.

'I can handle her,' said Wally, 'We have an understanding. And that's the best you can hope for in this life. An understanding. She's saving money to make a trip, to Europe.'

William took out his wallet and gave his father twenty-five pounds.

'Rose will appreciate this,' said Wally.

'It's for you,' said William, angry. 'Don't you see? You need to eat. Go to the shops and buy a sausage and an apple for yourself every day.'

'An old man doesn't need to eat much,' said Wally. He was looking at the notes in his hand, as if he had not seen so much money in his life.

There was the sound of boxes and objects falling outside the kitchen and suddenly the back door flew open and Rose burst in. She held the axe above her head. William stepped back from the table as she brought it down, the head embedding itself in the table top.

'It was our agreement,' Rose wailed at Wally, and lifted the axe again ready to bring it down on Wally's head. William leapt forward and again seized her arms, but he did not get a firm grip and the downward force of her stroke sent them both to the floor. But Rose was up first and had the axe above her head again.

'Call the police,' said William to Wally, scrambling to his feet. Wally did not move.

'Don't you dare use the telephone,' said Rose. With

William away from the light switch, she brought the axe down on the switch, smashing the wall and dislodging the switch plate. The kitchen light went out.

William raced into the hallway and seized the telephone. Rose came after him with the axe raised and brought it down on the telephone wire on the floor, severing it. William ran out the front door. He bounded across the veranda and onto the freshly mown grass, followed by Rose wielding the axe.

The neighbours opposite were strolling around the perimeter of their garden, examining their flora. They looked up when they heard the commotion at Badgers'. In the deepening dusk the axe was visible raised above the heads of two struggling figures.

William grappled with Rose and managed to wrest the axe from her. He stood with it raised above his head, holding it out of her reach, while she crouched in front of him.

'You're the cause of all this trouble,' she hissed at him.

William jerked his head toward the house, commanding her to return inside. Rose backed up the stairs across the veranda, bumping up against the screen door, so neatly repaired. William followed her, taking one step for every step she took, keeping the distance between them constant. Rose felt behind her for the handle of the door and in passing her hand across the wire she felt the patch that William had installed. She pressed with all her might against the wire, and the patch gave way. The old tear reappeared with the rectangular patch dangling from it. Rose found the handle and opened the door. William followed her inside into the dark, the axe still raised. He flicked on the hall light and jerked his head at the door to the lounge room. Rose backed in, her hands covering her eyes. William flicked on the light after her. She backed across the room until her calves touched the lounge chair and she flopped backwards onto the cushions. William went to put down the axe, and as he did Rose tensed, ready to spring for it. William picked it up again and held it aloft, and Rose sank back into the chair.

'Go across the road and call the police,' William said over his shoulder to his father, who had shuffled up the hallway and was standing behind him.

'She'll be all right, son,' said Wally. 'Just go now.'

'She'll kill me, and you,' said William. 'Call the police.'

But the police were already at the door and had burst into the house, where they found William standing with the axe over his head and a frail-looking blonde woman cringing before him in the lounge chair. They seized William from behind and in relief he gave them the axe. Inside he was smiling, thankfully, but whether this showed on his face he did not know.

'You'll have to come with us,' said one of the policemen.

'Of course,' said William. 'And her?' He nodded at his mother.

'She can come, too, if she wants to testify, but we've seen enough to make a charge.'

'A charge?'

'We'll have to charge you with assault,' said the policeman.

'Me?'

The policeman gave a pull on William's arm, nudging him toward the door.

'Are you all right?' the policeman asked Rose.

She nodded.

'Is he your son?'

Rose nodded again.

'We're sorry,' said the policeman. 'This often happens on Christmas Day. Too much drinking, too much stress and strain in the family. People can get killed.'

'But she was attacking me,' said William.

'That's not what it looked like. And it's not what the people who telephoned said. They said that a tall young man was threatening a woman with an axe.'

'Dadda,' said William, appealing to Wally. 'Tell them what happened.'

The policeman looked at Wally, who looked at the ground.

'Aren't you going to tell them?' William asked, then fell silent, understanding that his father was not going to defend him. His father had decided that William should go to jail and be charged with assault and that Rose and Wally should continue their lives as before.

William let the policeman lead him from the house to their car. As they went down the front path the bright yellow square of light behind the screen door in the hallway snapped off. As they drove off William looked back at the house, which was now completely dark. On the front patio opposite, standing in the dark so that they would not be conspicuous, were the neighbour and his family, watching.

Part III

William met Tillie his first night in Brussels, his second night in the northern hemisphere.

The bus that brought William from Heathrow to London left him at Victoria station. Although he had no plans, no destination, he strode through the station with purpose. As he walked with his duffle bag on one shoulder, he felt a presence at his side, a companion, silent but palpable, just out of sight beside the bulk of the duffle bag, slightly behind him. He stopped short. He had a companion, an invisible companion, and it was a woman. If he switched the duffle bag to the other shoulder he need only reach out the hand nearest her to place it flat on her shoulder blade, then her shoulder, and draw her to him. If he leaned down, his cheek would press her hair. If he turned, surely he would see her beside him. Nevertheless he kept his eyes forward. If she stayed beside him, fine. If she disappeared, that was fine, too. He needed no one.

He stood listening to the announcements of train departures, waiting to sense what his companion would do. She seemed to step away, toward the ticket booth and he moved there too, keeping the duffle bag between them. He found himself buying a ticket for the train to Dover, about to depart, connecting with the night ferry to Ostend.

In his compartment sat a young couple, probably students, and another couple, older, with a child who was drawing in his colouring book with crayons. One of the students, the young man, said to his partner, 'Let's play Chinese chequers,' and at that moment two young Chinese, a man and a woman dressed in identical checked pullovers, leant against the windowed wall of the compartment. The child, riffling through his box of crayons, chanted 'Brown, brown, where's the brown,' and he held up the brown crayon just as a tall, brown-skinned Indian passed by, paused, and looked into the compartment, almost as if he had been summoned, then moved on.

As William settled himself into his seat he understood that his companion was no longer there, and he thought of rushing off the train. Surely he had made a mistake. This train was not for him. But imperceptibly the train had begun to move and had already slid out of the station.

William's companion did not reappear. He reproached himself for being stupid enough to rely on something he could only describe as a presence, and putting it down to jet lag, he allowed himself to be carried along upstairs, downstairs, through immigration and customs and onto the ferry, where he found a corner chair and curled up, uncomfortably, with his head on the hard, rigid arm of the vinyl chair, like a child, until finally he had to stretch his legs out, resting his head on the back of the chair, staring up at the ceiling, then closing his eyes and trying to sleep, while dozens of travelling students with their rucksacks piled in a heap in the corner of the deck cavorted and drank beer. Ostend and beyond seemed as good a destination as any.

As he dozed, William dreamed that President de Gaulle of France had two legs made of Oregon pine, nicely sanded and finished, and that he was addressing the student dissidents of Paris. Even through the trousers of de Gaulle's uniform it was apparent that the legs were Oregon pine. He had made his speech to the students, a giant addressing dwarfs. '*Je suis dans la merde jusqu'aux genoux, mais vous êtes dans la merde jusqu'au cou.*' But while he was talking one of the students sawed skilfully through his legs, just above the knee, and when de Gaulle went to walk off, his calves and feet stayed rooted to the ground, like tree stumps, and he had to climb down and waddle away on his thighs, on the half legs that remained to him.

William started awake. 'It's all wood,' he heard a man's voice say authoritatively. It could have been a student talking or President de Gaulle himself.

In the dawn at Ostend, the passengers trudged onto the train for Brussels, which stood awaiting them. William, stiff and confused from his night askew in the vinyl chair, followed. As long as a train hurtled him along, he was going somewhere. Just where he was going would become clear sooner or later.

In the compartment of the Brussels train were five others, three men and two women. All acted as if they were alone. Not a nod was exchanged when William entered and sat down. He could have been invisible, not even a presence.

In the corridors students slept on the floor and had to be stepped over. Every now and then as the train traversed Flanders, William saw vacationing students lying on the platforms, their heads on their rucksacks. They seemed not to have a care in the world. Yet William had heard it was students like these who were causing upheavals all over Europe, peasants at the gates of the castle, challenging the established power structures, the political divisions, and the influence of the United States in Europe. The unrest and the calls for change had been set in motion by students in West Germany. The professors refused to discuss university policy and education with the students, who at first demanded reforms within the university, and then, in the factories and throughout the whole society. Sparked by the German students, all of Europe was alive with protests and reform movements. They were at the barricades in France, uniting with the workers. In Holland, Sweden, the United Kingdom, the United States, and in Belgium the students were on the streets. They were protesting against the war in Vietnam; the secret surveillance of the people by their elected governments;

the power of big business and the powerlessness of the
workers; nuclear proliferation; and the destruction of the
environment. They probably had never had to work, labour
at a tedious job, William thought bitterly, remembering
his years in Pens and Pencils and the time after that spent
digging holes and driving delivery trucks. He would not
mind a stint as a student, doing nothing but advocating
a change in the order of things and now and then going
off with a rucksack to have adventures, now that he had
escaped and was free.

In the cell at the police station in Sydney, where he
had been taken after Rose's assault with the axe, William
had found himself with half a dozen other men, most of
them drunk, several of them from the settlement of shanties
and caravans on the outskirts. Some had managed to bring
bottles of beer into the cell with them, which they swigged
from as they sat and waited. William stood in the corner
looking out. The lights were painfully bright.

'Those are good strong shoes,' said one of his cellmates.

William said nothing. He was aware that his good strong
sneakers were very dirty from the yard work he had done
that Christmas Day at the house of Rose and Wally Badger.

'Want to play poker? Put up your shoes?'

William shook his head. Four of the men set up a poker
game, staking possessions that they swore they owned and
could put their hands on the minute they were let out.

William had been told that he would be held in the
jail all night and all the next day, Boxing Day, a public
holiday, and go before the magistrate the day after that.
He would get a trial and be convicted, and then he would
begin his jail term. 'But I'm not guilty,' William said.

'The evidence says otherwise,' said one of the policemen.
'You might as well admit it and save us all time and money.'

As the men in the cell drank, they became rowdier.

The man who coveted William's shoes sat at his feet and every now and then touched the uppers of his sneakers. 'We could just take them right off him,' he muttered.

'The trousers, too,' said another, 'and the shirt.'

If they all got much drunker, William was sure that that was what they would do. They would attack him and take his clothes.

'I was only blowing up this bloke's house,' said one of the men playing cards. 'He was fooling with my wife.'

'What kind of bomb?' another asked.

'Petrol in a jar,' said the first.

William did not turn around but listened closely. He had to learn what he could in order to protect himself in the future.

'It's simple. You put ground-up matchheads in tin foil at the base of a candle, and stick it in the neck of the jar. Then you light it and go off home to dinner and while you're in your kitchen putting tomato sauce on your steak and eggs, it goes off. The candle burns down and heats up the matchheads and pow! And you're nowhere near.'

'Have you got cigarettes?' the man at William's feet asked.

William shook his head.

'What went wrong?' the man playing cards asked the bomber.

'Something tipped the thing over, a cat or something. It was just a little fire, not an explosion. They've got no proof it was me, though.'

William's aloofness and his clothes, which although dirty from his day's work put him apart from the others, had irritated the men from the beginning. The toff they called him.

'Hey, toff, be a man and have a game of poker.'

'Toff, here, have a swig, like a man.'

Later in the evening a scuffle broke out. The would-be bomber accused another poker player of cheating, and after what had happened with his wife he was sick and tired of cheaters. They started punching and one of the men fell against William. His opponent flew after him and after pounding the card player started punching William.

William fought back. The noise brought the guard, who opened the cell and indicated to William with a jerk of his head that he should emerge.

'We're letting you out for the moment,' he said, 'since it's only domestic violence you're involved in. And you're unsettling the others.'

At the desk William thankfully signed his name to his guilt, felonious assault.

'Here,' said the officer in charge, poking a piece of paper at him, 'your interim restraining order. That means don't go back to the scene and don't try anything else, because that'll only make it a double charge and a sentence twice as long. You seem a sensible fellow.'

William was told he had to appear in court in two days' time and that he could expect a year in jail or, if he was lucky, months since it was only violence in the home he was accused of.

Despite the restraining order, William walked back to his parents' house, taking a roundabout route, and sat in the car at the kerb until morning. He needed to think, and there was still something he had to see to.

At six, when he thought that they would surely be up, having gone to bed at eight thirty, he walked around to the back and stood at the kitchen door, the entrance to which was clear after Rose had knocked aside all the objects obstructing it. He leaned sideways to peer through the window. His father was in the kitchen putting the kettle on and gave a start when he saw William's face. He looked frightened. William opened the door and stepped in.

'I'm sorry, son.'

William waved away the words impatiently. He did not want to hear anything more from his father or his mother.

'I'm going,' he whispered. He did not want Rose to hear him. 'I just want one thing. I need my birth certificate.'

His father looked puzzled.

'I'll leave the country as soon as I can get a passport, and I'm going to have to show them my birth certificate.'

His father hesitated.

'You do know where it is, don't you?' William asked, suddenly afraid that the document did not exist.

Wally Badger nodded.

'I have to get out of here before she wakes up,' William pleaded.

Wally stood for a moment longer then went slowly to the dining room. William heard him opening the sideboard and moving glasses and dishes. He went to the door of the room to see what his father was up to. Wally Badger was kneeling down in front of the sideboard and groping behind the stacks of table linens. He pulled out a worn brown envelope, the envelope William had discovered years before, and peered into it, poking at bits of paper, until he fished out the document he was looking for.

Wally Badger replaced the envelope and linens, closed the doors of the sideboard and went into the kitchen. William stepped back into the kitchen behind him and held out his hand.

'I've got to go.'

Wally Badger held onto the piece of paper, shaking his head, before handing it over. Then he sat down. The kettle started to whistle and he leapt up, anxious to extinguish the gas flame so that none would be wasted.

'If they come asking for me, say you haven't seen me,' said William. 'That's the least you can do.'

In Brussels William ate breakfast at the Gare Centrale then left his duffle bag in a locker and sat for a while on the steps of the station overlooking the city of Brussels, waiting for a sign, or at least an idea. When none was forthcoming, when no companion had sat herself down beside him and indicated what he should do, he walked down the hill to a warren of cobbled streets filled with cafes and restaurants. Suddenly he was overcome with shyness, feeling conspicuous, a lone stranger, and he rapidly retreated from those streets, walking toward the less crowded areas, and then when he had gathered some confidence about walking through these strange streets he found himself passing an exhibition hall whose doors stood open, and he allowed himself to be drawn in.

In the vast hall, just inside the door, a man in a neat grey suit was swinging gently through the air in a sling, and a little farther on stood a woman in a pink uniform with curlers in her hair, and beyond her a man holding a miniature rake was reaching into the air. William could have been on another planet.

Beneath the man suspended in the sling drifting level with William's shoulder was a stand with a notice, rather like the signs planted throughout botanical gardens indicating the names of the adjacent flora. The notice informed William that the man in the sling was a Dutchman who had invented and built a machine that lifted invalids from their wheelchairs and lowered them into the bathtub.

This was the annual inventors' exhibition. Inventors from twenty-one countries with their inventions earnestly demonstrated their capacities and uses.

A German had constructed a collapsible garage which sprang up to form the garage when the car drove over a spring in the driveway and subsided to ground level when the car drove out.

A Belgian hairdresser had made curlers out of sponge rubber.

A Spaniard had invented a portable car float. When a driver came to a river he could inflate the float, drive on, and steer across the river, without having to look for a bridge.

A young Italian demonstrated an automatic card shuffler.

A Portuguese inventor had made the little rake that lifted olives from the tree four at a time.

William passed the day there, standing before each exhibit with its exhibitor. He tried to think of something he could invent, something that would save the world. When people asked him what he did he would reply, 'I am an inventor.'

As night fell William walked back to the centre of the city and paused outside the window of a small crowded restaurant, trying to muster the courage to enter. The light was warm and yellow, the laughter happy, the groups around the tables tightly packed. There seemed to be no room for him. He walked on, back up the dark hill, following the tramlines, until at the top he found a cafe with many empty tables and a few couples talking quietly. He stood outside examining the menu, calculating that a simple omelette would cost him four dollars.

Two women were seated at a small table near the open window of the cafe, speaking English.

'Did you stay in Madrid?'

'When we were in Madrid we did.'

William meandered on to the windows of a dress shop nearby and understood then that he was in the smart, expensive part of town, the Place Louise. He moved back to the cafe and stood near the door peering out across the Place before him, a broad intersection of tram tracks and roads. In the middle of the road, among the tram tracks, was a dark shape. Someone was hunched over on all fours, or rather, as William watched, was crawling, moving slowly along between the tracks.

'In Los Angeles I can give you a list of plastic surgeons who can be counted on to do good nose jobs,' said one of the women in the cafe behind him.

William stepped off the kerb toward the person on the ground—it seemed to be a woman—who was now kneeling, moving her right hand back and forth. He walked over to her, looking this way and that, but since it was late at night, the roads were fairly empty.

He imagined she had dropped a ring, an engagement ring, a diamond, and was risking her life, for love. 'Did you lose something?'

At his feet was a young woman who held a paintbrush. PAN EUR was painted in sloppy white capital letters on the asphalt. She looked up at him. Her dark hair was pulled fiercely back from her pale, long face.

'Just stand there,' she said brusquely in English. 'And if you see the police, grab this paint can and follow me.'

William stood beside her, looking around, more afraid of trams and cars than of police.

The young woman stood up. PAN EUROPE were the words left behind on the road.

'Follow me,' she said, and William obeyed, carrying her paint can, following her to the other side of the Place, where she fell to her knees and once more painted PAN EUROPE.

William observed a car moving slowly toward them with some kind of insignia on its side. 'I think it's the police,' he said.

The painter looked up, sprang to her feet. 'Quick,' she cried and raced to the side of the road, disappearing into an alleyway. William sprinted behind her. The door of the police car slammed and when William got into the shadows, he looked back to see two policemen standing over the painted word, reading it, walking around it, then looking up, peering in the direction that the two dark figures had run.

William ran down the alley, following this young woman and her long, dark ponytail around a corner, across another road, down a smaller street, to a Volkswagen parked in shadows, midway between two streetlights. She flung open the door and got into the driver's seat. She leant over and opened the passenger door.

'Don't just stand there,' she said.

William got in. The back seat of the VW was piled high with papers, pamphlets and magazines—for a moment it reminded him of the dining room at Rose and Wally Badgers' as he had last seen it—so he sat hunched up in the front seat holding up the paint can, careful not to let it touch his knees and ruin his trousers.

'Put it on the floor,' said the young woman. 'You don't want the police to see it, do you?'

'It'll spill. No lid.'

'Hold it with your feet then,' she said, and with a jerk the car took off.

This was Tillie Pepper, Englishwoman, political activist, working to tear down the boundaries that separated the peoples of Europe, questioning the dominance of the United States in Europe, calling for a radical overhaul of Western society, advocating that development for its own sake be questioned, challenged, and that the nations of Europe try to disarm—all novel and subversive notions.

Tillie tore through the streets of Brussels, heading first

south on the eight-lane boulevard that encircled the city, then dodging around a lumbering, late-night tram and speeding off to the southwest on the Chaussée de Ninove.

William concentrated on steadying the can of paint, which he now saw was a lilac color, not white. Tillie swerved right then left along a street called rue de la Campagne, lined with drab modest houses and not a single tree, not a blade of grass. Tillie braked in front of a two-storey red brick building, causing William to let out a cry as the paint sloshed to the rim of the can.

'Sh!' commanded Tillie. She leapt out and made straight for a wooden door that gave directly onto the street. She looked back and seeing William still seated with the can of paint she came quickly back to the passenger side of the car and yanked open the door. 'Come on, quick, bring it inside,' she hissed. "And be quiet. Here, I'll help you.'

William emerged from the VW and together with Tillie, with the paint can between them, like Jack and Jill holding their pail of water, tiptoed into Tillie's flat.

Tillie flipped on the light, placed the paint can on the floor and threw herself onto the sofa.

'I'll tell you what I'm sick of. I'm sick of doing that night painting by myself. Cato's been out of town for several weeks, Agnes is interviewing the student activists in Germany, and Marc slacks off when Cato isn't around to impress. I'm the only Barbarian willing to go out and keep up the struggle. And I'm sick of it.'

'Barbarian?' William repeated.

'You know, Barbarian, the new European. It's now recognised that the barbarians had a whole complicated culture that was obliterated, ignored, because there was a dominant culture. Then it was the Romans, now it's the Americans. For us barbarian is a positive concept.' Tillie waved her hand at the room, indicating that William should sit down somewhere. 'It's lucky you arrived tonight.'

The flat consisted of one room with two alcoves, one with a double bed in it, the other with a refrigerator, stove and sink. In the middle of the room was a large table, one half of which was covered with scraps of paper and books, the other half given over to a large jigsaw puzzle in the first stages of assembly. A plate with chunks of salami and sausage stood next to the puzzle.

'But Cato will be back tomorrow or the next day, thank God. Everyone gets lazy and malicious without him around. He's a genius.' She drummed her fingers on the arm of the sofa. 'You should know that Cato and I have this thing. We're together, really.' She stood up and came up to the table in order to contemplate the puzzle. After a moment she seized a brown piece of the puzzle and clicked it into place, part of the shadow of a tree. 'You can stay,' she said to William, 'but you'll have to be quiet, no moans and groans. The last man who stayed ground his teeth. It kept me awake, but the landlady, who must sleep with her ear to the floor, could hear it, too.' Tillie pointed at the ceiling. 'She lives above and she doesn't like men to be here at night.'

William looked at the white ceiling, then down at the table and the plate of sausages. He had no idea into whose shoes he had stepped and into what life he had walked. This Tillie seemed to have been expecting him.

She waved her hand at the sausages. 'The landlady gives me those all the time. She's a vendor of processed meats. And giving me gifts is a way for her to keep track of what I'm doing. You'll see. Always knocking at the door. Take some if you're hungry. She's probably being paid to keep track of me. Secret service. I wouldn't put it past them.'

William had not eaten since breakfast at the Gare

Centrale. He stood by the table eating slices of salami. The jigsaw puzzle, he saw from the box, was called 'A Scene from Enkhuizen', five thousand pieces, taken from a painting by Cornelis Springer, a Dutch painter he had never heard of. The four borders and part of a flagstone square in the foreground had already been assembled. William picked up the lid and read it. Springer was described as a painter, etcher and aquarellist, and William was overcome with such a deep envy and melancholy that he had to turn away. This man, Springer, could be described definitively in three words, painter, etcher, and aquarellist. William had not even one word to describe himself.

'There's a beer in the fridge, and I'd like one, too,' said Tillie.

William went to the kitchen alcove, got out two beers and gave one to Tillie. He had observed as they were running from the police that she was short and dark, but now he saw that her hair really was as dark as it had appeared outside in the night. It was pulled back tightly, as if she would tolerate no trouble or interference from the hair on her head, because she had better things to do than bother about hair and its good behaviour. She would be attractive really, if she were a little kinder to her hair. William thought he might suggest that she let it loose, if he got to know her better.

'It's going to have to change,' said Tillie. 'I can't go on doing it all by myself, *The Barbarian*, the planning, all the doing. *The Barbarian*, our magazine, has just gone monthly. A lot of work. I'm going to have it out with Cato. I don't mind *doing* things, but what they expect of me is too much. What's your name, anyway?'

It was a question that William continued to dread.

Before handing over William's birth certificate, Wally Badger had held on to it as if he did not want William to have it. William attributed the reluctance to Wally Badger's general contentiousness. He almost had to snatch the piece of paper from Wally Badger's hand. He took it with him out the back door, then paused beside the garbage can to unfold it. He had never seen his birth certificate and he read it with interest. He knew he had been born in London at the beginning of the war. But the name was not his name. He went back into the kitchen.

'This isn't Badger,' he said to his father, his astonishment overcoming the rage and pain of the past twenty-four hours.

Wally Badger hustled him out of the kitchen to the driveway at the side of the house.

'She'll be up in a minute,' he said, and seemed to be pushing William to the double gates at the street.

'It's not Badger,' said William and waited for an explanation.

'We weren't married yet,' muttered Wally Badger, opening one of the gates and trying to push William out. 'We got married when she came out here.'

William stood resisting him.

'That's her name, and yours,' said Wally.

'Fine,' said William stonily. 'Just as long as I know what's going on.'

He vaulted the gate and without even nodding a farewell at his father he drove off as quietly as possible, hoping that the neighbours and his mother had not seen his arrival and departure that Boxing Day morning. He wanted William Badger to have disappeared forever. He had never even been William Badger. The name on the handwritten birth certificate was Longleg. He was William Longleg after all. He liked the name. It was he who would take one long step off the coast of this continent and come down on another continent altogether. He was William

Longleg, and the police would look for William Badger.
When he was calmer he would have to go back over his
life, making it tally with this new information. He stopped
the car, remembering the rubbish from the yard he carried
in the boot, and hauled it all out, pushing it off the side
of the road into a ditch covered with undergrowth. He
drove on, the car empty and light, and rejoiced in his new
name which meant that he was a free man. The police
had charged William Badger with felonious assault, and
it was William Badger they would search for when he
did not turn up for sentencing. William Badger, Australian.
Meanwhile, William Longleg, Englishman, would take his
birth certificate to the British Consulate and get a British
passport and leave the country.

He had forgotten all about the purpose of his journey
home, to ask Rose why she had sung songs in German,
if she was really a German countess. Suddenly Meg's
fantasies seemed ridiculous, the constructions of an
immature girl. His escape, unlike hers, would be real, a
fact, and not imagined the way hers was. But he could
never see her again. Meg Meese knew William Badger,
not William Longleg. It was William Badger, not William
Longleg, who was in love with Meg Meese, salesgirl, future
secretary. He could not return to Pens and Pencils.

William Longleg returned to William Badger's boarding
house in Glebe only to leave Ralph's car at the kerb outside.
William Longleg found a room in another boarding house
in another part of town, down by the docks under the
bridge. He saved money by not taking meals with the other
boarders. He kept a pint of milk in the communal
refrigerator and ate cereal in his room in the mornings
and boiled eggs or heated a can of baked beans at night
on the hotplate that was for the use of the boarders. In
his single-mindedness and frugality he approached Rose

Badger, although the resemblance escaped him.

When William applied for a passport at the British passport office, they asked few questions. He had told the truth, that he had been brought to Australia as a child, that he had been included on his mother's passport which had expired long ago, and now he was applying for his own passport. If they had bothered to verify his story, they would indeed have learned that a Rose Longleg with her son had been issued a passport at the end of the war. Even if it had occurred to them to check with the Australian police they would have found no mention of William Longleg. William Badger, who was charged with assault and had disappeared, had no connection with the British authorities.

William's only moment of uneasiness came when the consular officer, checking the documents, compared William's birth certificate with his application.

'Longleg?' he queried, looking closely at the handwriting on the certificate.

'That's right,' William said.

'What kind of name is that?' the officer asked, pulling his chin in, squinting and frowning at the piece of paper.

William swallowed, nervous. 'Just a name.' His voice sounded like a squeak to him.

The officer shrugged. 'Well, if we can have Drinkwater and Ramsbottom, then I suppose we can have Longleg,' he said curtly.

'Well, what's your name? Tillie asked impatiently.

'Longleg, William.'

She considered the name for a moment and looked at William as if he were not telling the truth. 'Are you sure?'

William nodded.

'German?'

'English,' said William.

Tillie shrugged. 'Did you make it up?'

'Pardon?'

'Your name, did you make it up, to escape detection?'

William swallowed. 'Of course not,' he croaked. 'It's my name.'

'Whatever you say,' said Tillie. 'So, Longleg. Harmless as a Daddy Longlegs?'

'I don't like violence,' said William. In fact he disliked violence so much that it approached cowardice. It was fear of violence, after all, that had made him declare his guilt with undue alacrity in the police station in Sydney.

'Who likes violence? We certainly don't.'

'Are you a student then?' William asked. 'A radical?'

'Once upon a time I was a student, and so were Cato and the others. Now we're critics of society, workers, exposing the hypocrisy of the middle class and the corruption of post-industrial society and searching for solutions.'

'Right,' said William as he sat on the sofa, and overcome by a deep fatigue he rested his head in his hands.

The phone rang.

'*Oui, oui, non,*' Tillie snapped into the phone. She slammed down the receiver. William got up and went over to the jigsaw puzzle.

The phone rang again. Tillie listened, then hung up.

'Wrong number,' she said. 'Not likely. It's some kind of surveillance. They like to check that you are home before they break into your office and ransack your files, and they call you at your office before they break into your home and ransack that. It's happened to several of us Barbarians, but not to me, yet.'

William picked up a scrap of paper that lay near the puzzle and read it. 'Anti-imperialistic battle to join anti-capitalist battle; need to root out leftist factions in working class—define actions and agitation models and bring them together.' He replaced it on the table top, dubious. Suddenly he saw that a piece of the puzzle, a medium brown piece with a few golden tones, was the skirt of the little lady on the lid of the box who was walking in the background of Cornelis Springer's painting. He snapped it into place. The little lady was walking on the head of the larger lady on the flagstones in the foreground, offering William a lesson in perspective.

'I do jigsaws to give my hands something to do while I'm thinking,' said Tillie. 'Sometimes I even put off drafting manifestoes and agendas just to stand over this stupid puzzle.' She snapped a piece into place. 'It's a monumental waste of time, it causes eye strain, backache, frustration. It's a real weakness.'

William stood watching her, this stranger, who had taken him in and was confiding in him.

Tillie gave a snort of impatience. 'We should get some sleep. You can have the couch, but be very quiet.'

She turned her face up to William, and he found his hand reaching out to her, touching her cheek with the back of his fingers. She smiled at him and raised her own hand to touch his as it rested on her cheek.

'Of course, Cato doesn't know.'

'Know?' William asked. How could he know? William had been there only an hour.

'About the puzzle. He wouldn't approve. Of course I'll have to tell him, otherwise he'll see it when he comes over. We're kind of together, you see.'

Then Tillie turned her head slightly, so that William's hand was resting on her lips and she kissed his fingertips. William was happy, and for the first time in his life he felt a strong urge to talk. He wanted to tell Tillie everything about him, about his whole life. He needed to let her know all his torments, starting with Manly and continuing right up to the past Christmas Day when his father had betrayed him and he had discovered his real name. But Tillie seemed to want to do a lot of talking herself.

'As you know,' said Tillie, 'there's a lot of work to be done. There always is for critics of society.'

'I can work,' said William. 'I have sold pens and pencils. I've been a labourer. I've driven trucks.'

After he had got his passport, William had dyed his hair dark brown, in case the police started circulating his picture, taken a job as a builder's labourer, and as he worked he talked to no one, made no friends, and put money away ready for his departure forever from Australia. To his new workmates he was William Longleg, the stand-offish labourer, who worked hard without complaining, who was willing to do the dirtiest jobs while they stood around watching, and why should they object if it was what he wanted? He seemed a bit cracked. Only once, when he was standing at the Quay staring at the orange peels and rotten apples floating in the oil-slicked water, was he recognised. A young woman came up to him and said, 'Don't I know you?'

He gave a start, frightened, but he did not recall ever having seen this girl.

'Didn't you take that typing course?' she asked. 'At the Tech?'

He shook his head and moved away.

'Then it was your twin,' she called after him. 'Spitting image. Just like you.'

After that he stayed mainly in his room, lying on his bed, thinking, going over his life. He thought of that Manly boarding house and of Roy with his extravagant theories about the world and his strange mixture of cruelty and warmth toward the abandoned boy, William Badger. And indeed since then the world had come to seem like a seesaw precariously maintaining its delicate balance, always on the point of bumping out of control and stalling.

William would have laboured twenty-four hours a day if it were possible. And then it occurred to him that he should get a new driver's licence, with his new name, a truck licence which would enable him to get jobs with a taxi truck service driving at night and on the weekends, making deliveries and moving pieces of furniture, saving every penny possible.

Through summer and autumn he worked, and at the beginning of winter he dyed his hair back to its own blond colour and flew into the summer of Europe, where he intended to become a private secretary to a man of culture.

'There's always work to be done on the magazine,' Tillie said. 'I don't suppose you can type?'

William put his arm around Tillie's shoulders and gave her a squeeze. And she leant into him.

'Of course I can type,' he said. 'And shorthand.'

Whoever she was, this Tillie Pepper, she was certainly a do-er. And he would be a do-er, too. Already she seemed to be offering him a job. He turned her away from him.

'Stand still,' he said, and he fiddled with the rubber band that anchored her hair so firmly, tugging at it, trying to slide it off her hair.

'Ouch!' said Tillie. 'The magazine is just one of the avenues of action we use to challenge the traditional power structures and work for the elimination of national boundaries between all the countries of Europe,' said Tillie, 'and to work towards a less militarised Europe. The authorities hate us.'

'I've wanted to do that since I first saw you tonight,' said William. 'Let your hair out.'

Tillie looked annoyed. 'Here, let me do it.' And she quickly unwound the rubber band and shook out her hair. 'Do you realise that the national boundaries that are in place at the moment, which most people take to be permanent, have existed for only twenty-five years or so?'

'I had not thought about it like that,' said William. He turned her to face him. 'There,' he said, and with one finger hooked one side of her hair behind her ear and then pushed the other side forward a little.

'I can't see,' said Tillie, rumpling her hair with both hands and pushing it back from her forehead. 'It gets in the way. But now there are too many vested interests for change to be made easily. The Common Market serves the interests of big business, the multi-nationals, not the people. People have to be taught to ask questions, prodded into action.'

'You look beautiful with your hair out,' said William.

'You want me to look more feminine, right?' said Tillie. 'To mitigate the activism, right? It makes you uncomfortable to see a woman with opinions, right? All men are like that.'

'Every woman I've ever known has had opinions,' said William. 'It's just that you hide your lovely face by yanking your hair back so harshly, that's all.'

'And what are you hiding?' Tillie retorted. She had thrown her hair back from her face and was about to secure it again in its rubber band.

William took a deep breath. 'I'm a fugitive,' he said. 'I escaped from jail.' He held his breath waiting to see her response.

Tillie let her hair drop down over her shoulders. 'You're just saying that to please me,' she said.

William shook his head. 'It's true. The authorities are after me.'

Tillie's mouth opened slightly, in wonder, then she shut it tightly and stepped up to William, her eyes shining. She placed her hand against his chest to steady herself, then lifted his hand to restore it to her cheek.

'Fair enough,' she said, matter-of-factly.

William, used to keeping a straight face and betraying no feeling, clamped his teeth together to stop himself smiling, laughing, and he clenched his fists to stop them slapping his thighs and the table top in delight. This woman was impressed by his past.

'I'll tell you all about it,' he said.

Tillie held up one hand, a policeman calling traffic to a halt. 'I don't need to know.'

'I want to tell you.'

Tillie stepped back to get a fuller view of William. 'I knew it wasn't your real name. I'll tell Cato. But you should know, however, that Cato and I have this thing,' she said. 'We're together really.' But she let William draw her to him and kiss her. 'How did you know where to find me tonight?' she mumbled into his chin.

There was a knock at the door. 'Agnes!' Tillie cried, clapping her hand over her mouth. 'I forgot she was due back tonight.'

Tillie bounded to the front door and flung it open. A young woman stepped in, greeted Tillie without smiling, and looked at William without changing her expression.

'When did you get back?' Tillie asked eagerly.

'This morning,' said Agnes. 'We just had an executive planning meeting.'

'We?' Tillie asked sharply.

'Cato, Marc and me,' said Agnes. 'And a couple of the other Barbarians.'

'Cato's in Liège,' said Tillie. 'He's calling me as soon as he's back.'

'He's been back for days,' said Agnes.

'And you had an executive meeting without calling me?'

Agnes shrugged and looked at William. 'I can go back to Cato's to sleep if there's no room here.'

'I can leave,' said William.

Tillie looked past him, impatient. 'He's just been helping me,' she said, as if William were not even there. 'He's a fugitive.'

Agnes nodded.

To Agnes Tillie said, 'He can type,' and to William she said, 'Of course, you'll have to get a real job to earn money. Typing for *The Barbarian* doesn't pay anything. I don't suppose you have work papers?'

William shook his head.

'There are ways around that.' Tillie looked at her watch. 'I'd better phone Cato. He'll want to talk to me.' Tillie picked up the phone. 'He's sure to want me to go over right away. He never stops working. The big day has to be properly planned.'

'They're not home,' said Agnes. 'They were all going out to eat. I was too tired.'

'I was out painting,' said Tillie, indignant. 'All by myself. No one came to help me.' She put down the phone. 'Only William Longleg. He can sleep on the cushions on the floor. He can type, too. I'm going to bed.' She pulled the curtain across the alcove—William could still see her feet and he watched her pull off her shoes and kick them under the bed. He watched the jeans fall into a heap on the floor. He could see that she was furious. This Cato, whoever he was, clearly did not have as much of a thing with Tillie as she had with him, and he was glad.

Agnes, without saying a word to William, threw the cushions off the sofa and unfolded the bed. She threw one of the blankets on top of the cushions. Then, as if he were not there, she took off her jeans and her shirt, discarded them in a heap on the floor and threw herself under the covers.

William placed the three cushions on the floor, half under the table. He doubled the blanket, laid it neatly over the cushions and tucked it in all around, leaving a slot open at one end. He stood by the jigsaw puzzle, a piece in one hand, waiting for Agnes to fall asleep. Then once she had closed her eyes he adopted her nonchalance, took off his jacket and shirt and trousers, letting them fall into a heap on the floor. He slid carefully onto the cushions beneath the blanket, as if he were inserting himself into an envelope. He lay for a while on his back, his arms at his sides, papoosed, then turned first on one side, looking through the legs of the table, then on the other side, where his untidy bundle of clothes rested, his trousers and jacket and shirt all in a tangle together. He took one hand from under the blanket and separated the three items, at the same time trying to straighten the trouser legs. He closed his eyes, but the disarray of his clothes was too much for him. He slid out of his envelope and picked up the clothing, folding the trousers along their creases, and rested them over the back of one chair. He placed his jacket neatly over another chair and his shirt over the jacket. He gave them a pat, then knelt down and returned to his bed.

If he was to have a new life, this seemed to be it. It had been thrust upon him.

Cato lived at the end of the tram route on the other side of the city, beyond the avenue Louise. The house itself was a tumbledown two-storey structure that sat at a slant at the end of a long driveway that was more like a dirt road running through a field.

Tillie sped in and braked, sending the car into a skid

along the dirt. She hurled herself out of the car and headed
for the house, her feet stamping into the dirt of the path.
William tailed along, stepping lightly, as if leaving an
imprint on the earth would be too presumptuous of a
stranger like him. Tillie threw open the front door, and
William felt an urge to caution her, to reach out and hold
her back, to suggest that they knock. He was afraid of
taking people by surprise. But Tillie was already inside
and climbing the stairs. William, who then felt it was safer
to enter with her rather than hang back and have to enter
alone, saw that the ground floor served as a storage barn,
an open room with boxes and bicycles and shelves along
the walls piled high with books and journals, with a few
tables and desks covered with stacks of papers. Tillie's feet
were clattering on the stairs. William drifted invisibly
behind her, hidden in the gloom of the stairwell. Tillie
threw open a door at the top of the stairs and stood with
her feet planted apart in the light that came flooding out.

William remained in the shadow on the landing. Beyond
Tillie he could see a group of four people—he recognised
Agnes's blonde head bent over some papers on the table—
gathered at one end of a wooden table so long that it
had to be placed diagonally in the room, creating two
triangular spaces on either side. The group at the table,
three men and Agnes, kept up their conversation for a
sentence or two—William could hear it was in French—
before looking up at the dramatic stance of Tillie in the
doorway. He held his breath, judging that Tillie was going
to upbraid the great Cato for not telephoning her, for
excluding her from their executive meeting.

'Ah,' said one of the group without getting up. This had
to be the famous Cato. While William pitied Tillie for this
cool reception he simultaneously felt a surge of joy. This
Cato did not seem to have a particular affection for his

Tillie, and he, William in the space of one day, did. He had probably fallen in love with Tillie, with her little feet that stamped and her energetic hands that waved in the air, her earnest face and her black hair, which he would let loose again at the first opportunity. He would teach her about her loveliness. Along with this swell of sweet affection for Tillie came sympathy for her, for her disappointment and humiliation before this Cato, with whom she insisted she had a 'thing'. William had learned that Cato was perfect— university degrees from several countries and a past that included political commentaries for press and radio and a stint with the British Foreign Office before he gave all that up and went to Brussels to join the radical movement that was pressing for a new Europe, where he founded *The Barbarian*, the only journal that ventured to criticise the European status quo and advocate a Europe truly united beyond the economic union of the Common Market, to include the countries of eastern Europe, a Europe that could wrest itself free from dependence on the United States. These were radical ideas shunned by established govern-ments, and while the Barbarians were dismissed as ineffectual hotheads, nevertheless their phones were tapped and their members kept under surveillance. This was the well-travelled, well-bred, charming Cato, who spoke every European language, with whom Tillie, and no doubt women of all nations, had had a little thing. There he was sitting at the table engrossed in his work, lifting his head for a moment to look at Tillie. He was clearly a tall man, long and lean in body and face, with straight red hair that hung forward over his forehead, giving him the look of an enchanting, mischievous British schoolboy rather than a critic of society, an underground activist, a member of the counter culture. He did not even have a beard.

'We should plan some kind of action,' said Cato. The

other three also looked up at Tillie and nodded. While Cato was not actually addressing Tillie, he seemed to be inviting her in, including her. 'But we need a plan. We must devise a political spectacle so that our ideas will be taken seriously.'

Tillie walked over to the table and stood beside Cato, her hand resting lightly on his shoulder. Cato shifted slightly, leaning away from her.

'Cato,' she said, bending to give him a kiss on the cheek. Then, to the other two, 'Marc, Silvestro.' She nodded at Agnes, then sat down on the bench next to Cato.

William stood just out of the light that beamed through the doorway, wondering what to do with himself. The group at the table had certainly noted his presence, but since they had not even greeted Tillie, whom they knew, it was unlikely that they would greet him, even further removed from them. He would stand quietly at the top of the stairs, a loyal companion who knew his place, ever ready to help. And at the flat, when things went well, he would have her to himself. Tillie placed her sack on the table. 'I've brought all the stuff I've been collecting for the special issue on worldwide student action.' Tillie was tireless, dedicated, and not what could be called thin-skinned.

Cato grunted and nodded and murmured something. Perhaps it was 'Good, good.'

William felt a tap on the shoulder. He turned to find a young woman with cropped yellow hair smiling up at him.

'Mat,' she said softly and held out her hand.

'William,' he replied and shook her hand. A friend. She had said her name, she had offered her hand. A normal person.

Mat indicated the group in the living room with her head and rattled off a sentence in French. William caught words like 'intelligent' and 'problem' and 'idiot.'

'Sorry,' he said and shrugged apologetically, pulling his

mouth back into a rueful grin and wagging his head from side to side as if to say 'Wouldn't you know it, I'm such a dummy that I don't even speak French.'

Mat switched to English. 'They are always rude like that, those clever men who think they can change the world and solve the problems. They think they can leave behind good manners.'

This Mat looked like a little boy with her short hair, shorter than Cato's, and shining dark eyes.

'I should know,' Mat said. 'I married him.'

Him could only be Cato. William felt another surge of joy. Tillie had not mentioned this.

'Cato's wife?' he whispered, not wanting his deep voice to draw any attention to him and Mat on the landing.

Mat nodded. She looked as if she might burst into laughter. 'He likes to keep me a secret. He's afraid it is too bourgeois to have a wife. He didn't tell you, right?'

'I don't know him,' said William.

'We have a baby coming, so I said it was time we got married, and I even insisted on a honeymoon, although he cut it short to get back to his beloved *Barbarian*.'

The way was clear for Tillie to be his, William's.

'Come with me,' said Mat and took William with her into the kitchen.

Looking back through the kitchen door across the landing and into the room where Cato and Tillie and the others were huddled, William saw Cato look up and peer over his shoulder at the kitchen, talking the whole time. He was alert, registering everything, the way a cat, even while it eats, swivels its ears and monitors its surroundings, listening for signs of danger. Cato must have finally asked Tillie who the newcomer was, because William could hear Tillie's bright, firm voice saying, 'He has first-rate credentials. He has a jail record. I took him in. He can help us.'

Then Cato must have asked his name and who sent him to them.

'I don't know, but his name is Longleg,' Tillie said.

'What kind of name is that?' asked Mat, who could hear Tillie's voice as clearly as William could.

'Just a name,' said William.

'Probably not his real name,' Tillie was saying.

Mat looked at William, raising her eyebrows.

'It's my real name,' said William.

'I like it,' said Mat. 'Long legs.' She ran the fingers of one hand along the counter.

'Sounds German,' Cato said in the other room.

'True,' Mat said to William, nodding. '*Lang bein*. Very German.'

'I'm English,' said William.

'I've read about a Langbein somewhere,' said Cato. He was frowning, thinking.

William felt rather pleased at the attention he was now receiving. Although the group in the other room was not addressing him directly, he had been an item interesting enough to interrupt their planning session and occupy their time for several minutes.

Mat placed a paring knife in William's hand and indicated that he should help her chop onions and tomatoes and wash the lettuce while the others talked.

'We must bring Europe to a standstill for a few hours,' William heard them saying. They had switched to English. 'We have to challenge the status quo.' And, 'It's time to coordinate with the movements in other countries.'

Mat giggled as she tore up the parsley, which she then threw into the bucket of salad. 'We use a bucket,' she said, 'because we never know how many people will come to eat.' She swung the bucket as if she were a dairy maid skipping off to milk the cows. 'It's like feeding animals at the zoo,' she said. 'Zoo-rope. The new Europe.' This Mat seemed to be the happiest person alive. 'And to feed little Thor.' She patted her abdomen.

Mat pressed a handful of silver knives and forks into William's hand. 'You can put these on the other table in there. They'll simply have to stop their nonsense when I say so, when the food is ready, when it's feeding time.'

William stood in the doorway, afraid to step into the bright light of the main room. He went back to Mat. 'Do you think you could put them out?' He cleared his throat. 'I'm a bit, you know.'

'Shy?' Mat said, taking back the cutlery. 'I, too, have nothing clever to say about a united Europe or disarmament or challenging the power of the multinationals, except that I'm for and not against.' She dumped the cutlery in a pile on the long table. 'What I'm called on to contribute is my typing.'

Just then Cato stood up and stretched. 'We need something dramatic, to demonstrate how all of Europe is linked, how all the countries are interdependent.'

'William types,' said Tillie quickly, eyeing Mat. 'That's why I brought him. He can help. And he has good ideas, too.'

The four at the table looked William over. Marc, the youngest of the three men, said, 'Perhaps he can tell us how to unite Europe, the whole of Europe, east and west, at least for a few hours.'

William looked puzzled.

'Who's the new female?' Tillie asked Cato, referring to Mat.

Mat laughed and shook her head. 'Cato keeps such big secrets,' she said.

Tillie looked puzzled, and William wanted to put his arms around her, comfort her for her ill-judged brusqueness and for the forthcoming embarrassment when she learned who Mat was.

To protect her, to obscure her question, William asked gallantly, boldly, 'You want to make a spectacle?', blotting out any answer Cato might supply about Mat. He would tell Tillie about Mat's being Cato's wife gently, when they were alone later. 'I know how to make a foolproof bomb, with tin foil and a candle. And you're at home eating dinner when it goes off.'

They were all looking at him now. He had certainly succeeded in drawing attention away from Cato and the secrets of his personal life.

Marc was looking disdainful. 'But we're non-violent. Of course you couldn't know that.' Marc seemed pleased that the newcomer had blundered. 'And we have several excellent ideas already.'

'What we want is press coverage,' said Agnes, ignoring William. 'Something bold.'

'Something playful, mischievous, naughty almost,' said Cato. 'Yet making a statement.'

William suddenly remembered the naughtiest thing a boy could do. 'You could halt all the trains,' he said. 'You plant someone on every train linking the cities and at a certain time everyone pulls the emergency cord and the trains stop.'

The room fell silent. Cato scratched his head. 'Right,' he said. 'We'll stop the trains.'

William steadied himself against the wall, reeling from his sudden brilliance. He was a creator, an inventor of ideas.

'And then what,' said Marc, 'when you've stopped the trains?' He sounded petulant. 'It's a bit far-fetched.'

'It's a brilliant idea,' said Cato quietly.

Mat gave William a hug at this important endorsement. Tillie moved along the bench, making a space beside her, to let William know he should sit with them at the table.

'We'll do some of your ideas, too,' said Cato to Marc, placating, 'as preliminary steps to the big day, the day when all the trains stop.'

'I told you he had good ideas,' said Tillie. 'And better still, he types.'

When they were leaving William waited at the top of the stairs while Tillie said her interminable goodbyes to Cato and Marc, gradually making her way to the door then retracing her steps back toward Cato as a new thought on a certain issue occurred, then moving back toward the door.

'I'm going to bed,' Mat announced and removed herself.

Agnes stood with her hands in her pockets, leaning against the window sill, saying nothing, gazing out the window into the dark, now and then shifting her weight from one foot to the other. William could see that Agnes, too, was impatient for Tillie to shut up and leave. Having reached the door, finally, Tillie called, 'Aren't you coming, Agnes?'

Agnes shook her head slowly. 'I'm going to sleep with Marc tonight,' said Agnes.

If he had had a hat, or even just a little green cap, William would have thrown it in the air and let out a cry, a whoop of joy. He would have Tillie to himself tonight. He would not have the two of them, Tillie and Agnes, chattering on about this action and that action, about *la révolution* and *l'oppression*, as if he were not there, as they did in the flat, from breakfast onwards.

Tillie uttered a few more pronouncements from the doorway, and it was only when Cato turned his back on her and addressed Agnes in a low voice that Tillie crossed the landing, and waved William ahead down the stairs. She hummed a little and handed William the car keys. 'You drive.'

On the way home William looked sideways at Tillie. She seemed pleased with him and was attending to him. 'I know you are on the run from the authorities,' she said. 'I don't know what kind of political trouble you're in.' She held up her hand. 'And I think it's better if I don't know.'

William found himself stuck behind a tram, not daring to pull out and overtake it. He was driving on the right-hand side of the road for the first time in his life, changing gears with his right hand. He ought to tell Tillie that it was assault he was charged with, nothing glamorous. He ought to tell her about Rose and the axe.

'But I respect your cover,' Tillie continued. 'It's safer if I don't know the details.' She hummed a few more bars, then said, 'I have to do a series of interviews for the magazine, with the student leaders. The Germans are especially active. Cato said he'd run anything I wrote in *The Barbarian*. He's quite remarkable, isn't he, Cato? I didn't think much of the new girl. She seems empty headed.'

This was the moment. 'You mean Mat?' said William.

'Right, the new woman.'

'She is Cato's wife. He married her.'

Tillie said nothing, stayed immobile. She seemed not to be breathing.

'She says Cato liked to keep her a secret. But he should have said something to you.' William thought he might as well tell her everything. 'They're having a baby. That's why they got married. That's why they were away. A honeymoon.' He added, 'I'm sorry,' although he was not sorry at all.

Tillie was still silent. Then she said, 'What a disgustingly bourgeois thing to do.' She looked sharply at William. 'You don't think I care, do you? You don't think Cato matters to me, do you?'

Tillie sank into silence. At one point as William crept

along behind another tram, Tillie snapped, 'Haven't you got the courage to overtake? Must you always follow?'

And she had known him only a few days. But back in the flat Tillie drew William into the alcove, her cave, and onto the bed. 'You can put your arms around me, but that's all,' she said and drew the curtains across the foot of the bed at the entrance to the alcove.

'Longleg is my real name, you know,' said William.

'Right,' said Tillie. 'The less I know the better.'

'Do you want me to tell you how I came by that name?

'No,' said Tillie.

It was easy enough for William to remain silent. He was ready to lie happily on the bed, with his arms around Tillie all night, obeying her orders. He moved his hands over her body once or twice—he told himself he was not really doing anything, not really going against her instructions, since his arms were merely around her, even if they were moving, and she had said she would allow his arms around her. But when she sighed and moved close to him, placing her arms around him, pressing her hands against his shoulder blades, in no time at all he was making love to her, happier than ever, making love over and over, claiming Tillie in a kind of celebration of himself, crowning the glory of the evening in which he had spoken boldly to a group of strangers and outlined a daring plan, a plan which had been greeted almost unanimously as brilliant.

When he awakened, Tillie had slipped away from him and was in the kitchen making coffee. He heard her unlock the back door and throw it open. He heard her inhaling and exhaling noisily. The alcove curtains had been thrust to one side, and when he propped himself on one elbow, he could see her on the cement square outside the windows of the flat. She was standing in the sunlight wrapped in her robe, her face to the sky, her eyes closed, and her arms outstretched, just breathing in and out. For a moment, watching her from the dark little cave of the sleeping alcove, William feared she might begin to twirl.

William watched Tillie for several minutes, his perfect woman, a goddess. She had allowed him to make love to her the whole night and now definitely he loved her. He was alive, living, at last. He stayed sitting on the bed, without moving, in case any sound from within disturbed Tillie from her breathing, her moment of quiet, and snapped her back into the present and her business for the day. Once she was dressed she would be off to do something or other with the Barbarians.

There was a knock at the door. William leapt out of bed and pulled on his clothes watching Tillie outside the window. She lowered her arms slowly, and then came back into the flat, pulling her robe around her and fastening it tightly.

'It's probably Agnes,' she said.

'Tillie,' he murmured, reaching out his hand, just wanting to touch her—on the cheek, the elbow, the shoulder to confirm their night together, to claim her in some way before she was spirited away.

But Tillie stalked past him without giving him a glance, leaving him standing slightly dishevelled in the middle of the room, his mouth open ready to utter an endearment, his arm outstretched to her. He closed his mouth and used the outstretched arm to pull the curtain across the alcove in order to hide the rumpled bed, the shrine of his love. He did not want Agnes to have any part of it, did not want her eyes roving over the evidence of his passion.

'Ah, *madame*,' he heard Tillie say dully.

Tillie backed into the room followed by a woman, quite young, perhaps in her thirties, plump, with yellow curly hair and a pink face. '*Bonjour, mademoiselle*.' She was wearing a floral dress, a housedress William would have designated it had he been pressed to categorise it, and an apron of a different floral altogether, made, William could see, from an even older dress. She was holding a bone-handled carving knife in one hand and its mate, a fork, in the other, and all smiles, she wielded these implements back and forth, jabbing the fork forward and then sawing the air next to it with the knife.

'*Bonjour, monsieur,*' she said, eyeing William.

Tillie raised her eyes to the ceiling, and William understood that this was the landlady, who lived above them.

She had come to upbraid him for the vigorous night he had spent in the bed that she was renting to Tillie. William clicked his heels and bowed to her, without taking his eyes off the blade and tines, which were slicing the air recklessly.

The landlady was looking questioningly at Tillie.

'This is my husband,' Tillie said.

The landlady gave a cry of delight. 'I am very happy that a young woman, who has been alone, has now found a life partner. *Monsieur* and I are partners and do everything together.' She winked at William.

She and her husband were butchers, she told William, winking again. Charcuterie. Salami, sausage and black pudding. She looked at the knife and fork in her hands and gave another cry. How silly of her to have forgotten why she had paid this visit in the first place. The surprise of learning that the young lady, now the young *madame*, had a gentleman guest, and then learning that this gentleman was her husband, had distracted her. She and her husband had many sets of these knives and forks, which they gave away to clients at Christmas. And she had thought that the young lady might need a carving set, and now that the young lady was married and had a husband, well, the carving set was more like a wedding present. She placed the knife and fork in Tillie's hands.

'And *madame*, when you're just setting up a home, when you're just married, you need things.' Then the landlady laughed and took the knife and fork back from Tillie. She placed them in William's hands.

'It's *monsieur*, is it not, who should carve?' She laughed and winked at Tillie. 'We women have to let the men do things, don't we, if we want to keep them happy and make them feel important, make them think they are the strong ones, and to carve meat is one way.'

'Thank you, thank you very much,' said William, bowing again, holding the knife and fork as if they were drumsticks and he was about to begin a roll. 'Very, very much. Muchly. Thank you.'

Tillie gave a stiff, polite smile and pulled her robe more tightly around her, hugging herself, then making a move to raise her left wrist to look at her watch then changing her mind and returning the wrist to her waist.

The landlady laughed and shook her head. 'Very nice, very nice.' She went over to the windows that gave onto the cement terrace and ran her forefinger along the window sill. 'Oh, this dirty city,' she said. 'I clean my windows and dust the sills every day, but still this dust and dirt. I apologise for my dirty city, this Brussels.' She went to the kitchen alcove, holding her dusty finger aloft, and turned on the faucet. From the pocket of her apron she drew forth a folded rag, dampened it under the faucet, then ran it along the window sill, after which she turned the cloth up to contemplate the dust, with some disgust. She dashed the cloth under running water in the sink and quickly squeezed out the dust and dirt. Then she took her leave.

Tillie went and stood by the table, contemplating the puzzle. William looked at the implements in his hands for a moment then placed them gingerly on the bed, as if they were loaded and might go off. His heart was pounding. He wanted to take Tillie in his arms and draw her back into their cave behind the curtain. Tillie. His wife. She had actually told the landlady that they were man and wife.

'She would have thrown me out,' said Tillie, snapping various puzzle pieces against the table. 'She hates me to have men here and I had promised I wouldn't, mainly because I can't be bothered to look for another place.' Tillie glanced at William, the first time she had looked at him since he had awakened, since their night of lovemaking.

'You could tidy up a bit around here,' said Tillie, 'while I make sense of these notes.' She continued to stand by the jigsaw puzzle. 'And clean. The landlady requires that, spic and span. I promised her.'

William was glad to be of use, grateful even, to help this tiny dynamo of a woman who, although she had been lying to the landlady, had nevertheless designated him as her husband. Perhaps she would grow to love him.

Tillie sat frowning at the papers spread before her on the table. To William she looked adorable.

'I have to get over to Cato's and help edit the proofs for the next issue,' Tillie said.

William stepped over to her and placed his hands on her shoulders.

'Maybe we could really get married,' he said. 'I,' he cleared his throat, 'I believe I love you.' He had never said those words to a woman. Never to Meg, stuck back in Sydney with her dreams of Olga, nourished by mere fantasies of a glamorous, cosmopolitan life, although he had certainly considered making such a declaration to her. He, William, not Meg, was the one who had actually taken action. He had left her, not she him. He had done something, found a new life, and really fallen in love. Tillie was dazzling.

'Love?' said Tillie, surprised. 'That's a word that has no meaning. The landlady would have thrown me out for having you here.'

She dressed, placed a black leather cap on her head, threw a long black and white striped scarf around her neck and raced out, then poked her head back in the front door. 'You could do the vegetables for ratatouille. I might bring people back with me. And tomorrow you could look for some kind of job.'

While Tillie was away, William cleaned the flat with great zeal and precision. He felt like a dancer. As he dusted and swept and picked up Tillie's tights and scarves, he could see the woman who lived in the house at the back begin to clean her windows, inside and out. Their industrious duet pleased him. He, along with all the women of rue de la Campagne, was sprucing things up.

William found the BBC Home Service on the radio. After a word quiz game called 'Just One Minute', in which four exceedingly articulate participants spoke for exactly one minute on a surprise topic—bats or beaches—without hesitating or repeating any words, 'The Women's Hour' came on. William leaned against the door jamb, gazing at the woman washing her windows and thought that he could be a radio personality. He could devise a program for women, organising snippets of this and that for an audience of millions, who would fall in love with him, with his voice, and with the skilful transitions he would write and narrate, uniting the segments of his program. 'Did you hear William Longleg this week?' the women of the world would ask. 'Isn't he wonderful?'

In the meantime he would lick envelopes, fold fliers, type Tillie's manifestoes, make soup and vegetable stew for the social critics who were shaping a new Europe.

In a way that was even more exciting and important than anything Meg had envisioned for him.

As he dusted, William held up the scraps of paper on which Tillie had scribbed her notes and smiled a lover's smile as he read snatches of sentences like 'Anti-West German role with Rhodesia and South Africa. Relations with West Berlin—learning process—how to work and learn conflict model from Cuba. (Study W. German investments in Portugal).'

When he had finished cleaning and tidying he peeled the eggplant and zucchini and onions that Tillie had waved her hand at as she left. He would rather she returned alone, so that he could have her to himself that night, but in order to please her he did as she had ordered and made double the amount. He could see from the way Cato and the others had treated her the night before that she was not as important to them as they were to her, and this realisation of her vulnerability, her neediness, and the probability of her getting hurt and rejected by them in the future made him love her the more.

Suddenly William stopped peeling, aware that tears were welling up and flowing down his cheeks. But he did not know if he was happy or sad.

At the end of the day Tillie swept in and threw her cap onto the bed. William was bent over the 'Scene from Enkhuizen'.

Tillie stood beside him, close enough that her arm brushed his. He liked the touch, was delighted, and stopped trying to place the little orange puzzle piece, keeping his arm against hers.

'They all *wanted* to come back with me,' said Tillie. William was about to begin nudging Tillie toward the alcove. He would take her to bed and make love to her, erasing *The Barbarian* completely. 'But we decided that I should be the one to go to this meeting tonight,' Tillie went on. She placed her hand on his arm and looked into his eyes. 'And I really need you to come with me.'

And William had to discard his plan for complete erasure in the alcove. Nevertheless, Tillie needed him. 'What kind of meeting?'

'Cato would have come with me but he had to finish something first. Marc and Agnes are doing something— although if you ask me I think they were trying to get out of doing any work. It's a good cause. Just a bunch of Common Market civil servants.'

William felt uneasy, a certain fear. He had imagined envelopes, and typing, and making quantities of food, but he was not at all sure about public meetings.

'We have to dress up a bit,' said Tillie. 'Do you have something resembling a suit?'

William hauled from the duffle bag his remaining clothes, which although neatly folded were rumpled from having been squashed in the sack. Tillie waved her hand at the cupboard that contained an iron and he pressed the worst of the wrinkles out, resting the trousers on the sofa.

Tillie went into her alcove, drew the curtain halfway, and emerged in a skirt of some synthetic material permanently creased into a series of sharp knife pleats, a blouse buttoned to the neck, stockings and high heels. William followed her to the car, noting that the pleated skirt made her rear end look too large, thinking that he would tell her this one day. He knew a thing or two about women's clothes. In the car Tillie put on lipstick, making a face.

'But don't expect me to do anything, or say anything,' said William as Tillie jerked the car out into the street and careered off into the city. 'I'm not the type.'

'I know your type,' said Tillie. 'You're just passing through, right? A man of few words and little action, right?'

But William was too much in love to be hurt. 'I can be of help, in all kinds of other ways,' he said, rather wishing he had pleaded fatigue and remained at the flat.

'We have this chance to change the world,' said Tillie, 'and you're shrugging and saying sorry, you're not the type?'

'Not everyone can be like you,' said William.

'It's easy to be like me,' said Tillie. 'Anyone can do it.'

They sped past the Place Louise, over Tillie's painted PAN EUROPE among the tram tracks, dodging buses, trams and cars.

'Highest rate of traffic accidents in Europe,' said Tillie, swinging the Volkswagen around a tram, onto the adjacent tracks and into the path of an oncoming tram, then ducking back again in front of the tram she had overtaken.

For years in Belgium anyone who turned eighteen could drive a car without a licence, lurching through the road-works, capering through the narrow streets and dodging around the trolleys. Although road tests for new drivers had been introduced, the tradition of wild driving persisted.

Tillie parked outside a glass box of a building and led William into a large meeting room where tiers of seats and desks descended in a semi-circle to a podium.

A hundred or so newly employed Common Market bureaucrats, fresh from their universities with their degrees, the young elite of Europe, were meeting for orientation. Their new shoes squeaked and their hair shone. It was an honour to have been chosen to come to Brussels to be international civil servants. William and Tillie passed unnoticed into the auditorium and slid into a row halfway down.

The Director-General of the European Economic Community gave the welcoming speech from the podium. The personnel chief talked about the duties of an international civil servant. When he had finished and just as the applause from the employees subsided Tillie climbed onto her seat and stepped onto the desk top in front of her.

Her shins were at William's nose.

'Get down,' he hissed, pulling at her leg. He had had no idea that she was going to do this.

But Tillie was too far above him to hear, and too excited. As she spoke, yelled, she rocked onto her toes and stayed there on tiptoe, one knee ticking back and forth as she pronounced the words. William could see up her pleated terylene skirt.

'We are here,' Tillie shouted 'to protest the tyranny of the European Economic Community over the people of Europe,' and then repeated the sentence in her perfect French, like a simultaneous interpreter. 'We young Europeans refuse to work under rigid old dictators, the same old dictators we have always had. Our telephones, the telephones of five thousand of us civil servants are bugged by our own employers. We refuse to sit here on our buttocks,' and when she repeated that in French there was a gasp from the audience, 'on our rear ends,' and she slapped the pleats over her own buttocks, 'in this, this . . .' and she waved her arms at the auditorium, indicating the whole building, 'here in this slum, and listen to you telling us to be obedient slaves.'

There was a shocked murmur, louder this time. '*Ces baraques*,' she had called this most gloriously modern building in Brussels, in which they were delighted to be sitting.

'We refuse to sit in this slum,' Tillie repeated, savouring the effect she had had with that single word, as if she believed that she had swayed them all, 'in this dump, and be spied on.'

'Where's your proof?' someone cried from further down.

'We'll get the proof,' said Tillie.

Then the new civil servants jumped to their feet, giving out a roar of rage. At first it seemed that Tillie had indeed aroused them to action and single-handedly started a revolt. But the young civil servants were shouting not at the Director-General but at Tillie.

'We want reform, and a say in how things are run, and an end to surveillance,' said Tillie.

The young man who had been sitting in front of her was now on his feet, turning and grabbing at Tillie's ankles, pulling them toward him, trying to topple her. Tillie tried to stamp on his hands. She began to fall backwards. William stood up to catch her around the thighs. Several people in the row behind leant forward and caught Tillie's shoulders. And Tillie was lifted up and passed over the heads and shoulders of the international civil servants, up the tiers to the doors, where she was ejected from the auditorium.

The president of the staff association stepped up to the podium, his arms outstretched patting the air, calling for calm and quiet, and he apologised to the Director-General. He said he had no idea who the barbaric intruder was, but she certainly was not a bona fide international civil servant, that much was clear. He kept bowing and expressing his profound regrets, hoping the Director-General would graciously overlook the affront and be assured of their loyalty and civility.

William shrank back in his seat and waited a few moments, then got up, manoeuvering past the still indignant civil servants in order to go and find Tillie.

'He's one of them,' a couple of the young Europeans yelled. 'Get his name. Get his identity card.'

William was at the top of the steps, almost at the door. Two young men leapt out of the back row and tried to grasp him. One got hold of his jacket, causing William to stumble, but the force of his flight propelled him forward, yanking himself and his jacket free, and he raced through the door and out into the dark streets to the car where

Tillie was sitting in the passenger seat rubbing her elbow.

'Why did you do that?' William gasped, sliding into the driver's seat. 'You united them, all right, *against* you.'

'Quick,' said Tillie, handing him the keys. 'Get us out of here.'

'And you forget, I can't afford to fall into the hands of the police.'

Then as William started the car and lurched forward, Tillie said calmly, 'It's just a political tactic, you should know that.'

William changed gear, clumsily, causing the car to dance along like a startled horse.

'Jesus,' Tillie muttered. 'And when we get hold of that document and publish it—it *does* exist you know, they *do* tap the phones—they'll begin to take us seriously.'

'Seems stupid to me,' said William. He was badly shaken up.

'Don't you know anything about political tactics?' Tillie was exasperated. 'Where have you been? What kind of training did they give you? What kind of fugitive are you?'

Tillie directed him past the Gare du Sud and onto the Chaussée de Ninove and into rue de la Campagne. William parked and rested his cheek on his hands on the steering wheel, staring at Tillie, who leapt out and went to unlock the door, her pleats swinging after her. When he got her to talk to him again, William would tell her about her hair and about skirts, tell her that something flared would suit her lovely body wonderfully, far better than pleats.

While Tillie muckraked and planned for the day of action, the halting of all the trains of Europe, William found work as a secretary—although he had to admit it was more like being an office boy—for two reporters, an American who wrote for a New York newspaper and an Englishman who wrote for a London paper. An English speaker with no official work papers, he had been lucky to find the job. He was paid his weekly wages out of petty cash.

William made tea and coffee for his employers, who were only a year or two older than he. He transmitted on the telex their reports to New York and London, clipped articles they had marked in every major European paper and filed them under headings like 'African Association', 'Cartels', 'Oil', and 'British Problems'. The New York reporter had written a book on the success of the Common Market, the rough draft of which William was retyping on a manual typewriter set up in a pantry next to the telex. If William showed promise the reporters said that he might at some stage be able to write a few of the lighter stories for them; if it worked out, they might be able to help him get started in communications.

As William typed he could hear the voices of his two employers in the next room. If he leant back in his chair and turned his head, he could see them as they leant back in their chairs, swapping leads and insights.

'He can tell us if he learns anything important—reporters are part of the establishment,' said Tillie to Cato and the Barbarians, feeling the need to justify William's job with employers whose efforts helped to maintain the status quo.

Since William could simultaneously type and think about something else altogether, he rarely took in what he was typing for the reporters. He thought he might become an essayist, and as he typed he thought of the title for his first piece: 'The Doom Buggy', which would demonstrate that the world was driving to its doom, that the Western world was in decline.

When William was alone in the office he answered the phone, saying 'Hello,' without the 'h,' as if he were speaking French. Although he had begun studying French,

the language seemed to become more elusive the more
he learned and the more he heard around him, and it was
at its absolute worst when he was with Tillie, who spoke
the language flamboyantly, boisterously, more Belgian than
the Belgians themselves, even more French than the French.

He had learned to say two things into the telephone:
'*Il n'est pas là,*' when no one was there, and '*Ils reviendront
plus tard,*' when he thought the reporters would be back.
And then he struggled to take down the names and numbers
and messages repeated to him several times with escalating
impatience.

Tillie spent all her days, including Saturdays and
Sundays, zooming all over Brussels from one meeting to
the next, delivering proofs, picking up drafts.

Marooned in the flat William sometimes imagined the
phone ringing and his straining to understand a voice telling
him in French that Tillie had been severely injured, perhaps
killed, in a crazy traffic accident on the Place Louise, where
he had first seen her, kneeling between the tracks, or in
the tunnel running under the avenue that Tillie took to
get to Cato's place. On Saturdays William tidied and
cleaned the flat, which gave him time to work things out—
go over what he would do that day, apart from cleaning
and making a lot of food in case Tillie actually returned
and brought with her a lot of people for dinner; and the
next day, Sunday, which was to buy the English newspapers
at the English bookstore on the avenue Louise and to hope
that Tillie would be sufficiently offended by the humiliating
treatment accorded her by the Barbarians that she would
stay with him all day; and in the future, for the rest of
his life, which was not clear to him. He knew he wanted
to stay beside Tillie, if she would let him, and *do* something,
something brilliant.

On Saturday mornings everything seemed possible,

becoming less and less so as the evening approached and Tillie did not return. Sometimes she did not get back until after midnight. The BBC Home Service helped him through the day and the evening; just the sound of voices speaking his own language comforted him after his week of struggling with French in the trams and in the shops and on the phone at the office and having constantly to turn to Tillie for help, when it all became too much for him. A man of few words and little action, as Tillie said, even though he was the one who had thought up the spectacle of stopping the trains of Europe. He was working on several new ideas for essays. One was called 'Modular Man', with the subtitle 'The Staff of Life Becomes a Toasted Bread Cube', in which he would show society's decline through the degeneration in the character of bread in less than a century, from the fine crusty loaf to the toasted cubes the astronauts took into space. Bread, like man, had changed its nature to conform to what the machine could produce.

He would be William Longleg, commentator, communicator, personality—three words.

And every Saturday when he cleaned the flat he dismantled parts of the 'Scene from Enkhuizen', very cleverly so that Tillie would not notice. He did not want the puzzle to be completed, because when Tillie became absorbed in it, it meant that they could spend several hours together.

On Sunday mornings, William drove the car to pick up the London papers, which offered another refuge. Once or twice a month, when fog on the English Channel delayed the ferry bringing the papers, he waited at the newsagent's thumbing through the new English novels. He stood with the expatriate British and Americans who milled about, awaiting their reading matter, listening to them greet one another in English and refer to Chicago or Hampstead as if they were suburbs of Brussels instead of miles away in other countries.

One Sunday Tillie came home early, stormed into the flat just a few hours after she had left to do a day's work at Cato's. She sat herself down on the sofa, announcing that she was depressed and angry once again about the way the Barbarians regarded her.

'That's wonderful,' said William. He was practically jumping up and down. 'We'll take the Sunday papers and lie together in the forest, the Forêt des Soignes, and read.' He thought the word 'together' might set Tillie off, make her retreat, so he repeated the sentence in an amended form. 'I'll drive you to the forest and you can lie down and read the Sunday papers in peace and quiet.'

He had already been to the avenue Louise and bought the papers—and there had been no fog on the channel, a good omen for this wonderful day.

'What's so wonderful about them giving me the layout to do?' Tillie asked. 'I'm always the one who has to fiddle with that. And they had an editorial meeting last night and Marc did not call me. And Cato said nothing, no apology, nothing, when I heard about it. Nothing. Marriage has made him weak.'

William touched Tillie's shoulders tentatively, moving his fingers slightly to suggest a comforting massage-like movement. Tillie wriggled her shoulders to indicate that he should proceed.

'Or we can drive a little in the Flanders fields, where the poppies grow.' William patted Tillie's shoulders then raced to the kitchen alcove and threw some bread and cheese into a bag. He wanted to get going before Tillie recovered from her depression.

Later, as William drove through the fields of wheat that rose taller than Tillie's little car, Tillie said, still brooding over the injustices meted out to her, 'I'll show them they can't do this to me.'

They emerged from the wheat and found themselves in a village of a few houses.

'Let's get some beer,' said William, pulling over and stopping. 'We can take it into the fields.'

Tillie sat, not moving. And William sat, looking expectantly at Tillie, waiting for her to get out to buy the beer.

'I'll tell you what else I'm sick of,' said Tillie. 'I'm absolutely sick of having to do everything. I work like a dog at *The Barbarian* seven days a week, and you expect me also to shoulder the burden of the little transactions, like buying bread, or, or, beer.' She waved her hand at the cafe on the other side of the street.

'But you're the one who speaks French,' said William. 'I make a fool of myself.'

'We're in Flanders now,' Tillie snapped. 'Their French is as bad as yours. You buy the beer.'

William got out and went into the cafe, past the Belgians drinking at the little tables. He pointed to the beer, his face red, determined not to speak.

'This beer or that one?' the girl asked.

William pointed, and paid.

In the car Tillie took her beer and said, 'That wasn't hard, was it?'

Mortified yet unwilling to surrender this day with Tillie, William drove back into Brussels and parked near the Place Louise. He did not want to return to the flat in case Agnes was waiting for them, ready to reclaim Tillie.

'I want to go home,' said Tillie.

'I'm taking you to the movies,' said William, man of action, and led her to one of the English cinemas. And Tillie followed, uncharacteristically meek. 'And afterwards we'll eat mussels. Mussels in Brussels.'

As he watched Anthony Quinn and basked in the English language, William held Tillie's hand. And she allowed this.

'I'm going to take a leak in the garden,' Quinn growled. The subtitle in French read, *'Je vais prendre un poireau dans le jardin.'*

'A leek!' Tillie whispered, laughing, leaning against William. By now he knew his vegetables in French and was able to laugh, too. He put his arm around her shoulder. And she allowed it to stay there.

They were still laughing as they walked down the cobblestones of one of the little streets in the centre of town, where William had walked his first day in Brussels, alone and afraid to go into a cafe to eat.

'If you were relying on the subtitles you'd still be wondering why he never came in from the garden with a leek, *un poireau*, in his hand.' Tillie was gasping with laughter.

William had never seen her so lighthearted. 'Unless you thought it was a ritual performed by English-speaking people,' he said, 'running out into the garden to pluck leeks at certain times.' Tillie was actually skipping along beside him. He felt fantastically able as they walked, his Saturday feeling, as if everything were possible, that he needed only to approach an idea in his mind for it to be totally realised. He held Tillie's hand tightly, as they mingled with the good citizens of Brussels. He would tell Tillie jokes and make her laugh even more as they sat and dipped into the pot for mussels.

William stopped and kissed her. 'Marry me, Tillie,' he said.

Tillie was still laughing. 'Silly Billy, so silly,' she said. 'Come on, mussels in Brussels.'

They walked along, their boots clattering.

'How do you imagine the students are able to pry loose

cobblestones like these and throw them, the way they're doing, here, and in Paris, and everywhere? The cobblestones seem so fixed, so permanent,' William said.

Then ahead of them he saw Cato and Marc and Agnes and some others, without Mat, standing outside Chez Guevara, where the Barbarians liked to go for a cheap omelette. Seven of them. William nodded and went to pull Tillie past, hoping she had not seen them. But Tillie had stopped.

'Hey!' she called. She pulled William right into the middle of the group. 'Where are you all off to?'

From Tillie's first joyful shout of recognition William could see that this would happen, and he wondered how Tillie could cast aside her hurt feelings so easily, how she could relinquish their happiness together as they walked hand in hand toward their mussels. She stood delighted in the middle of the group, as William stood behind her and whispered, 'Mussels in Brussels, remember?' Then, when Tillie showed no sign of having heard, he pinched her hand to let her know that he did not want to eat with seven politically concerned people that night. Again Tillie gave no sign of having understood him.

'Come on,' said Agnes, 'I'm hungry.'

'I don't want to eat with them,' William whispered to Tillie and pinched her hand again, hard.

Tillie turned sharply and glared at him, a stranger, no longer the woman who had let him lead her down the cobblestones, who had giggled at Anthony Quinn taking a leek in the garden.

'If you pinch me once more I'll hit you,' she said.

So they joined the Barbarians for dinner. William wished Tillie had hit him, so that he could have left her joking and laughing and gone off alone, walked home. Or he could have driven away, leaving Tillie to walk home or get a lift from her multitude of interesting friends. Perhaps she would not have come home at all. By the time William had those thoughts, they were sitting at a long table in the cafe, Tillie in the centre laughing, William at one end, out of it, everyone at the table leaning away from him toward Cato and Agnes, opposite Tillie, who was gesturing exaggeratedly and pushing her lips forward as she spoke, to show the whole of Brussels that she was completely at home with this language and in these surroundings.

Tillie was discussing what she would write for the next month's issue of *The Barbarian* and declaring how glad she was to have acquired the layout experience on these past issues. William's feeling of fantastic capacity and capability had evaporated completely, and he turned leaden, his limbs becoming ever heavier, so that it took a great effort to pick up a fork, to chew, to stop the eyelids descending. He felt he was slanting in his chair, as if the world were tilting, and he had to lean to one side to remain upright and not fall to the floor.

William sat tilted, his eyelids moving to a close, watching Tillie asking Marc in English why he did not let himself have more fun and if he ever wanted to go to the movies one afternoon instead of working he just had to mention it to her. Marc laughed, pulling down the corners of his mouth.

'And don't forget he has brothers,' said Agnes, also laughing. 'They might need to go to the movies some time, too.'

'Are they as handsome as you?' asked Tillie.

'Of course,' said Marc, as Agnes clapped her hands over her mouth, over her laughter. 'But alas, they are in Paris.' They were mocking Tillie and she did not know it.

William would have laughed out loud at Tillie, making a fool of herself like that, if his cheeks had not been made of lead, too heavy to rise into a laugh.

On the way to the car, Agnes and Tillie moved ahead of William, and as he stared they both became pieces of wood, logs, stumping along, clumping along, primitive puppets.

William himself was scarcely able to place one foot in front of the other. He was working hard at not falling against a wall, at staying upright, moving, doing something to stop himself from slanting to one side, subsiding onto the cobblestones and never getting up.

'I'll drive,' said Tillie when they got to the car, and Agnes held the seat forward so that William could climb in the back.

William crawled into bed, and when Tillie finally cast herself down beside him, neither said anything. William lay on his back, his hands clasped under his head in order to stop them finding their way to Tillie next to him. In any case, Tillie had left the alcove curtain open, and beyond, Agnes lay on the sofa, tossing and turning.

The next morning, he still felt empty and incapable. He heard Tillie in the kitchen with Agnes, making coffee, planning the day's work.

The only Barbarian William liked, the only person he could talk to was Mat, the wife of Cato. She was the only person who showed any interest in him.

'If you'd talk a bit more, make an effort,' Tillie said if he expressed this complaint, 'they'd take you in. You do nothing to help yourself.'

When Cato and Mat's baby was born, they called him Thor and decided that he should call them by their first names to help him escape the oppression of a mother and a father. William imagined that it was Cato's idea and that Mat had been pressed into agreement, that she would have preferred Mummy and Daddy, Mother and Father, Mami and Papi.

'Oh no,' said Mat, when William suggested that this might have been the case. 'It was my idea completely.'

They were in the kitchen preparing salad as usual while Cato, Tillie, Agnes, Marc and the others were gathered around the table in the next room, proofreading and conferring. Baby Thor crawled at their feet.

'What did you call your parents?' Mat asked William.

William blushed.

'Come on,' cried Mat.

'Well, Dadda,' said William, and Mat shrieked with laughter. 'And Mumma.'

Mat had to lean against the counter so that she would not fall over from laughing.

'That was when I was little,' William said over Mat's laughter. 'I changed it to Father and Mother.'

Then William too, began to laugh, and together they giggled as they tore up parsley and scattered it in the salad bucket.

'Sometimes,' said Mat, hauling Thor away from the bucket, giving him a sprig of parsley to contemplate, 'sometimes I think Cato and all of them are stupid. Dummies, as you say in England. And yet they all have the air of being super-clever.'

William loved hearing this. He nodded, wanting Mat to go on. The tears were running down his cheeks from the onions he was now chopping.

'In bed he talks about nothing but *The Barbarian*,' said Mat. 'He is always so tired. *The Barbarian* uses him up, and there's not much left for me.'

'Do you want to leave him?' William asked. 'Don't you want to run away?'

Mat laughed. 'Of course not. I love him. I don't really mind. And it is a good cause, to change the world, so that the world will survive. They are absolutely right about the state of Europe, the corruption, the immorality of the governments, everything. Eventually what they're saying now will be generally accepted, but the Barbarians will not get any credit for having done all the thinking. And Cato is happy doing this work.'

'But you're not,' said William. He took the mountain of chopped onions and as he went to scrape them into the bucket, he trod on little Thor with the heel of his boot. Thor screamed, William picked him up, thinking he had crushed some vital part of this little person, maimed him for life.

'I didn't mean to,' he stammered.

'It's all right,' said Mat, taking the bellowing baby, now red-faced, blanketed in tears, a big round black hole for a mouth. She put Thor's fingers into her mouth to suck the pain away and comfort him.

Cato came running in. 'What's the matter? What has happened to my son?' And he seized Thor from Mat and clutched him to his chest, opening up the hurt hand to see if it was damaged. Thor screamed more loudly.

'He's all right,' said Mat calmly.

'I'm sorry,' said William, 'very, very sorry. I didn't see him on the floor. I didn't mean to step on him.'

Mat put her arm around William to comfort him. 'Babies are always getting trodden on.' She paused for a moment, then added, 'It's a baby's destiny, really, to get trodden on.'

Tillie came in. 'What did William do to Thor?

William stood with his head bowed. He could always run out of the house and never come back, running up hill and down dale and disappear, a little black dot, over the horizon. That option was always open to him. 'Didn't mean to. Very, very sorry.'

Tillie and Cato took Thor with them into the living room. Mat kissed William on the cheek. 'I am happy this way, you know. It's my destiny. This is my place. But I think you are not sure if it is yours? I think you can always recognise when you have to take a new path and when you should stay where you are.'

William saw himself as that little boy in pyjamas at the fork in the road, in the book that Rose had insisted on reading to him. He stood having to choose between the beautiful, easy, enticing road and the narrow, thorny, difficult road. Surely he had always chosen the difficult path, the correct path.

'How do you recognise the path?' he asked Mat.

'You just do,' said Mat. 'And already you have taken a new path. You left your home and your people. That was courageous. I could never do that. My family, my parents whom I love are here in Brussels. I didn't have to make any decision.'

'Leaving was easy,' said William. There was no courage involved. It would have taken courage to stay. He had taken the easy path, after all. He wanted urgently to tell Mat about the axe and Rose and Wally and about the discovery of his real name. But he turned away from her. It was tremendously exciting, the thought of taking out his past, his secrets, his treasure, and showing it to someone special, a woman. But it should be his love, and that was Tillie, who received this gift.

'And now I have Thor,' said Mat. 'I could never leave.'

'My mother left me, once,' William said. This confidence he would give to Mat.

'Why?'

'I don't know,' said William.

'Didn't you ask?'

The Barbarians in the living room were laughing. The

think-tank was over for the time being, which meant that Mat and William could join them and sit drinking wine. Mat carried the plates in. Didn't you ask? Mat had said, and then whisked herself away from him. She was already in the other room laughing and tickling Cato. How could she say what she had said in the kitchen about Cato and now act as if she was the happiest wife in the world?

William entered with the salad. Tillie was frowning at Mat's display. William put down the salad and touched Tillie's hair, trying a little display of his own. Tillie pulled away, shrugging him off. Even in her sleep she pushed him away, muttering 'Stop fiddling with me,' as he tried to lie with his arms around her unobtrusively. When Cato pushed Mat away, she simply smiled and rumpled his hair.

'Just bring in some wine,' Cato said, and Mat, winking at William, got up and went into the kitchen.

It was British Trade Month in Brussels, a festival whose purpose was to encourage the Belgians to buy more British exports. At work William was to write a brief feature on the activities of the British, an assignment passed on to him by the two reporters, who were busy with Market meetings. The London reporter said, 'See what you can do with this,' then the New York reporter said, 'We're giving you a break. You said you were interested in writing.'

William had started the piece with, 'The unsuspecting tourist in Brussels this week may think that his travel agent had delivered him to the wrong city. Hundreds of Union Jacks are flapping in the autumn breeze and red double-decker London buses cruise the streets of the Belgian capital.' He read it aloud, saying terrorist instead of tourist, for a moment transforming his dull paragraph into something interesting.

The reporters returned early with documents and reports

under their arms. William proffered his feature story, and they read it in turn while William stood to one side, beside their desks, like a schoolboy who had handed in a composition.

'A bit twee, isn't it?' said the London reporter handing it back to William, and the two reporters turned to each other in their chairs and began discussing the confidential report that had just been leaked to them, about electronic eavesdropping devices installed by the Common Market security service on all telephones in the Common Market headquarters. As he retreated to his chair in the pantry, William recognised that it was the document Tillie had been wanting to get her hands on. William leant back in his chair. The reporters were leaning back in their chairs, their hands behind their heads, their feet on their desks, and were arriving at the conclusion that they should not use the confidential report on bugging since it would compromise their sources and stir up the already volatile situation vis-a-vis the students, who had taken to the streets in all the countries of Europe. They did not want to foment the unrest. They would ignore the document for the time being. And off they went again to cover something else.

William tore up his meek paragraphs about British Trade Month and used the official handouts provided by the British information people. The document Tillie wanted rested on the desks of his employers. If he told her about it, she would force him to steal it, and he could not steal. He had pleaded guilty to a charge of assault; he had originated a plan to stop all the trains of Europe; but he did not want to steal. He, too, decided to say nothing at all about it.

While he was in the lavatory filling the kettle, a boy from the street walked into the office. At first William thought he was delivering something and he called out that he would be there in a minute. Then the boy ran out, and when William went back to his desk and found his jacket on the floor he understood that the boy had stolen his wallet. He chased the boy down the stairs onto the street, shouting, 'Stop, thief!' But the boy had disappeared. William called the police and haltingly explained the theft, searching for the words for thief, for steal, for wallet. Then when the police asked for the address and his name, he hung up, remembering who he was, afraid that it would be discovered that he was working illegally and somehow that he was William Badger, wanted for assault in Sydney, Australia.

When the reporters breezed back in, they listened to William's sad story of the theft, looked at each other, then the American reporter simply opened the petty cash box and took out some money, a few notes, and without looking at him held them out in William's direction, as if they were carrots for a horse, and started discussing the confidential report again. William hesitated, humiliated, wishing he did not need the money. The American reporter jabbed the notes at William, then let them drop onto the corner of his desk, and began making phone calls to contacts.

William looked at the men, then down at the money, and because he needed it he reached out and picked it up, knowing that as soon as the reporters went out again he would indeed steal their document and begin photocopying it to give to Tillie.

'I love you,' he told Tillie that night, holding onto her in bed rather more earnestly than usual. He would surprise her with the document when he had finished copying it.

'That is a word that has no meaning,' said Tillie, but gently this time. She had had a good day with the Barbarians.

William was photocopying the confidential report on electronic eavesdropping when the phone rang.

'*Héllo, non, il n'est pas là,*' said William slowly.

But the voice on the phone was speaking English. It was the foreign editor of the London paper calling from London.

'For God's sake, what are you doing there?' the voice cried, and William guiltily held the report to his chest. 'There's a fire, the fire of the century, in that old bookstore.' The voice paused. 'Are you there?'

'Yes,' said William.

'Just down the hill from you, in that big building,' yelled the editor. 'That architectural treasure. You know it, don't you? Horta or someone?'

'There's no one here at the moment,' said William. 'They'll be back later.'

'We've picked it up on the wire service. We need something of our own. People are dying.'

William looked out the window and saw the smoke down the hill in the centre of the old city. It had taken a call from London for him to learn that Brussels, almost where he stood copying a secret document, was burning. The London reporter was at a meeting of ministers, and the New York man was at Casteau interviewing a NATO general.

'You do it,' ordered the London editor. 'File something, quickly.'

William locked the door of the office and walked as slowly as he could down the hill toward the fire. This was his big chance, to write the story of the worst fire in Europe in the twentieth century. The narrow streets were blocked with cars and trams and several red double-decker buses sent over from London and fire engines trying to get through. William had not even heard the noise.

The burning building was a huge, art nouveau structure, its main feature the enormous windows, several storeys high, leaded into small squares. It stood in the middle of the old city, surrounded by lanes and cobblestoned streets, now festooned with red, white and blue streamers for British Trade Month. The Union Jack draped across the front of the burning building, above the entrance to the bookstore, which was featuring work by British writers, caught fire and disappeared in a blaze of light. A record store nearby piped Beatles songs onto the street. A Scottish military band in kilts stood in the middle of a little square, having stopped playing their bagpipes, and were watching the smoke and flames, becoming spectators rather than performers, blending with the horrified crowd.

William watched the flames leaping behind the beautiful windows and the faces of the shoppers and office workers, distorted by their screams, pressed against the leaded squares. They had broken the squares of glass and could reach their arms out. Three storeys up a mother was forcing her child through one of the tiny openings. The child had been poked through feet first and although its legs were cut by the glass, all had gone well until the shoulders. The legs were waving in the air and the body was stuck at the shoulders.

The faces turned from the windows, the arms went up over the heads, and William saw the bodies engulfed in smoke and flames. The child's body stayed wedged in the square of lead.

William tried to write what he had seen, mentioning the screams and the child. The whole afternoon he wrote and rewrote the story.

In the end he filed two sentences, typing them out on a sheet of paper and then transferring them to the telex. 'A fire destroyed a historic building in Brussels this afternoon. Hundreds of people died in the blaze.' He had heard the crowds talking about the hundreds trapped. Then he changed 'died' to 'perished.'

The London office telexed back immediately. 'When we say brief we don't mean two sentences telling us what we learned from the wire hours ago. Get rid of that nincompoop, for God's sake.'

William was about to stuff the reprimand in his pocket when the London reporter returned. 'There's a serious fire down the hill,' he said, taking the telex message from William's hand.

He did not even look at William. Neither of the reporters looked at him, ever. Bending over the telex, without sitting down, the reporter typed out the London connection and let them know a new story would be on its way shortly. He made a few phone calls, then went down the hill to get interviews and vivid details.

'It may well be the worst fire disaster in modern times,' he wrote when he came back. 'It may well be' was the phrase he liked to use in his news stories when he did not have the precise facts. He gave William the story, page by page as he typed it, and William telexed it as quickly as he could for the next day's paper in London. The story was full of colour. Screaming victims were trapped on relentlessly moving escalators that carried them up into the searing flames. The books in the ground floor bookstore fuelled the fire. Within minutes the building was like a furnace. The smoke blotted out the exit signs. Millions of francs were lost in property damage. Hundreds of people were missing. There was no mention of the boy stuck in the little lead window square, and William nursed this image, this private horror and did not tell the reporter about it.

He wanted only to lie with Tillie in her dark cave and beg her to wrap her arms around him.

The London reporter came in with the next sheet of his story and stood by the door, waiting for William to get off the phone.

'You can go home,' he told William when he had finished telexing the fire story, as if he wanted him out of sight. Afterwards he never mentioned the incident, never referred to William's inadequacy and the reprimand from the London office, but just kept giving him the filing, the typing and telexing, and the errands. And William left, with the copy of the secret document folded into the newspaper he was carrying.

The fire had disrupted the whole city and the traffic, congested at the best of times, sat still on all the roads. William walked home. He stopped to buy tomatoes, selecting them one by one with his right hand, holding them away from his body so that the grocer would not suspect him of stealing. His left arm with the newspaper and stolen document was clamped against his body.

'Ten,' he said, '*dix*,' and counted them out, '*un, deux, trois*,' and as he counted out the tomatoes, holding each one and slightly moving his fingers without squeezing to ascertain the degree of ripeness, he thought of soft flesh in flames and felt he might well collapse. '*Quatre, cinq, six, sept.*' On everything he looked at was superimposed the after-image of the child trapped in the window.

As William sat on the sofa, his head in his hands, waiting for Tillie to return, the phone rang. He was afraid to answer it, but since it might be the police calling to say Tillie had been killed in an accident, a fire, he picked up the receiver.

'*Qui, oui, non,*' he stammered and tried to explain in French that the caller had made a mistake, had dialled a wrong number. He hung up, unnerved by the call. Then the phone rang again, and again the caller hung up.

Just then Tillie opened the door and dashed in. 'There's been a terrible fire,' she said.

William nodded. 'I have seen people burned to death.'

Tillie knelt on the floor beside William's legs and leant forward to put her arms around his waist, resting her head against him.

'Come and lie down,' she said. 'Tell me about it.'

Gratefully William let her lead him into the alcove and nudge him gently onto the bed. She lay down beside him, patting his shoulders, holding his head to her, murmuring his name. William fell in love with her all over again.

'I'll tell you why I was in jail,' said William. And he told Tillie everything, about the axe and Rose and Wally, but despite his great love for her, he stopped short of telling her about the discovery of his real name. He wanted to keep something in reserve. 'Are you disappointed?' he asked her. 'You thought I was some hero.'

'That was heroic,' said Tillie. 'To take the blame for the violence of someone else.'

William clung to her and after a while asked, 'Do you love me?' His voice was husky, as if he had been crying, although he had not actually shed tears.

'Sh, sh,' said Tillie, holding him close. 'That sort of question has no meaning.'

William fell asleep, although it was still early in the evening, and he slept for several hours, until something awakened him. He sat up straight, trying to fathom what was on his mind. Tillie was asleep beside him. Then he remembered. He shook Tillie awake.

'I have something for you,' he said, slipping out of bed and switching on the light. He had remembered the stolen document folded into the newspaper. The sofa bed was unfolded, and in it was a sleeping mound, no doubt Agnes, who grunted and sat up.

'What's going on?' she grumbled, closing her eyes against the light.

'The newspaper,' gasped William, searching around

Agnes's bed. He had left it on the sofa. Or had he left it in the grocer's. Had Tillie thrown it away?

'Go back to bed,' Agnes growled.

William was on his hands and knees beside her, peering under the sofa, where he found the newspaper. With a cry he drew it out and shook out the document, which he seized, and rushing to Tillie he thrust it at her.

'Look what I have for you,' he said, 'Just look.'

'Can't all this wait?' Agnes asked.

But Tillie, half-asleep, shaking her head and groaning, actually took the sheets of paper and began reading them.

'My God,' she said. 'Agnes, Agnes!' She leapt out of bed and shook Agnes to awaken her thoroughly. 'Look what we have, for *The Barbarian*.' She turned back to William, standing modestly by the bed, his hands behind his back, looking at his toes. 'William, you are a hero. This is what we have been trying to get our hands on.' She began to read the document. 'Those bastards,' she muttered from time to time. 'You're simply not supposed to tap people's phones in a free society,' she said. 'But they do, and *no one cares*! No one wants to hear about it.' She read on, then looked up. 'Why,' she asked, 'why don't people see that this kind of intrusion, this kind of activity means that *all* rights are at risk?'

Tillie was right. William understood that. 'People aren't ready to hear what you're saying,' he said. 'It is too frightening.'

'You really are a hero,' Tillie sang, looking up from the document. 'Cato will be so pleased.'

Back in bed, William held her again, and she did not push him away. He sighed. 'I love you, Tillie, I really love you.'

And gently she said, 'It isn't love that you are feeling.'

Cato and Mat were staging a party outdoors in the overgrown field next to their old, tilting house to celebrate the acquisition of the secret document on wiretapping. It was midsummer's eve.

Dozens of Barbarians and their friends were milling about, talking and eating. William quickly withdrew to the periphery, protected by the deepening dusk.

The Barbarians moved this way and that in a choreography they all knew. Cato presided over the fire, poking sausages with a fork, squirting mustard on a sausage when someone held out a plate. The groups formed, chattering in French, German, Dutch, Italian. Tillie was talking rapidly, her lips puckered, her voice rising and falling, a splendid performance. Even Mat was performing, flitting around, flirting with her friends.

William lay down in the grass. Marc crashed past him into the bushes to pee, blotting out Tillie's words, then as he returned, he stepped on William's hand and tripped over his legs. Marc picked himself up and gave William an indifferent look. William scrambled to his feet.

'Marc just took a leak in the garden,' Tillie howled and told everyone about Anthony Quinn and the leek, broadcasting to the cast of thousands their private joke.

Mat banged a stick against the salad bucket then raised her glass. 'You must all drink to William Longleg, who stole the secret document, and to a new, enlightened Europe,' she commanded.

'Europe!' they all cried, as Marc dashed to seize a glass and hold it aloft.

Then William heard his name. Tillie was telling them all the story of William's life, about Rose and the attack with the axe and his escape from jail. His precious life, his secret, had become just another anecdote. She would have told the story of his name, too, if he had been foolish enough to confess it.

William edged up to Tillie and told her he wanted to leave.

'You can go,' she said. 'I'll come later.'

And William left.

At the flat, William stood before the 'Scene from Enkhuizen'. It was still early, only ten o'clock. Four hours later, he finished the puzzle. He lay heavily in bed, the bed of Tillie and William, and did not sleep until the birds started to sing just before dawn. Tillie was there when he awoke, asleep beside him. He lay still, his head propped up on one hand, and looked at her, her mouth straight and stern in sleep, her hair adorned with twigs and grass from the party. The alcove curtain was not drawn and he could see that Agnes was not on the sofa. He went to the kitchen and sat down, very quietly drinking coffee. His back ached from the hours bent over the jigsaw puzzle the night before. William and Tillie had spent perhaps a hundred hours together working on it. She had never seemed to notice that he kept dismantling it, a few pieces here and there, while she was away.

William swept the kitchen floor, massed the bits of paper that Tillie had scribbled on into one pile, and dusted around the puzzle. He was going to preserve it. He would lacquer it and frame it.

'Why did you tell them all about me?' he asked Tillie when she awoke. 'All my secrets?'

'You have impressive credentials,' said Tillie. 'I thought you'd like the attention.'

When the special issue of *The Barbarian* appeared, it became a news item in all the major European papers, and even in *The New York Times*. *The Barbarian* was finally being noticed. There was an outcry against the Common Market's tapping its own employees' telephones. The Director-General said he knew nothing about it, but promised to discontinue the practice and dismantle the apparatus. *The Barbarian* had become a legitimate journal.

At the office, the two reporters were furious, and they told William they no longer needed him.

'We don't know who leaked the document,' the American reporter told William, 'but we have been compromised. And you have connections with *The Barbarian*, we know that. Our sources within the Market may never tell us another thing.'

'Congratulations!' Tillie cried, when William told her he had been fired. 'We've done what we needed to do. Thanks to you.'

'Will you marry me?' William asked. Tillie's praise made anything possible, miracles, anything.

'I tell you what. Let's go away for a couple of days. A seaside holiday. Ostend, Knokke. Just you and me.'

'And you'll marry me?'

Tillie took a deep breath. 'Maybe.'

William spread his arms and snapped his fingers, letting out a hoot. He thought he might just dance, dip and stamp in an abandoned way. Tillie frowned and pointed at the ceiling. William stopped his noise and stood with his arms open, and Tillie, still frowning, stepped to him, so that he could enfold her and kiss her. Then he led her to the puzzle.

'A gift,' he said proudly, 'The "Scene from Enkhuizen" is completed. We'll pack it carefully in the box without disturbing it too much, and then we'll have it framed.'

Tillie looked at him for a moment, smiling, then picked up the edge of the puzzle and gave it a flick.

'Don't!' William cried.

Tillie flicked the puzzle again. The pieces fell apart.

'We've spent all this time doing it,' said William. He placed his hand flat on the half of the puzzle that remained intact.

Tillie pushed his hand away and smashed the whole thing, picking up the groups of four or five pieces that stayed attached to one another and scattering them on the table.

'Why did you do that?' William asked, heartbroken.

'You always want to hang on to everything, don't you? You cling to the status quo, like an entrenched government,' said Tillie. 'Listen, we'll go away to the seaside, and then, then, okay, we'll definitely get married.'

William cleaned the flat then retyped an article that Tillie had written for the next issue of *The Barbarian*, on the American presence in Europe, so that she would be free to go off with him to the seaside, just the two of them, no Agnes, no Barbarians of any description. He had packed their bags and all that was required was Tillie's return from Cato's. He had planned their route, wandering through the countryside rather than going directly along the highway to the coast.

It was midnight when Tillie came in, radiant. She was carrying a box of balloons and a footpump. William was sitting on the sofa dozing. Tillie went over to him and sat close beside him, snuggling against him.

'It's all ready,' she breathed. 'We'll go in the morning.'

William startled, sat up. 'You're so late,' he mumbled. 'We were supposed to leave today.'

'You're in charge from now on,' Tillie said. 'I'll do whatever you say, as long as we end up in Ostend tomorrow evening.'

'What's the hurry?' William asked.

'There's just something that has to be done in Ostend, and then we'll be free.'

William explained to her his plan, to meander through Flanders.

'And so we shall,' said Tillie. 'We can still make it to Ostend in time.' She held up her hand in case William should object. 'And look!' She reached behind her head and cheerfully snapped off the rubber band that held it back so tightly and shook her hair free. 'There, that makes you happy, doesn't it?'

Because of the heavy early-morning fog, William drove slowly south a little, then west, his own gloom deepening in proportion to Tillie's cheerfulness, which had only grown since the night before. Her hair, still loose, blew about her face in the breeze from the open window, and she was smiling. If this elation of hers continued, she would not need him at all.

On the back seat were the box of balloons, the foot pump, and a Belgian flag. They were to go to the Kursaal in Ostend, where an exhibition of turn-of-the-century art and civilisation was due to open late that afternoon. They were to inflate fifty balloons, drape the flag over themselves, and while the mayor was making the opening speech, William and Tillie were to pop the balloons in quick succession, obliterating what was certain to be a fatuous address and symbolically rendering harmless the guns of the militarists.

'We've told our contacts at *Le Soir* and the other papers to expect something,' said Tillie. 'Cheer up, it'll be fun. It'll give our seaside holiday a purpose.'

They stopped for lunch at a shabby-looking cafe called The Constantinople, which stood alone at the edge of a country road, surrounded by fields of wheat still shrouded in fog. Beside the cafe was a small clearing, reclaimed from the wheatfield, where several cars were parked, and a few jeeps stood on the dirt shoulder of the road. Because it was midday, the fog was bright and white, almost dazzling.

The cafe was surprisingly dark. The windows were covered with black cloth, and candles in chianti bottles seemed to provide the only illumination. Faded paper chains, which must have been up since the New Year, dropped from the burlap covering the ceiling. In the corner was a pinball machine.

William and Tillie stood for several moments in the doorway while their eyes adjusted to the gloom, listening to the hum of voices and rowdy laughter.

There were only a few customers in the cafe, all men, all in uniform, and they were speaking English.

'The U.S. military,' exclaimed Tillie. 'They must have driven over from Casteau or somewhere.'

'Let's go somewhere else,' William suggested. The tone in Tillie's voice promised trouble.

'No, we'll stay here.'

She led William to a table in a corner, and as they sat down a large, pretty young woman, her face glowing in the candlelight, got up from the table where she was sitting surrounded by American soldiers and came over to them.

'Rosa, Rosa, come back here,' one of the soldiers called after her, his speech slurred.

'Moment,' she called back, then winked at William and shrugged. 'Your order?' She spoke in Flemish.

'Rosa, come back,' the soldier called and waved a twenty-dollar bill in the air. 'This is for you.'

'I have big debts,' she said apologetically, explaining her fraternising with the soldiers. She switched to French, guessing William and Tillie to be French-speakers. 'And I have a son to take care of.'

Rosa took their order for beer and shashlick, which was the only food offered, broiled behind the bar and smothered in tomato sauce. 'Americans like it like that,' Rosa said, when she brought the food. She returned to sit at the table with the rowdy servicemen, fiddling with the candle wax dripping down the side of the bottle and laughing at the jokes of the soldiers.

'Capitalism corrupts,' said Tillie. 'There you have a living lesson in front of you.'

The Americans were drinking spirits and cognac, paying with large notes and telling Rosa to keep the change. Rosa was animated, leaning on her elbow, jumping up to gather the empty glasses, swinging around the bar, making the new drinks.

'She only wants to get money from them. She has to make a living, too,' said William.

One of the soldiers pulled his chair close to Rosa and put his arm around her shoulder.

'Look how he is demeaning her,' said Tillie.

'She knows what she's doing,' said William.

'Rosa,' Tillie called out.

The soldiers at Rosa's table turned at the sound of another woman's voice.

'Rosa, *s'il vous plaît, encore une bière.*' Tillie called for another beer, trying to rescue Rosa.

Rosa went to get up, but was held in her chair by her soldier. 'Just leave her alone,' William whispered.

'You leave me alone,' Tillie hissed back. 'I know what I'm doing.'

William got up angrily and went to the pinball machine in the corner.

'Here,' the soldier called to Tillie. 'Drink. Here. With us. *Avec nous.* Go get her,' he said to one of the other soldiers, who got up and made his way to Tillie, clicking his heels, saluting, bowing and waving his hand towards Rosa's table.

He addressed Tillie. 'Please, silver plate, *mademoiselle*, come and drink with us.' He raised one hand to his mouth in a drinking motion and then pointed at the table.

'*Laissez-moi*,' Tillie replied.

William, his back to it all, resisted turning. He knew that Tillie was enjoying pretending to be a Belgian, enjoying the whole situation. He knew that Tillie intended to get involved, no matter what he said, in order to make some kind of point. P'p'ping, went his machine, ping, ping, ping. As long as she did not expect him to do anything. P'p'ping.

The soldier took Tillie's hand, and she allowed herself to be led over to their table and seated in the chair that the others pulled up for her.

One of the soldiers, reeling a little, went over to William at the pinball machine and stood watching his progress.

'You know the Berlin Wall?' he asked after a while.

William nodded.

'You think the American government didn't want the Russians to build the Berlin Wall, right?'

William nodded. 'Right,' he said.

'You thought the Americans might go to war over that wall, right?'

'Right.'

'Wrong. Dead wrong.' The soldier looked around, then whispered loudly. 'We, the Americans, let the Russians put it up. We gave them *permission* to put it up, don't you see? We as good as *asked* them to put it up. The Russians would have stopped if we'd done something, but Kennedy said, "Let them put up a wall. It's what we want, too." Don't you see? We don't want the Germans united. We want them divided. And we get brownie points for saying it's the Communists who do things like that.'

'Two *mademoiselles*,' Rosa's soldier shouted from his table. 'Our lucky day in this dead country.' Then to Tillie he said, 'Got any sisters back home?'

Tillie frowned, questioning, feigning incomprehension.

'Sister, sisters, like you. Any more back home.'

One of the soldiers made the silhouette of a woman with his hands and whistled.

The soldier at William's side tapped his arm. 'You ask how I know this? Right?'

'Right,' said William. 'How do you know this?'

'My brother was there, in the army, like me now. He heard Kennedy's order relayed on the military radio. "Let them build their wall. It's what we want." He heard that loud and clear.'

'Rosa, leave these military pigs and sit with us over there,' Tillie said loudly in French.

Rosa shook her head slightly and leaning against her soldier smiled up at him and said, 'More? Cognac? Double?'

'Double cognacs all round,' said her soldier. He stood up, surprisingly short, perhaps only as tall as Tillie, and much shorter than the robust Rosa.

'He's a Napoleon,' Tillie said to Rosa. 'No good, trouble, Rosa.'

The little soldier counted heads. 'Six double cognacs,' he said. 'Sis.' He held up six fingers. 'Urn, der, twa, carter, sink, sis,' then looking over at William at the machine, 'set,' holding up seven fingers. 'One for the pretty boy in the corner.'

He pulled out several notes and flourished them under Rosa's nose. She grabbed them quickly and went to the bar. 'Keep the change, sweetheart,' the soldier called after her.

Rosa blew him a kiss and brought back the cognacs and placed them on the table.

'Drink, drink,' said the soldier, pushing a glass toward Tillie. 'Take it.' And he kept pushing the glass, flicking it with his finger, as if it were a marble. Tillie made no move to take it, and he would have pushed it right off the table into Tillie's lap, if Rosa had not picked it up and placed it firmly in front of Tillie.

'I drink only beer,' said Tillie.

Rosa whispered, 'Please, for me, please, take it. Don't cause trouble.' She picked up William's glass and took it to him at the pinball machine. 'Compliment,' she cried gaily, and sailed back to the table. Still standing, she took her own cognac, raised it aloft, and said haltingly in English, 'To friends.' She pretended to drink, then resumed her seat.

The men downed their cognacs. Tillie did not lift her glass but pushed it farther from her. Rosa laughed, reminding them all that they were having a good time. 'Let us have fun,' she said. Rosa reached into her soldier's pocket for one of his cigarettes, patting his chest as she drew it out, and leant toward him for a light. He held his lighter several inches from Rosa's cigarette, compelling her to lean forward even more, and then he held it over his head.

'Ah, Statue of Liberty,' said Rosa and stood up to get her cigarette to the lighter.

The soldier then stood up, his hand still raised, and Rosa, laughing, reached up to grab his wrist to bring the light to her. The soldier stood on his chair, the lighter now out of Rosa's reach again.

'*Attention*,' said Rosa. 'The paper.'

She pointed, and the soldier saw that the flame of his lighter had come close to setting the paper streamers alight. He moved it even closer to the streamers and with his other hand pointed at Tillie.

'Drink your cognac,' he ordered.

'Only beer,' said Tillie.

'Drink it.'

William went to Tillie's side. Rosa was standing on her chair pushing the soldier's raised arm away from the paper chain.

'Drink it and come away,' said William quietly.

'English!' shouted the soldier. 'She's English, and so's he! And she won't drink with us.' He set the streamer alight. The flame gobbled up the paper.

Rosa shrieked, '*Merde*,' and dropping her unlit cigarette tore the burning streamer down and stamped out the flames. Then she got down on her knees to retrieve the cigarette.

William grabbed Tillie's arm and hauled Tillie back to their corner table. 'For God's sake stop meddling,' he said. 'This is her turf. Let her do what she wants.'

'Pigs,' said Tillie. 'Someone's got to take a stand some time. They've spoiled this place, the military has spoiled the whole world, and they're corrupting an innocent Belgian waitress.'

Rosa was now sitting with her back to William and Tillie, her cigarette lit, and she was talking with the soldiers as if nothing had happened.

'I don't know about innocent,' said William. 'Let's get out of here.'

'No,' said Tillie. 'This is part of our education, don't you see that?' She looked ready to jump up again and continue her battle.

William grasped her arm. 'Do you want to know what I just learned?' He would tell Tillie about the Berlin Wall in an effort to distract her from whatever action she was planning against the table of soldiers.

'It's not true, that the Americans were against the wall.'

'Against what wall?' Tillie asked absently.

'The Berlin Wall. They allowed it to be built. The Americans lied.'

Tillie was still staring over at Rosa and the soldiers. 'Of course they lied. Governments always lie to their people. Always.'

'Your American cigarettes so good,' Rosa was saying.

The soldier took the whole pack from his pocket and placed it on the table.

'Yours,' he said. But when Rosa reached out to take it, he placed his hand over hers. 'But not yet.'

The three other soldiers at their table drifted to the pinball machine, leaving Rosa and the little soldier together.

'I'm from Texas,' he was shouting now, 'and I have money to burn.' He took out five ten-dollar bills and placed them on the table. 'Hey!' he called to his friends.

The soldiers, mumbling and stumbling, went back to the table. 'Not today. Not again.'

'Sure,' Tex said. 'It's the only fun we get.' Rosa did not know what was happening. Tex picked up one of the notes. 'Yours,' he said to Rosa.

She sat still, puzzled, smiling.

'Yours,' he said again and waved the note up and down in front of her.

Rosa hesitantly reached out to take it, and he whipped it away.

'What can we do?' said Tillie. 'We must save her.'

'She wants the money,' said William. 'Leave her alone.'

The soldier took out his lighter and held it next to the note. 'Yours, Rosa.' He set the note alight.

Rosa grabbed it from him, extinguishing the flames in her fist. She opened her hand, uncrumpled the note to see how much damage had been done. One corner had burned slightly, but the note was intact. She put it in her pocket.

'Yours,' the soldier said, and set fire to the next note.

Rosa, gasping as she understood his intention, reached for it, extinguished the flames, and again spread it out carefully. She folded it and put it in her pocket.

'Gutsy,' said the little soldier. He lit the third note, which Rosa grabbed. She was sobbing now.

'Should we call the police?' Tillie asked.

'No,' said William, surprised that Tillie should think of resorting to the system.

'Rosa,' Tillie called, and Rosa turned to look at her.

'Yours,' said the soldier again, and Rosa turned back, but the fourth note had burned too far for her to save it, and she watched it shrivel and turn to ash.

'So, you don't need money?' asked the soldier. 'What was this story you were telling, about debts and the boy in the hospital, eh? I'm only trying to help you.'

'Leave now,' said Rosa to the soldiers.

'We'll call the police,' said Tillie, standing up and addressing the whole room.

'No,' Rosa said quickly. 'No police, just go.'

'Ah, the English girl finally condescends to talk to us,' said the little soldier. 'Call the police and I'll tell them this barmaid is getting us drunk and stealing our money.'

He blew the ashes of the fourth note off the table, then he picked up the last note. 'Yours,' he said quietly, setting it alight.

Rosa flattened it against the table with her hands, then bundled it into her pocket.

'Now we're ready to leave this dump,' said the little soldier, 'this slum,' and stood up. He picked up the pack of cigarettes and walked to the door. Rosa stayed sitting at the table, looking at her hands, crying.

The soldier turned. 'Here's your tip for giving us some fun. It was all just a joke. A practical joke.' He took all the cigarettes out of the pack he was holding and threw them at Rosa. They hit her and scattered over the floor. 'I told you they were yours,' he said.

The soldiers left.

William and Tillie ran to Rosa, who had crossed her arms and wedged her hands tight under her armpits. She pushed them away.

'Leave me alone,' she said. 'I made a lot of money today, for once.'

Rosa picked up the cigarettes, one by one, William and Tillie helping her, in silence, before she went to the sink behind the bar and placed her hands under the running water.

In the car William, his hands on the wheel, was sitting without starting it up, shaken from the incident in the cafe. 'Now shall we begin our seaside holiday?'

'There's an article for *The Barbarian* in this,' said Tillie.

So that was why she had been so willing to get involved with Rosa and the American servicemen.

'No,' said Tillie, when William expressed this thought. 'It was you who caused that scene at the cafe. I was just trying to protect another woman. If you had kept quiet and not spoken to me in English, that Hitler wouldn't have gone on like that.'

Again William was overcome by the now familiar, dizzy weightlessness. If he succumbed and just lay down on the ground, he need never get up again.

'What was all that about the Berlin Wall?' Tillie asked.

'I'll tell you in Ostend,' said William, starting the car, now feeling an urgency to reach the coast, to get away from the cafe.

Tillie tapped her fingers on the dashboard in front of him, d'd'dit, dah dah dah, d'd'dit. Suddenly she turned to him. 'Maybe Cato is right about you, fugitive or no fugitive.

Your name probably really is Longleg and your whole family has a dubious past. He wanted to know what they were up to in the thirties and during the war.'

'Leave my name out of this,' said William. He drove to the highway, where he headed for Ostend, having lost the desire to dawdle in the countryside.

The fog was still heavy, even in mid-afternoon, a freakish phenomenon. Although visibility was ten yards, the drivers were still doing forty miles an hour, as if it were a sunny day. Suddenly the cars in front started jack-knifing, banging into each other in a massive chain collision. As each new car collided into the one in front, they seemed to move in a flock, like sheep, pushing crazily first in one direction then another.

William jammed on the brakes. There were seven trucks and thirty-nine cars in the pile-up. Their car was the fortieth. William stopped just inches from the tangle of vehicles, rising like a heap of junk in the fog.

William parked beside the sand dunes just south of the Ostend promenade and in silence he and Tillie pumped up the balloons, stuffing each one into the trunk of the car and, when that was filled, into the back seat and the front passenger seat. William imagined the car rising into the air and floating off. Tillie had suggested that they disguise themselves as clowns, with make-up, so that people would guess them to be a part of the open-air entertainment offered on the promenade, and they would not be recognised later. But this was too much for William and he refused.

They left the car and went to look at the exhibition before the mayor's speech, to get a sense of the layout of the hall.

'Now tell me about the Berlin Wall,' Tillie said and

listened thoughtfully as William recounted the soldier's story.

'I want to ask you to do something for me,' Tillie said quietly. 'I want you to burst the balloons on your own. I'm taking the train back to Brussels, just for tonight. I'll be back tomorrow. You can do what we have to do here alone.'

'But why?' William asked.

'I have to go back and write about what just happened in that bar, include it in my article.'

'But the article is written and on the way to the printer already.'

'There's time to add another page or two. It's what the article needs, a specific incident to bring home the problem. Cato says my writing is still too dry, too impersonal. I must put in that bit about the Berlin Wall.' Tillie squeezed his shoulder. 'You're the one who unearthed that little gem. It also shows how Europe is shaped by American decisions.'

'Please stay with me,' William said. They were walking slowly away from the hall.

'Don't you see,' Tillie snapped. 'Someone has to do it. I'll rewrite the article. You'll carry out the action in Ostend. It'll be easy. And then we'll get married. Okay?' She was quickening her pace, heading for the station.

'There's just one thing I've been meaning to tell you,' said William.

Tillie raised her eyebrows.

'You know that maroon pleated skirt?'

Tillie nodded.

'It looks terrible on you. It makes your backside look like the side of a bus.'

Tillie walked away from him then turned back for a moment. 'You know that idea of yours about stopping the trains? Well, we abandoned that some time ago. I forgot to tell you. It was a stupid idea. Cato said it verged on the violent, and the Barbarians are nonviolent. Marc thought of something much better, with the balloons.' And she walked off noisily toward the trains.

William stood contemplating the exhibits—the penny-farthing bicycle and Sarah Bernhardt's sky-blue silk dress embroidered with bees swarming in relief around the hem and up to the navel. A nineteenth-century painting by Surand showed naked nymphs dancing around a praying priest. On a table lay a fan in the shape of a woman's face with the wings of a beautiful insect forming the hair. In one poster a group of happy Belgians proclaimed that all intelligent people in Belgium read *Le Flirt* at ten centîmes a copy. *Le Petit Journal* of Paris was opened to a coloured illustration in which assassins were putting an end to a startled President McKinley at a Buffalo exhibition hall. In an alcove near the exit William stood before the sombre, tormented face of Edvard Munch, a self-portrait. He turned away.

William went back to the car. The freak fog was lifting. He stood before the car crammed with inflated balloons. A small group of children and older people out walking had gathered to stare. When William opened the car door, one of the balloons blew off. The children, laughing delightedly, chased it, and when it flew off over the dunes they came running back to the car to see what this strange man would do next. William smiled at them, then opened both doors of the car and set all the balloons free. The children, squealing and yelping, ran off after them. One balloon, lodging under dune scrub, was pecked at by a seagull and burst. From time to time reports of bursting balloons echoed across the beach. The strollers continued on their walks, some of them saying what a nice young man that was to do such a nice thing for the children, letting balloons blow off across the dunes so prettily.

William could not face Tillie now. He could not report this final failure and hear her telling him again he was a man of few words and little action and no doubt refusing to marry him. He left the car where it was and walked along the promenade, joining the strolling Belgians, and when he came to the dock, he simply walked onto the ferry for London. Tillie would never find him. Perhaps this was the new path, and he had recognised it after all, as Mat had predicted, and his name, with the good, long strides it suggested, would help him along it.

Part IV

Amanda was the leader of a group of American students spending their first summer abroad, in London. William Longleg was the driver of the bus Amanda hired to convey her students through their introduction to British culture.

William started watching Amanda in the rear vision mirror the first day, when he drove her and the students past the statue of Lord Baden Powell and listened to her describe it as the only statue in London that paid tribute to a man in shorts. And she remarked that it was fortunate his legs were so handsome.

At first William found Amanda merely fairly attractive, large, the same height as he, like a fine horse, but interesting.

He continued to watch her as they passed the Victoria and Albert, Kensington Gardens, Amelia Pankhurst, the Houses of Parliament, and the cottage that resembled The Old Curiosity Shop, all the way to the British Museum.

While Amanda assembled her students and told them about the treasures of the museum and how to conduct themselves once inside, William sat on the steps and smoked a cigarette.

Standing in groups on the steps were dozens of American academics, professors from Berkeley and Chapel Hill greeting professors from Ann Arbor and Boston, whom they had not seen since the previous summer. They let each other know which journals were bringing out their latest articles in the coming year, and they also worked into their conversations their successes in placing their graduate students in a tight job market.

Amanda herself broke away from her students to greet a man she knew from Chicago. William watched her gesturing, smiling, shifting her weight from one leg to the other, then he noticed that she had moved to the step below the Chicago academic, so that she now looked up at him. She seemed slimmer, altogether more attractive than he had thought in the bus. Amanda waved her students into the museum and stayed talking with the man from Chicago, at one point reaching out to touch his arm, a fleeting public caress. William stubbed out his cigarette. He had begun smoking after he fled Belgium. Even after these years in London, he imagined that Tillie might turn up and confront him with his inadequacies, and the cigarettes seemed to help ward off this possibility, to offer some comfort.

'What are you working on, Ray?' Amanda asked, her mouth returning to an expectant smile between her bursts of words.

William hated questions like that.

'I drive a bus,' he said these days, quietly, if anyone should ask, trying not to sound defensive as he went about in the uniform of the private bus company he worked for— navy blue shirt and trousers and a navy blue windbreaker. Bus driver. Two words.

That afternoon he had thought of buying two tickets for one of the Shakespeares, *Coriolanus* or *All's Well That Ends Well*, to impress Amanda. He had even imagined asking her to accompany him.

The man from Chicago shrugged modestly at Amanda's question. 'Just the same old research. Contemporary culture.'

Amanda laughed. Why did women laugh like that, William wondered, when there was nothing to laugh at? And they laughed without discrimination, for any man at all, squandering their lovely bounty. Amanda seemed aware of William's watching her. She checked her laugh abruptly and looked down at her sandals.

A second American professor loped diagonally across the steps to Amanda and the critic of contemporary culture. He clapped the man on the back, then to Amanda and the world in general he said, 'I see him in Chicago, I see him in London, I see him in Rotterdam, Brussels and Munich, and he never tells us what he is really working on. We all think he's CIA, of course.' He let out a long laugh, then placing his hand on the scholar's elbow, he drew him away, and they turned their backs on Amanda.

Amanda sat down beside William on the steps. 'Could I have one of your cigarettes?' she asked, and to his surprise she patted his shirt pocket and drew out the cigarettes for herself.

William said nothing. He was working on nothing, writing nothing, he knew nothing that would entertain this intelligent woman, more experienced, older, wiser than he, a woman of culture.

'Sometimes it is frightening,' she said, 'the way we feel we must travel, trudge about the world. And it's supposed to be broadening.' She waved her arm at the museum, to indicate her students. 'And after this they do Europe.' She looked at William. 'But you don't need to do that, do you? You seem secure, content.'

William wanted to tell her that he was not content at all, that he was on the contrary really an interesting person. He had trudged around half the world, had experimented with alternative lifestyles, had had his encounters with contemporary culture, had been miserable in love, and he had been in jail.

'I drive a bus,' he said. 'All over London, sometimes all over England. That's travel.'

Amanda laughed, this time for him, touching him lightly on the knee and exhaling the smoke of the cigarette in a small cloud, and suddenly she had become incredibly lovely, gentle-looking, and altogether more fair, more blonde.

'I wish I could drive a bus,' she said. 'But these narrow streets must present problems. Perhaps it will be easier for you in the countryside, when we go to Oxford and Coventry and places.'

'You get used to buses,' William said. 'Turning corners can be tricky, in those tiny village streets.'

They ended their afternoon tour in a pub to show the students that important feature of British culture. Amanda invited William to join her and the students for a drink. He sat at one end of the long, wooden outdoor table, a little apart from the students, who fooled around, talking too loudly.

Amanda sat down beside him. 'This job isn't as easy as it looks,' she said. She patted his pocket again and helped herself to a cigarette, resting the heel of her hand against him. William loved her doing this, like a horse reaching for sugar. He could feel her hand on his chest through the cloth of his shirt.

One of the students, an earnest boy, joined them and began discussing Wren's architecture, directing his observations at Amanda. Another, a young woman William and Amanda came to call Baby Bunting, sat down with them, making pronouncements about life, about the fame of her father in the motion picture industry, about the extent of her travels and experiences in her twenty years on this earth. As she talked she hitched her skirt above her knees, crossed one leg over the other, and jiggled her feet in their yellow high-heeled espadrilles, moving her ankle this way and that.

Amanda raised her eyebrows at William, and they both laughed. And as she laughed and swept her hair back from her face, William rather thought that Amanda winked at him.

William played basketball and soccer with Amanda's students in the park near their dormitory. They were full of energy after sitting for hours in William's bus and in theatres and pubs. William generally hurt his knee or jolted his back when one of the strong young bodies crashed into him. He often had a bruised elbow or limped for a day or so, pleased nevertheless with the opportunity to leap around in front of Amanda. The students liked to call him the old man, and even this pleased him.

William told Amanda about his shabby flat on the canal near the zoo in Regent's Park.

'It sounds charming,' she said.

And William invited her to tea.

On the opposite bank of the canal, visible from the kitchen window, was a school, and twice a day, during the morning recess and at lunchtime, when William was between jobs, the squeals of the children reached him, a constant background noise rather like the insects and the lawnmowers in Sydney when he was a boy. And every day the same set of girls practised handstands against the wall, their skirts falling down over their faces. William savoured the melancholy that came with the voices and activities of the children, a comforting melancholy.

Today, while Amanda prowled around the living room and William in the kitchen placed biscuits on a plate, two boys climbed onto the roof of one of the outer school buildings and then slid down to a ledge from which, should they miss their footing, they would fall about thirty feet to the footpath beside the canal. William watched them, expecting them to fall. When the kettle boiled he made the tea, and when he looked back, the boys had disappeared. He placed the teapot on the tray, refusing to go to the window to verify whether or not the boys' bodies lay on the footpath, and bore the tray in to Amanda.

Afterwards they walked up Primrose Hill, right to the

top, where they sat down on a bench and looked at London spread before them. Amanda sighed and stretched her legs out, hitching her skirt up a little to catch the weak afternoon sun on her legs.

A father, with two young sons and a baby girl, sat on the grass nearby. The boys ran down the hill and up again in a mild sort of race, but they were kind to each other, the older boy explaining to the younger why he was able to run faster and the younger boy accepting the explanation rather than bursting into tears. The baby girl lurched about.

'They are like my children,' said Amanda. 'But younger.'

Every day Amanda bought something for her children, a model car kit, a jigsaw puzzle, a book of paper-doll cut-outs, and sent them off to Chicago. So many presents, enough for ten children. Sometimes she bought a tie, of silk or hand-woven linen, or a book for her husband.

William was jealous of Amanda's husband and did not want to know anything at all about him. He hoped only that he was boring, pompous, and frightful to behold.

Amanda shook her head, watching the children playing, then said, 'The children are with my husband this summer. They say it's good for husbands and wives to spend time apart.'

From this William knew that Amanda was not a happily married woman, and this knowledge bathed him in happiness.

They walked down Primrose Hill, past the zoo, and all the way to Amanda's little flat, which was in a close near Soho. Amanda held William's elbow as he led her across roads and she touched his shoulder to draw him aside to read the plaques affixed to certain buildings describing their previous famous occupants. He loved receiving this public, physical display. And again, as he stood on the cobblestones and watched Amanda unlock the glass doors that led into the tiny building that contained her flat, he marvelled at her loveliness.

Amanda took her students for a picnic on Hampstead Heath. William accompanied them. He had discarded the navy blue shirt of his bus driver's uniform for the occasion and wore a white shirt. This day he felt he could see around the leaves on the trees as if light did not travel in straight lines. William knew he was in love with Amanda, really in love this time, something he had not intended, to love a married woman, or even to take the risk of loving again and being miserable.

They sat with the students on the grass, drinking wine and eating bread and cheese. They played word games and gossiped. Amanda kept tidying up the picnic things, packing them into the basket. William kept standing as if it was time to go. He felt that Amanda, too, wanted to end the picnic quickly, so that they could be alone. But one of the students, that Baby Bunting, the one who had ruined several outings by looking sulky and wearing unsuitable shoes, this time stumbled against a tuft of grass in her yellow espadrilles and wrenched her ankle as they walked down the slope to the bus. William and one of the young men made a seat with their hands and carried her, penny-a-ride, to the edge of the heath, and by the time they found a taxi and got her to casualty at the hospital, the moment for William and Amanda to be alone had passed.

'But let us have dinner together tomorrow,' William said, boldly, yet expecting Amanda to look at her watch and say that she was too busy. But her face lit up and she agreed.

'I'd love to,' she said. 'There is no schedule planned for the weekend. Many of the students are going to France.'

William rang Amanda's doorbell and through the glass doors he saw her running down those stairs from her flat, in that way she had, slightly aslant, her hair still wet, her skin wet, patches of wet showing through her bathrobe, which she held together with one hand. He had arrived early and she had been in the shower.

Amanda came running down the stairs, with that smile, for him. William stood leaning against the wall of the building, laughing.

William had filled in time all day, doing this, then that, trying to nap, just waiting until he could set out, far too early, from his flat on the canal to go to Amanda's flat in the close. The students were at last taking care of themselves for a whole weekend—most of them were in another country altogether—and William's only duty was to take the lovely Amanda to dinner.

He rang the bell at the building that was like a doll's house, something from a fairy tale, and there she came down the stairs to the front door, smiling at him, laughing really, in her wet bathrobe, saying that she was not quite ready. She seemed pleased to see him, with that twinkle in her eye.

William wanted to wrap his arms around her and feel her wet hair against his cheek, her body against his. Later she told him that she, too, had wanted to put her arms around him at that moment.

Instead William stood leaning against the wall and laughing because he was a little early and she was a little late. He wanted very much to make love to Amanda, although he also knew that anything could prevent it— a flash of lightning, a phone call, anything. And of course she might be affronted, a married woman, not willing to indulge in love and passion, not prepared to ignore the rules of respectable society, as William suddenly was.

William had chosen a French restaurant, rather beyond

his means. He had thought that Amanda would like, expect, this kind of place. They ate gravelax and lamb cutlets, while a waiter asked between the courses if everything was to their liking.

'I was thinking that we might see *Coriolanus* together,' William said, under the impression that someone like Amanda could never tire of culture.

But Amanda looked doubtful. 'I don't think I could bear to sit through it another time. It's so long, so grim.' She placed her knife and fork on the plate. 'Let's get out of here. Let's walk back to my place and have coffee there.'

They walked along the river, onto the bridge to stand for a while, and back again, Amanda's skirt brushing against William's trousers as they went, William savouring every moment, in no hurry to get back. He felt that they were doing a slow and deliberate dance as they moved toward the flat. But when Amanda suddenly said she was weary, William hailed a taxi.

Then, when finally they were on the cobblestones in the close, almost at Amanda's flat, there before them was one of Amanda's students, the earnest boy who loved literature and culture. He had not gone to France but to the Shakespeare and was walking past Amanda's flat on his way back to his dormitory hoping to run into her.

'The Shakespeare presented a refreshing interpretation of the lovers,' said the boy. 'They were portrayed as ludicrous, and I agree with that rendition.' He fell into step beside them, accompanying them right to the door of Amanda's building. This was the bolt from the blue, the *deus ex machina*. If Amanda invited the wretched boy up, he would sit talking ponderously about directors and dramatic interpretations and so on, and William's moment with Amanda would have passed, yet again.

The boy continued to stand and talk in an unnecessarily

loud voice. 'I've just realised,' he said, 'that the name Amanda probably comes from *amare* to love, the gerund or something, feminine.'

Someone poked a head out of a window farther along the close and said, 'Pipe down. People are trying to sleep.'

'Pardon me,' said the boy. 'I should be going.' He seemed to be waiting for William to go off with him. Then, looking from William to Amanda, he pronounced, 'I have found British theatre on the whole disappointing,' and left, looking back at them once, a delayed reaction, as if it had suddenly dawned on him what they might be about to do.

William and Amanda sat in the miniature living room. Amanda took off her sandals and wriggled her toes. William poured port.

'Let's go for a long walk,' Amanda said. 'Let us get away from this London and really forget these students of mine. We can go walking in the fields of Suffolk. Perhaps tomorrow morning?'

Amanda took out a guide book, a large one with coloured photographs, and gave it to William. He balanced it on his knees, bending studiously over it, aware of Amanda's feet on the carpet, aware of her setting down her glass and walking to his chair, aware of her looking over his shoulder at the pictures of the pebbles on the beach at Aldeburgh, the church tower at Dedham, aware of her sitting on the floor beside his chair, so that she could see the pages better. He pointed at the ruined martello tower at Orford. She nodded. William took one hand from the book and placed his arm across her shoulder. She looked up at him. His hand moved down to her shoulder blade. She smiled. He moved his hand across her back. She reached up to draw his face to her, and William kissed her. Surely he had done this before. Or was it familiar because this was what had been intended for him all along? Had he reached his destination?

They stood up and put their arms around each other. Amanda said, into his shoulder, 'I have wanted to do that since the moment I saw you today. And for many days.' She led him into the bedroom and with a small movement of her hand waved him to the bed.

They made love and whispered the whole night. William felt that they were actually inventing lovemaking. Amanda told him she had been miserable for years. She and her husband rarely spoke, they talked only to the children, they never did anything together, she had thought of leaving him many times, but she hated the stigma of divorce, she led the student groups abroad as an escape, she loved her children, she hated her life in Chicago, she felt trapped. They slept at three or four and awoke at six. When William opened his eyes, Amanda was lying there beside him, her head propped on her hand, just looking at him.

'I have not been as happy as I am now, not with anyone, ever,' Amanda said, and she nestled in William's arms again. 'I have to do something about my life,' Amanda said.

William lay in bed with Amanda's head on his shoulder and believed that he would be her means for change, and she his. William believed now that Amanda would return to Chicago and divorce her husband, and that he and she would be together forever, in the not too distant future.

'I think I am in love with you,' said Amanda.

A sparrow flew in the open window of Amanda's flat and commenced to batter itself against the walls and windows so that it was soon flying in a dizzy, weaving way. William and Amanda stayed under the sheet, shrinking from the fluttering creature, startled by this violent intrusion. It was Amanda who got out of bed and picked up the injured thing in a newspaper, after it had lodged itself under the bed. She looked at William. He shook his head, indicating that he had no idea what she should do with it. She hesitated, then dropped the sparrow out the window, into the concrete yard two storeys below.

'It's too late now to go to Suffolk,' she said. 'We'll go another day.'

William made a charming lunch, with slices of ham and wonderful tomatoes and beer, which he laid out artistically for Amanda, as if to compensate in some way for his inaction with the sparrow. But the image of the bird stayed with him, and while he avoided the window for a while, he finally allowed himself to be drawn to look down into the yard. He could see no smashed corpse and found it hard to imagine where the bird had gone.

'I'll call you later this afternoon,' Amanda said when William left to return to his flat on the canal. She had some people to see. 'I'll call you when I know what I'm doing, when I'm free.'

William felt a certain foreboding at leaving her. She would disappear and he would not find her again. His telephone would be unaccountably out of order and Amanda would try to reach him, to tell him that she had been summoned to Chicago, that one of her children had been injured in a car accident.

When he rounded the corner of his street he saw that the road outside his flat was torn up. Several workmen were standing in a ditch outside his gate attending to wires and cables. Barricades were up and repair trucks were parked at angles to block traffic. This had happened in the space of a night and a day, while he was away making love to a married woman.

'An explosion,' the workmen told him. 'The electricity and telephones are out.'

William went inside and stood for a while, leaning his forehead against the window and looking over the canal.

During the night that he had been away a brightly painted barge with geraniums in pots along the roof, the kind rented by American families wanting a novel holiday in Britain, had docked opposite his window, and now the family was emerging, the mother, the father and several children popping their heads one at a time through the hatch then climbing out, ready to see London by night. The lions and birds in the zoo nearby and the ducks on the canal were making their customary evening cries and calls. William thought that Amanda's husband surely would be relieved to have their unhappiness brought out into the open, would surely be glad to be left to his research and to let Amanda and the children go to William.

It was five o'clock. The men were still outside his gate, working on the repairs. William's phone was still dead. He ran back to the bus stop and leapt on the bus to Amanda's. He ran to her door and rang the bell. She was not there. Perhaps he was too late. Her husband had telephoned and begged her to return, he was missing her, loved her, and could not bear to be without her any longer. William sat down on the front step, in front of the glass doors, staring at the cobblestones. It was dusk when he heard the clattering footsteps and he looked up. Around the corner came the lovely Amanda in a white cotton dress and sandals. She was thinking, frowning slightly. When she saw William sitting on her doorstep the frown deepened, then she smiled.

'What a surprise,' she said, mildly.

He ran to her. 'You must have been trying to reach me. The phones were out of order. So I came to you. Is everything all right? You're not leaving?'

Amanda shook her head, puzzled. 'I was busy all afternoon. I was going to phone you later.' Then she took his hands in hers. 'Of course I'm glad you're here already.' She unlocked the glass doors and led William up the stairs into the flat. 'A cup of tea?' she asked, moving toward the kitchen, then changing her mind she turned back to William, shaking her head. 'Come,' she said, and William moved to her and kissed her, somewhat cautiously, still surprised at the ease with which the lovely Amanda continued to receive and accept him. It was exactly what he wanted. And still he hesitated.

'We must make the most of these days together,' Amanda said.

These days together. William was thinking in terms of years, a lifetime, together with Amanda and felt a certain dismay at her words. But then he was in Amanda's bed once more, making love to her as night fell, astonished and grateful that he, careful and solemn William Longleg, was capable of such copious caresses, such petting words, capable of casting all reserve to the breezes. 'I love you,' he ventured.

Amanda sat up, tapping her fingers on William's chest, smiling down at him—coquettish, William thought, looking at her carefully. This magnificent woman was also a coquette and he, William Longleg, was her gallant lover. He closed his eyes, overcome with the simple joy of loving, the joy of loving Amanda.

The tapping on his chest became stronger, approaching thumping, as she demanded his attention. William opened his eyes. Amanda gave his chest a final firm pat and then swung her legs over the side of the bed. William reached out to hold her to him. 'I don't want to lose you,' he said. 'I love you.'

She pulled on her jeans and a strapless tube of a top, which left her shoulders and arms bare. 'Come, tonight I shall take you out.'

William reached for her shoulders. He had to keep on holding her, touching her.

'We'll be back here later,' she said, grabbing her jacket and slinging it on. Then she sat and watched William as he unwillingly heaved himself out of bed and into his clothes.

Amanda hailed a taxi, directing it south then east, to the docks, until they reached a dim little cafe beside the wharves. Amanda leapt out of the taxi before William could open the door for her and led the way to the cafe. As they entered, Amanda took off her jacket and said over her shoulder at William trailing close behind her, 'This place is Greek.'

The cafe was packed with strong-looking dark men, Mediterraneans, William guessed, Greeks of course, who looked as if they had just got off one of the ships moored nearby and had decided to go no farther, as if by staying near the water they remained as close to their homeland as they possibly could. And William thought of Rose, his young mother, who having alighted from her ship onto the tilting ground, had proceeded to Wally Badger in the west, far from the sea that connected her to her homeland. But then William saw that the women with these dark, strong men were brightly dressed, in tight short skirts, sitting easily, drinking and laughing. And he saw that the men were not as dark and strong as he had first imagined, in fact that they were not seamen at all. Most of them were wearing black turtleneck sweaters and black jeans and had the faces of the young men William saw every day on the streets of London going to their offices to work.

The tables were placed close together around the periphery of the room, leaving a square of floor empty in the centre. Amanda stood for a moment surveying the cafe. Everyone turned to watch this fine, fair woman with the bare shoulders, dangling her jacket carelessly from one finger, and the tall fair solemn young man beside her in blue jeans and neat shirt. William felt he was blushing

and was ashamed of himself. How could he blush when
he had just spent several momentous hours making ceaseless,
passionate love to this golden woman beside him? As he
stood there he made a low humming sound, pretending
a carelessness that he did not feel at all, and with his fingers
on his thighs he beat out a rhythm to help him to remain
stern and unflinching.

A waiter with a long white apron tucked into his brown
trousers approached and greeted Amanda, bowing to her,
touching her elbow as he straightened up, as if he knew
her, then indicated an empty table against the far wall.
Amanda led William through the crowd and threw her
jacket over the back of one of the chairs and sat down.
William threw himself down into the chair opposite, and
assumed a careless pose. When he looked around the cafe,
the other faces were all turned away, talking and gesturing
as they had been when Amanda and William entered.
Perhaps they had not been staring at the newcomers at
all, had not even noticed them. Had William imagined
their stares, as if he were still a self-conscious child?

'Do you know him?' he asked. 'The waiter?'

'I try to come here every summer,' said Amanda. 'I never
bring the students. I like to keep some secrets to myself. I
like a chance to unbend. Even my husband doesn't know.'

William looked down at his knees. Amanda had allowed
a third person, that husband of hers, to join them here,
spoiling it all. Amanda smiled dazzlingly across the small
table and leant forward, beckoning William with a slight
movement of her head to lean forward, and William did
so, then allowed her to kiss him, banishing the husband
as he wooed her in the presence of hundreds. 'I love you,'
he said, when he drew back, and clasped her hands in his.
He had no other words for her. And he would never tire
of saying them.

A second waiter, bored, hardly looking at the lovers, slid onto the table a menu, a sheet of paper in a sleeve of yellowed perspex. He leant over and wiped down the oilcloth that covered the table, pausing while they lifted their hands, then placed at the edge of the table a burning candle stuck in a bottle.

'We'll have ouzo,' said Amanda.

Without uttering a word or showing that he had heard, the waiter tucked his cloth in his back pocket and walked off. Amanda leant forward again to be kissed, at the same time reaching for one of William's cigarettes, as she had that day on the steps of the museum.

'We should go to Greece one day,' she said. 'Have you been there?'

'I've lived in Europe,' said William. 'Wally Badger was there. In Greece, at least near Greece. It's where he got his leg.'

'His what? Who is Wally Badger?'

'His leg. Wounded,' said William. 'My father.'

'Tell me about your parents,' said Amanda, inhaling and looking up at the tin ceiling of the cafe as she expelled the smoke. 'And why your father has a different name from yours.'

The music that had been issuing softly from a dark corner of the room was building to a crescendo, and suddenly four of the waiters, including the one who had greeted them and the one to whom Amanda had given their order, were standing next to each other in the square of space in the middle of the room, their hands resting on one another's shoulders.

'This is very ethnic,' said Amanda. 'It's the place to come these days.' She had forgotten her question. William was a little sorry. He wanted to present to her his story.

The waiters were moving in unison, left foot forward,

right foot forward and back, and then a bobbing rhythmic movement as they progressed across the space, like four brown ducks tacking across a lake.

Several of the customers in black leapt to their feet and surged onto the floor, linking arms with the waiters and forming a circle. Then several of the young women in bright, short skirts joined in. Once the dancers were established, dipping and capering in their circle, the waiters having set the night's entertainment in motion extricated themselves and continued their work.

At first William looked away from the men dancing. But the music was romantic, vigorous, suggesting other more passionate worlds than those he had known, and the movement of the men was so entrancing and unrestrained that he turned his eyes back to watch. One of the dancing men was staring in the direction of their table. No matter which way his body turned as he circled, his eyes stayed fixed on their table, on Amanda.

Amanda squeezed William's hand. 'Come, let us dance.'

The waiter strolled up to their table and placed their drinks before them.

'I don't dance,' said William.

The dancing man in black, a black swan, still had his eyes on Amanda.

'Don't?' Amanda asked.

'I have never danced.'

The black swan was turning slowly, his hands above his head, fingers snapping.

Amanda laughed. 'Then tonight you shall dance.' She stood up and tried to pull William up beside her. 'Come, it's easy.'

William pulled her back down to the chair. 'I don't want to dance. I want to get back to the flat.' He leant forward. 'I want to make love to you.'

The black swan broke away from the group of dancers and William saw that he was coming to their table and would force Amanda to dance with him.

'Let's go back to your flat,' he said.

'We've just got here,' said Amanda.

The black swan was approaching. Amanda sat relaxed, gazing off, stroking the back of William's hand. The black swan was beside her chair, bowing slightly. Amanda looked up, not at all puzzled or surprised. She, too, had known he was coming to get her.

William stood up. 'Teach me to dance,' he said, pulling Amanda after him to the dance floor.

The circle of bobbing men and women opened up to admit them, and Amanda, light on her feet, lovely and fair, laughing, watching the feet of the dancing men and women, went around and around in the circle, her boots moving smoothly one in front of the other. William, his hand on her bare shoulder, his arm along her arm, followed her, his eyes fixed first on her feet and then on his own to make sure that they did his bidding and did not wander off on their own. Amanda's shoulder shone golden in the light. Around the circle they swirled until, after a while, he did not have to look at Amanda at all. His feet could dance on their own. He was able to throw back his head and laugh and dance. He dipped, kicked, sidestepped, swooped and turned, as if he had been born to dance.

He raised his arms to the side, then bent his elbows, so that his hands were above his head, snapping and clicking. And slowly he propelled Amanda with him into the centre of the circle of dancers and began to rotate. He looked back over his shoulder at her, she looked back at him, mirroring his movements. The other dancers were circling, watching. The men who were not dancing were clapping and hooting, the women were squealing and stamping their neat feet on the floor. The waiters, standing at the edge of the dance floor, were stony-faced. For them this was a routine night, and their surliness was part of the ambience.

Then William heard a plate crash to the floor, and his first reaction was to feel a concern for the unfortunate person who had dropped it, a public disaster. He looked around, toward the sound of the smashed plate, and saw on the floor fragments of crockery. He found himself humming, chanting, in time to the beat of the Greek music. But he was still dancing. And so was Amanda. Instead of drawing back, the other dancers swarmed forward to stamp on the pieces of broken plate. The dancers were chasing the pieces scattered across the floor and jumping on them. No one was attempting to sweep up. William's feet crunched down on fragments of the plate. Then another plate shattered. The dancers hooted. Amanda laughed. Another plate broke. Then William saw that on one of the tables at the edge of the dance floor was a pile of plates, and one of the waiters was throwing them, rhythmically, dashing one to the floor as soon as the one before had shattered. William turned his head first to one side, then the other, his fingers snapping, his shoes crunching on the plate fragments, grinding them into the floorboards.

One of the men in black, the black swan, who had approached Amanda earlier, was now throwing the plates. When Amanda looked over at him, he held out a plate toward her, beckoning her to him.

Amanda slid away from William, dipping and looping, moving toward the table with the plates and the black swan beside it. She seized the plate offered her and cast it among the dancers, as if she were skimming a flat stone onto the surface of a lake. The dancers skipped lightly to one side, shouting. William danced over to Amanda, took a plate from the table and hurled it, and again the dancers clapped and sprang aside. The black swan took Amanda's hand and danced her onto the floor. William kept throwing the plates, and after a few random throws, he began skimming the plates across the floor toward Amanda and the swan. Several times the man had to jump back to avoid the plates breaking around him, their fragments leaping up to beat against his black jeans. Broken crockery now covered the entire floor, like broken sea shells, forming little piles. The dancers kicked and scraped the debris as they leapt, tumbled, screamed and roared.

One by one William threw all the plates onto the floor, at first in the direction of the dancing black swan, then directly at his legs. The last plate hit the man's ankle, causing him to hop awkwardly on one foot to keep his balance. Then he knelt down on one knee to examine the ankle more closely. William raced over to Amanda in order to haul her away to the far side of the dance floor. When the black swan stood up, Amanda was dancing again with William, trampling on the white crockery pieces. William could see that the knee of the man's trousers where he had been kneeling was torn, ripped by fragments of the hurled plates, and that the crescent of exposed skin was bleeding. The man stood for a moment, as if he might approach and try to repossess Amanda, before turning and limping off the floor. William leaped and plunged without reserve, totally absorbed and exhilarated by his frenzied dance, until Amanda, gasping and flushed, more beautiful than ever, gripped his arm and pulled him toward their table in the gloom near the back wall.

'I have to rest,' she said, fanning herself. 'I'm getting too old for this.'

William seized her hand and then pulled her forward so that he could rest his lips on her wrist. 'More beautiful at forty than in the flush of youth,' he murmured.

Amanda pulled her hand away, leaving it suspended above the table for a moment. 'I'm not that old,' she said, laughing. Then she placed her thumb nail against the flame of the candle in the bottle. Before William could reach out to stop her, the nail polish caught fire and Amanda held out her thumb, flaming, to William. He blew it out, like a candle on a birthday cake. The nail was scorched black.

'Come,' he said, standing up and gently pulling Amanda to her feet. 'Now we shall go back to your place to be licentious and immoral. Come.'

Without a word of protest Amanda followed him out, a few steps behind, holding onto his belt as he steered through the revellers.

The next day William and Amanda walked in Suffolk. They took a footpath through the fields from Stratford St Mary's, following signposts to Dedham, heading for the church tower in the distance. One of the signposts directed them into a field of sheep, bound on two sides by a river, on one side by a ditch filled with water, and on the fourth by a fence. William and Amanda climbed over the fence and walked along the river, their arms around each other. But they could find no way out of the field. They walked all around the perimeter, two figures in nylon windbreakers, red and navy, but they could not get out, except back the way they had come. The sheep panicked at the intrusion and dispersed as they approached. It became clear that Amanda and William would not reach Dedham and that the church tower would remain unattainable, in the background, and they returned to Stratford St Mary's where William ordered beers in the pub.

He tapped his glass against Amanda's. 'Upon not reaching Dedham,' he said, lovingly. 'But we have reached something else, more important.'

Amanda smiled, but looked down at the table. William, who until then had never reached any destination, never attained any goal, never found the path, despite the promise of his name, had reached Amanda.

'I realise that if you meet someone else and I lose you, it's tough luck for me, hard cheese, as they say,' Amanda said.

The phrase shocked William, seemed even callous. 'Perhaps you'll find when you get back that your husband will want a divorce. Perhaps he will have run off with someone else.'

Amanda thought about that. 'That would certainly make it easier for me,' she said coolly.

William could see that she was annoyed. She gave him a little smile and placed her hand over his. 'I'll write once I get home,' she said, 'when I'm sitting in the den, after my husband is at work and the children at school.'

This cosy picture of home was Amanda's revenge for William's suggesting that her husband might be unhappy with her. 'You love the status quo, don't you?' he snapped.

They were almost quarrelling.

They drove along the coast. William took one hand off the steering wheel and held Amanda's hand against his cheek. He led Amanda to the ruined fort at Orford and they climbed to the top. He led her to the beach at Aldeburgh, the rain slapping against the pebbles. They picked up stones and threw them into the waves, toward Europe.

'I do love you,' said Amanda.

But William now wanted to hear much more than a declaration of love. He was sure that he needed only to say the right combination of words, provide the right cue, and she would tell him that she was definitely planning to leave her husband and come to him. 'I must do something about my life,' Amanda said, providing the cue William needed. 'I don't want to lose you.'

'People change,' William said carefully, then added tentatively, 'divorce is common now.' As soon as he uttered it, William regretted the word, so harsh, so uncouth, in the midst of their love, and so tactlessly soon after their near quarrel in the pub.

'Divorce means failure,' Amanda muttered.

'What's wrong with failure?' William said sharply. 'Staying married when you're miserable and lonely is a failure.'

'I need time,' Amanda said. 'I have to see what things are like at home.' And for the first time she seemed to dismiss his passion, his devotion. 'And the children.'

She bent down to examine a pink pebble. 'This one looks like a bird.' She handed it to him.

William examined the stone in the palm of his hand, a pink bird nestled in a ball, its head under its wing. 'This beach is so different from the beaches I knew,' he said, and making another mighty effort to bind Amanda to him, he told her rapidly about Rose and Wally Badger, about the episode with the axe, about being left by Rose Badger at Manly. It was his ultimate declaration of love.

'Why did she abandon you there?' Amanda asked.

'I don't know,' said William.

And when Amanda asked why his father had let him take the blame for the assault, William answered again that he did not know.

'You really ought to have asked,' said Amanda.

'And I'll tell you about my name,' said William. They had left the beach and were walking past a row of shops.

Amanda caught sight of a canvas fisherman's shirt in a window and veered toward it. 'I won't be a minute,' she said. Then, inside, she said, 'I'm looking for one of those shirts for my husband,' looking at all the salesmen and pointing out the who who came closest to her husband's size.

William left the shop. He fingered the bird in his pocket. She had said that she loved him, that she had never been as happy with anyone, ever. How could she bear to buy a canvas fisherman's shirt for her husband, for someone she did not love?

'I have to take something back,' Amanda said when she rejoined him with her parcel under her arm, 'something substantial. It would look odd if I didn't. He is my husband.'

That night, their last night before going back to London and the students, they drank champagne in a hotel room in a village on the coast overlooking the fens and a windmill. Amanda had wanted to wait in the car outside while William registered, then scurry directly up the stairs to their room. She said she did not want anyone to see her.

'Who would know?' William asked. 'Why do you care?'

'People from Chicago are everywhere,' said Amanda. 'And I don't want to appear to be just another one of those self-indulgent, married women that you come across everywhere having an affair in some hotel room.'

'This is not just some affair,' said William. For a moment he did not know whether to shake her or to sob. 'I'm sick of it,' he said, 'doing everything, helping you to hide.' Then he grabbed her hand. 'You have to have some kind of courage,' he said and took her with him into the hotel lobby, and made her stand beside him as he signed them in.

'We are lovers,' William said, when they were in their room. 'We love each other.'

From the bar downstairs the piano pounded out 'Foggy,

Foggy Dew', and 'Roll out the Barrel'. William and Amanda lay in bed and watched *Limelight* on television.

'I shouldn't have fallen in love with you,' said Amanda.

'It isn't a terrible thing,' William said. 'This is what happened. And you love me. You said you loved me.' But love suddenly seemed a puny, irrelevant, unpersuasive notion.

'Maybe they're trying to telephone me back at the flat,' said Amanda. 'Maybe something terrible has happened at home. The children could be hurt, ill. I'm married, remember, with a family.'

'You are not letting me forget that for a minute,' said William. After a while, he put his arms around Amanda. 'Am I the first man you've fallen in love with? Is this your first love affair?' He was asking questions.

'Of course not,' Amanda said. 'I have fallen in love before, when I'm away like this. It's part of living. It's not the same as marriage.' Then as William let his arms fall away from her she said, 'But you are special. It has never been like this before.'

William awakened to find a seagull perched on the windowsill. Its beak was hooked, its head and neck were as large as a cat's. The long double windows had stood open all night, and William had lain watching the sky, watching the dawn, before falling asleep. Now the seagull stood there, perhaps for fifteen minutes, staring at William, and then with a nod of its head it flew off, as if it had learnt something important and carried this something away with it.

Amanda was sleeping beside him. Tall, blond, married Amanda. William got up and stood for a while, leaning his forehead against the window and watching the turning windmill. He ought to leave London, to leave Amanda before she left him. He ought to take the train to France, anywhere, after his last bus-driving assignment. He would have to forget her, this woman who took lovers.

But when Amanda stirred, he whispered, 'Come to France with me.'

'There's nothing I'd like more,' she mumbled.

In Oxford, William was walking with Amanda by the river. The students had been sent to tea. This was their last weekend before returning to the United States, before Amanda flew off to Chicago. It was what was called a hot day. William's spirits lifted. But when he went to put his arm around her, she backed away. 'The students,' she said. 'We can't enact our melodrama in public.'

'Let us sit on the bank,' William said. As soon as they sat down, it became overcast and cool.

William took Amanda's hand and led her toward the town. She pulled away. 'The students,' she said. 'Don't spoil these last days together.'

She had slipped away from him, away from William Longleg, the felon. They were passing Blackwell's, the bookstore, and William saw in the window dozens of copies of *Dunkirk, The Great Escape* piled in a pyramid.

'I do love you,' Amanda said, as they lurched down the lane, out of step with each other, stumbling on the uneven surface of the pavement. 'You know that, don't you?'

It was after midnight when William's bus deposited the students at their dormitory, back in London.

Amanda was dozing in the seat behind William.

'I'll drive you to your door,' he said.

'That's silly,' she mumbled. 'I can walk from here.' And she dozed off again.

William started up the bus and took it through the streets of the West End toward Amanda's flat, turning into streets that became ever narrower. He edged his bus along to the entrance to the close, almost wedging it in the archway, which was the only obstacle preventing him from taking the bus galloping right up to the door of Amanda's flat. He turned off the engine.

Amanda jerked awake. 'That was a pretty stupid idea,' she said, 'bringing this bus along a tiny street like this.'

'You were asleep. I wanted to bring you home safely.'

'You'll never get out. You can't turn around.'

William's bus filled the street. A solitary car, coming up against the bus, stopped and backed away to find another route.

'You go ahead,' said William to Amanda. 'I'll see to the bus. It'll be simple.' He wanted her out of the way. He feared she was right and he did not want her to see him stranded with his bus jammed in a tiny London street. 'I'll be fine. See you tomorrow.'

Amanda went off under the archway, her shoes echoing on the stones.

William turned on the ignition. The engine roared, then panted like a huge breathing animal. One or two lights went on and heads looked out windows. He started to inch the bus backwards, knowing now that the cars parked at the corner would block his exit, prevent his backing the bus around. The bus sat askew, blocking the intersection.

William had to call the police, and the police had to ring the bells of all the flats in all the buildings, arousing the good citizens, asking them to move their parked cars so that this tour bus, this white elephant in their neighbourhood, could turn the corner and lumber off. William was booked, for driving a bus on a prohibited street, and fired by his company.

But none of this he told to Amanda when he saw her the next day.

'Did you get home okay?' she asked him.

'Oh, that,' he said. 'It was simple.'

Part V

Wally Badger, white-haired and tiny, was sitting on the front veranda, his leg propped against the veranda rail, when William picked his way up the front path through the chunks of loose concrete that wobbled and cracked when he stepped on them. Wally Badger was still alive.

The old fibro house stood battered and seemed to lean to one side. The yard, overgrown, was now bounded on both sides by blocks of flats of liver-coloured brick. Opposite stood a man watering his garden with a green hose.

William had left his suitcase in a locker at Central Station and come straight out from the airport.

'Unusual name,' the immigration official had said, turning the passport over, riffling the pages.

The official's movements were deliberate, unhurried, and he seemed elaborately unconcerned as he punched William's name and passport number into his computer. He was even humming under his breath. William could almost catch the tune. He thought they must be trained to do that, to feign disinterest when they were onto something, about to arrest a criminal.

William fixed his eyes on the official's hands, resisting the urge to look around to see if the airport police had been alerted and were about to close in on him.

'Staying for long?'

'A few weeks,' William said. It seemed as good an answer as any.

'First visit?'

William nodded. His passport, renewed several times, showed no sign of his ever having been in Australia. The immigration official looked up at him, as if questioning the veracity of the reply, and William switched from nodding his head to shaking it, switching from a lie to a truth. It was possible that the record of William Longleg's leaving would show up on the computer.

'I was here as a child,' he said.

'And your Sydney address?'

'I don't have one.'

'Isn't there a friend, some name you could give as a contact?'

'There's no one,' said William. That was true. He did not know if Wally Badger was alive. As for Rose, he knew nothing of her either. She might well have gone off, disappeared.

'Just a sec,' said the official and took William's passport off with him through a door next to a framed grey mirror.

William swallowed. How could they possibly connect William Longleg with that William Badger of so many years before? There was nothing to be done now, no escape. He simply had to wait. Then the immigration official was returning, slapping William's passport against the black trousers of his uniform. His lips were pursed, possibly whistling.

The official handed the passport to William. 'Enjoy your visit,' he said.

As William passed through the customs barrier, choosing the gate for passengers with nothing to declare, a customs official halted him and indicated that he should go to one of the counters to be inspected. A customs officer went through William's suitcase carefully, with the same deliberation and studied lack of concern as the immigration official. She, too, seemed to be humming. Then she, too, wished him an enjoyable visit and waved him on.

William was sweating, as he issued forth from the customs enclosure, feeling that he had had a close shave, had escaped detection, until he heard his name called over the loudspeaker.

'Paging William Badger. Please report to the

information desk. William Badger.' His name, what sounded like his name, his old name, was now being shouted out all over the airport.

He contemplated making a run for the taxis to get away. He was wearing sneakers, good escape shoes. Then he reminded himself that he was not William Badger and no one, simply no one who had known him in his Badger days, could possibly have learned that he was arriving in Sydney. He had not been in touch with Wally Badger at all since that Christmas, the day after, Boxing Day, to be exact, years before, when he had discovered that his name was Longleg. No one knew he was coming. He had told no one. William placed one of his suitcases, the smaller one, on its end in the basket of the baggage cart, so that it blocked his face, and he wheeled the cart toward the information desk, fearing to see a phalanx of policemen rattling handcuffs. But gathered at the desk were only three ordinary men and two women. Of the three men, one was middle-aged, in a business suit, and one was slightly older with wispy brown hair, wearing brown trousers and a brown cardigan clinging to his curved back. It could have been Wally Badger come to claim him, to whisk him away, back to the western suburbs and jail.

The third man was tall, slender, about William's age and height, with dark curly hair and olive skin, in jeans and sneakers and a leather jacket, rather similar to the clothes William was wearing. As this young man finished his business at the desk, he looked at his watch, then dashed off toward the departure gates.

Emboldened, William nudged his cart to the desk.

'William Badger?' he asked the clerk.

'William Badger,' the clerk repeated, coughing as she said the name, one hand over her mouth. 'Excuse me. He was just here.' The clerk looked up quickly then back at

the papers before her. Had she really said William Badger?
Or was it William Padgett?

'Padgett?' William said, questioning.

'Right,' the clerk said. 'Padgett.'

But it sounded like Badger.

'Badger, right? William Badger?' William asked.

'Yes, Padgett, Padgett,' the clerk said irritably, 'that's
what I said, Badger,' and turned away.

At least William Padgett—or was it Badger?—was
departing as William was arriving, keeping the balance.

'I do love you,' Amanda had whispered, then turned
away from him, irritable at her own declaration. They
were in London, at Victoria, and she had kissed William,
first looking quickly around her. Then she said that she
and William would see each other in the future quite often,
whenever she needed to pass through London to go to
meetings or led students groups, perhaps once or twice
a year, in June and maybe January.

'That's not what I'd call often,' said William. Where
had he gone wrong? When had he lost her?

'It's better than never seeing each other at all.'

'I would come to you, if you wanted me to. I would hop
on the plane to see you for just one day, just one hour, if
you needed me.' He knew he was capable of such a grand
gesture. If he *begged* her not to let him go, would that work?
He remained standing at the door of the train that would
take him back to Europe, to the night ferry to Dunkirk, yet
wanting desperately to get off and remain at Amanda's side.

Sitting by the window was a man, grumbling, mumbling.

'I'm going to come and fetch you, soon,' William said
to Amanda on the platform, but it was more like a question
than a statement.

Amanda looked down and poked at a cigarette butt

with the toe of her sandal. 'William, please, I told you. I can't leave my family. It would upset the children too much.'

As the train began to pull out, the man who had been muttering angrily jumped up, pushing William out of the way. 'This train is not for me,' the man said. 'I'm not leaving on this train.' And he leapt onto the end of the platform, obliterating Amanda from William's view.

William knew he had learned a lesson, that married people complaining about spouses they had lived with unhappily for many years did not actually want to give up the unhappiness, even if they fell in love with someone else. He began to understand that he had actually helped Amanda endure her unsatisfactory marriage. He had shored it up, supported it.

On the ferry he found his corner chair, stretched his legs out and stared up at the ceiling for a while before closing his eyes and sleeping. Then he found himself on the train to Paris, and instead of alighting there he let the train bear him south along the Rhône. At Nîmes, at midday, as if he knew exactly where he was going, William waited at a bus stop outside a restaurant called the Café des Fleurs. The sun was beating down, and there was only a sliver of shade by the wall of the cafe, where the passengers stood as well as they could, holding up newspapers or scarves to protect their faces from the sun. When a green bus pulled up, William boarded along with the others and allowed himself to be taken up into the hills of the Cévennes. As the bus climbed higher, they passed a boy in a boy scouts uniform walking a donkey.

'He thinks he is Robert Louis Stevenson,' the bus driver called to his passengers. 'Every summer there are boys who do this, who travel with a donkey.' He winked over his shoulder. 'They say Mr Stevenson mistreated that donkey of his. Poor, dumb creature. But then, he had been unhappy in love, with a married woman.'

At the end of the route, William walked through a village and along a path across the fields to a ruined church, a Protestant temple, with a dilapidated tower, and as he walked across these fields toward the broken tower his arm was around Amanda. He was afraid to look down, so certain was he of her presence, so certain that he would lean down to kiss her.

William climbed to the top of the tower and leant upon the broken stone of the parapet. And suddenly he hated being here, in Europe, in the south of France, because it placed him so far from Amanda, now on her way to America. Then simply he returned to Nîmes. In the early evening he walked to the Roman arena. Dozens of tourists were climbing the stone tiers to the top of the amphitheatre. The mothers and grandmothers laboured to get up, the children and the young men in white loafers leapt, like mountain goats climbing from rock to rock. At the top these families—they were all in pairs or groups, there was no one alone except William—ranged themselves in rows to be photographed and then climbed down again. In the middle of the arena workmen were erecting a wooden platform and lights, ready for *Holiday on Ice* from America. Down below, the stage on which they were beginning to spray the water to make the ice was tilting and William, dizzy, had to steady himself with one hand against the stone wall of the arena. The whole of France, the whole of the northern hemisphere, was tipping, leaning, and William knew it was time to fly back home, to the southern hemisphere, to set things straight. As it was, he was simply going round in circles.

William made his way out, feeling his way carefully down the worn stone steps, which seemed now to undulate, and back to the station. On the train, at Lyons, a talkative Frenchman got on with his tall, yellow-haired wife, and asked William where he was from. 'You anglophones travel too much, I think. You are everywhere.'

The Frenchman's wife sat near the window reading one magazine after another, chewing gum, patting her hair, flipping the pages, never looking up.

'We French have no need to travel,' said the man. 'We are in France already.'

When Wally Badger saw William approaching him up the front path, he patted his cardigan pocket, reaching for his pipe.

'You look older, son,' he said. 'Are you married yet? Have you found a woman who'll have you?'

William stumbled on one of the chunks of cement that lay on the cracked path. He righted himself and stood stiffly at the bottom of the steps to the veranda. One of the steps had broken, and one was missing altogether.

'They want to buy me out, demolish the house,' said Wally, 'but I'm not budging, not me.'

'Why did you let me go to jail?' William asked. 'Why didn't you tell them how it all happened? That she started it?'

Wally Badger examined his pipe, tapping out the old ashes and patting his other pockets to find his tobacco tin. 'If you must know, she had me over a barrel, by the short hairs, between the devil and the deep blue sea. That's the issue here. In other words, she would have dobbed me in.'

'Mother would have turned you in? What for?'

Wally frowned, tamping down the tobacco. 'What for? Who?' he queried.

'Rose, where is she?' William felt he was leading his

father through a catechism, one question following the other. 'Mumma.'

'She went off,' said Wally Badger.

'She went away? Or do you mean something else?' He was an inquisitor. He stepped onto the veranda and stood towering over Wally Badger.

Wally clamped his teeth on his pipe and broke it. The bowl fell into his lap, scattering the tobacco over his brown trousers and onto the floor around his rocking chair. 'They took her away.' He pointed at the floor with the stub of the pipe stem, shaking his head. 'The ground, son. Too uneven for her.'

The ground? A grave? An uneven, untidy grave? Pushing up the wildflowers, as Rose might have said sarcastically, and before William could ask her why she had left him at Manly. Rose Badger was dead. Wally Badger looked pretty close to death himself.

'How do you manage, then?' William asked, looking away from his father. He sat down on the veranda floor, his legs hanging down beside the dilapidated steps.

'The pension, meals on wheels, and they send someone to do a bit of tidying up and washing from time to time,' said Wally. 'The woman who comes calls me Tiny. "How are you going today, Tiny?" she asks. I don't like that at all. She comes and calls me Tiny. Thinks it's funny.'

William sat for a while watching the man in the house opposite, possibly the same man who had witnessed the assault with the axe. The man was watching Wally and William as he moved his hose in an arc from side to side.

William stood up, realising that the neighbour might recognise him and call the police. 'I have to go,' he said, then as he looked at his old father added, 'Do you think you ought to come with me?'

'I'm not budging. They'll have to carry me out in a wooden box.' Wally Badger jerked his thumb toward the side of the house. 'In the sidecar of the Harley they'd have to carry me out—it's still there out back. And you can't stay here. There isn't room. The house is too small.'

William took a deep breath. He had not meant it, the offer to take his father with him.

'It's time for me to turn in,' said Wally Badger. 'It's getting dark. Turn in,' he repeated, pondering the phrase. 'She would have turned me in, son, that's the issue here. She was a do-er, in the sense that she does what she threatens she'll do. I know that much about her.'

William moved behind the veranda post, out of sight of the neighbour. He still had questions. 'What had you done?'

'Done?' Wally Badger brought his bottom lip up over his top lip. 'I didn't *do* anything. I've never *done* anything.' Wally Badger placed his leg on the floor and began to push himself out of his chair. 'Stop interrogating me.'

'Wait,' said William. He still had a question. 'Was she German?'

'Why should she be German?' Wally Badger asked crossly.

'My name. Everyone says it's German. And she sang in German.'

'She sang because she's Irish. They can't help it. The name's as Irish as you can get. But she pretended she was English. A bit of a snob. Same thing. And she liked to make things up. White lies, she called them. But there's no hiding it. The Irish all sing. Her father was a tram driver. He sang. He would put on his uniform, drive his tram, and sing. I saw him. Heard him.'

'He wasn't a soldier?' William asked. 'In Germany?' That was what he had been imagining, with his name that others insisted was German and Rose's love of uniforms and Tillie's dark innuendos.

'An Irish tram driver. In London. He sang in his tram in the middle of London. Like my Rose used to sing in buses.' Wally Badger was on his feet. 'They couldn't help it, that family. All mad, if you ask me. Couldn't stop singing and dancing.'

Wally Badger hobbled across the veranda to the front door. There was no screen door at all now. William imagined that it was probably out the back somewhere in a pile with all the other testimonials to Wally Badger's broken-down past. 'But women like men in uniforms. Her father a tram driver, and her father's father. He was a policeman. He sang, too. She wished they had been English generals, not just an Irish tram driver and a singing Irish policeman.'

'Longleg is an Irish name?' William asked.

'Longleg?' Wally Badger paused at the front door. 'Longleg? What do you mean Longleg?'

'The birth certificate,' William said.

'Langley,' said Wally Badger. 'That's the name. Langley, Langley, Langley. Can't you even read a name straight? What's this Longleg business?' He stepped into the hallway. 'What kind of a name is that?' And he disappeared into the gloom.

William closed the front door, then jumped from the veranda onto the earth beside the path, giving one of the chunks of cement a kick and sending it rolling. He walked quickly and quietly to the front gate, without looking up. Langley. William Langley. An Irish name. Not only had he never been William Badger, he had never even been William Longleg. He had misread the handwriting on the birth certificate.

At the gate he hesitated. He had not asked Wally Badger where Rose was buried. Not that he wanted to visit her. But it seemed right to know, or to wish to know.

'Excuse me?'

William looked up. The man across the street, in what used to be Stanleys' place, was calling to him, coming toward him. The man was unlatching his gate, calling to William, who thought of sprinting to the corner and disappearing, taking off like a bride's nightie as he remembered someone saying to him once, long ago.

'You must be the son,' the man was saying.

William nodded slightly, ready to deny it if the neighbour brought up the matter of the axe. Yet this man seemed to be a different person altogether. He was young, with dark curly hair, and plump. William could easily outrun him if he turned nasty. But he was nodding and smiling.

'We saw what happened to Mrs Badger,' he said, clicking his tongue, shaking his head. 'I was standing right there at the letterbox and saw it all.'

William swallowed. 'How did it happen?' he managed to ask, fearing what he might learn.

'One of those bits of cement,' said the neighbour. 'It's a good thing you're back. Those steps need fixing, and the uneven path. Something will have to be done, so that the same thing won't happen to Mr Badger. A fall could kill a tiny old man like that.'

William put his hand to his forehead. Rose had been killed by a chunk of cement?

'Do you know where they took her?'

'He didn't tell you?'

'Rookwood?'

'Rookwood?'

'The cemetery,' said William lamely. 'It's the only one I've heard of. Of course there must be others.'

The man gave a little laugh. 'Ah, yes. You like a joke, don't you. A bit of a tease. She's in hospital, of course. It happened the day after we moved in.' The man gestured at his newly acquired house opposite. 'This is an up-and-coming area. The prices haven't gone sky high yet, and we got a good buy.' He nodded at the Badgers' house behind William. 'Your house, being in such bad shape, helped. It's the edge of the veranda she tripped on.'

'What hospital?' William asked. It seemed Rose Badger was still alive, and he had questions to ask.

'Went straight down onto her knees, onto those bits of cement, then her hip. Very nasty business.' The neighbour touched his own right hip. 'I saw it all. She was carrying something, a box, into the house. She couldn't put her hands out to break her fall.'

Rose was alive and Wally Badger had not told William, did not want William to know.

'Near Parramatta they took her. The big hospital.' The neighbour looked at the Badgers' house and shook his head. 'It's dangerous, a house in such bad nick, and now it's holding down the value of my property. You should get him to sell, make a tidy packet, and they could pull it down. Otherwise I might have to complain to the council.'

'When did it happen?' William asked.

'The accident to the old lady?

'She's not that old,' said William.

'A few weeks. And she looks old enough,' said the neighbour. 'Very frail bones. She hadn't been eating right for years, I heard.' He nodded and turned to cross the road back to his own property. 'Tell your father I'll buy his house, help him out. I'll even give cash if he gives me a good price.'

It was easy enough for William to locate Rose Badger's room in the hospital. He hesitated outside the ward in the corridor, standing next to a row of empty wheelchairs for so many minutes that the nurses gave him looks as they scurried back and forth.

'Why don't you go in,' said one, 'instead of blocking the gangway.'

William peered carefully around the door. In the ward were a dozen or so beds, all occupied by women, any one of whom could have been Rose Badger. William looked at each pallid face surrounded by wispy hair. Even young, dark-haired women seemed to fade in that setting. But which one was Rose William could not tell. That one with the lank curls and pink nightie? The one propped up on the pillows, sleeping with her mouth gaping wide? The one lying still, on her back, her head turned, staring beyond a bunch of bananas on the bedside table, beyond the woman sitting up in the next bed, and out the window?

'Who is it you want?' a nurse asked brightly, piercingly.

All the heads in the beds turned to look, except the open-mouthed sleeper and the one gazing out the window.

'Rose Badger,' William whispered.

'Badger, Badger, Badger,' the nurse said, pointing her finger and allowing it to scan the room slowly, past the beds, until it came to a stop, indicating the woman staring out the window. 'That's her. Rose!' she called.

'No, don't,' said William, trying to stop the jarring announcement. 'No need.' He wanted a chance to look at his mother first, and he hated the familiarity with which this young woman addressed her. 'I'll go over to Mrs Badger myself.' But it was too late.

Rose Badger turned her head and was looking directly at William.

'Visitor for you, dear,' cried the nurse.

William trod carefully over the linoleum floor, placing the ball of his foot down first, and Rose Badger watched him come toward her. An igloo, covered by a sheet, rose up from the foot of her bed. So tiny did Rose Badger appear, lying there, her head on the pillow, her arms beside her body on top of the sheet, which lay straight and tight across her chest and under her armpits, that she could have been in a capsized kayak. Her hair was short and straight, still blonde, parted on one side, with a child's plastic barrette holding the hair tightly from her face. She looked like a ten-year-old girl. William wondered if the barrette had been snapped severely into place by the nurses. It was not something he could imagine Rose choosing for herself.

Then, as she recognised William, she rose on her elbows and started to haul herself to a sitting position.

'Help me up,' she said to him, after hesitating only a moment.

William placed his hands under her arms and hoisted her up, arranging the pillows behind her back. He could feel the bones through the skimpy flesh.

'You've finally come for me,' she said. 'I've been ready for weeks, waiting.' She waved her hand at the lockers at the end of the room. 'I'm all packed. Bring me one of those wheelchairs they've got out there. Help me into my dressing gown. Then we'll go.' As she spoke she moved her skinny arms about like a dancer, indicating the corridor, the robe at the end of the bed, and the provisions on the bedside table. 'Throw those articles into that little bag!' She was shrieking.

William looked about him desperately. The woman in the next bed, perhaps in her thirties, although it was hard to tell, wearing a flannel nightgown with a peter pan collar buttoned to the neck, caught William's attention, and he turned to her, imploringly.

'She always does this,' said the woman. 'Don't worry. She says she can leave, but the nurses say it'll be some time.'

'Nurse!' Rose called.

'Her leg in plaster like that.' The woman in the flannel nightgown nodded at the igloo on Rose's bed, then without warning she blinked violently several times. The blinking was so powerful that her cheeks and mouth were also fully engaged in the effort and moved upwards with each pursing together of the eyelids.

'Pass me my dressing gown.' Rose reached out and poked William on the arm to reclaim his attention. She jabbed him again with her forefinger. 'If you break her, the rose will stick you with her thorns, so that you'll always remember her.'

William ducked out of the way, stepping back a pace. Rose was staring off now, past William, and had begun to sing softly. *'Knabe sprach, ich breche dich, Röslein auf der Heiden! Röslein sprach, ich steche dich, dass du ewig denkst an mich.'* Her eyes turned to rest on William. 'Come on,' she insisted, pointing at the dressing gown lying at the foot of the bed, her voice no longer soft. William reached toward the garment.

The woman in the next bed shook her head. 'No,' she mouthed, wagging her finger. 'She's not allowed to get up.'

Rose subsided onto the pillows, apparently fatigued by her efforts, but making a beckoning movement at the dressing gown in William's hand. 'I'm ready to leave. I've been packed for days.' She closed her eyes and sighed.

William let the robe drop onto the bed, on the far side of the igloo, out of Rose's sight.

'Excuse me,' said the woman in the next bed, plucking at William's sleeve, 'but could you be so very kind as to pass me one of those bananas. Thank you very much.' William handed her a banana. 'Thank you very, very much, indeed,' the woman said.

In the doorway to the ward appeared a man, about sixty, short and tanned with silky, silver hair, which although cut traditionally short at the back and sides nevertheless waved about the crown of his head unaffected by gravity. Flanking him, slightly to his rear, and looming above him was a boy of fifteen or sixteen, tall, lean, his back bent over, wilted like the stem of an indoor plant deprived of water. His hair was long, covering his ears.

The older man, who William guessed was the boy's father, looked around, beaming like a little boy, and then charged across the room as if into battle, toward William standing awkwardly between Rose's bed and the bed of the blinking woman. William thought he might bowl him over, so unusually rapid was his approach. The son followed slowly, unsteadily, like an old man, and because he moved clumsily and self-consciously, he gave the impression of being slow-witted. As he walked he kicked the legs of a chair in passing and the wheels of several trolleys stationed in the ward, causing metal implements and glass beakers to vibrate and rattle. It was as if his feet, so far from his head, had plans of their own, were throwing off the authority of their master above and were attempting to go off on their own.

'Good afternoon, my love,' the man cried, stretching out his arms and narrowly missing William, who had stepped swiftly to one side. The man seized the blinking woman in his arms and embraced her. She let out a small cry of pain.

William squeezed out of the space between the two beds and withdrew to Rose's other side.

'Don't move, don't inconvenience yourself,' boomed the man. 'There's plenty of room for all in this spacious land of ours.' He pointed at an empty chair for the tall boy to sit on. As the boy lowered himself, all the while gazing off into the distance, he kicked the beside table and in sliding onto the chair he pulled the sheet of his mother's bed with him.

'Jason!' snapped the father, having finished embracing his wife, who had fallen back onto her pillow, her hand pressed to her right side as she regained her breath.

'Well, well.' The silver-haired father was rubbing his hands together, beaming across at William. He reached over Rose's small body to shake William's hand. 'Tiny,' he said. 'Tiny Armstrong. Call me Tiny. We're Tasmanians.' He inclined his head at his wife. 'On holiday, which has been ruined by her appendix.'

William was startled into taking the man's hand. 'How do you do, Tiny?'

The man laughed boisterously. 'Hear that, Jason? Tiny! He called me Tiny.' The boy looked away and said nothing. Then to William the man said, still chortling, 'Tony, not Tiny. I can see you like a good tease. Tiny!

'Lena Armstrong,' said Tony, indicating his wife, who nodded, smiled, and gave a fresh series of urgent blinks, three short, three long, three short. Her eyes were blinking out a message. D'd'dit, dah dah dah, d'd'dit. Help.

'Thank you very, very much for passing me that banana just now,' said Mrs Armstrong. 'Very much indeed. He was really so very kind to do that for me. I couldn't do it myself. It hurts me to reach.' She bit her lip and touched her side again.

'And Jason,' said Tony, continuing the introductions and

pointing at the long boy, who grunted. 'Maybe you thought he was a girl with all that hair.'

'Shut up,' muttered the boy and commenced gazing at his knees.

'What was that, son? Speak up!' said Tony.

The wife, smiling and grimacing, leant toward her husband and patted his forearm. 'Leave him be,' she said softly.

The son, without raising his head, rolled his eyes up to witness this patting, then lowered them again to his knees.

Tony Armstrong stood beside his wife and looked about the room as he spoke. Now and then he tapped his hand on his wife's arm or shoulder or thigh, as if he were giving a lesson in body parts.

'And you?' He was addressing William.

'Me?'

'Your name?'

William cleared his throat. Rose appeared to be asleep.

'Langley,' William said quietly, then 'William Langley', a little more loudly. He was speaking his real name for the first time.

Rose opened her eyes for a moment and looked from William to Tony Armstrong, then she closed them again.

'Arm strong,' said Tony Armstrong, pretending to flex the muscles in his arms. 'I'm a timber merchant.' And as if William had inquired further about the timber business, he continued. 'Tasmanian timber is exported to every country in the world, including Oregon. You might think that was like sending coals to Newcastle, which just goes to show you what fine wood we have, if they want it in Oregon.'

'Tasmania is the last unspoiled place on this earth,' said Lena Armstrong.

Tony Armstrong surveyed the room then checked his watch against the clock on the wall. 'This is a business trip for me, and a jaunt for my wife and son here.'

Lena Armstrong nodded. 'We were trying so hard not to get in his way, weren't we, Jason?' She blinked urgently at William several times. 'Then I had to spoil everything for them and end up here. I keep telling them to go on and have a good time without me.'

Jason fiddled with the cuffs of his shirt. He was the unhappiest boy William had ever seen. He surely had not smiled in years. William nodded at the boy, to show he was a friend. The boy looked away.

Tony Armstrong was rocking on his toes, his hands behind his back. 'Our boy fits right in in Sydney,' and he leant over to flick Jason's hair with his finger. 'In Tasmania, that's where we're from, same size as Belgium, that hair didn't go down too well. My business partners had begun asking if I had a sissy for a son.'

Jason ducked away from his father's hand.

'Rubbish!' said Rose suddenly, her fingers grasping William's trouser leg. Her eyes were wide open, and she was sitting up, not leaning on the pillows. 'It's Badger.'

'Sh,' said William, embarrassed. 'Not so loud. It's on the birth certificate. I've seen it, you know.'

Rose pursed her lips and gave a little snort. 'In any case, you've been far too long coming to get me,' she said.

'Mother,' said William, leaning down to her.

Rose looked away, as if the form of address pained her.

'Rose,' William tried again, then, 'Mumma. What did he do? What did Wally Badger do, that you could turn him in?'

Rose made a sweeping movement toward the door with her arm. 'You had better get a wheelchair before they're all gone.'

'Tell me,' said William. 'What did he do wrong?'

'Give me my gown now,' Rose hissed. 'Take me away from here.'

'What did Wally Badger do?' William asked. He picked up the robe so that Rose could see it. She reached for it. He jerked it farther away from her.

'Tell me,' William insisted. 'I know you weren't married at first, so don't think that's a secret any more. But what did he do? He said he did nothing.'

Rose glared at William for a moment then beckoned him close. He bent down to her. Muttering, angry, so that William could barely hear, she said, 'Better to ask what didn't he do? He was a do-er all right. There was a wife already.' She grabbed for the robe. William whisked it behind his back, then bent back down to Rose. 'He didn't expect to see me out here and with a boy,' she went on. 'He didn't know anything about my boy. I'd called him the same name, too. He said I could have knocked him down with a feather, when he saw me and the boy on his doorstep.'

It was as if Rose were talking about someone else altogether, not her son, not William, who stood next to her bed in the hospital.

Rose tried to reach around William to get her dressing gown. William stepped back and held it up, making it do a little dance, like a puppet, out of Rose's grasp. She poked his thigh. 'I'll stick you.' She held up her hands and looked from one to the other, flexing the fingers. 'These are my thorns. And they can hurt. Remember that.'

'Where was the wife, then?'

'She had wandered off,' said Rose. 'A wanderer. Like me. Only I had to give up wandering. I had to make him pay for what he did. I couldn't just go off. He had to pay.'

'Where did she go?' William was breathless with the exhilaration of asking Rose question after question and getting answers.

'She had a boy, too. I didn't know where they went. Those boys were the same age, the first one, the only one he knew about until the new one showed up, was a bit younger. That meant he left me in London and immediately took up with the other one, got himself another boy. He was called William, too.' Rose began to cry, hunched up, her hands over her face. Then she continued, as if she wanted to finish her story. 'Spitting image, they say. It was simpler for him just to marry me and take me and my boy in and say nothing, since the other one had gone off with that other boy.'

'My boy helps out in the business,' Tony was saying to no one in particular. 'Also, I own the oldest bookshop in Australia, if not the southern hemisphere.'

'Oldest,' said Rose, nodding her head. 'You see what I mean? It never stops.'

'I'm not your boy,' Jason muttered. He was watching William's hands drumming on the iron rail at the foot of Rose's bed as he absorbed this new information offered by Rose.

'And when the other bookshops get going—we've just bought into a chain of bookshops—my boy's going to get involved in distribution, right? And because it's family and we have to put in hard work to make it pay at first, he's going to do it for free.'

'May I be excused?' said Jason, rising from his chair. Because of the crescent formed by his curved back his head hung over his father for a moment before he stumbled away, bumping into a stand with roses on it, which he managed to steady with his hand and prevent its crashing over.

'Don't go far,' the father called after him. 'You don't want us to miss the train and get stranded out here. He's a hard worker, not like those other kids who ask for money to buy rubbish. Not my boy. His hair is the only problem.'

As William watched Jason lope out of sight, he let Rose's robe fall, holding it only loosely in his fingers. Rose reached forward and grasped it, triumphant, and tried to put it on as she sat in the bed, weighted down and immobilised by her leg in its cast.

'You might wonder at my going into the book business,' the timber merchant continued, as his wife's face flashed another series of messages. 'You might think that books are a big change from timber and many have commented on that. But it's all wood, I always say.' He looked at his watch. 'We're a very happy family, as you can see. We all get along swimmingly, right?'

'We're very, very lucky,' said his wife. 'And very, very happy.'

Tony Armstrong placed his arm along the back of his wife's bed. She recoiled a little, as if expecting him to touch her, to hug her, and hurt her. 'We're really very, very lucky,' she said and blinked again, three short, three long, three short. So exaggerated was the blinking that after the first three longs it looked as if she might not be able to get her eyes open again. William held his breath and suspended his tapping, waiting for the three final shorts to resolve the crisis.

'Time to go,' said Tony Armstrong. He nodded and smiled around the ward and bowed slightly toward William. 'Good luck to you all.'

'Time for me to go, too,' said Rose. The dressing gown was draped untidily around her. She was pushing off the covers and grunting as she attempted to manoeuvre her legs to the edge of the bed. 'You've probably made me miss out on a wheelchair by now. I'm a wanderer. I have to go.'

'What about Manly?' William asked.

Rose pursed her lips, then unpursed them briefly to say, 'I'm not saying another word,' before clamping them together again.

'Tell me about Manly, then I'll bring the wheelchair,' said William. 'Why did you leave me there?'

Rose darted a look at him, then spoke. 'I had to track them down, didn't I? That Ama told me all about them. She's a meddler, and she never liked me. She told me I was not Mrs Walter Badger at all. I wasn't even a wife. But I got even with Wally Badger, didn't I? I spoiled it for him thereafter, didn't I? I really spoiled it for him.'

'Why didn't you just leave me at home with Dadda?'

'He couldn't know, could he, or he'd stop me, wouldn't he? So I gave you a nice seaside holiday while I looked for them. I never found them, however.'

'Maybe Ama wasn't telling the truth,' said William. 'Maybe she liked to tell untruths, white lies.'

'That Wally Badger never comes to see me,' said Rose. 'When I get out, I'll show him. I'll spoil it for him all over again.' And she started to sing again, loudly this time, her hand resting on her breast bone, below her throat. '*Und der wilde Knabe brach's Röslein auf der Heiden, Röslein wehrte sich and stach,*' and she jabbed a finger at William, '*half ihr doch kein Weh und Ach, musst'es eben leiden.*'

William placed his hands over his face, as if he were splashing water over it.

'He tried to break her but the rose had to defend herself. She *stuck* him, and now *he's* the one hurting. And when I get out, I'll do it all over again,' said Rose. She began to hum.

'I have to go,' William said. 'I'll be back some other time.'

'The wheelchair,' Rose said, indignant. 'You promised. You can't just leave me here.'

'I'll be back soon,' William said, and made his way out of the ward, reeling a little, feeling his way past the row of beds.

'I'll spoil it for you, too,' Rose called after him, 'when I get out of here.'

William wandered about the station at Parramatta. As he passed the newstand he saw the boy Jason rummaging through the magazine rack. He took out a *Playboy* and began to thumb through it, then, as William watched, Jason slipped the magazine under his shirt, and lurched off, coming to rest in front of the train indicators.

'Jason!' Tony Armstrong's voice was calling through the station.

Later, on the platform where they waited for their train to Central, William saw the two of them, the father's face upturned toward Jason, who arched over him like a ceremonial umbrella. He had discovered the *Playboy* and was wagging his finger under the boy's nose. In the other hand, pinched by a finger and thumb, dangled the magazine.

'Vile, filthy rubbish,' the father exclaimed and let the magazine fall into a bin.

'It's all wood,' Jason said.

Then the timber merchant reached up and seized Jason by the shoulders and tried to shake him back and forth. But the boy stood so rigidly that all the older man's violent rattling did not budge him. The only person who rattled was the father.

On the train William was actually lighthearted. He was William Langley. Plain William Langley, who had found the answers to his questions. He could fly if he tried. Now, finally, he would try to *do* something. He sat with his elbow on the window ledge, smiling out the window, but when the train passed through a tunnel and he saw his reflection in the glass, he saw that his face was as serious as ever.

The seat next to him was empty, but opposite and also alone was a solemn boy of about ten, his elbow also on the ledge, staring out the window. William watched the boy's reflection in the glass, and as he watched he saw that the boy's eyes were brimming with tears.

William waited for a couple of stations, then leant forward to the boy.

'I'll tell you what,' he said, 'I've got something here that might come in handy.' He reached into his bomber jacket for a pen and something to write on and from an inside pocket fished out his aeroplane ticket and boarding pass, the back of which was blank, suitable for writing. And rapidly he wrote out the first letters of the morse code alphabet, dot dash, dash dot dot dot, dash dot dash dot.

'That's ABC,' William said. 'What's your name?'

'Jack,' said the boy.

Quickly William wrote out the name. 'And this is SOS, three shorts, three longs, three shorts. You might need it.'

The boy took the card and examined the dots and dashes, then handed it back to William to finish all the letters.

'Could you do the numbers, too?' he asked.

'Not only numbers, but punctuation,' said William. 'You can write secret letters this way. You have friends, don't you?'

The boy shrugged.

'No friends?'

'Not since we moved,' said the boy, watching as William wrote.

'What's the problem?'

The boy shrugged again. 'My stepfather made us move here. I hate it. I hate him.'

'Listen,' said William, giving the boy the boarding pass with the morse code completed. 'You'll be needing this in emergencies. I'll tell you what." And he told the boy that this moment and all the other moments in his life, sad and happy, would become his past, his history, the one thing, the only thing, that a person could truly possess.

'No one can take your past away from you. It goes with you wherever you go. If you think about it, it's a comforting thing, a blessing, not a burden. Your past is your treasure, your secret hoard, your own story. You can take it out and enjoy it whenever you want. That father of yours . . .'

'Stepfather,' the boy corrected tersely.

'That stepfather of yours one day will be simply part of it, and you will see that he is just an ordinary man, and after a while he will be an ordinary, perhaps cowardly, old man.' William was for a moment surprised at the word cowardly that unexpectedly issued forth.

William told the boy that it was a child's destiny to be stepped on, to be hurt from time to time, and all of it, including the tragedies and trauma, became part of the secret hoard.

'There's a beauty to it all, to the patterns and paths,' he said, and paused to murmur again the word beauty, once more surprised at the word he had chosen. 'And there's even a special word for it!' He struggled now to remember that word, frowning out the window. 'Aesthetics!' he cried, turning to the glum boy opposite him. 'It's a kind of aesthetics.'

The boy gave William a dubious look, verging on disdain. 'Aesthetics,' William repeated. He liked the word very much. He felt as if he had invented the meaning of life. 'Just write down what happens—in morse code, if you like. Morse code is beautiful, too, to look at.' He wanted to shake the boy, who appeared not to be listening at all. 'And after that the main thing is to be a do-er. That's the issue here. You have to be a do-er, accept what has happened, and get on with it, really do something.'

William looked out the window, exhaling, slumping against the back of the seat. Simply an ordinary, cowardly old man, he had said. Again he felt he was smiling, because suddenly he had answered one more question. He could understand that Wally Badger had not wanted Rose to go to jail, had protected her, his Rose, who knew too much. But why, if someone had to go to jail, had Wally Badger not offered himself first? Why had the father surrendered the son and watched him suffer? But he was simply an ordinary, cowardly man, already a prisoner in a jail of his own making, and William, the son, was now free. Although he was unloved, at least at the moment, he had certainly loved and would surely love again. He was capable of it. He knew that. He had had some individual instances of good luck in the journey so far. And the planet was still spinning. There was a certain beauty in it all.